I0585945

MOONLIGHT GAUNTLET

MOONLIGHT GAUNTLET

Maddison Greer is the author of the *Maldwyn & Harlan Series*. Born in Australia in 1994, Maddison Greer has lived in several cities, including Sweden's capital Stockholm where she lived for a few years at the start of her high school education.

Later, Maddison returned to Australia where she completed her Bachelor's Degree at the University of Newcastle. She currently resides and writes in Melbourne, Australia.

MOONLIGHT GAUNTLET

by

Maddison Greer

SCAR TREE
AUSTRALIA

**SCAR TREE
AUSTRALIA**

Moonlight Gauntlet
ISBN 978-0-6488029-6-9

First published in 2022 by Scar Tree Australia

© Maddison Greer, 2022

The moral rights of the author have been asserted.

All rights reserved. Except as permitted under the Australian Copyright Act 1968 (for example, a fair dealing for the purposes of study, research, criticism or review), no part of this book may be reproduced, stored in a retrieval system, communicated or transmitted in any form or by any means without prior written permission.

All inquiries should be made to the author.

Editing by Ashley Greer

Disclaimer

The material in this publication is of the nature of general comment only, and does not represent professional advice. It is not intended to provide specific guidance for particular circumstances and it should not be relied on as the basis for any decision to take action or not take action on any matter which it covers. Readers should obtain professional advice where appropriate, before making any such decision. To the maximum extent permitted by law, the author and publisher disclaim all responsibility and liability to any person, arising directly or indirectly from any person taking or not taking action based on the information in this publication.

To those struggling in the wake of the last few years, shuffling along as I have in survival mode. May this book shine some light back into the world.

CONTENTS

PART ONE

CHAPTER ONE

Family Matters

I T WAS QUITE A SIGHT at this time of year. Small, dark timber cottages were dotted across the powdery, snow-covered hills. The moon seemed to be humming with a pure brightness, gleaming down over the icy town, making the snow shine in stark contrast with the black, night sky.

Plumes of smoke billowed out of the chimneys poking out of the thatched roofs, coiling up into the night sky, and releasing the warming, almost spicy, smell of burning wood. Yellow lights from the fuming hearths lit the tiny gaps in the tightly closed window shutters, keeping out the icy breeze.

There were very few trees spread about the hillside village and, with their bare limbs, they reached out to catch the gentle falling snowflakes. The open, white fields were free of any animals. Most of the cattle would have been gathered together under a large shelter that would keep them safe from the fierce cold of winter. Although it was a simple town, it was a beautiful sight.

Exhausted, Maldwyn stopped in his tracks, relieved to see his hometown Alander on the horizon. An exquisite feathery snowflake fell into Maldwyn's view from the dark clouds overhead. A frosty gust swept around him as he stood fixed in place. He pulled his wool coat tighter around his shoulders and his hood lower over his face to better block the freezing wind. His shoulders were sore from the heavy pack he carried, which had been digging in deeper throughout his trek.

Sighing heavily after the weeks spent journeying on foot, Maldwyn rubbed his forehead and pressed on toward the cluster of buildings that marked the village centre. The ground had a thin layer of ice that crunched beneath his boots as he made his way over the countryside. His shoes were thick with muck. All around, everything was quiet. Not even owls could be heard hooting.

Having travelled a long way to Dresden's most northern border, Maldwyn was looking forward to reaching a proper shelter where he could have a decent night's rest. In the time that he had been making his way to Alander, Maldwyn had spent a lot of it dwelling on his mother's condition, hoping he would make it in time to say goodbye before her passing. She had been ill for a long time, and news that her health had worsened worried him. Still, there was a part of him that was apprehensive about seeing his mother again.

For most of Maldwyn's life, his mother had been a point of contention for him. She had raised him and nurtured him in many ways. She had been the person who cared for him and placed food on his plate, sometimes foregoing her own meal just to make sure he was well looked after. Despite all her motherly tendencies, Maldwyn's mother also taught him to fear his power, even to despise this part of himself.

He slowed his pace and took a moment to settle his growing repugnance which left a bitter taste in his mouth. His dry tongue felt glued to his palate as a multitude of emotions bubbled to the surface and his stomach knotted. Returning to the place he had intended to leave behind was like stepping through time to a point where shame crept into every corner of his life. Taking in a deep breath, Maldwyn took note of how little appeared to have changed about the town.

As Maldwyn walked the empty streets, he noted how quiet they were in comparison to the city he had become accustomed to since leaving this place behind. The silence was almost unnerving. The paths through the village had been cleared so that all that remained was brown sludge, and the snow had been piled up into mounds on either side of the muck. Boot prints marked the roads which snaked through the simple wooden buildings. Splinters jutted out of the roughly crafted planks the buildings were made from, and frost covered the exterior walls leaving the dark wood with a feathered, greying effect. Sharp icicles of a range of lengths dangled overhead from the eaves, on the verge of cracking free from the thatching and falling to the ground in a heap of shards.

Knowing every turn to take by heart, Maldwyn followed the muddy roads and halted before the house in which he had grown up. The place was small and the corners of the building were not square. In fact, the door frame itself had a slight lean. Stepping forward, Maldwyn lifted his hand to knock on the door. He felt warmth flowing from inside. He shook his head, relieved to know there was someone inside.

He banged on the door when he heard the tragic sound of his mother coughing. Even from outside, he could hear how difficult it was for her to breathe.

Muttered voices exchanged a few words before footsteps moved toward the door. Maldwyn wondered who was inside. He hadn't expected anyone other than his mother to be there. As the door opened, Maldwyn was greeted by Owen, his mother's neighbour.

Owen hadn't changed much, except for the length of his beard, which was now almost touching his collarbone. His hair was a sort of inky black colour and when he smiled Maldwyn was reminded of the wide gap between his front teeth.

'Maldwyn, welcome home!' Owen offered as he stepped aside, letting Maldwyn pass through the door. His rotund gut obstructed the doorway a little, making Maldwyn have to pass by at an angle. 'I trust you are well.'

'Fine, thank you.'

Maldwyn checked the area that had once been his home, looking around at all the familiar things that somehow now felt foreign.

Inside, it was a humble house. The small open space had a brightly burning open hearth in the centre, offering warmth and light. A beaten kitchen counter occupied the corner opposite the door. Some shelves lined the wall near the bench holding jars of dried herbs, large cast-iron pots with preserved fish and cooking implements of a range of sizes with large handles designed for hanging from the ceiling over the open fire. A quaint, rough table with four chairs around it was placed between the counter and the open hearth. The chairs around the table had uneven legs and wobbled when someone sat on them. For as long as he could remember, they had been this way.

Beyond the open fire, which had smoke billowing up to the small opening in the thatched roof, was his mother's bed in the far corner. From where he stood, he couldn't quite see her for the roaring flames, but he could make out a lump beneath the layers of furs which were heaped over the figure.

A tall timber weaving loom, almost as tall as Maldwyn, stood in the final corner of the room. A half-woven piece of linen with threads, which were tightly woven on the top and hanging loosely on the bottom, was suspended in the frame.

On the floor, by the loom, was a thick fleece rug, softening the hard floor so that one could bear the hours spent standing to craft finely woven fabrics. Beside the loom was a plain, wooden rocking chair with a cushion on the otherwise hard, flat seat.

'Veronika and I have been taking turns watching your mother.' Owen had lowered his voice to a whisper and scratched the side of his beard. 'We wanted to make sure she wasn't alone.'

'I'm sorry I wasn't here.' Maldwyn shrugged, wondering what else he could say. 'When I got your message, I was worried I wouldn't make it in time.'

'You're here now.' Owen frowned and patted Maldwyn on the shoulder comfortingly. Lowering his voice further, he said, 'She doesn't have long though, Mal. Maybe a few days at most.'

'Thank you,' Maldwyn murmured under his breath.

Owen went over to the bed. Maldwyn followed him through the little house, walking around the hearth. Taking off his heavy pack, he placed it on the floor by the loom.

'Renate,' Owen said with a quiet voice. 'Maldwyn's home.'

Maldwyn's mother managed to turn her head and gaze at him, standing behind Owen. She was sickly pale and her gaunt face was heavily wrinkled, making the skin around her neck seem rather saggy, especially as she tried to smile up at him. Maldwyn was saddened to see that the rims around her eyes were reddened, and the whites of her eyeballs were yellowed and worryingly veined. Her greying hair was limp and had matted into her pillow. He wondered how long she had been bedridden.

'Maldwyn?' Renate sounded incredulous as she peered up at him. He felt guilty that she may have thought he wouldn't come.

'I'm here mother,' Maldwyn reassured her as he kneeled beside the bed. He pulled off his gloves and took up her cold hand. She gripped his hand tightly and began to cry at the sight of him. He felt tears welling in his own eyes but held them in so as not to make her cry more. 'I'm here.'

Owen looked awkwardly between them. 'I'll leave you two to catch up. If either of you needs anything, feel free to stop by next door. Veronika and I are always here for you both.'

After they both thanked Owen, Maldwyn walked him to the door and saw him out. Owen was quick to disappear into the night, rushing home to his wife. Closing the door, Maldwyn felt strange to be home. It was quiet, but his mother's breath continued to wheeze in the background.

Maldwyn walked back over to the bed and sat by her side, holding her hand. 'I wished you would come,' she told him.

He sniffed, still on the verge of tears. The guilt for leaving Alander and abandoning his mother began to crush him. 'I'm sorry mother. I never meant to hurt you by leaving.'

Renate lifted her hands and cupped Maldwyn's jaw as a tear ran down his cheek. 'I could never blame you for leaving Maldwyn. After your... friend died. I know it was hard for you to be here.'

Maldwyn pulled back a little. Renate had always denied the truth about his relationship with Will, refusing to acknowledge the love they had shared. After Will had been murdered, Renate practically ignored what had happened. 'He didn't just die mother, he was killed... by someone here, in this town.'

'I know that, Maldwyn.' Renate shook her head as if she had heard this all before. 'That's all in the past now. I'm sorry I wasn't what you needed back then.'

Maldwyn let out a heavy breath as his chest tightened. He had never imagined a day would come when his mother would apologise for failing to support him through his grief. He felt a tear finally stream down his cheek and settle on his upper lip, leaving him with a briny taste on the tip of his tongue.

'I handled you all wrong.' His mother's hands were shaking as she reached for him again. 'I always have. For that I am sorry.'

'You did the best you could.' Maldwyn knew this was the truth. She had been alone and had little support to raise him.

The only support she had was from her brother, Flynn, who was a brutal drunk. Maldwyn did not have many fond memories of his uncle and was even relieved when he passed away a few years back.

Raising Maldwyn on her own as she did could not have been easy, especially once she learned he was not an ordinary child. The day they both realised he had abilities had been one of the hardest in his life, but they were beyond that now.

'If I could go back, I would do everything differently.' Renate held his hands in hers, gripping them softly by the wrist. Her eyes glistened with tears. 'I would never have reacted the way I did.'

He knew what she was referring to. In the early days, fearing his magic, his mother had thought his power came from his hands, so she had bound them tightly in an attempt to stop him from using his abilities. Of course, she had been wrong and the bindings had not stopped his power from escaping his grasp, but they had left a taint in his memory.

'I'm sorry for everything,' she sobbed.

Maldwyn leaned down and pulled her into a warming embrace. There was a certain gentle musk scent about her. For some reason, hearing Renate's words made all of his resentment wash away and he felt that for the first time he understood his mother's struggles. He felt how unfortunate it was that they should reach this moment only now, as she lay on her deathbed.

'I forgive you,' he told her. As he pulled away, she gave him a motherly smile and wiped his dampened cheeks. She began to cough. It was a chesty cough full of phlegm. Maldwyn stood and pulled the sheets back up over her as she covered her mouth with her hand. 'You should rest, mother.'

Nodding, she struggled for air and laid her head back on the pillow. Maldwyn watched her for a short while as she fell asleep. He thought of how their roles had reversed, how she now relied upon him for care and comfort. It was ironic, the way a parent would become a child with time.

Maldwyn went to his pack and pulled out the book that had been given to him by the Erendil, *The Power of Divinity*. He had only managed to read a few passages since departing from the city. Mostly, it was too dark on the road to read the pages once the sun settled and he hadn't been able to read while keeping a good pace on the road.

He grabbed the rocking chair and brought it over to his mother's bedside. Sitting by the flames he opened the book to where he had last been reading. The chapter was titled: The Swan Sigil.

The power of divinity, our power as gods, is greater than any power in the nine realms and, much to the dismay of the giants, remains unmatched. Everything around us hums with the gift the Yawning Void birthed in us, and the artefacts we create are seldom spared from our divine energy, often imbuing ordinary items with unusual effects.

Few such relics exist beyond the divine realm, and of those few, most were created by the smithy god, Wayland. Having spent time in captivity in the mortal realm, Wayland created many pieces of jewellery and weapons which were gifted with his divine touch. Every such item created by the smithy god was dedicated to his wife, known as the Swan Maiden, and marked with a swan insignia.

Maldwyn paused as he considered the beauty of this notion, that even in the darkest moments as a prisoner, it was the smithy god's love that anchored him. He smiled wistfully at the thought as he gazed over to smouldering flames, wondering how many relics crafted by Wayland remained in this world.

* * * * *

Maldwyn jerked awake in his seat, which rocked slightly forward as he moved. The book was open, resting face down in his lap where it had landed. There was a faint wrinkle in the leather spine and the pages had crumpled against his thighs. He had been tired when he arrived and supposed he had fallen asleep reading.

He gazed over at his mother, who was lying flat on her back, breaths rattling. Maldwyn felt odd about their exchange the evening before as if he had dreamt of their peacemaking. Still waking, he rubbed his eyes and lifted the book from his lap, trying to fix the creased pages.

The flames from the open fire had perished down to glowing embers and the cold air was seeping through the walls. Getting up from his seat, Maldwyn grabbed some small timbers and kindling from the pile near the front door and fed the dying fire. After a while, the fire reignited and grew livelier, once again radiating warmth and light.

Satisfied that he had been able to salvage the embers, returning them to a bursting flame, Maldwyn decided to make some breakfast for them both. He felt a pang of hunger as he walked over to the kitchen, inspecting the food stored on the shelves.

Whatever he was going to serve, it would have to be something that would be warm and not involve too much in the way of chewing. He didn't want his mother to gag on her breakfast. He had come a long way and planned on caring for her, until the end.

Opening a jar filled with barley, Maldwyn settled for cooking some porridge as Renate's supplies were quite limited.

He poured some of the flakes into a cast-iron pot and covered the grains with water from a jug. Grabbing a mortar and pestle, he crushed some cinnamon and nutmeg and sprinkled the ground spices over the saturated barley, stirring them through with a wooden spoon.

Maldwyn covered the pot with a lid and placed it over the fire where it hung by its handle from an iron hook. As the porridge began to warm and the grains soaked up the water, swelling to a reasonable size, Maldwyn looked through more jars until he found dried apples.

He took some of the dried slices out and placed them on the flat surface of the benchtop. He took a kitchen knife from the utensil holder on the countertop, checked it for sharpness and began chopping the slices into tiny pieces which would be easy for his mother to swallow.

Once the barley had been boiling for a while, he lifted the lid and caught a waft that smelled of spiced straw. Renate stirred behind him in the bed. Maldwyn glanced over his shoulder to check on her and saw that her eyes were open.

'Good morning,' he offered as he added the diced apples for sweetness to the mix and stirred them through with a wooden spoon. 'How did you sleep?'

'Better than I have for a while, I think.' She tried to push herself up to sit, a feeble attempt since she was bedridden. Maldwyn rushed to her side to help her, pulling her up the bed and stacking pillows behind her back to keep her upright. She smiled at him. He smiled back. 'You're cooking?'

'Unfortunately, it's just porridge.'

'You always were good in the kitchen,' she praised as Maldwyn pulled mittens over his hands and lifted the pot from the fire by its scorching handle. He ignored her remark and served their breakfast in two basic wooden bowls after giving it a moment to cool.

Sitting on the rocking chair by his mother's side, he placed his bowl in his lap and proceeded to feed her with a spoon. She was too weak to keep her arms up to feed herself. The cinnamon and nutmeg reminded him of the smell in the village markets around the time of the winter solstice festival. Maldwyn's mother had a wistful smile that beamed, telling him she too was reminded of fond memories that the spiced scents brought to mind. The fine creases around her eyes deepened with her half-smile.

She blew on the spoon, cooling the hot porridge before pulling it off with her stained, aged teeth. Her lips were dry and glued to the sticky spoon. Maldwyn was unsettled by how difficult it was for her to swallow the gelatinous porridge. He placed both bowls on the floor and sprung forth from his seat to grab a cup of water to help her push the food down.

After sipping at the water, she breathed in deeply as if relieved and rested back against the pillows. Maldwyn gave her a moment to catch her breath, reaching for her with his free hand, wishing he could help her through the pain.

His magic seemed to come alive, flowing through him, trying to break free. Despite that Maldwyn and his mother had put an end to their past misunderstandings the evening before, he knew she was still likely to frown at his power if he allowed it to escape his grasp.

He closed his eyes and focused on his breaths, trying to calm himself and maintain what little control he had over his abilities. As the surge began to subside, his mother gave him a grave one-sided smile.

'Your magic still troubles you.' Maldwyn looked down to the floor, pulling his hand back, and gripping the cup of water with both hands. Her voice was seething with judgement. 'You must never use your power Mal,' she scolded. 'You know it is forbidden.'

'You know I can't help it sometimes.' Maldwyn shook his head, bothered by the turn of events. 'It's stronger than me.'

'How many times do I have to tell you to keep it in?' She lowered her brows, corrugating her forehead, and fixed her admonishing stare on him. The veins in her eyes seemed to pulsate. 'You have to be stronger than your power. It isn't a choice.'

'You don't think I try to stop it?'

Renate frowned at him. Maldwyn knew she would cross her arms and wag her finger if she had more energy. 'You just need to control it better.'

'Is stuffing it down really controlling it?' He snapped.

Renate pulled her head back, aghast at her son's boldness, and looked up at him with a sad expression, as if he had wounded her deeply by questioning her and testing her patience.

'I only have your best interest at heart, son.'

Maldwyn leaned his elbow on the arm of the rocking chair and rested his head in his hand. 'I know you mean well mother, but you just don't understand how hard it is keeping a part of yourself suppressed all the time.'

Her bottom lip trembled, quivering with sorrow. Maldwyn watched her as she stared at him. He wondered what she was thinking. Was she horrified, condemning him yet again for things that were out of his control? She pushed herself forward a little. Perhaps she was about to offer an apology. What he had said was the truth, she could never understand how his power felt.

'It's time I told you the truth.' Maldwyn's mother mumbled. Her voice took on a regretful tone.

Worried by his mother's sombre expression, Maldwyn moved forward to the edge of the rocking chair he sat on. The seat leaned forward with him as if mimicking his troubled curiosity. 'The truth about what?'

A cold draught crept through the thin gaps in the timber walls. The heat from the hearth was enough to keep it at bay, but not to defeat it entirely. Maldwyn drew his woollen coat tighter about his shoulders, shivering a bit, feeling much colder now that he wasn't cooking over the fire.

'The truth about where you come from.'

'Mother, what are you talking about?'

Maldwyn glanced sideways and lifted his brows with curiosity as he scratched his chin with his dry hands, noting that they still smelled of the spices and chopped dried apples. He contemplated whether he was about to learn the identity of his father or the cause of his strange abilities.

Renate weakly lifted her hand to her mouth, as if covering her words might soften the coming blow.

'The truth is, you're not my son… at least, not by birth.'

Maldwyn felt the muscles in his forehead tense. He tried to comprehend the fact that the woman he had known as his mother had lied to him his whole life. His chest tightened as he grew anxious about her confession, wondering who his true parents might be and how she could have kept something like this from him for so long.

As he sat still, considering what to say to her, he noted that he felt an underlying frustration growing at the fact that the truth of where he came from was only coming out as Renate lay dying. He pondered whether she ever would have told him the truth if she weren't ill.

'What are you saying?'

'I'm sorry. I should have told you sooner,' she pleaded, folding her aged marked hands together as if in prayer, begging for Maldwyn's forgiveness. The fire in the background popped as a welcomed interruption. 'I am so sorry, Mal.' She wrapped her emaciated fingers around the furs and gripped them as tight as her weak hold was able.

Maldwyn rubbed the side of his face to soothe his shock. He frowned at his mother, no longer feeling quite as sympathetic to her illness as he had moments before when he had been feeding her breakfast. He felt that she was always using things to manipulate him, even now she was using the truth of his parentage to keep him in line. He thought she was about to warn him yet again about using his abilities because of where they came from.

Clipping one of the bowls with his boot, he moved forward in the rocking chair. The bowl spun on the floor, spinning in an unstable, wobbling fashion, yet somehow managing not to spill the food all over the floor. The seat inclined toward the bed with the shift in his weight.

'I don't understand. Whose son, am I?' The words sounded strange as they passed his lips. The very notion seemed ridiculous. She hesitated, turning her gaze away from his to avoid the question. 'Well?' Maldwyn pressed. 'Whose son, am I?'

'I don't know,' she stammered, hands trembling, gripping the sheets. 'You needed a home, and Leith and I wanted children—at least I thought we did.' Intrigued, Maldwyn perked up. Before now, his mother evaded the topic of her former husband, Leith. Maldwyn had assumed it was because, for some reason or other, it was too painful for her to talk about. 'We took you in to raise you as our own.'

Maldwyn's mother began to cough. Phlegm bubbled in her throat as she tried desperately to catch her breath. Her cheeks were wetted by her tears which settled in her wrinkles.

'I don't know what it was, but, I suppose, he realised what it was to have a child, and Leith left us while you were still a baby. He struggled with how much having you changed our lives.' She wiped a tear from her cheek and sniffed. 'Maybe he never wanted children,' she muttered to herself. 'I'm just glad he was gone before you came into your powers. I hate to think how he might have... reacted.'

There was something about the way she hesitated at the end of the sentence which made Maldwyn question if she had thought he may have accepted his powers, perhaps even encouraged them. Maldwyn's mind was filled with questions, but he wanted to wait and see how much more his mother would tell him.

A silence settled between them and the flames were all that could be heard spitting and exploding with heat. The smell of the cinnamon and nutmeg spices had been drowned out by the woody smoke. A haze formed along the ceiling, spiralling up through the gap in the thatching that worked as a chimney. The house was poorly built.

Maldwyn watched the dancing smoke as he waited for his mother to continue, but more words never came. He wasn't sure what he expected. Anything, even a morsel, of information that may have helped him to understand who he was, or rather what he was. Yearning for meaning, he chewed the inside of his cheek.

'That's not it, though… surely?' Maldwyn steepled his fingers together, resting his elbows on his knees. His mother remained quiet. Her gaze darted about the room, avoiding looking in Maldwyn's direction. 'Where did you find me? Who gave me to you? Whose son, am I?'

Renate wept in reply, choking on her tears as she coughed. He felt bad for badgering her and sat back in the rocking chair. He breathed in the thick smoke-filled air. He laughed in an unbelieving awkward manner, livid that he had been lied to for such a long time, and that she chose to leave telling him the truth until she lay on her deathbed.

All her torments that he had endured, all the ways in which she would criticise every aspect of Maldwyn and his choices, and she wasn't even his mother. Maldwyn shook his head.

He realised he had never needed her acceptance. It simply didn't matter. She was not his mother. Yet, in the face of the truth that had been laid out before him, Maldwyn felt a knot in his stomach at the thought of turning his back on Renate. He frowned as he considered the fact that she remained the only mother he had ever known, despite her deceit.

Right now, because of Renate's lies, and the anger Maldwyn felt as a result of her actions, he knew he needed space. A place to go where he could come to terms with this new information, and reconcile the warring thoughts and emotions he now bore towards her. A place away from Renate where he could leave her to rest. When he had let the anger go, he would return and speak with his mother calmly, to learn all that he could.

'I can't listen to this right now,' he said quietly, trying not to provoke another coughing fit as his mother began to regain her breaths. He held up his hands to silence her as she began to protest.

She coughed as he stood from the bed, grabbed his gear and made his way over to the door. He looked back, saddened that his life up until this point had been a lie. He pushed the door open and stepped out into the street.

CHAPTER TWO

Orphan of the Unknown

ALL AROUND, the world outside was painted in shades of grey. The cloud-covered sky was like a low-sitting veil of mist. The buildings were iced over and the frosted paths were no longer cleared. The streets were quiet as everyone remained inside, soaking up the warmth from their wood fires, which spewed smoke into the air that could be smelled for miles.

Feeling alone, perhaps more than ever, Maldwyn walked through the undisturbed blanket of snow. The thin layer of ice which had formed on the surface cracked beneath his boots, freeing the powdery texture below. Aimless, he meandered through the streets, heading toward the hills. Now and then, Maldwyn passed by a lone person walking with a purposeful pace toward the town centre for supplies. He would offer a polite curl of the lips, keeping his stare to the ground as much as possible to avoid entering into any unwanted conversations.

When he reached the hills, the burial grounds to his right grabbed his attention. Maldwyn recalled that he had not visited this place for quite some time and felt a pull in his chest, calling him toward the barrows. Marching through the knee-deep series of snow-clad earthen tombs, Maldwyn felt a profound sadness resurrect within him as an intense and sharp feeling of pain settled into an aching in his chest.

He pursed his lips as the memories came back to him, feeling a little nauseated. It had been summer when Maldwyn had lost the person he had loved. Back then, the burial mounds could easily be mistaken for hills from the way the grass would grow tall, like barley, and sway with the gentle breeze.

Now, in the dead of winter, the freezing, bitter wind stung his eyes, making them water from the chill. The frosty breeze crept through the gap between his sleeved shirt, the cuff of his jacket and his woollen gloves that had gathered at the base of his hand. Maldwyn pulled his gloves back up past his wrist, tucking in his sleeves to keep out the cold air.

Knowing his way through the graves by heart from the regular pilgrimages he used to make to visit his beloved, Maldwyn felt a wave of guilt surge over him, making him lightheaded, as he recalled how long it had been since he had last come by these grounds. It pained him that he was beginning to forget the image of Will's face in his mind.

Stopping by a perfect white mound, Maldwyn went down to his knees, sinking into the freezing snow. He studied the rise and fall of the mound that marked the grave of his former love. It was flawless. A perfect mound, protecting the body of what had been a gentle person. He reached out to touch the burial tomb, as though it would bring him solace.

'I miss you,' Maldwyn mumbled to the snowy mound. He knew better than to expect an answer, but he dreamed that Will had heard him. 'I should have been with you. If I had…' Maldwyn would never forgive himself for not being with Will when he was killed. He remembered how happy and safe Will made him feel. Many times, Maldwyn had played the events over in his mind, turning up just in time to use his gifts and save Will from death. Every night he would save him, but every day he would wake up and be faced with the sad truth that what he had conjured up was merely a dream. 'If I could trade places with you, I would do so in an instant.'

Maldwyn sat there on the cold hard ground for a long while, nursing his guilt, head hanging hopelessly. Time felt as though it had no meaning in the stillness outside. The clouds were fixed in place in the sky, unmoving with the light wind. In the complete and utter silence, his thoughts grew louder until his vision was blurred by the tears welling along his lower eyelids. It was cold, and he began to shiver.

'I thought I might find you here,' a familiar voice said to his back. Maldwyn sniffed, wiping his dripping nose on the back of his glove. He turned to see Dimitri, Will's father, standing behind him. He was a man of average height and build with a square set jaw and a thin mouth. He had grey hair and kind, moss-green coloured eyes. Lines were marking the years on his face and a patch of scaly skin where winter's touch had graced him with dryness. The several layers of thick clothing he wore made him look more round than usual. 'I just ran into Owen and he mentioned you were back.'

Maldwyn stared, dumbfounded. He hadn't expected that he would see Dimitri so soon. In a strange twist of fate, Maldwyn had come to visit the love he had lost and wound up being greeted by this man's father.

Picking himself up off his knees, he stood to face Dimitri. 'Dimitri... I'm sorry.' Maldwyn hadn't spoken to him since Will's passing. He had blamed himself and feared Dimitri would feel the same way. 'I didn't expect to see you here.'

'I went by your mother's and she told me you had left a while ago.' Dimitri was standing very erect with his arms hanging loosely by his sides. 'She told me that you were upset; that the two of you had argued about something.' Dimitri scratched his head as if he were trying to find the right words. 'I guessed you would have come here.'

'I came to pay my respects,' Maldwyn said, sounding a little defensive as he tilted his head. Stepping away from the burial mound, Maldwyn lowered his gaze and offered a kind and gentle smile to Dimitri before turning to leave.

'I talk to him sometimes too.' Dimitri said as he held up a hand to halt Maldwyn in his tracks and wave him back a step. 'I wanted to speak with you.' Maldwyn felt a tightness in his stomach, worried about what Dimitri wanted to say to him. 'It's just that you left so suddenly back then and I wanted to check that you are in a good place.' Surprised by Dimitri's well wishes, Maldwyn parted his lips as he took in a relieving breath of air. He had expected Dimitri to be angry with him and to ask him to leave the grave. 'Your mother's illness must be quite triggering for you. I know that the two of you aren't exactly close.'

That was an understatement, Maldwyn noted. His relationship with his mother was complicated, perhaps even more so now. 'I'm fine, thank you. My mother just said some things that… well, I guess that I wish she hadn't.'

Seemingly unsure of what to say, Dimitri gestured to the grave behind where Maldwyn was standing. 'Will would be happy to know you've visited.'

Bleary-eyed, Maldwyn stepped back on his heel and wiped his dampened cheeks, hoping his face wasn't too blotchy. He supposed the redness of his face from the cold would have masked his tears well. 'I miss him. He always knew how to make everything better. He gave me a quiet mind. I suppose I just wanted to feel close to him again.'

'I understand.' Dimitri rounded his shoulders. The corners of his lips were turned down a fraction as he attempted to muster a half-smile. He looked away as if he didn't want to dwell on the sadness eating away at him. 'How is your life in the palace?' He asked, changing the subject.

Maldwyn welcomed the change, relaxing his stiffened stance. He considered how best to answer the question. He wasn't quite sure what to say given that it was an incredibly complicated answer.

Since living in the city and working in the palace as a servant, Maldwyn had been taken on a journey where he and the prince were taken captive. On a few occasions, his magic had escaped his grasp, and, at other times, he had gained some control over his power, able to summon it at will.

Unintentionally, he had gotten himself involved with sorcerers, seers and curses. There were secrets and lies in abundance in the palace, but one person was struggling to make sense of things almost as much as Maldwyn, and that was the Crown Prince.

In the time that Maldwyn had lived in the city, he had grown unexpectedly close to the prince, enjoying the simplicity of lingering in his company. The memory of the kiss they had almost shared in the woods, under the moonlight, came to his mind, making Maldwyn feel horribly remorseful as he stood before Dimitri. He felt as though he had somehow betrayed Will.

'It's complicated.'

Dimitri nodded, accepting the answer as the honest truth. 'Are the rumours about the princess true? Is she on the run for using magic?'

'Yes, unfortunately, they are.' Maldwyn hoped the princess had made it out of the kingdom by now. Knowing that she had fled with Mikel was worrying.

Mikel was a slimy sort of person, determined on exacting some sort of revenge upon the royal family in Dresden for executing his aunt, Queen Sonia. Although Maldwyn hoped he had prevented Mikel's plan to curse King Viktor, he could not be positive that it had worked and he had not been able to stop his plans completely since the man had escaped custody.

Maldwyn had been bothered by a few things about the day Mikel had been arrested. It was odd that he would have shown up in the courtyard for the king's speech at the exact moment the prince and Maldwyn returned to the castle following their captivity. There was a part of him that wondered if he wanted to be captured. The other issue that had troubled him was the matter of the curse on the queen's triple horn pendant.

Although Maldwyn had disposed of the cursed pendant, he wondered who had cursed the piece at all. He trusted that

Princess Cassara and Erik were not to blame, and Mikel was not trained to use sorcery. Such curses were well and truly beyond his ability. Thus, Maldwyn was left speculating if there was another sorcerer in the palace, one that had cursed the pendant at Mikel's request. If so, then many of the people he cared for in the castle were still in danger.

'You've been on the road so long you have probably missed the latest rumour in the princess's case.' Maldwyn raised a curious brow at Dimitri's remark. 'She's made it out of the city. The rumours say that she and the man she's travelling with have come north.'

'North? She didn't head west?' Maldwyn checked, expecting that Mikel would have tried to lead her back to Mordiallok, avoiding the Erendil.

If they had headed west, then they could have passed over the southern end of the mountain ranges, avoiding the danger in the disputed territories along the Anhalt Mountains. Those disputed regions were under the lordship of Karana Downs. Maldwyn couldn't understand why Mikel would have brought Princess Cassara closer to danger.

'No, supposedly they came north. Let's hope that doesn't cause trouble around here. We may be further northeast than the disputed territories, but we don't need her bringing danger to Alander.'

'Yes… let's hope she doesn't pass this way.' An awkward gap in conversation made Maldwyn uncomfortable. Without warning, he thought of his mother and of how she was probably struggling to breathe as she lay helpless in her bed, worried about Maldwyn. 'I should go back to check on my mother.'

As Maldwyn walked away from the burial mound, Dimitri grabbed him by the arm. 'I'm sorry about your mother.' Maldwyn offered Dimitri a small, sad smile. 'If you need anything, I'm here for you.'

Maldwyn nodded, feeling oddly filled with pride. As Dimitri dropped his hand, letting Maldwyn go, he turned to face the white mound with a sad expression. Maldwyn turned again to leave, not knowing whether there was anything he could say to Dimitri that would take away the pain in his gut or the weight from his shoulders.

'One more thing,' Dimitri called, lifting his head, as Maldwyn continued along the path out of the burial grounds. 'Your life in the city… are you happy?'

Maldwyn couldn't lie to Dimitri. He meant well. The truth was, happiness was hard to find. It could be found in moments, maybe even held onto for a short time, but it was an elusive feeling that so easily slipped through one's fingers.

'I'm doing better there than I would be if I had stayed here,' Maldwyn answered honestly, as he paused and looked back over his shoulder.

'Will would be glad to know that.'

'Thank you,' Maldwyn said as he turned away and headed back toward the town, leaving the barrows behind.

As Maldwyn walked up the hidden path that was marked by his and Dimitri's footsteps, he looked back over his shoulder and saw Dimitri leaning to one side, head hanging solemnly.

Seeing Dimitri had been strange. He was glad to know that he didn't appear to blame Maldwyn for his son's death. Letting out a heavy sigh, Maldwyn contemplated how he was going to return to his mother and deal with the news of his adoption.

The streets around town remained barren as people still huddled in their houses and workshops for warmth away from the sting of winter. There were noises from the animals gathered in an enclosed shelter near the centre of town. The mouth-watering whiff of the baker's cooking was calming and the laughter from inside the closed houses reminded Maldwyn of the life hiding inside the walls.

As he passed by a large building with an open area covered by an oversized awning, under which orderly piles of tools were spread about workbenches, he heard the loud clanging of the town blacksmith working hard inside the forge. The scent of burning metal and coal hung low in the air as he passed, filling his nostrils with the pungent aroma.

Absorbed in the town's atmosphere, Maldwyn allowed his mind to wander, and consider the pieces the blacksmith was forging. He imagined the smith might be working on u-shaped, iron horseshoes, pointed heads of spears and arrows for hunting moose and reindeer in the woods, or blades of small daggers and knives for gutting prey. It must be therapeutic, Maldwyn supposed, working metal, shaping it to your will, and being able to make anything of it when under different conditions it would appear unyielding. At times, Maldwyn felt that life was as unbending as metal, and wished he were able to craft such artwork of his small existence.

Nearing his home, two women stepped out of one of the frosted houses as Maldwyn crossed his arms over his chest, trying to keep warm against the biting breeze. One of the women was rather short with frizzy mouse-brown hair, wearing an avocado-coloured dress with cream leggings, white woollen gloves and a blue scarf wrapped around her neck to keep her warm.

The other woman was tall and heavy-set with wiry black hair. Her clothes were similar to the shorter woman's in style, but the colours were brighter, more of a golden-orange saffron colour with forest green accents on the dress. They were muttering something about trouble in Aberdeen, the nearest town to the remote village of Alander.

Aberdeen lay many miles to the east, separated from Dresden's borders by a wide river that placed Aberdeen within the limits of the neighbouring kingdom, Haradnor.

The two kingdoms were allied and relied upon their mutual trade agreements. Aberdeen was a large supplier of wool, and, if issues in the area affected the trade industry, then the problems could lead to harsher winters ahead for the entire kingdom.

'Excuse me,' Maldwyn said to the shorter woman, who looked up at him with a befuddled expression. He unfolded his arms to seem more approachable. 'I just overheard you talking about problems in Aberdeen.'

'Yes. The winter has hit them hard this year and many of their livestock have died. They're low on food stores and supplies for trading. The whole town is suffering.'

'That's awful,' Maldwyn said, genuinely concerned for the people of Aberdeen. 'What is King Sebulon doing to help the people?' King Sebulon wasn't known for charity.

The taller woman shrugged. 'Nothing so far. Word is, he's in denial, ignoring the issue this could pose to his kingdom.'

'Supposedly he's been advised not to acknowledge the problem,' the shorter woman added. 'If he admits to the tragedy of what's happening, then it will draw too much attention to the difficulties this will cause to their economy, which he fears will impact his reputation and the kingdom's trade relationships.'

'If the king can find another town to supply the wool,' the taller woman continued in a monotone voice, as if she was just reciting well-known facts, 'then he can cover up what has happened in Aberdeen, and he can secure his trade status. As long as other kingdoms get what they need, they'll turn a blind eye.'

'I can't believe it! That's terrible!' Maldwyn stood aghast in shock at the news. The two women agreed with his remarks, shrugging as if there was nothing more to say about the topic. 'Thank you,' he said, bidding them goodbye and continuing back along the trodden, mushy path.

When he made it back to his mother's house, Maldwyn took in a deep breath, collected himself and pushed the door open. The hinges made a squeaking sound and the base of the door scraped against the floor. The fragrant woody smoke funnelled his direction, racing out the open door, as a wall of heat smacked him in the face. Maldwyn's cheeks suddenly stung as they defrosted. His nose dripped; a winter hazard.

After closing the door behind him, Maldwyn slipped off his gloves and placed them on the kitchen counter as he made his way back to the simple rocking chair by his mother's bed. Her gaunt face was looking up at him. Her bloodshot eyes were jumping around his face, searching for something he wasn't sure he could yet give: forgiveness.

Maldwyn sat in the chair, avoiding the cups and bowls which were still on the floor, resting on the plump cushion, clasping his hands together and placing his forearms on his knees.

Looking squarely at his mother, Maldwyn frowned, seeking the words without the anger. His mother waited, patient.

'Why did you lie for so long, mother?'

She bit her lower lip. 'I always planned to tell you the truth, but I was selfish. I wanted you to be my son, not someone else's. I worried that if you knew, you would find your real parents and you would wind up using your magic. I feared that, in time, you would be killed.'

He didn't like the answer but knew her too well to think it was another lie. His mother, Renate, had always been a woman ruled by her fears. Maldwyn had tried his best to be different from his mother and to live his life without making decisions based on fear. There were times though, that his mother's voice would play inside his head and he would fall victim to her thought patterns.

'Whose son am I?'

'I don't know, I never knew.' She laid her frail, thin arms timidly over her chest, one hand on top of the other as if she had been laid to rest in a coffin. 'Leith and I had been trying to have children for a few years. We had almost given up when you came into our lives.' Covering her mouth, she coughed up a mouthful of phlegm.

Maldwyn went to a nearby set of drawers and pulled out a small, square handkerchief that had a pink, floral pattern. He passed it to her and poured another cup of water as she wiped it around her mouth. She sipped the water, taking a moment to catch her rattling breath.

'Leith and I were in a bad place when we couldn't conceive. I prayed to the gods that they would grant us a child, and, eventually… they did. I found you in the hills.'

It seemed so surreal, learning that he had been dumped in the wilderness; an infant left to fend for himself. He pitied himself. Unworthy and unloved from birth, only to fall into the hands of a family that would teach him to hate himself.

'You were just a baby, wrapped in nothing more than a blanket. Your arms and legs were tucked in tightly by the swaddle. You were lying in the grass, crying.' Again, she coughed, body spasming with the sheer effort and energy it took from her. She spat out a ball of mucus into the handkerchief and leaned back, measuring her breaths. 'I didn't know how long you had been there, or who your parents were, so I took you home and convinced Leith that we should keep you, to raise as our son.'

Maldwyn moistened his lips. 'So, you don't know who left me in the hills? I was just there, alone?'

'Yes,' his mother sounded sombre, keeping a grim façade. 'I don't know what, or who your parents were. I don't know where your power comes from.' His mother let out a feeble cough. 'Can you do something for me?' Maldwyn gave her an unsure expression. 'I want to show you something,' she said with a little sensitivity creeping into her tone. 'I think it's from your parents, your real parents.'

'Alright,' Maldwyn agreed.

Lifting one of her arms weakly, as though it might drop at any moment, she pointed to the set of drawers. 'Go to the bottom drawer. Beneath the clothing, there is a small, green blanket and a letter. Take them both out please.'

Maldwyn did as his mother requested, pushing the clothing in the drawer aside until he found a petite, rectangular, folded blanket that seemed to be made of the finest silk and was pale chartreuse. He unfolded the blanket.

Leaves with yellow flowers were embroidered around the border. In one corner, was a falcon perching on a branch, stitched with a high-quality brown thread. Perched on the branch beside the falcon was an eagle, sewn with a darker strand for its body and an ivory thread for his face.

In the opposite corner, was a winged, black horse, rearing on its back hooves fiercely, like a warhorse riding into battle. Inside what had been the neatly folded swaddle, was a piece of parchment. Holding both items, Maldwyn returned to sit by his mother's side.

'These were the only things with you when I found you— other than your clothing. I never understood the meaning, but I kept them for you.'

At his mother's behest, Maldwyn opened the parchment feeling more confused than ever as he stared at nothing more than the symbol of an eagle, wings spread out wide as if preparing for flight, and its head angled to the side with its beak open. When he flipped the page, the other side had a pair of pure, black wings. Written beneath the wings in a cursive hand were the words: *Keep him safe.*

'I don't understand. It's just a picture of an eagle and a pair of black wings. It's basically the same as what's on the swaddle. Except the black wings are a flying horse on the blanket, which has the addition of a falcon.' Maldwyn looked at his mother, further frustrated by the useless letter. He didn't know what he expected really, but this certainly wasn't it. 'What is this even supposed to mean?'

'I don't know. Maybe nothing.'

It occurred to Maldwyn that some believed him to be important; a powerful figure of prophecy, most often referred to as Firebird. What that title had to do with an eagle and a flying horse was beyond him. It all seemed so bizarre and of no use.

'Whatever it means—if there is indeed a meaning—I am certain it is meant for you.' His mother started to cough again, body jerking helplessly. 'Whatever you do about this, Maldwyn, you must be careful.' Despite the cold air, beads of sweat were forming all over her gaunt, wrinkled face.

Maldwyn stroked her hair back to put her mind at ease. He folded the parchment back along the creases and wrapped it inside the swaddle. After stowing the blanket safely in his pack, he went to the kitchen where he poured water from the jug into a bowl. He dipped a linen rag into the water, dampened the cloth and came back to his mother's side where he wiped her face clean. He lifted the sheets higher over his mother. Exhausted, she fell asleep.

CHAPTER THREE

The Swan Sigil

PRINCE HARLAN CROSSED the polished granite floor to the other side of the throne room. Pillars ran the length of the room, holding up the magnificent vaulted ceiling. Decorative metalwork swirled up the length of the stone pillars, glimmering faintly, reflecting the beams of light breaking through the dark clouds outside.

Glancing out the huge, arched windows, Prince Harlan spied snow drifting through the air, bouncing on the slight breeze like weightless feathers, as he made his way toward where his father waited for him, sitting on the throne. The once-green vines that dangled over the outside of the impressive windows like living curtains were grey, hanging stiffly, encased in a thin layer of icy crystals.

Sighing to himself, Harlan breathed in the somewhat peppery air as he glanced up at his father, smirking from his grand throne.

Over the past few weeks, King Viktor had been in a horrible mood, prone to rages where his arms flailed about wildly and the veins in his neck would bulge beneath his skin. Everyone—servants, royal soldiers and members of the court alike—in the palace had been keeping a safe distance, treading carefully when in the king's presence.

There were several reasons that King Viktor was frustrated at the moment. The raids throughout the palace, the city and its surroundings had been largely unsuccessful at identifying anyone even remotely associated with the forbidden practices of sorcery. There had been fewer arrests than expected.

In addition to the raids, Princess Cassara and Mikel had not been seen since they had escaped the dungeons. Rumours of their whereabouts were most often precious little more than the whispers of clueless townsfolk spreading stories as legends told to their children. Some reports seemed to be more promising leads than others, but once investigated, nothing solid would be established and the trail would go cold.

On top of the lack of arrests and the rumours about the princess spreading, the king had been most maddened that the late queen's triple horn pendant had gone missing. Harlan guessed that it was perhaps because he had been warned that it would be stolen through his own daughter's dreams—dreams that King Viktor and Prince Harlan had only recently learned were the results of her being a seer.

Anyone in Dresden with sense knew how much the king hated magic and could guess how enraged he was with his daughter's aberration. In short, to simply say that King Viktor's temper had been unpleasant in recent weeks, was an understatement.

Prince Harlan slowed as he approached the base of the wide steps leading up to the podium where the king sat on his mammoth, finely carved throne. The grey granite stairs had dark spots speckled through the stone. The oak throne itself was sculpted like a piece of art, with delicately crafted feathers and leaves swirling together in a gentle lace-like pattern.

'Father,' the prince announced as he bowed out of respect to his superior, as was the proper custom. 'The invitation was sent as requested.'

King Viktor's eyes were dark and calculating as he slithered into his seat. The black streak on the side of his head cut through his greying hair. The subtle age lines that marked his face were like crinkled parchment. The crown he wore was gold and crafted to resemble leaves connected to twisted branches.

Pleased with the prince's report, King Viktor nodded and ran his hand over his clean-shaven chin. Prince Harlan waited for something to be said by his father but was not surprised by his continued silence.

'Forgive me for overstepping my bounds,' Prince Harlan began, clasping his hands before him and below his belt, a little confused by his father's request to send a summons to the Lord of Karana Downs, 'but should we not just punish Lord Darius for his insubordination?'

The guard to Prince Harlan's left gulped loudly in response to the Crown Prince's audacity to question the King of Dresden. Keeping his expression neutral, the prince waited for his father to respond.

Leaning forward, King Viktor rested his elbow on the arm of his throne. The fabric of his thick, wool coat which was lined with fur along the trim made a quiet rustling sound as the king shifted. The dim light from the setting sun, which hid behind grey-purple hue clouds, shaded the recesses in King Viktor's face.

'No. I want to see how deep his betrayal goes. Besides, he has been a trusted member of this court for years and I'm interested in hearing his explanation. It is possible that Mikel manipulated Lord Darius. He deserves the benefit of the doubt.'

The king got up from his throne. The guard to Prince Harlan's left bowed to the standing king, waiting to be permitted to straighten his stance. With a flippant wave of his hand, the king nonchalantly signalled for the guard to rise. King Viktor paused, assessing the quiet guard closely for a moment before lowering his voice to dismiss the soldier's presence.

Irked that his father would send away his guard so casually, especially given it was the king who had ordered Harlan be kept under watch at all times since his return from the Anhalt Mountains, caused the prince to tense the muscles in his face. Clenching his jaw slightly, Harlan understood his father's actions as no more than an ostentatious display of his power as the king of the realm. The constant escort had nothing to do with Harlan's safety, rather it was his father's way of keeping an eye on him whilst preventing him from being able to move about the castle freely. He and the king had been at odds since Princess Cassara's arrest, before her escape. The guard was his father's way of reminding Harlan of his ultimate power as the King of Dresden.

As a final gesture of respect, the guard bowed once more and backed away a few paces before turning around and walking out of the throne room. His boots clicked on the stone floors, and his pace seemed rhythmic. The enormous doors creaked as he opened them just wide enough to slip through.

Harlan remained neutral as his father came to stand at his side, staring toward the huge doors behind the prince. 'Tell me, Harlan, has your sister tried in any way to contact you?'

The prince gave his father a sort of side-eyed expression. He had heard the rumours that Cassara and Mikel had fled beyond the city walls, but the few guards loyal to Harlan that he had sent to search for her had all returned with little more than hollow whispers spread by simple villagers.

The prince knew all too well that little faith could be placed in local talk ever since he had learned the truth about his mother's execution. In a race with his father to find the princess first, Harlan considered what he could do to protect his sister from their father's rule.

He had thought about trying to smuggle her over the kingdom's border, but that was only half of the solution. Even if he did manage to contact Cassara and see her safely out of the kingdom, where then would she go? He didn't like the idea of her going to Mordiallok. Mikel was just one reason for Harlan not to trust that side of the family.

Prince Harlan locked eyes with his father's questioning stare and supposed he should answer him, lest he may enter a fit of rage. 'No, Your Majesty. The last I heard, she was already beyond the city's reach.'

Dipping his head doubtfully toward Harlan, King Viktor pressed his forefingers against his thumb in a supposing gesture. 'If I find out you helped her escape—'

'Father, rest assured, Cassara's escape was not orchestrated by myself.' Harlan couldn't help but enjoy seeing his father squirm at his lack of control over his son and daughter. 'I had only arrived back in the city that day. I could not have had the time to plan such a scheme... even if I had wanted to.'

'I'm warning you, son... don't get in my way.'

'How could I?' Prince Harlan shot back, keeping his appearance calm and cold.

He was growing tired of being under his father's constant scrutiny. Having his movements watched limited his ability to take measures to protect his sister. Despite the added difficulty in operating privately, however, he had found ways of passing messages to those he trusted and making plans without his father's knowledge.

The prince's ability to contact others without his father's awareness was—in large part—thanks to Master Damyan, Master of the Staff of Servants. Prince Harlan had agreed to keep Master Damyan's history of smuggling known sorcerers safely from the city a secret in exchange for his loyalty and assistance when called upon.

Thus far, Master Damyan had been an invaluable ally. He had even managed to sneak in a local cobbler by the name of Carlin, rumoured up until this point to have worked for Lord Darius himself, into the prince's private quarters without King Viktor learning of the meeting. Carlin had brought a great many interesting insights regarding Lord Darius with him. All the same, nothing mentioned by Carlin had been criminal, but the stories about Lord Darius's prostitutes certainly painted the man in an unsavoury light.

Of course, the information from the cobbler would not be enough to persuade King Viktor to remove Lord Darius's title, nor to have him sentenced for treason. However, Carlin had managed to unwittingly leave Harlan with an alternative lead. This new thread mentioned a woman by the name of Moya, the most trusted lady in waiting for Adria, Lord Darius's wife.

Harlan had never met Adria. Lord Darius didn't usually bring her on tour with him when he attended assemblies for the court in Dresden. Thanks to Carlin, he had learned that Moya and Adria were supposedly as close as sisters. They shared everything. Since Adria was likely the keeper of her husband's secrets, Harlan was hoping that Moya might be able to shed some light on Darius's activities and that she might be able to give him some information to help bring the traitor down.

Harlan knew getting Moya to open up about Lord Darius was going to be difficult, which was why the prince had gone along with his father's request to send a summons to Lord Darius. Knowing that it was Moya he wanted to speak with, Harlan had addressed the order to both Lord Darius and Lady Adria. A small detail he had neglected to share with his father. Prince Harlan figured that Moya would likely be brought to Dresden to attend to Lady Adria and then Harlan would be able to find a way to get her to talk. Trying not to grin at his covert investigations, particularly given that he was being followed by his father's guards at all times, Harlan lifted his brows somewhat to his father.

'You're the king. I can't do anything without you knowing about it.' In truth, the prince was aware that many of the servants were also keeping tabs on him, but was comforted to know their reports would be funnelled through Master Damyan, who would make the necessary edits before passing on the accounts to the king.

King Viktor sneered, curling the corner of his upper lip and giving the prince a doubtful expression. 'Be that as it may, if you attempt to help her, you will be punished.'

The threat felt a little empty to Harlan, given that he was the Crown Prince. As heir to the throne—especially given his sister's sentence to be executed—there was only so much his father could truly do to punish him.

Staring out the arched windows again, the prince saw that the snow had grown heavier. The darkening grey sky held its pale purple tint. Soon the servants would move through the castle unseen, like spectres, as they lit the torches and lanterns to brighten the castle in the blackness of night.

'So, father, when can we expect Lord Darius to answer your summons?'

Rubbing his chin, the king's stubby nails scratched along his jaw. 'He and his company can be expected to arrive within the fortnight.' King Viktor crossed his arms and paced with deliberate steps toward one of the huge windows, bathing in the dying light. 'Thank you for your report. You are dismissed unless there is anything else you wish to discuss.'

'No, father.'

King Viktor watched him from over his shoulder for a moment as Harlan kept an impartial demeanour. 'That'll be all. You may leave.' The king turned his back and spun away from the window, making his way up the steep stairs to his throne.

Prince Harlan bowed politely. 'Your Majesty,' he properly bade his farewell to his father, the king, before turning on his heels and heading out of the throne room.

When he passed through the massive doors, the royal guard accompanying the prince was waiting for him, arms folded over his chest. He wore the lightweight, deep blue leather armour of the palace guards, which made a series of creaking sounds when he bowed to Harlan, the Crown Prince of Dresden, as he passed by.

Indubitably, this was not the only royal guard that had been assigned to escort the prince through the palace since his return. The person allocated to undertake the task would vary with the changing of the palace guard, as one shift would end and another would begin.

Harlan felt a little bad that he couldn't remember this man's name, even more so since it was not this particular guard's first time chaperoning the prince about the castle. It was probably because Harlan felt the chap was an utterly dull fellow who, although he was a highly capable soldier, was an odd sort of man with squinty brown eyes, and who spoke in short sharp sentences and as little as possible. His responses to questions were limited to 'yes' or 'no' wherever feasible. The few times the prince had taken the time to attempt to learn more about the man, Harlan had been left completely uninterested, finding him one of the more boring people he had ever met. He would often find the guard standing at attention and staring at the blank palace walls, with a similarly blank expression on his face.

Harlan sighed as he considered that this was normal behaviour for the royal guards. There was just something about the way this guard remained so motionless, so completely still as if his own boredom had turned him to stone. Most of the other guards at least appeared to have more zest for life. Perhaps it was the difference of a simple twitch in the corner of one's mouth that made others seem more alive than the guard trailing a few paces behind Harlan.

His presence was made worse by the fact that the prince found his silence quite awkward at times. As Harlan glanced to his left, he spotted the clothing of a servant retreating behind one of the small doorways for the palace staff. For a moment, the sight of the retreating servant reminded the prince of Maldwyn, and he thought of how he yearned for his company. Anything to spare him from his bodyguard's insipidness.

Harlan smiled to himself as he thought how Maldwyn usually had something to say. The prince didn't mind that he often spoke out of turn, given his station. In truth, Harlan found Maldwyn's honesty refreshing.

Turning around a corner, the prince wound his way up a spiral set of stairs, leading him higher to the royal chambers. Many of the torches in this part of the palace had already been lit by the well-concealed staff lurking in hidden passageways, spitting and crackling at the slight draught as he passed.

In the distance, Harlan saw royal soldiers making their rounds, patrolling the greater corridors. Their shoes pounded on the ground in a seamless marching beat. Security in the palace had increased since the princess had escaped.

A soft smacking sound came from a nearby alcove, drawing the prince's attention to take a peek as he passed. Beyond the small recess near an outdoor balcony that had dried, iced vines hanging over the doorway, Harlan caught a glimpse of Theodor leaning over an auburn-haired servant woman. She was looking up at Theodor with a starry-eyed expression, oblivious to any passers-by. Lips curled into a happy grin, Theodor's gaze remained fixed on the woman and he never even noticed that the prince had witnessed their tender moment.

Filled with a strange sense of emptiness, Harlan's mind jumped back to Maldwyn as he was reminded of the moment they had almost shared in the woods before returning to Dresden. He still hung onto the what-ifs that swirled around his head since that day, occasionally indulging himself by replaying the moment in his head, changing the way things had turned out to suit his mood. He clenched his jaw and swallowed, pushing his thoughts away as if afraid that the guard following him might somehow read his mind.

Rubbing his forehead, the prince passed through the reception area in his residential wing, walking up the long wide corridor to where he entered his chambers, ordering the guard to remain outside.

Inside his private quarters, everything was in its place. The bed had been freshly made and the curtains were pulled back, welcoming the full view of the white snow-covered courtyard as the grey-purple clouds parted a little to reveal the darkening sky as the sun set. The fireplace before the upholstered lounges was popping and warmth billowed from the open hearth. The flat, muddled papers on his desk were undisturbed.

Although the room was faultless, Harlan had noticed that the servant who was tending to his rooms since Maldwyn had left the palace was a fraction less fastidious. The difference was so minute that he had wondered if it was just his mind playing tricks on him. Then again, when retiring for the evening, he had remarked on more than one occasion that the sheets were not so tightly tucked into the bed frame. This was a detail of which he could be certain.

Making his way over to the lounge area, Harlan noticed that there was something new, something out of place. A small envelope was resting on the fine, maple timber mantelpiece which had a fleur-de-lis incised in the centre of its buffed surface.

Picking it up and flipping it over in his hands, Harlan saw that the envelope had a wax seal depicting a bow and arrow, the mark of the worshippers of the bowman god, the symbol of the Erendil. Knowing that it would have been placed in his chambers by Master Damyan, Harlan tore open the letter to read the words of the Erendil's sovereign, Jerrik.

Your Royal Highness,

I trust that this letter has made its way safely to you and thank you for reaching out to me, especially given the risk posed to you by the tightened security in the palace since the princess's escape.

Unfortunately, I am not able to be the bearer of good news. Although Princess Cassara remains unaccounted for beyond whispers, the latest rumours have led my people to believe that she has made it as far as Karana Downs where, I fear, Mikel may have led her to seek refuge with Lord Darius. This is something he has done in the past.

Regrettably, I am not able to give you an insight into the association between Mikel and Lord Darius. Previously, when my people were tracking Mikel after he fled the Anhalt Mountains, we were not able to gain any information regarding his dealings with Lord Darius, and he had already been taken in as the liaison representative in the palace. Once Mikel was in the city of Dresden, we were no longer able to track him or his communications.

Despite the fact that I cannot assist with the investigation into Mikel and Lord Darius directly, nor give you the location of Princess Cassara, I would like to inform you that the disclosed summons from your father does not bode well for the princess if she is residing in Karana Downs—as I believe her to be—especially if your father should decide to discipline his unfaithful court member. Your sister will be at the mercy of Lord Darius's soldiers and I am not in a position where I am able to bring her safely to the Anhalt Mountains. We Erendil remain in hiding to preserve our ways and do not have the capacity to fight both your father and Lord Darius on what would become two fronts.

Having said that, I am willing to expend efforts to assist you with the collection of evidence against the Lord of Karana Downs where possible. I believe this is in the best interests of everyone.

On another note, please be reminded of our deal, and the condition of your release from our custody. I look forward to news of Kristian's ring, may he finally find peace in the afterlife.

Yours faithfully,

Jerrik Taramae

Harlan sat before the warm flames on the plush couch, soaking up the emanating heat as he held the envelope in one hand and the letter in the other. Tossing the envelope on the seat, he raked his fingers through his hair and considered the news that his sister may have sought shelter with Lord Darius in Karana Downs.

The lord was a corrupt man who had betrayed the crown, the man whom the prince was currently trying to have removed from power so he could no longer facilitate Mikel. Harlan felt torn between his allegiance to the crown and his sister, longing for something, a sign perhaps, to make his path forward clear, but no such signal would come.

Knowing that the way ahead had just become far more complex, Harlan tried to push the worries aside by focussing on Jerrik's reminder regarding their deal for the prince to retrieve Kristian's ring. When Harlan had sent word to Jerrik seeking news of Princess Cassara or evidence of Lord Darius's betrayal, he had purposefully not mentioned that he had already located Kristian Sadler's ring. Although the prince intended to return the ring to the sovereign, as agreed, there was a curiosity that had been sparked deep within him. He suspected Jerrik had been less than honest about the ring and wanted to understand its importance.

Resting now before the radiant fire, the prince pulled out the ring that he had been keeping on the chain he wore around his neck. He pulled off the chain and examined the ring closely. The band was wide and had dark, red jewels set on the surface. The silver band the stones were set in was beautifully crafted, with swirling motifs embossed upon its surface. As the prince turned the ring over in his hands, admiring its beauty, he noticed an engraving etched on the inside of the band.

He angled his head and brought the ring closer to his face so that he could better see the markings on the inside. He noticed that the imprint was a sort of symbol. He tilted the ring toward the light of the fire and discerned that the engraving was that of a swan. He thought it odd and considered why a swan would be etched on the inside of the ring.

Wanting to show his discovery to Maldwyn, Harlan suddenly felt alone in the palace and yearned for his return from Alander.

CHAPTER FOUR

The King's Crusade

WITH A HEAVY HEART, toiling through the snow-laden path, Maldwyn fixed his grip on the prickly rope handle of his mother's beaten, rough-looking coffin, aided by the trailing funeral procession bringing her to her final resting place. He had thought it would have been a grey day, full of clouds and falling snow, the day she was set to move on to her next life. But the sky was oddly blue; clear of grim clouds, clear of eddying smoke, clear of humming birds, and clear of all life despite the burning brightness of the sun, gleaming like a yellow ball of fire overhead.

Maldwyn thought the presence of the sun was merely a trick, visiting to dupe them into believing the day may be spared from winter's bite. His cheeks tingled from the sharp, glacial breeze. His nose felt numb. His fingers, which were locked around the rope, were bare so that he could feel the bitterness burning his hands as the bristles on the handles stabbed into his palms.

As he stepped in synchronisation with the rest of the escort, the memories of his mother's final days clouded his mind. Even though he had been prepared, knowing this would be the end of her time in this life, nothing could have readied him for just how confronting it was to watch her deteriorate.

Towards the end, she was slipping in and out of consciousness, forgetting where she was, calling for her mother to come and hold her. As she slept, Maldwyn had thought that he could get some reprieve from her cries only to be tormented by her gasps for air as she struggled to breathe.

The day of her passing left Maldwyn emotionally conflicted, making this one of the stranger days of his life, leaving him with an inexplicable sense of emptiness, like he had been consumed by an ever-darkening abyss. He had tried to gently wake her, wondering if she were just sleeping after having finally been able to breathe without choking on her phlegm. As he shook her carefully, she stayed motionless and unresponsive, seeming to continue dozing peacefully.

Maldwyn knew that she was dead, and nothing further could be said between them. That was it. The feeling that she may still wake at any moment haunted him. A shiver travelled down his spine at the memory of her death, and the pain of it all.

Unable to find the words to sum up her life adequately, painting her in a kind, positive light, especially given Maldwyn had spent most of his life angered by his mother, Maldwyn remained mute, moving along with the rest of the cortège. Owen led the solemn group in prayers to the gods, following close behind where the coffin was being escorted. His voice was loud and clear and seemed to have more weight than usual.

A dark stain in the blank, white ground marked the spot where his mother's grave had been dug among the other barrows. The mass of dirt piled to the side ruined the otherwise perfect, unscathed, powdery snow. Shovels were sticking out of the pile of dirt like needles poking out of a pincushion.

There was something about the way the hollow grave mimicked how he felt in his core, as if it were a cruel depiction of his soul at this point in time, that disturbed him, making him feel horrid, rotten even. The abyss inside Maldwyn threatened to swallow him, just as the ground would swallow his mother in her casket.

When he and the rest of the train of people stopped to lower the coffin into the hole, Maldwyn noted the ground at the bottom was not level. Looking down, avoiding the sight of the box containing his mother's body, he saw that his hands were red and raw from the coarse rope chafing against his skin. Time felt slow as if the moments between blinks were unusually long, and the eyelids themselves opened and shut upon his conscious command.

Maldwyn looked up to the sound of sniffling. Veronika was a petite woman with long honey-coloured hair that highlighted the subtle amber tones of her brown eyes which were glinting with tears. Maldwyn noted that her lips were dried and cracking. A result of the harsh winter. Looking down, she clasped her hand around her husband's, interlocking her fingers with his. Owen pulled her in close and placed a kiss on her forehead.

The crowd began to hum and make guttural sounds, singing in low, baritone voices that sounded more like chanting as they laid Renate to rest. Together, the voices of the townsfolk were divine, capturing the pain of loss, giving Maldwyn goosebumps and sending chills over the burial grounds.

Numb, Maldwyn stood frozen, eyes transfixed on the dirt. There was an unusual beauty to the depth of colour the ice had given the soil; a certain sort of richness from being buried beneath the thick blanket of snow, which gave it a near-blackened, burned effect that was in stark contrast with the pristine white hills.

The background song brought Maldwyn to tears, which he stifled as best he could. He was slightly bothered by the weeping faces as he scanned the crowd. These people did not know her, not the way he had. Renate was not a kind woman. She was cold, aloof, and highly reactive, barely worth liking in many respects. These were sides of his mother these people hadn't witnessed, but Maldwyn knew them all too well.

He wondered why he felt sad. Although he had just learned that this woman was not his birth mother, Maldwyn couldn't help but feel connected to her as the only family he had known outside his uncle who had died years before. He supposed that, despite all her faults, and that Maldwyn had spent his childhood feeling afraid and unsafe because of Renate, the realisation that he was alone was an overwhelming sensation of hurt which left him deeply heartbroken.

When the song was sung and silence returned to the hills, Owen turned and reached for one of the shovels, tapping

Maldwyn on the arm as he passed it to him. As if sleepwalking, Maldwyn took the shovel by its handle in a grip that felt as though it weren't his own.

Taking the lead, Maldwyn dug the shovel into the pile of dirt, loading it with a generous amount of soil, and poured it over his mother's coffin. Owen and the rest of the group that had helped carry the casket picked up the other shovels, helping Maldwyn build the earthen mound that would mark his mother's tomb.

After what seemed to be hours, the casket was buried, and the barrow formed. Maldwyn knew that, over the course of time, the burial mound would eventually be covered with grass and sprouting flowers. For now, though, it was a dark mark marring an otherwise pristine white, snow-covered hillside.

The crowd left, retreating from the cold, yet Maldwyn remained. The clouds rolled overhead. Snow fell from the sky, making his bare hands burn. Alone, he stood to watch over the dirt as the snow slowly covered the grave, morphing it through various shades of grey until it settled upon white.

He felt like a statue, frozen by the waves of emotions overwhelming him, such that he was unable to state his exact mood. The cacophony of sentiments churning about his head deadened him as if murdered by the onslaught.

As the sun began to set, an unpleasant chill in the air made him shake uncontrollably, shivering from the harsh, frigid wind. Finally, Maldwyn headed back to the house, pausing in the doorway as he took in the picture of a life that had been lived. The cup she had been drinking from was on the floor by the bed, which had been soiled shortly after her passing. The house was filled with the smell of her urine. A square rag with frayed edges hung over the side of a bowl of water. Maldwyn had used the rag to wash the sweat away from her face and body, giving her dignity in death.

Maldwyn set the hearth alight to heat the home and battle the strong stench in the air, which was clinging to his nostrils. He stripped the bed of the soiled sheets and tossed them into the fire, burning the mess away. As the room began to lose the chill in the air, Maldwyn stripped off his woollen coat, hanging it on the back of one of the dining chairs. Grabbing a huge pot, Maldwyn made several trips outside to collect enough ice that, when melted over the roaring flames, filled the pot.

As the water warmed, he picked up the cup, rag and bowl from the floor, placing them inside the pot of boiling water to sterilise them. He wiped the dusted surfaces, swept the floors, put the delicate wooden carving of a wolf that reminded him of his mother in a drawer, and carefully washed the clothes in which she had died.

He sniffed and wiped the drip on the tip of his nose on the back of his hand as he stepped back to check the state of the room. Satisfied that the place was sufficiently tidied, Maldwyn packed his bag, glad to be leaving this place behind in the morning and returning to the servant halls of the palace, where he was a misfit among misfits.

Thinking of Dresden Maldwyn wondered what he had missed and what might have changed in the palace in his absence. Perhaps Prince Harlan had contacted Jerrik about Kristian's ring. It occurred to Maldwyn that he may have even returned the ring to the Erendil by now, as had been agreed.

When he was packed and ready to depart the next morning, Maldwyn sat in one of the chairs by the dining table. It wobbled beneath his weight. Rubbing his forehead, Maldwyn let out a weakened breath. He closed his eyes, trying to get some relief from the day. Head in hand, he finally allowed himself to cry, giving in to the despair that had been suffocating him most of the day.

The fire crackled softly. The wind whistled through the gaps of the window shutters, howling every so often. The boiling pot bubbled and gurgled at irregular intervals.

Maldwyn felt weak and tired, as though there was nothing left in him. He wiped the tears from his cheeks with the palms of his hands, sniffing, sucking in a huge breath. No longer feeling anything, Maldwyn sat in the quiet, eyes downcast, focusing on the uneven floorboards. Even his thoughts were mute.

A piercing scream from somewhere in the distance seemed to cut right through Maldwyn's gut, catching him by surprise. A loud bang, like the breaking in of a thick, heavy door, declared a cause for concern. Lifting his burdened head, Maldwyn listened to the sounds coming through the closed shutters.

Metallic ringing, like that of scraping steel, and the sounds of metal clashing together, were accompanied by an orchestra of terror, screams singing the songs of death. Unsettled, Maldwyn rose to investigate the ominous noises.

Making his way over to the door, he placed his hand on the warm knob, ready to yank the door open. Then, there was silence. Complete quiet. The momentary calm sounded like a warning, cautioning Maldwyn from opening the door to the world outside.

A whooshing sound swept around his house, like a wave of destruction, collapsing the humble homes of his neighbours. The wall to his right groaned, murmuring to tell him to step back before it gave way.

Unsure what was going on, what to do, or where to go, Maldwyn raced across the room to the dining table and pulled on the coat he had hung over the back of the chair, slipping his arms through the sleeves. Grabbing the pack which had been placed on the floor by his mother's loom, which had a half-sewn linen piece hanging within the frame, Maldwyn lugged the backpack over his shoulders, tightening the straps through the buckles a little. The wall erupted, engulfed with the raging fire, hissing at Maldwyn to leave his home as if it were a snake claiming his house as its territory.

Searching for a way out of the deadly blaze, Maldwyn felt his heartbeat pounding in his chest from terror. Flames climbed the roof, reaching out to lick him. He ducked to dodge the inferno, holding his hands up to protect his face. Maldwyn's effervescing power soared, exploding forth from his control with a roar of its own.

The world went mute. Moving his hands away from his view, Maldwyn saw that the flames had stopped advancing, no longer burning through the walls on its warpath. The screaming outside had ceased. The clanging metal quieted. Everything was silent.

Having done this once before, Maldwyn knew that the slowing of time would only last so long before the world would catch up with him. He dashed across the room and rushed out the door, jumping over the fiery threshold while the flames were subdued. He slipped on the icy path, losing his footing a bit as he ran out into the street, stumbling to where he saw the true extent of the madness he had heard from inside.

For as far as he could see, the buildings were burning, devoured by red and orange infernos. Black smoke was rising into the night sky, blocking the stars from the view on the street. Men wearing the heavy golden armour of the royal palace guards stood in threatening poses with their weapons raised, blood spattered over their breastplates, and their faces were hidden by polished helmets. People huddled together on the open streets like lambs to the slaughter.

A young girl with tear-soaked cheeks cowered into the snow beneath a frozen guard, who was driving his sword toward her chest. The sword began to continue its path. The screams sounded strange, deeper and lower in pitch than they should have been. Roaring flames began to growl.

Worried for the girl's life as time slowly resumed, Maldwyn looked around for a weapon but saw nothing that could help him. As the girl's crying returned to normal and the sword sped along its path, Maldwyn reached his hands out toward her, helpless. Feeling his pulse pounding through his hands, his fear for the girl released another burst of his power, knocking the sword from the guard's grip. The man looked up and locked eyes with Maldwyn.

'We've got one!' The man shouted, turning toward Maldwyn and pulling out a large knife from his hip. A few guards came to aid their shouting comrade. 'Get him! He used sorcery!' The man instructed, remaining behind with the gathered crowd.

Backing up, Maldwyn reached for his power and threw out his hands, feeling nothing answer his call. Wishing he had better control, he realised he had nothing to defend himself from the advancing group of guards. Stepping back on his heels, Maldwyn spun around and ran for the hills.

Guards jumped out from behind the burning buildings. Maldwyn ducked and weaved through the danger. Spears and swords stabbed at him, narrowly missing Maldwyn by a hair's breadth. Just as Maldwyn thought he had outrun most of the guards, a hand caught his coat by the arm and swung him around, making him fall over on the icy path, crashing through the wall of a mostly burned building. A few flames still sizzled on the charred, blackened planks. A small chunk of wood cut the hand he had reached out to break his fall.

Wincing, he pushed himself to roll over to his side. A bald man with a scar across his left cheek, wearing no helmet but holding a spear, stepped into the wreckage. Embers flickered as he kicked a plank of blackened wood out of the way with his boot. Maldwyn blinked, feeling his eyes itching from the ash in the air, and held in the desire to sneeze as the cinders filled his nostrils.

'Give up, sorcerer.' The man told him, lowering his spear to Maldwyn's chin. Terrified, Maldwyn swallowed. The metal spear was marred with blood. 'There's nowhere for you to run.'

A silhouette of a man of average height and build quietly came up behind the guard, picking up a burned plank without making a sound. Confused, Maldwyn watched the man swing the plank at the back of the soldier's head. The guard's eyes rolled to the back of his skull. He fell to his knees. Blood ran from the back of his scalp down the side of his neck. The spear hit the ground with a loud clunk.

Shocked, Maldwyn lay still in the rubble. The silhouette, stepped forward, into the light, extending a hand to help him up to stand. Maldwyn took the man's help with his good hand and recognised the square jawline and moss-green eyes of Dimitri.

'Why would you help me?' He asked, bettering his footing in the debris, genuinely baffled that Dimitri would risk his life to protect Maldwyn.

Dimitri looked back over his shoulder, checking that the guards behind weren't following. 'I know you have magic.' Maldwyn felt his heart skip and land in his throat, forgetting that his hand was bleeding. 'Will told me the truth about you the day before he died.'

Stumped by the confession, Maldwyn drew his brows together. 'You knew all this time?'

'Yes.' Dimitri grabbed him by his shoulders in a tender, almost fatherly way. 'I saw what you did back there. You moved with impossible speed and then disarmed the guard without saying a word.'

Maldwyn shrugged. 'I couldn't let the girl die.' He stepped forward, lowering his voice to a whisper. 'I don't have control over it though.'

'You can't control it?'

'Not always.' Dimitri nodded as if finally making sense of Maldwyn. He dropped his hands from his shoulders. 'About Will... I would have saved him if I could have.'

Dimitri frowned, looking at Maldwyn with sad eyes. 'Maldwyn, I know you weren't with him when he was killed. I don't blame you for what happened. I never did.'

'I wish I felt the same,' Maldwyn admitted, remembering the cut across the palm of his hand, suddenly noticing a throbbing pain there. Hearing guards shout to each other on the street, Maldwyn looked over Dimitri's shoulder, confirming they had yet to be spotted.

'The guards, they know you used magic. I don't think they realised there were no spells involved and that the power was your own. You're not safe by any means. Not to mention, I don't know how well they saw your face in the dark. You have to run before they catch you.'

'Come with me,' Maldwyn said in a hushed voice.

'No. I'm still searching for the truth about what happened that day. Searching for who killed Will and why. If I leave, I may never know the truth. Besides, I can hold the guards off while you make your escape.'

'Don't risk your life for me. They kill people who are deemed to be magic sympathisers.' Maldwyn tensed as he heard voices getting closer. 'I would never forgive myself if you died because of me.'

'I'll be careful, Mal. Just get as far from this place as you can.' Maldwyn hesitated, letting out a heavy breath as he weighed his options. He considered allowing himself to be captured to spare the lives of his neighbours, however, he also knew the king was likely to execute them all as a message to other towns harbouring sorcerers. Perhaps it was safer for them all if Maldwyn wasn't caught. Those left alive may be spared while investigations were conducted to catch the escaped sorcerer. 'You need to leave.'

Finally, shaking his head, Maldwyn gave in to Dimitri's pressing. 'Okay, I'll go.'

Dimitri pulled Maldwyn into a warm embrace, one that reminded him of family, something he had lost. Dimitri patted him on the back before letting him go.

'I hope you find the truth,' Maldwyn offered, stepping back.

Dimitri smiled at the remark. 'Good luck.'

Maldwyn took a deep breath, neared the gap in the wall that he had been thrown through and peered out to the street, checking whether the path ahead was clear. There were some guards to the right, looking between the gap of some buildings. If he were going to make it out of the village alive, then now seemed as good a time as any to run for the hills. He gave one final smile to Dimitri before rushing out to the street.

Maldwyn was careful as he ran through the rest of the town, keeping a keen eye out for guards in the area. When he reached the edge of the village before the hills, Maldwyn was conscious that there would no longer be any cover to keep him from their view, and, despite Dimitri's best efforts and the darkness of the evening sky, he would likely be spotted as a dark shadow running up the pristine, white hills.

Feeling jittery and breathing in short, rapid breaths, Maldwyn began to run away from the burning town. Behind him, as he ran up the nearest hill, Maldwyn heard the soldiers shouting at each other. Afraid to risk slowing by looking back, Maldwyn pressed on harder, racing up toward the crest as he thought he heard arrows whistling through the air after him. Reaching the top of the hill and hurrying beyond their sight, Maldwyn heard what sounded like a group of men being ordered to track him down.

Breathing quickly, he ignored the pain he felt building in his calves and pulsating in his hand. Knowing that he couldn't stop now, Maldwyn surrendered to the chase and sprinted away as fast as he could, hoping to put some distance between himself and the royal guards.

CHAPTER FIVE

The Arrival

'LORD DARIUS! Your arrival honours our great city, Dresden!' It was an unctuous, address from the king, intended for avoiding ignominy before the crowd, which had gathered to witness the arrival of the Lord of Karana Downs.

The courtyard hadn't been this full since the prince had returned from captivity last fall, the day Harlan's sister had been arrested for sorcery. The prince cringed at the memory, skin-crawling at his sister's sentence.

The open square before the palace appeared to glow as the sun peeked through the clouds to kiss the snow-covered ground, which reflected its golden-hued light. The palace's rugged stone walls were decorated with dead, grey vines that were crisp to the touch. Prince Harlan was standing on the palace steps with his father, King Viktor, to greet the arriving guests. Harlan's escort stood behind him on the other side. A grand balcony hung off the front of the rugged castle overhead, casting a wide, dark shadow on the ground.

A large, horse-drawn carriage with iced fleur-de-lis carvings embellishing the wooden frame, and massive, sturdy wheels that were covered in muck, halted before the palace. There was a small contingent of guards and servants. Harlan wondered which of the maidservants was Moya, the woman he was seeking. The curtains in the window of the carriage swayed as the door opened.

Lord Darius, a burly, barrel-chested man with thinning wheat-coloured hair and heavy-lidded, tawny eyes, stepped out of the carriage. He was wearing leather travelling clothes of a dark, almost black, chocolate colour and a massive grey fur coat made out of a wolf pelt. The snow on the ground stuck to his black boots. He held out his hands, as if presenting himself to the crowd, and bowed before King Viktor.

The watchful crowd stirred. People at the back pushed their way forward to catch a glimpse of the happenings at the royal palace. The guards lining the courtyard were on high alert, standing to attention, examining the citizens as they shoved each other to take a peek.

'Your Majesty! It is I who is most humbled and honoured to be your guest!' Everything about the lord of the northern regions was a performance, nothing more, and the very presence of the man put Harlan on edge. 'Please, allow me to introduce you to my wife, Adria.'

Lord Darius reached back and held a hand out toward the carriage door. A small, freckled hand stretched out and wrapped around Darius's dirt-stained fingernails. When Adria slipped out of the carriage, she wasn't what Harlan had expected.

She was a petite woman with a heavily freckled, round face and shoulder-length, curly ebony coloured hair that was parted to the side in a messy half updo. The shape of her eyes made them appear sad and they were a sort of pewter grey shade. As she moved forward, he could tell she was bowlegged and pigeon-toed. The simple, forest-green travelling dress she wore wasn't well-tailored and did little to hide the way she walked.

Bewilderingly, Lord Darius was considered very charismatic despite his appearances and, for this reason, Harlan expected the lord's wife to be a stunningly attractive woman. As Harlan thought about it, he supposed that she wasn't unattractive, rather it was her appearance that didn't match the near-perfect vision of her he had built in his mind.

He tried not to show his surprise at her appearance as both the lord and his wife approached the prince and the king, standing on the palace steps. The crowd cheered when the Lord of Karana Downs waved to them as he left his envoy behind. Lord Darius flicked his gaze to the guard standing behind Harlan. He wondered whether the lord had been informed about the growing rift between the prince and his father and that Harlan was under constant watch.

'Your Majesty! Your Royal Highness!' Adria properly addressed them both, curtseying before royalty. From this distance, Harlan could smell the strong magnolia perfume she was wearing.

'Lady Adria,' the king started, his voice as smooth as velvet. 'How lovely it is to meet you after all these years! Welcome to

Dresden.' The king turned to Lord Darius, narrowing his eyes and lowering his voice so that the crowd could not hear. 'I have been informed of your association with Mikel.' For the first time since Harlan had known Lord Darius, he saw a glimpse of panic touch his face as he gulped. 'I am interested to hear your side.'

Lord Darius gave a slight nod and gulped, terrified that the king may have him executed on the spot for treason. 'Of course, Your Majesty.'

King Viktor gave a greasy smile, showing the whites of his teeth, and with a flick of his hand, bade his people farewell before leading the guests up the rest of the palace stairs. The escort had been left in the courtyard to make their way through the servant halls to where their lord and lady would be quartered for the duration of their stay. Prince Harlan felt quite satisfied to see Darius be made to feel uncomfortable by his father, the king, especially since he had never much liked the slimy lord.

The massive reinforced doors creaked open. The expansive foyer with vast, vaulted ceilings had an array of sculpted patterns in the stonework. There were torches on the walls, but they weren't lit as there was plenty of light pouring in through the arched windows, illuminating the space from floor to ceiling. The clacking of their boots echoed in the cavernous entrance hall.

Lord Darius and Lady Adria knew better than to make small talk given the circumstances. They followed, quiet and obedient, through the corridors and climbed the grand staircase higher into the castle. The corridors in the palace were magnificent and there was a sort of ardour about the place, even in the freezing chill of winter. Tapestries of ancient fables and paintings of previous monarchs hung from the motley, stone walls.

The halls grew wider and grander until they reached the massive, oak doors to the council chambers. The king's sentries stood by the entryway, wearing heavy, golden armour that was so perfectly polished that it glimmered in the dim light in the corridors. The guards stepped aside and opened the doors, making way for the king and his company to pass into the chambers. Harlan's escort waited outside by the door with the rest of the guards.

Inside, the council chambers had a slight musty smell from the winter's cold, despite the expansive size of the room and its array of opulent furnishings. The long, heavy timber table was flawlessly smoothed and had eight bulky, high-backed chairs tucked around it. An open fireplace was set in the wall nearest the long table and was bursting with a warming flame.

In a small room to the side was a large, ornate desk with just one seat behind the table. A wide, low line, walnut hallstand had piles of parchment and scrolls that lined the lengthy shelves. Candelabras with whirling, sculpted metal hung from the roof, wax dangling directly above the council meeting table.

The balcony beyond an open archway could be glimpsed through the gaps of the hanging dried, frozen ivy and had a few inches of snow blanketing the stone balustrade. Surprisingly, the room managed to stay relatively warm despite the open archway.

Lord Darius and Lady Adria waited for the king to instruct them to take a seat before moving to the far end of the table. They dragged the chairs on the floor, making a low droning sound. King Viktor sat at the head of the table, on the opposite end to the lord and lady of the north. Harlan locked eyes with Lord Darius and grinned as he sat to the right of the king, taking his place as the Crown Prince of Dresden. The room was silent.

King Viktor leaned back and rested his elbow on the arm of his chair, leaning smugly to one side. 'Well… Lord Darius.' He threw his hands up as a blasé gesture. A feeling of dread settled in Harlan's gut. Ever since Lord Darius had achieved the impossible feat of winning the Battle of the Shadow Plains during the war between Dresden and Mordiallok, when the prince was but a child, King Viktor had given the lord certain concessions. 'Here we are.'

'Your Majesty… if I may,' Lord Darius's words were cut off by the king holding up his hand. Harlan was pleased to watch him sink back down into his seat and see that his father hadn't immediately fallen fool to the lord's influence. Lady Adria shifted nervously beside her husband and coughed a little pathetically, holding her hand over her mouth.

'We have it on good faith that you helped a member of the royal family of Mordiallok—our enemy—to gain access to the palace.' King Viktor cleared his throat as the fire crackled. 'What do you have to say for yourself?'

Lord Darius hesitated, as though he were considering his answer very carefully. 'Your Majesty, I have always been loyal and dedicated when it comes to serving the crown. Before today, I would have considered us as more than mere acquaintances… I would have considered us friends. Please, before condemning me, I would like to know the source of your information, so that I can properly comprehend the allegations.'

King Viktor turned to his son and signalled for Prince Harlan to take the lead in offering a full explanation of the accusations. It had been Harlan who had brought the news of Lord Darius's betrayal to Dresden. Taking a moment to determine exactly how much information to give to the lord, Harlan rested his hands on the table, keeping his palms flat on the smooth tabletop.

'I am afraid I can't name the source to you,' Harlan started as he glanced to his father to gauge whether he considered this an acceptable response to the lord's request. With his father's nod of approval, he continued, 'But what I will say is that you were directly identified as being in league with Mikel Wolff who planned to make an attempt on the crown.' Lady Adria gasped and reached for her husband's hand. Harlan noticed that the lord pulled his hand away and rubbed along his brow, looking a tad concerned. 'As it was on your orders that Mikel was accepted inside the palace as a representative of Karana Downs, can you enlighten us as to why you sent an imposter into the castle?'

'Thank you, Your Grace,' Lord Darius began as he scratched the side of his cheek. 'I appreciate you discussing this matter with me. Mikel came to me under the guise of Mikel Tanzer. I believed him to be of noble birth from our allied kingdom, Haradnor.'

Lady Adria sat tall and stiff as she stared down at the table as if studying the direction of the wood grain and trying to ignore her husband churning out lies. The expression on her face was deeply suspicious and gave away that she knew the truth of Lord Darius's intentions. Harlan hoped this knowledge had been shared with her maidservant Moya.

'I took him in on good faith, which I take full responsibility for, Your Majesty.' Harlan clenched his jaw, frustrated as he watched his father soften, accepting the lies as soon as they were uttered. 'I was impressed with the way the man conducted himself in the short time he was with me in Karana Downs, and, when the previous liaison's wife fell ill, I felt Mikel would be suited to the role. Thus, I sent him to the palace with the letter of recommendation.'

'You never tried to verify this man's position with the court in Haradnor before placing him under your protection?' King Viktor asked sounding genuinely curious. Harlan was impressed his father seemed to be remaining clear-headed.

'No, Your Majesty.' Lord Darius's voice feigned remorse incredibly well as he hung his head low. 'I was too trusting of the man.'

'You always were overly trusting,' King Viktor agreed, scratching behind his ear. Harlan stiffened, noting the change in his father's tone. 'Still, an intrusion such as this can't be ignored. We need to counter King Filip's infiltration and find out what he's planning.'

Feeling the need to redirect the conversation back to the lord's guilt, Harlan broached a new topic. 'Mikel escaped custody a short while ago with the help of my sister. As of yet, we have not been able to locate them, but rumours have suggested that they headed north, to lands under your protection.' A sudden change in the air wafted the smoke from the burning wood his way. It was a warming and comforting sort of smell. 'If Mikel was not in league with you, why would he seek refuge in your region?'

Raising his eyebrows and tilting his head to one side, acting unimpressed by the question, Lord Darius bit his lower lip. 'Well, Your Grace, the eastern border of Dresden is lined by a large channel of water running directly back to the ocean and would take the two of them further away from Mordiallok; not to mention that they would wind up in unfriendly territory by entering lands allied with our great kingdom. The Erendil litter the Anhalt Mountains to the west of the country and are concentrated heavily to the northwest. The only other way out of the kingdom to return to Mordiallok is north, through Karana Downs and the surrounding lands.'

'Are you suggesting that it would be easier for them to slip through Karana Downs than through the Anhalt Mountains?' Harlan angled his head, scrutinizing the lord across the long table. 'Are the borders to the north not secure?'

Lord Darius was careful not to smile at the prince's point. Lady Adria clasped her hands on the table and brought them closer to her body. King Viktor wore a dubious expression, glancing over to Harlan from the corner of his gaze. The sound of a pin dropping in the council chambers would have seemed deafening in the silence as they waited for an answer.

Shaking his head, Lord Darius let out a heavy sigh. 'Your Majesty, Your Grace, for some time our region has borne the brunt of the disputed territories, being in constant battles with the Erendil in the mountains. As you know, we have already been cut off from accessing the mine in this region. As a result, our efforts are focused on the northwestern borders, so it would make sense for them to aim to slip through the northern border which has poorer protection.'

Clenching his hand into a fist, Harlan sat back, feeling that he should have seen this coming; that he should have guessed the lord would use the well-known disputes to cover up his aiding Mikel and Cassara. A glance at his father and Harlan could tell the king was buying into the falsehoods. The feeling in his gut left an unpleasant taste in his mouth. Harlan grew more irritated as he watched his father willingly fall victim to whatever schemes Lord Darius had in the works, all the while he was losing his own father's trust one day at a time. Harlan was a patient man and buried his anger deep down with years' worth of slow-building rage.

'Hmm,' the king started, 'the Erendil have plagued our lands for too long.'

'Yes, Your Majesty, they have.' There was a spark of heat in his voice. Lord Darius aimed a finger at the prince. 'I hear Prince Harlan has recently returned from captivity with the Erendil himself. Perhaps the tales of my involvement are the embellished rumours of the Erendil.'

And so, the story was set, Harlan told himself. King Viktor was won by Lord Darius's well-spun mistruths. Knowing that the source of the information was the Erendil—a people hated by the king—Harlan folded his arms. He knew when a battle was lost.

'His capture was most unfortunate, but he proved himself most capable by finding his way out of their stronghold.' King Viktor smiled at Harlan as though he were a proud father praising his son. 'We have yet to sift through the lies they told him. I am glad to at least be able to exonerate you as an accomplice to Mikel Wolff. We have a festival coming up to honour the gods and pray for a safe winter in the coming weeks. Please stay for the festival as our guests.'

Lord Darius and Lady Adria both offered overly joyous expressions as they accepted the king's invitation. The king relaxed his arrogant composure and sat taller in his seat. Things had not gone well, but Harlan had half expected this to be the case before the arrival of the lord. Still, he was disappointed in his father.

Harlan was glad that the stay had been prolonged. It would give him more time to meet with the maidservant Moya to learn any information she had about the lord's actions. More than that, the recent exchange had shown Harlan that the lady herself was not as close to her husband as one might expect. He guessed that with the right appeal she might be open to sharing everything she knew. Harlan just needed to work out how to buy her faith.

King Viktor stood abruptly from his seat. If it weren't such a heavy seat, he would have knocked it over onto the floor. 'Please, allow my guards outside to take you to your rooms.'

Harlan stayed in his seat as the king left the chambers. Lady Adria sashayed as she walked, following the king through the large doors. Stopping beside the prince, Lord Darius leaned down to the seated Harlan and whispered near his ear, 'What you have done by having me brought here, Your Grace, is merely the movement of a weak man.'

In no mood to banter with the man, Harlan remained motionless in his seat until the lord straightened and slithered through the doors to trail the king's lead. Folding his arms across his chest, Harlan weighed up his options.

Two loud knocks banged on the servant entrance to the council chambers. Harlan glanced up at the sound, surprised. The chambers would have been cleaned earlier in the morning. There was no reason for servants to return to the chambers until the following day.

'Enter,' Harlan called to the door, curious to see who was waiting in the servant corridor.

An older gentleman with silver streaks gleaming through his hair stepped through the small, creaking door and bowed. It was Master Damyan. Harlan hopped up from his seat and slowly made his way over to the Master of the Staff of Servants who had a satisfied look on his face.

'Your Royal Highness, I come bearing good news.'

'Oh?'

'Ser Theodor has information regarding Mikel and he's waiting in the hall for you, sire.' Concerned about how much information had been given to one of his father's knights, Harlan rubbed his forehead, considering whether or not to permit the knight entry. 'Your Grace, forgive me for talking to him without you, but I promise you he can be trusted. He is not as loyal to your father as you may believe.'

Harlan finally nodded and agreed to let him in. Master Damyan went back to the servant door and led Ser Theodor into the room. The knight was a kindly-seeming person with a square jawline and prominent cheekbones. As was usual, he wore the lightweight brown leather body armour and trousers of the knights of Dresden, with his sword housed low by his hip.

'Your Royal Highness,' Ser Theodor addressed Harlan properly, bowing low with a perfectly straight back.

'I am told you have news regarding Mikel.'

'I do, Your Grace.' Theodor had a worried expression. 'The night your sister escaped, I learned that your mother's missing pendant was to be used in a plot to curse the king. A curse that would mean his death. Mikel was in league with a sorcerer, sire, and this sorcerer may still be in the castle.'

Harlan paused; his mouth was slightly agape. He placed his hands on his hips. 'How could you possibly know this and why would you not have told my father this?'

Ser Theodor and Master Damyan shared looks that told Harlan they had some sort of secret agreement. Letting out a heavy breath, Ser Theodor shot his eyes to the floor. 'Your Grace, I need to ask for immunity before I answer those questions.'

'Immunity? For what?'

'I can't say until I have your word, sire.'

Harlan wove his brows together and gave Master Damyan a questioning expression that went unanswered. 'I can't give you immunity if I don't know what for.'

'Your Grace, when you were in the woods with Maldwyn, by the lake, the night that we found you, I saw something that I have shared with no one.'

Harlan's heart began to race as he held his breath. Dread settled in and made its home in the pit of his stomach. Master Damyan dropped his hands which were clasped in front of his hips to his side, shocked. Harlan ignored the change in the master's posture.

'Are you blackmailing me?'

'I would of course prefer not to Your Grace, but if it comes to that, then yes, I am blackmailing you.'

Harlan shook his head, feeling at a loss. He was not having a good day. 'Alright, fine. You have immunity.'

'Your Grace, I am Master Damyan's accomplice.' Master Damyan winced and gave the prince a sincere look that told Harlan the knight was being honest. 'I am the one that helped him get many people safely out of Dresden and away from your father's wrath. Master Damyan hid them, and I moved them when it was safe to do so. We saved many lives.'

'You mean sorcerers.'

'No, Your Grace, I mean lives.' Ser Theodor neared Harlan, a presumptuous move. 'Like your sister, whom you are trying to protect.'

Harlan didn't know what to say to that. The truth was, he knew Ser Theodor was right, but his father had raised him not to see sorcerers as people. It wasn't until his sister had been cruelly lumped in among sorcerers and condemned to die that he was almost able to understand Ser Theodor's point.

'My questions still stand. How did you come by this information and why haven't you told anyone this until now?'

'Your Grace, the information came to me by a sorcerer who also saved your father that night. This person was the one that removed your mother's pendant, which was cursed, from the castle and I helped them do it.' A crow landed on the iced balustrade of the balcony and let out a sharp, shrill call. 'The information about the curse came from Mikel himself. I told the king about his plans against the crown, but I didn't share the story of the curse for fear that the man who saved the king would be executed.'

The response made sense. 'You won't tell me who this person was, will you?'

The knight sighed and shook his head. 'I promised not to betray their identity, Your Grace.' Harlan wondered if the promise extended as far as concealing the man's identity from Master Damyan.

'You have good intentions. I respect that,' Harlan told Ser Theodor. 'I won't ask who this person was, but I want to know if you have any hard proof of the allegations. Something more than hearsay.'

Master Damyan and Ser Theodor both had regretful expressions on their faces. 'Nothing solid, Your Grace. Just my word. However, I agree with you, sire. Lord Darius is not a man to be trusted and I believe he helped Mikel gain access to the palace. I want to help you find out why and how far his betrayal extends.'

Master Damyan stepped forward, loosening his posture. 'When Ser Theodor mentioned what he knew of Mikel to me, Your Grace, I had an idea.'

'What was that?' Harlan asked, quite confused.

'Your Grace, Ser Theodor's family control a fifth of the king's soldiers. He can volunteer himself and his family's forces to be your personal guard, permanently. Then you don't have to fear that you are being watched at all moments by your father's loyalists. The reports to the king would be filtered through Ser Theodor.' Master Damyan gestured a hand toward Harlan. 'You would essentially have your freedom back, sire.'

Harlan stroked his chin as he remembered the guard waiting for him outside the council chambers. 'How would we get my father to agree to that?'

'It would be quite easy, sire,' Ser Theodor said. The crow outside let out another loud call. The patrol in the lower courtyard could be heard marching heavily through the snowed grounds. 'My family is held in high esteem by His Majesty. Having a permanent solution to guarding you would mean that he could better control you and prevent rumours from escaping the court. The king could also tell the public the added guards to your detail were for your protection since returning from captivity.'

A soft, cold breeze drifted through the open archway. Harlan folded his arms close over his chest again, trying to keep warm from the icy weather outside. The fire gave off a sudden pop.

'Alright,' Harlan said, a little hesitant, 'if you pledge your allegiance to me, I'll accept your help.'

'Then it is done, Your Grace,' Ser Theodor said with a confident edge to his voice. He got down on his knees in front of Harlan and lowered his head as a sign of respect. 'I pledge my life to your service, Your Royal Highness. I will follow you into battle. I have known you most of my life. You are the king I would choose.'

'Thank you.' Harlan offered a hand to help him stand. Master Damyan, although not a man to usually give away his thoughts, seemed happy with the turn of events.

'Before either of you go, is the news about Aberdeen true?'

'I am afraid it is, Your Grace,' Master Damyan answered. His voice was low and filled with worry. 'Time will tell how bad things get in Haradnor. Let's just hope this winter is kinder to our fair city. If they can't find a new wool supplier, we could be in trouble.'

The freezing wind swept into the room again. Harlan dismissed them with a kind word, then slipped his hands into his pockets to keep them warm. He sighed and made his way through the doors leaving the council chambers, where his escort waited for him.

CHAPTER SIX

Lord of the Downs

L ATER, AS THE EVENING was beginning to settle in, Prince Harlan was in his private chambers, sitting comfortably at his desk and flicking through the archived notes from past council meetings. The room was lit by the many buttery candles which were placed within the arms of the delicately crafted, freestanding candelabras that stood about the room like trees holding up their widely splayed canopies, battling the creeping darkness. The fireplace by the sitting area roared with heat, hissing at the logs which were stuffed in its mouth. The curtains were mostly drawn over the glass windows to keep out the cold air as much as possible, but there remained a slither through which Harlan glanced.

Outside, the sky was dark and heavily clouded, cloaking the stars from view. Snow drifted through the evening dim, like minuscule, white, daisy petals gliding toward the ground, swirling about in the undulating wind which rattled against the tightly closed windows.

Ignoring the wind, howling ever so often as if to draw his attention away from the reports, Harlan reclined back in his seat, palms wrapped around the ends of the armrests of the chair, feeling a little defeated that he had yet to learn anything useful. Having spent hours reading archived accounts from the royal council, which had been secured inside the annexe behind the chambers, Harlan rubbed his sandy eyes.

Specifically, he had focused on the notes written by Kristian Sadler from the time he sat on the council as King Viktor's magical advisor, before magic had been outlawed in Dresden. Harlan had hoped to find something among the scrolls that would tell him about the sacred ring Kristian had worn. He was trying to work out whether there was something special, perhaps magical, about the piece and if Jerrik may have any ulterior motives.

As of yet, nothing in the reports had been useful for much more than painting a picture of the man his mother had loved in his mind. Skimming through the numerous reports, Harlan had come to see what his mother must have admired about Kristian. There was a softness, an almost lyrical touch to his words that conveyed an unexpected kindness, sweeping Harlan into a world where magic was more than useful: it was beautiful. However, there was no gleaming piece of information that explained the way events had unfolded, nor any hint of the ring having been spelled.

If there was anything more to the ring than being a sacred relic to the god Uller, then the council were likely not aware of it. More to the point, there was no indication that the sovereign had any secret intentions, and if he did, then Kristian had not seemed to know of his plans. The pages revealed that everything had occurred in exactly the way Harlan had already been told by both Master Damyan and Jerrik.

He shifted the crinkled piles of reports over to the side of the desk. They rustled at his touch. A small piece of parchment that had been rolled into a tight scroll and had been squashed between the layers of papers, slipped out onto the desk. Harlan reached for it and picked it up. Gently, he slipped his thumb under the edge and worked it open.

The note smelled of old, dusty shelves and had quite obviously gotten damp in the annexe from the way the words bled into small lines that distorted the clarity of the script. Despite that the note was a little marred, Harlan could tell it had been written by someone with a neat and beautiful hand, clearly gifted at the craft of writing. He squinted his eyes as he read the blurred, cursive lettering.

I believe that my husband is beginning to suspect something. We are in grave danger and the shame of our affair prevents me from turning to my family in Mordiallok for support. I have kept the knowledge of Cassara's gift secret. My greatest wish is to guide her in understanding how to read the flowing streams of time so that she can interpret her dreams. I fear that will not be possible and worry how Viktor will react if he ever learns the truth. The gift of a seer is uncommon and many do not know of its presence amongst my family.

With that in mind, it is my responsibility to protect my children and my son faces a heavy burden. His destiny has yet to be realised but has long been written by the gods and it is our duty to bring it to fruition. I cannot entrust this task to another. As his mother, I owe it to Harlan to be the one to complete the ritual on him. Meet me later tonight, in the courtyard by the dining hall. We must seek the goddess's blessing.

Harlan felt a rush sweep over him, reading his mother's words, and his chest tightened with worry. Thoughts raced through his mind wondering what she had meant by his destiny and how soon after this note was written had his mother and her lover, Kristian, been apprehended for their affair. He cupped a hand over his mouth as he considered whether the mentioned ritual had been completed and what it might have done to him.

He rolled up the tiny note and tucked it safely in the drawer, which was mounted beneath the desk's tabletop. Feeling quite overwhelmed by what he had read, especially given that it was his mother's own words, Harlan pulled at the chain he wore around his neck and studied Kristian's sacred ring, red gems glistening from the firelight. He considered the etching of the swan in the ring's surface, curious to know what it meant.

Supposing it was nothing more than a signature from the jeweller, Harlan placed the council records in the drawer to conceal the small note. He accidentally knocked over the long, spotted, grey-feathered quill that had been standing tall in its holder as he went to rub his forehead. The fierce, sharpened tip was like a barbed arrowhead and pointed to the small, wide, round bottle of black ink that twirled on the desk. The candle on his table swayed, disturbed by the movement.

Beyond the large, smooth, oak door that marked the main entrance to his chambers, Harlan heard lowered voices making a series of short, sharp exchanges. He recognised one of the voices as the man assigned as his guard for the evening but wasn't able to make out the other voice which was muffled through the thick door. When the back-and-forth remarks ended, Harlan heard footsteps leading back down the hall.

A few loud bangs pounded on the door. Sitting bolt upright with a perfectly straightened posture, Harlan tidied the desktop and permitted whoever was outside his chambers to come inside, interested to know what was happening.

Instead of his personal guard entering the room from the hall leading to the rest of the prince's residential rooms, Harlan was surprised to see Ser Theodor. The knight walked confidently into his chambers, one hand resting on the hilt of his sword hanging by his hip. The knight bowed, low and respectful, and then closed the door behind him before nearing where the prince sat.

'Your Royal Highness, I come bearing good news. You will be pleased to know the king has approved my proposal to be responsible for your observation and protection.'

Harlan leaned forward, resting his elbows on the desk. 'He has? How did you get him to agree to that so quickly?' He allowed a hint of astonishment to underline his words.

The corners of Theodor's lips drew back up his face into a slight grin, forming small wrinkles on either side of his nose that met with his mouth. 'I made him think it was his idea, Your Grace.'

'You did?' Harlan locked his ankles under his chair, watching Theodor for a moment, who lowered his head as a sign of respect and honesty. 'Of course,' Harlan uttered, to himself as he let out a slight laugh that was more like a heavy breath. His father's arrogance never ceased to amaze him. 'He would think that.'

'Your Royal Highness, His Majesty mentioned that he wants you to attend a banquet with the lord and lady of the downs.' Harlan scowled at the suggestion of mingling with Lord Darius. 'He has had the servants working hard to hold the event for this evening. Most members of the court will be in attendance.'

'This evening?' Harlan knew he shouldn't be surprised to see how fast Lord Darius had landed back in his father's good graces. 'Well, that didn't take long.' He crossed his arms and slumped his shoulders forward. He was in no mood to watch them schmooze over dinner, but also welcomed any distraction to take his mind off his mother's note. Harlan felt it would be important for him to make an appearance so that he could keep up the guise of a filial heir. If nothing else, he supposed he could attempt to pry some information from the lord. 'Thank you, Theodor. Please, have my father informed that I'll be attending.'

'I'll make sure a message is sent to His Majesty, Your Grace.'

Harlan rubbed his chin with his coarse hands which were dry and slightly scaly from the cold weather. The prince stayed quiet, considering whether the knight might be of more use to him. Theodor waited patiently to either receive further orders or to be dismissed. The window battered against the frame, hammered by the brutal gust.

'Your affiliation with Master Damyan, tell me more,' Harlan said.

Theodor looked questioningly at Harlan. 'What exactly would you like to know, Your Grace?'

Harlan shrugged. 'Why did you decide to work with Master Damyan to protect sorcerers?'

'You are a few years younger than me, sire, so you probably don't remember that the years following your mother's death were particularly... turbulent.' Theodor broke his stare with Harlan, looking a touch regretful. 'Although your father didn't outlaw magic immediately after her death, he began to encourage the condemnation of sorcery more than ever, and he publicly blamed magic as the cause of many issues across the country. I saw so many people suffer, long before anything was classed as illegal, because of your father's prejudice.' Theodor's nostrils flared as he tried to conceal his anger toward King Viktor. 'Your Grace, I was a young noble back then—when I witnessed these things—not yet a knight and barely able to protect anyone. As I grew older, sire, and your father grew crueller, I decided to use my position to become a knight so that I would be better placed to help those who could not protect themselves.'

Pursing his lips, Harlan considered his next question carefully as the fire spat at a cold current of air that swept down the chimney. 'How did you and Master Damyan become associated in protecting those accused of sorcery?'

Theodor wetted his lips with the tip of his tongue. 'I caught Master Damyan hiding the son of a sorcerer in the servant rooms. I had the choice to apprehend him or help him. We discussed things and quickly realised that we held similar views. So, I helped him get the boy out of the castle.'

Struggling with his mother's sympathetic words and his father's hateful interpretations, yanking Harlan down two different paths, the prince clenched his jaw. He hesitated to learn more and studied the smoothness of his desktop to mute the buzzing thoughts in his head as he wondered which of the two sides he should heed.

'What is your opinion?'

'Sire, with respect, you are asking me to discuss a matter that is forbidden.'

'There is no one here, but me. I have no intention of sharing the details of our conversation as it would also place me at risk. As you have said, my father would be very angry to know the details of anything we have already been discussing.' Reminding himself of his position, Harlan kept his expression cold despite the sincerity he maintained in his voice. 'Let me also remind you that I am the Crown Prince, and you have sworn allegiance to me.' Theodor straightened his posture, hands now clasped below his belt, and, once again, bowed his head to show his respect for the prince, apologetic for troubling him. 'I suppose, I am curious to know your thoughts about it all.'

'Well, Your Grace,' the knight started, as if he had caught a glimpse of Harlan's candour, 'I believe that magic is a tool. Like anything, it can be used to help or harm people. It was once the most respected craft. Those that use sorcery to help others don't deserve to be executed, sire.'

The knight's words struck a chord with Harlan as he considered his mother. He thought about how he had never been close to his father and that they were often at odds, yet, despite this, up until recently, Harlan had always remained obedient and followed his father's orders completely. Had he been wrong for never questioning his father's actions?

As if out of nowhere, it occurred to Harlan that Theodor mentioned remembering the time around Queen Sonia's execution. He wondered if there was anything the knight could tell him that might explain the words in the queen's letter.

'Can you tell me anything about the night my mother was arrested?'

'Sire,' Theodor turned his stare down, his face saddened, 'Master Damyan told me that you are aware of your mother's affair and her execution. If this is what you are referring to, then I do not know what more I can tell you.'

'Do you know how my mother and her lover were discovered? How they were captured?'

'Your Royal Highness, I am only aware of a few rumours that have been shared among palace staff. Some say that the king witnessed their affair personally; others say that he learned of the affair from a misplaced love note. I couldn't tell you which is true.' Theodor stepped closer to the desk, gesturing to the prince himself. 'I can tell you one thing that many of the servants—perhaps, even Master Damyan—do not know because I was there… in the royal gardens that evening.' Harlan leaned forward, interested to know Theodor had witnessed his mother's arrest.

'You were there?'

'Yes, sire. Though I was a child, I had been in the grove to pray for forgiveness.' Theodor laughed at some memory of the past. 'My mother sent me there for being disobedient. I was supposed to kneel in the grove, praying to the gods, until she came to get me. When I heard voices coming up the path that sounded hushed and desperate, I felt I shouldn't be in the area. So, I hid among the shrubs.

'Your mother and her lover were arrested together in the sacred grove, and, of the three arresting officers, only one is alive. Two died in the war. These officers were all of a low rank back then, but fiercely loyal to your father. Though I was a boy, as a noble among the court, I knew the three men that were by your father's side that rushed into the grove to arrest them.' A low-burning candle behind Theodor died, no longer able to bear the gleaming flame. 'This surviving man I mentioned has been awarded a high rank and led a battalion into the war with Mordiallok. He won a battle in the Shadow Plains, and was given a lordship.' Theodor's face turned sly. 'Lord Darius was there the night your mother and her lover were apprehended, Your Grace.'

Shocked, Harlan reclined, scratching his chin as he felt a lump form in his throat. The knowledge that Lord Darius had played a hand in his mother's execution made his blood boil. The window banged against the frame again, battling the gust that howled in the courtyard. The fireplace popped.

In an attempt to soothe his rising hatred of the lord, Harlan turned his mind to another matter and considered Theodor's blackmailing him. 'Why did you never say anything?' Prince Harlan frowned, whispering the words as if he were far away, wary about going down this line of discussion.

Theodor hesitated to answer, unsure about what he was being asked. He laced his brows together, his confusion evident upon his face. 'Sire?'

Harlan allowed his cool, royal veneer to fall from his face, feeling each muscle tighten. He wanted to know why the knight had never mentioned what he had seen in the woods and why he had chosen not to report it to the king. Most of the other knights or officers would not have kept the knowledge to themselves if faced with a similar situation.

'Why did you never say anything about what you saw that night, in the woods?'

As soon as he uttered the question in full, his mind became a flurry of ideas of what the knight's answer might be, and each thought was a tad more worrying than the last. He reminded himself that Theodor had always been a loyal and trustworthy person to him in the past.

'At first... I wasn't sure of what I had seen, Your Grace.' A little awkwardly, Theodor gulped and tapped his fingertips on his sword hilt. 'I knew I had interrupted something... intimate.' Standing stiff, but leaning to one side, Theodor turned his gaze down to the floor.

Harlan looked away remembering the moment in the woods, recalling how little space had been between him and Maldwyn. Back then, Maldwyn had seemed sad and reflective, and Harlan had wanted to comfort him. Theodor went silent, picking his next words with great care.

'When we were travelling back to Dresden, sire, it became evident what that moment had meant as neither of you spoke. Maldwyn fell back into his role as your servant.' Ser Theodor locked eyes with the prince, holding a firm stare. 'Your Royal Highness, I let the matter go, assuming there was no reason to be concerned.' Ser Theodor itched the side of his head.

'That doesn't exactly answer my question.' Harlan wasn't sure why he wanted an answer so badly as if he were yearning to be at ease with his struggles, maybe even validated in the way he felt. 'Why did you never say anything to my father about what you believed you had witnessed?'

'Your Grace, I never said anything to your father out of loyalty to you. I would never have betrayed you like that because I meant what I said. I know you to be a good man and you are the king I would choose.' Theodor pinched his lips together in thought. 'I don't care who you hold affections for, but His Majesty wouldn't appreciate it, given he is a palace servant.'

'And, you would?'

'Your Grace, there is someone I care for, and I understand how that can compel you.'

Remembering having seen Theodor sneaking about the palace with a red-haired, green-eyed servant woman, Harlan softened. 'The servant girl?'

'Ailaya.' Ser Theodor smiled wistfully, looking a little surprised at Harlan for having noticed their trysts and keeping this to himself. 'She's the most beautiful woman I have met and I tried to ignore it, but after a while, I... couldn't. If anything happened to her,' Theodor clenched the hilt of his sword with his fist as he gritted his teeth, 'I don't know what I would do.'

'You worry about the danger you place her in?'

'She's a servant, of the lower class. Our union is not permitted by His Majesty because of her status.' Ser Theodor made a presumptuous move and grabbed one of the chairs around the prince's dining table and carried it over to where Harlan was sitting at his desk, placing it opposite the prince. He sat down and looked Harlan dead in the eye. 'What we have can only be in secret. But, Your Grace, without her, I am sleepwalking through life.'

Something was reassuring about Theodor's words that made Harlan feel as though someone understood his struggles. He felt relieved as if a weight had been lifted by being able to speak openly with the knight. The two continued to talk for a while about a range of issues from personal to political. Harlan filled Theodor in on everything since Mikel arrived in Dresden and, after some time, Harlan dismissed the knight so that he could ready himself for the banquet.

As Theodor opened the door to leave, he turned to face Harlan. 'By the way, Ailaya is Maldwyn's best friend,' he said with a wry look on his face.

* * * * *

When Harlan made it to the dining hall with Theodor close behind, he was the last to arrive, just as he intended. The room was noisy, bustling with nobility, mingling in deep conversations. Servants kept their gaze on the floor, some moving through the masses like spectres carrying platters of food and pewter jugs, while others swept through the space cleaning the messes left by their betters.

A passing plate of bite-sized, salty pork pies caught the prince's attention. He grabbed one straight off the platter before it was gone, shrugging at Theodor who looked at him with a judgemental expression. He bit into the pie, it was sweet and salty.

Looking around the room, Harlan spotted candles and torches in abundance lighting the whole hall with a warm glow. Massive, dark-stained timber beams, which were roughly buffed with large dents from the black knots in the wood that dug into the planks, reinforced the open, arched, stone roof that was spotted with an assortment of shades of grey. There were long tables that were lined up and down the hall. Through the many heads, Harlan spotted his father seated with the Lord and Lady of Karana Downs at the largest table, situated at the head of the room where they could watch over the rest of the court. There was a spare seat to the king's right, which had been reserved for the Crown Prince.

Harlan crossed the room, barely acknowledging the bowing nobles moving out of his way. When he reached the table, he could see that Lady Adria had braided her hair and changed into a sleek, navy-coloured dress that was made of a thick fabric with fur lining the neckline and sleeves. Lord Darius was wearing a high-necked jerkin, which was made of an almost silky, dense, barley-coloured linen.

On the other hand, King Viktor was in a heavy, gold-coloured, smooth jerkin, with a subtle pattern woven into the cloth. The crown atop the king's head was a plain, gold circlet with bevelled edging and was, on the whole, much simpler than his usual crown. Harlan was greeted with a false warmth as he took his seat. Ser Theodor stood behind him, making sure not to relax by eating or drinking while guarding the prince.

'Your Grace,' Lord Darius exclaimed, thrusting his arms out as if to welcome him. His eyes shot to where Theodor stood, betraying that he had noticed the change in the prince's guard. 'We were beginning to think you weren't going to make it.'

'Lord Darius, I wouldn't miss this,' Harlan replied in a scathing tone, flashing a cold glance at his father.

King Viktor sprawled back into his chair, hooking out a stick of rosemary that was caught in his teeth, unbothered by Harlan's remark. 'We have been discussing the matter of control over the mine. Lord Darius has suggested a coordinated assault in the region to regain control from the mountain dwellers.'

Harlan propped one arm on the table, which had platters piled high and was covered with masses of peppery meats, salty bread rolls and tangy, cooked vegetables. One of the ladies across the room let out a shrill laugh.

'Surely that is out of the question. Lord Darius. You ask far too much,' Harlan cautioned.

'What would you have us do, Your Royal Highness?' Lord Darius picked apart a piece of bread, loading an array of foods inside the roll. Lady Adria was shaking her head at her husband's appetite, clearly disappointed with how much he had eaten. 'Appeal to them? Negotiate? This has been tried and failed. They don't want to make a deal.'

'Your Majesty,' Harlan started, turning to his father who remained unaffected by the lord's remark, 'with the lack of supplies coming out of Haradnor at the moment, winter is not the time to be sending our men into difficult terrain to fight an almost unseen enemy.'

'I must agree with my son here, Lord Darius,' King Viktor declared with a strong sense of confidence as he waved a drumstick in the air, strings of meat clinging to the bone. Lord Darius glowered at his wife as if making sure she kept quiet. 'Besides the lack of supplies, we must consider the raids that are currently underway to root out the scourge of sorcery still plaguing our lands. Asking the villages to go to battle against the Erendil in the present circumstances would be asking for a civil war.'

'The people of Karana Downs are with me, Your Majesty.' Lady Adria glanced sideways as Lord Darius spoke. Harlan could tell she had her own opinions about the mine but had been silenced by her husband and dared not to speak out. 'This is what they want and I want to give it to them.'

Harlan laughed at the lord's remark, wondering if Theodor was as amused as he was. 'Of course, the people,' he mocked, intending on getting under the lord's skin. Lady Adria locked eyes with Harlan, looking at him as though she were ashamed of her husband, before diverting her gaze and staring at the mingling nobles that wandered the dining hall. 'An army of untrained citizens waging war against the well-trained, swift masses of the Erendil. What a battle that would be!'

Biting into his overflowing roll, which had layers of food spilling out the other side, Lord Darius remained smug. Harlan recognised Ailaya sweeping across the far side of the hall, clearing emptied platters from the nobles' sight, her long ginger-toned hair was pulled back into a ponytail. She was wearing a simple, moss-green coloured dress with a brown, linen shawl to keep her warm.

She dared to gaze at Theodor, standing behind the prince. No one, other than Harlan, appeared to notice her flirt with the knight. Ailaya arched her brows, grinning as she averted her gaze. Harlan was pleased to know they had managed a stolen moment before she snuck away, arms filled with empty dishes.

'I have emphasized conducting these raids in my engagements with the public,' Harlan heard his father say, tuning back into the conversation, 'and, after what happened in Alander, we are going to have some damage control to do.'

'Alander?' Harlan felt his mouth drop as a sudden rush left him shaken. Master Damyan had told him that this was Maldwyn's hometown and the place he had returned to care for his dying mother. He felt a pounding in his chest. 'What happened in Alander?' Harlan asked, trying to hide the feeling of alarm deep in his gut.

Appearing to relish in some misstep of the king's, Lord Darius worked hard to conceal his pleasure by using his tongue to lick the fat dripping down his chin from the overstuffed roll he munched into. King Viktor wrinkled his forehead as he winced.

'Lord Darius and Lady Adria brought news with them from the northern villages.' Harlan was determined to relax his stiffening posture, but each time he forced himself to relax, he would immediately tense as soon as he lost his focus. 'We sent a small group of soldiers to move through the northern villages and carry out the raids to search for evidence of sorcery. For some reason, the people of Alander had not been informed that the raids were being conducted within their region and they resisted, believing they were under attack.' Behind him, Theodor scuffed his boot on the stone floor as a gentle reminder for the prince to remain calm. 'We believe one of the guards went beyond their orders, harming the wife of a farmer, causing the confusion. The soldier is being disciplined, however many of the villagers were killed that evening, and the few survivors were arrested.'

Biting his cheek, Harlan shuffled forward to the edge of his seat, disturbed by the news. The sounds of cackling ladies, knights pulling meat from the bones of glazed pheasants, and muttered conversations passing gossip around the room irritated Harlan. He wanted to yell for the room to be silent but made sure to keep his composure.

'What happened with those that were arrested?'

'We received the message when we were already heading south. One of the soldiers was on his way to the castle. He told us the prisoners were being brought back to the palace,' Lady Adria told him, finally joining in on the conversation.

Her voice was croaky, signalling that travelling to the palace in the cold had taken its toll, despite that it was still early in the season. She had been watching Harlan intently since the mention of Alander. He wondered if she had seen him stiffen, or noticed the slight drop in his face.

'It was a most unfortunate outcome,' the king said, rubbing his forehead.

Harlan wanted to get up and run toward Alander. The sound of Theodor pulling on the hilt of his sword, as if to draw it free from its scabbard, drew Lord Darius's attention and prompted Harlan to take a sip of wine to distract himself.

'When are the prisoners expected to arrive?' The touch of melancholy in his voice was masked by coughing as he breathed in the pungent fumes of his strong drink.

'According to the messenger, they should arrive in a few days,' said Lord Darius, whose voice was muffled between chews. 'They are a larger company than our small escort, so they were travelling slower than we were.'

Harlan listened to them prattle on for a long while about politics around the country. He tuned in and out of the conversation, occasionally snacking on the food in front of him as he stewed over the news about Alander.

After an appropriate amount of time and mingling, Harlan excused himself from the table and left the dining hall, wanting a moment of fresh air to clear his head from the long day which overwhelmed him with information. Nobles were chatting in the halls and one of the knights was staggering, drunk, hand guiding him along the wall.

Pausing by the huge archway just beyond the corridor to the dining hall that led outside to a quiet courtyard, Harlan considered that this was where his mother had intended to meet Kristian and was reminded of the letter he had found. Wishing he was able to remember more of what had happened in the past, he stepped outside into the sting of winter.

The courtyard was small and crisp, with snow-covered hedges tracing along the stone walls. In the spring these hedges would be kept well-trimmed and beautiful blossoms would burst forth from the glossy green leaves. For now, though, they were stowed beneath iced, white blankets, and the frosted ivy which wrapped around the castle walls was frozen in place, glued to the stone.

It was cold, and steam emanated from Harlan's mouth as he breathed. Feeling a little hopeless, he looked up and saw that the stars were covered by clouds. Everything was quiet. No insects were chirping or birds hooting. The only sounds were coming from the dining hall.

'Do you think Maldwyn's dead?' Harlan said to Theodor, whose boots crunched on the icy ground behind him.

'No, Your Majesty.' The steadfast look on Theodor's face was as if he knew something the prince didn't. Harlan admired his resolve. 'Perhaps he is among the prisoners.'

Harlan nodded, trying to remain focused until he knew more about what had happened to Maldwyn. 'Lord Darius wants to control the iron mine in the mountains. He's prepared to start a war over it, I want to know why.'

'We'll find out what he's up to, Your Grace.'

Harlan lingered in the snow for quite some time before the cold got the better of him, and he headed back to his chambers. He may not have gotten much information from the lord of the north, but the prince was glad he wasn't returning empty-handed. When Harlan got back to his chambers, he wrestled with everything he had learned, wishing he knew more. His determination to unravel the mysteries of the past was renewed, sparking within him.

CHAPTER SEVEN

The Ruins of Templestowe

WILD BEASTS IN THE FOREST howled long and mournful cries. Exhausted, breaths ragged and harsh, Maldwyn breathed in the pungent, tangy pine trees hanging in the cold, night air. He leaned on the tall, coarse trees that had dropped their leafy canopy, their naked branches poking towards the stars with their widely splayed, gangly limbs, and, with his hands, used the rough, icy trunks to propel himself forward on his aching feet, calves burning. The luminous moon shone through the thin veil of glowing clouds that it used to hide behind as if to give Maldwyn a whisper of hope in the immense darkness.

His injured palm, wounded from crashing through the bones of the scorched building back in his hometown, stung beneath the makeshift bandage he had cut from a linen shirt he carried in his pack. His face was so cold that it had become numb, tingling every once in a while. A frozen, crusty layer of snow coated Maldwyn's thick cloak, icing his dark hood with a layer of white.

He had been running for days; so long that he had lost track of time. Short of breath, Maldwyn stumbled forward over a raised, bumpy tree root which was masked by the copious shades of grey that went for as far as his eyes could see. He no longer had any idea what direction he was running, or how he had gotten to wherever he now wandered alone. All he knew was that he couldn't stop running.

The guards that had been tracking him were relentless. Each time he entertained the idea that he had outrun them, he would slacken his pace and try to work out where he was, and then, in the distance, he would eventually hear their loud, hoarse voices calling to one another. He would notice the sounds of their boots smashing on the ground as they caught up to him, leaving Maldwyn with just enough time to slip away. Too often he had been forced to use his gifts to help him flee, and too many times the king's guards had almost captured him to have him executed.

The left strap of his pack had slipped off his shoulder. Maldwyn slackened his pace to catch his breath and readjust his heavy backpack. His feet throbbed. His hand ached. The back of his throat was reddened and felt raw from the gasps of the abrasively cold night air he drew in through his mouth. He gulped back saliva to try and soften the scratching, painful feeling in his oesophagus. His pulse raced. The cold air met with Maldwyn's hot cheeks, searing them as if ice were being pressed against the hot plate of a frying pan, causing sweat droplets to form on his forehead, that were quick to freeze. Steam teemed from his open mouth.

In the distance, Maldwyn heard the wind whipping through the arms of the trees, rustling the pine bristles. His eyes began to water from the frost, distorting the black shapes of the trees around him into indistinct dark blobs. Wiping his eyes to clear his vision, Maldwyn was able to make out the silhouette of a strange set of shapes through the bodies of the trees. Squinting, Maldwyn noted that what he saw was a tall, large building with multiple pitched roofs, which were suspended by long pillars.

Tired, Maldwyn pushed on, heading for the lone structure in the middle of the forest. The ornate, stave temple was crafted out of remarkably smooth timber planks and had several tiers with overhanging roofs. Carved dragon heads for eaves rested atop the sloped, gable roofs.

If there was a path leading up to the temple, it was concealed by the knee-deep snow, but Maldwyn had been able to navigate his way up a frosted, wide set of steps in the ground. The closer he approached the temple's shadow, the more Maldwyn was able to tell that the building was run down with gaping holes in the roof shingles.

Reaching the top of the stairs, he saw that the doors were just hanging onto the broken hinges and had been left a fraction ajar. Each door had a dragon head carved in the centre as a handle. Gripping one of the dragon heads, Maldwyn pushed his weight against the door, forcing it open and scraping its base along the floor, the door wobbling on its loosened hinges.

A freezing gust of air rushed out of the gap, hurrying to be released.

Maldwyn checked behind him that there was no sign that the royal guards had caught up with him. When he was satisfied that the path behind was clear, at least for the time being, he stepped inside.

Within the temple, it was dark and, as far as Maldwyn could see, there was no sign that anyone had passed through for many years. Although it was difficult for him to distinguish much in the night, Maldwyn was able to discern the large, open area that lay beyond the door.

Smooth, timber archways lined the central space and supported the upper landing. White, almost glowing, chiffon drew his eye to the far end of the temple, flowing gracefully in the breeze behind a low-lying altar that appeared to be about hip height. Maldwyn noticed that a jumbled mess of bowls and rotten fruits was spread all over the floor around the altar.

Curious, Maldwyn moved further into the temple and slipped on pieces of parchment that lay strewn about the temple floor, which he hadn't seen in the darkness up until this point. He paused, standing in the centre of the room on the piles of paper and took in the oddly grave, yet beautiful, structure, imagining the grandeur of this temple in its prime days of worship.

Approaching the altar, Maldwyn turned the large, round, silver bowls back over and placed them on the table, finding it strange that no jewels or valuable offerings were remaining. Gazing over the long, wide bench Maldwyn took note of the red, linen cloth which had been bunched up and hung off the sides of the altar unevenly. Along the edge of the tabletop were cursive carvings that Maldwyn thought appeared similar to the script of the language of the gods inscribed on the cover of the book he carried with him: *The Power of Divinity*.

There was an unusual skull as a centrepiece that weighed down the red cloth, keeping it from being blown away by the wind tearing through the holes in the roof. One half of the hideous face had been left bare, dust piling up on the eye socket, the other half was quite stunning and had been painted with black, gold and red patterns swirling over the bone. Tilting his head to the side, Maldwyn questioned what the two faces meant.

Besides the skull, was an ornate urn with bevelled, gold detailing around the top and bottom which glinted in the moonlight pouring through the open doors. The surface of the urn was painted black and depicted a pack of silvery wolves that seemed to glow with a metallic shimmer. He noted that they were baring their teeth with low heads as if growling at some sort of formidable opponent. With a careful hand, trying not to bother his aching palm, Maldwyn spun the urn just enough to see the rest of the picture and saw the image of a massive dragon beating its wings, looking down on the wolves.

As the tips of his fingers touched the surface, a cold chill swept over him like a wave of death. Quickly, he retracted his hand, feeling overcome with a horrid sensation of oblivion, as if he had been filled with a yearning for complete annihilation.

Stepping away from the wicked altar, Maldwyn glanced around with an overwhelming sensation of hopelessness settling deep in his gut. There was nowhere for him to go and he no longer had the energy to keep evading the royal guards. Having completely given up, Maldwyn looked around at the dilapidated temple he believed would be the scene of his death.

'Maldwyn,' a familiar, although ethereal, voice called on the wind. Searching for who might have spoken his name, he stepped forward, staring into the blackness. The longer he stood fixed in place, staring into the bleak night, the more his vision was consumed into nothingness.

'Who's there?' Maldwyn finally called out to the abyss, hoping for an answer.

No such answer came to him. There was merely a lingering silence that tormented his mourning soul, mocking him from the shadows. A snowflake fell through a hole in the roof, slow and tragic, as though it had fallen from the grace of the gods. An obscure shade, cast by a cloud moving over the moon, which was gleaming through a hole in the roof, seemed to walk up a set of stairs to Maldwyn's right. Dread crept upon him and made its home in his gut.

Miserable, he breathed in deep, wishing that death would arrive sooner rather than later, as he followed the ghostly shade climbing the stairs, wanting to know who had spoken. The floorboards creaked and the balustrade wobbled. Piles of debris lay under the moonlight, glinting where the flecks of snow had fallen. There was a hint of the zesty, pine scent of the forest creeping through the broken openings in the roof, which mixed with the smell of the damp, musty timber of the ruined temple.

Upstairs, was a simple landing that wound around the walls with a large, central, open space that watched over the altar below. Tall, decorative bookcases were built into the walls, and there were even more dusty papers scattered about the floor as if someone had carelessly stripped the shelves. Maldwyn supposed it was the wind that had blown the scriptures around the temple, but wondered, just for an instant, whether something depraved had happened in this place.

In the distance, on the other side from where he was standing, was a narrow corridor, peeling off to the right. Despite feeling hollow, having lost everything he had ever known, a curiosity sparked inside Maldwyn. Walking slowly, and taking in everything he could in spite of the darkness, he moved to make his way down the confined corridor where he found a small, panelled door.

Foggy, he closed his eyes, as if to muster a pathetic amount of strength, and opened the door. The room beyond had cobwebs hanging off every surface and there was a single window on the far wall, which had bulky, slatted shutters that were pulled closed. A wide, modest desk sat near the window, with a high-backed chair behind it.

There was a small, neatly made-up bed against the wall to Maldwyn's left, with a flat-topped chest at the foot of the bed and, to his right, there was a quaint nook with a fireplace and a sitting chair by a short shelving unit. This had been the priest's chambers.

Maldwyn went over to the nook and saw a pile of remaining firewood below the thick layer of powdered lint. Being so cold, he stacked the wood into the hearth. Focusing his mind on setting the timber alight, Maldwyn's power failed him. He supposed that his exhaustion had taken all of his energy and that he didn't have the strength left in him to even spark a simple flame.

Having lived a humble life, and been a servant for a long time, Maldwyn was no stranger to lighting fireplaces. Although it took some time and effort, he was able to get the dry timbers to light. The logs fizzled at the layer of dust, filling his nostrils with the smell of burning dust and hair.

Turning to the armchair behind him, Maldwyn jumped at the sight of a well-dressed and webbed skeleton seated in the chair, hands dangling off the armrests. There was an open book placed face down in its lap.

'Maldwyn,' the distant, silvery voice beckoned to him again. He jumped up, alarmed that the voice had returned. 'Maldwyn,' the ghostly voice whispered.

'Who's there?' Maldwyn asked the shadows, unsure as to whether he should expect a reply from the voice in the air.

'A friend.'

'My friends don't lurk in the shadows.'

'You don't recognise my voice?' Maldwyn lowered his head trying to place the tone and the pitch, but he couldn't quite pick it as the voice sounded far away and eerie, as if calling to him from another life. 'Has it been that long?'

A tug in his chest made him hold his breath for a moment at the realisation of whose voice was beckoning from beyond the grave. Maldwyn cocked his head and asked, 'Will?'

'Yes, my love.' Maldwyn's lower lip began to quiver as he wondered what sort of a place he had stumbled into. Was this real, or was it all in his mind? Was he that delirious from running for so long that his head had begun to play tricks on him? 'I see in your eyes that you're lost and confused. Your mother died. Our town is ruined… you're all alone.'

Although there was nothing to see, he still searched for Will with his eyes, scanning the area. 'This can't be real,' he said flatly, shaking his head, unsure as to whether he should believe what he was hearing. 'You're in my mind.'

Will's silvery voice became a touch colder. 'Dreams are not real, yet we remember them.'

Frowning, Maldwyn turned as he heard the wind rattling against the closed shutters. An unnatural rumble in the air stormed the temple. 'What does that mean?'

'Maldwyn, I know you.' The voice seemed to whisper, becoming a little breathy as it circled the spot where Maldwyn stood fixed in place. 'You're adrift and in need of strength. Let me be your confidant like I once was.' Will's voice saddened, becoming a little throaty. 'Let me save you from this life.'

Maldwyn's head shot up. Horror struck him at the realisation of what may have been suggested. 'This life?' He stepped away from the nook, backing himself closer toward the desk, back facing the window.

'You don't have the strength to go on. Come. Join me.' Trembling, Maldwyn looked over to the skeleton sitting in the chair. It turned its head to smile at him, bones cracking as it moved. A piece of flesh dangled off the cheekbone. 'It doesn't hurt, much.'

Maldwyn held his hands to his face, covering his eyes. 'You're not real! Will would never ask me to do that.'

'You've proved to yourself that you can't go on.' The silvery voice changed tact, growing more forceful in tone. 'I heard you surrender by the altar. Come, be with me.'

Maldwyn cupped a hand to his mouth, shaking his head. The skeleton began to laugh; it was a wretched sound, teeth clacking together as it chuckled. Stepping backwards, Maldwyn bumped the table, which knocked the arms of the high-backed chair, pushing its weight off balance. The chair slowly, as if thinking about landing on its feet, leaned back, crashing into the shutters and forcing them open.

'Let yourself be free from the pain. Join me… in death.'

Maldwyn turned his head out the window as he heard the mournful howling of the wolves. Outside, he noticed a white lynx with glossy fur, black spots marking its coat and dark tufts sticking up off its ears. The lynx was stalking forward with its head lowered and back arched.

Following the direction of the lynx with his eyes, Maldwyn noticed the large, fluffy, howling wolf, which jumped a little playfully to the side, testing the lynx's patience. After tolerating a few taunts, the large snowcat charged at the wolf, who turned and ran back into the woods with its tail between its legs.

The minor distraction from the voice was enough to remind Maldwyn of the lynx on the crest of Prince Harlan's armour. A fondness soothed his anguish as the events of the past few months flooded Maldwyn's mind and taunted him through the voice of this spectre.

He recalled the many people in the palace that he cared about: Ailaya, a simple servant woman who had become his dearest friend; Greg and Erik, two hunters that had welcomed Maldwyn for his skill; Theodor, the man who had recently learned of Maldwyn's gifts and sworn to protect him; and, of course, Prince Harlan, a man who had awoken a piece of Maldwyn that he believed had died.

He considered that none of the guards pursuing him had seen his face. There was no reason he couldn't return to the palace and resume his life as a servant. All he needed to do was to get out of this wicked temple and run far enough away from the guards that they lost his trail.

'No,' he told the voice, filled with a new will to live.

Maldwyn looked back to the smiling skeleton, bearing the open book in its lap, and saw that it hadn't moved since he had lit the fire. Realising that the images of it laughing had been cruel tortures placed in his head by whatever dark powers haunted this temple, Maldwyn clenched his fists, preparing himself to run on his pained feet.

'Whoever you are, whatever you are, I won't do as you ask.' Maldwyn dashed across the room, grabbed the book in the dead man's lap, and ran out the door, down the stairs and out of the dark temple.

CHAPTER EIGHT

Priest of the Blood

MALDWYN RAISED HIS SORE HAND to shield his eyes. The wind had picked up since he left the temple and snow stung his face like burning needles driving into his skin. The sky was still dark, but the moonlight that was reflecting from the snow was blinding.

Keeping his head low, chin tucked into his chest, Maldwyn held the hood of his coat over his face with his other, gloved hand. His footsteps were slow, and his boots sunk into the ankle-deep snow. Knowing that each stride he took brought him further from the king's guards, Maldwyn stayed on his path, hoping to find shelter sooner rather than later.

His renewed strength was waning, and his pack was heavier since stuffing the priest's notes inside. He considered throwing them aside, leaving them to be buried by the snow, but he wanted to understand what had happened back in the temple. The voice mimicking Will left him tortured.

He was glad he had been able to break away from its beckoning and find a spark of hope from the memory of his life in the city that awaited his return. He thought of the soft look the prince's eyes held, something Maldwyn suspected was just for him.

In his mind, he painted the prince's face, noting his perfect jawline, his thick, fawn-coloured hair and his crystal blue eyes. In his delirium, Maldwyn romanticised the image in his head, envisioning the prince's tall, well-muscled physique, and imagining he was helping him along this difficult, never-ending path. It was a comforting vision, which gave him the strength to continue into the night until he finally found a large niche in the rocky mountainside he was trailing, which was deep enough to provide him with partial cover from the blizzard. Huge, frosted boulders kept the recess well hidden.

Maldwyn took his pack off and set up his bedroll for the evening. He started a small fire and curled up to finally rest, pulling the bedding tight around him. Keeping the picture of the prince in mind, Maldwyn allowed himself to drift off to sleep.

* * * * *

The next morning, Maldwyn awoke when the sun was already high, and the crows were cawing loudly at the day. The warm, crackling fire had died. Not even the embers remained in the iced, black pit. The wind had ceased, and Maldwyn was relieved to see that the snowstorm had ended. The sky was blue, marked only by a few clouds. Slowly, he pulled himself up, took off his gloves and snacked on some dried fish and bread he kept in his pack.

As Maldwyn sat there resting, he noted that his feet were throbbing, and his calves and thighs ached from the rigorous journey. In the distance, he spotted a dark, almost black, moose meandering through the trees, its twig-like antlers blending into the woods.

Maldwyn, pleased to see a soothing presence in the woods, remained still, so as not to scare the calm, massive creature. The moose paused and nibbled on the low buds from a scarcely dressed pine tree, picking off the needle-covered twigs in small bites. When it was done snacking, the moose slowly turned and made its way deeper into the trees until it was out of sight.

As the area remained quiet, and there was no sign of his pursuers, Maldwyn decided to rest a while longer, hoping that the storm had hidden his tracks. The pulsating, aching of his injured palm reignited after Maldwyn used his hands to pull apart the bread he carried, and he supposed he had better take it easy, for as long as he could. The burning of the soles of his feet heated his boots, reinforcing his desire to wait a while longer before setting out again. He pulled out the priest's notes from his pack to pass the time.

When Maldwyn opened the plain, leather cover, he looked at the large script, written in the common tongue, and traced the letters with his finger: *Morloch Brandt, Priest of the Blood.* Knitting his brows together, Maldwyn grew even more curious than he had been before entering the temple the night before. This was a priest of the blood, a member of the highest order of worshippers of the Queen of the Netherworld, Hel.

Maldwyn had read about her handiwork in *The Power of Divinity*. She had been described as a terrible beauty with long, white hair and black eyes that were cold and seemed to see into the hearts of people. What was most notable about her was her face, which was split into two distinct halves: one was fair, reflecting beauty and grace, and the other was hideous, flesh rotting away to reveal her skull.

Hel was the queen of the world of darkness, a place which was said to lie both northwards and southwards. The shore to her kingdom was told to be a sea of corpses and her castle was filled with hissing serpents. Her hounds, massive, black wolves, shepherded the damned, while scaled dragons guarded the entry to her realm.

Kvasir, the God of Knowledge and the supposed author of *The Power of Divinity*, had portrayed Hel as an enemy of the gods. She was said to be a woman driven to seize power, destroying the nine realms and everything the gods had worked to create so that she could build a world of her own. A cold wind rose, making Maldwyn pull his coat tighter. He pinched the crinkled, aged parchment at the top corner and turned the page over to read more of the writings of this mysterious priest. The crow sitting proudly in a tree nearby flapped its wings and cawed as if warning him from reading on.

As Maldwyn thumbed through the scribblings of what appeared to be the notes of a madman, he learned that the priest believed there was a place in the mountains which was an ancient prison. A tomb where dragons had been left to guard a monster, incarcerated by the gods for the crimes committed against Wayland, the smithy god.

Maldwyn knew from his readings that Wayland had once been captured and forced to craft divine jewellery and weapons in the mortal realm. According to the priest's notes, Wayland had been taken by Hel's son, who Morloch referred to as the Bringer of Oblivion.

Maldwyn paused, eyes studying the bringer's title. Something about the words on the page filled him with dread, deep in his gut. Glancing up to take a break from staring at the priest's notes, Maldwyn stared at the crow sitting silently on the branch. There was a wise, almost knowing look in its eyes.

Needing to know more, Maldwyn continued to read, letting the morning pass by with little care. The sun moved higher in the sky. Eventually, the clouds turned darker and the breeze picked up, once again carrying the aromatic smell of the damp woods.

Morloch mentioned that Hel's son was tasked with leading the charge in an ancient war against the gods; a war that ceased when the gods freed Wayland from the bringer's grip and caged Hel's son in a prison among these mountains. The gods left behind great dragons to guard the bringer in his tomb and raised a veil between the worlds of life and death to protect all that had been created from Hel's destruction.

As Maldwyn sat beneath the half cover of the rocky mount, enthused by the priest's writings, he heard a sudden, sharp snap from somewhere in the woods. A voice called, shouting something about a broken branch. Maldwyn had been stumbling in the snowstorm the night before and had been careless, breaking low, thin branches as he staggered, lurching from tree to tree. The time that he had gained by pushing on late into the night had been lost.

Quiet as he could, Maldwyn closed the book and stuffed it back in his bag. After pulling the straps over his shoulders, Maldwyn drew his gloves over his hands, hurting his tender palm by placing more pressure than intended on the wound when he tugged the glove over the bandage, wiggling it down his hand. Slowly, Maldwyn leaned forward and poked his head out from behind the rock, searching for the whereabouts of the guards.

Kneeling by a wide, lumpy tree trunk, was one of the king's soldiers, heavy, golden armour shining under the sunlight, examining the broken limb of the fat tree. Another taller, thicker-set man, came up behind him and removed his helmet, revealing his bald head to take a closer look.

Looking around for somewhere better to hide, Maldwyn saw that the stony mount was relatively flat and reached high up into the heavens. Out of options, Maldwyn readied himself to run with a few quick, short breaths.

The guards stood and looked around. Pointing toward where he was hidden, they began to march in Maldwyn's direction. Panicked, he darted out from his cover, bounding into the labyrinth of trees. His calves and thighs burned. His feet stung.

The guards shouted. Their armour rattled as they chased him. Their boots beat down to the ground with a heavy clunk.

Ducking and weaving through the trees, he ran parallel to the mountain face. Maldwyn fought the urge to look back over his shoulder. His pulse raced. His hands sweated inside his leather gloves. His hood fell back.

Charging onwards, he struggled to maintain a consistent breath, tiring quickly as his muscles seared. The guards yelled for him to stop. He reached for his power, but it did not answer. He was too distracted by his need to run.

A dagger missed him by the width of a hair. A sudden whistling sound shot by him. Behind him, a guard made a tragic, gurgling noise, as others shouted, raising alarm.

Muttered, confused calls between the soldiers, and the silence of their boots chasing him, made Maldwyn stop. He looked back and saw an arrow sticking out of the neck of a collapsing guard, desperately clawing at his throat. Another whistle and Maldwyn caught sight of an arrow shooting straight by his head, landing right in the eye of another guard. Blood exploded from his helmet, dripping like thick, red sap down onto his golden, plate armour.

Looking up in the direction of where the arrows were firing from, Maldwyn saw a dark, hooded figure leaping from branch to branch with impeccable ease. He smiled at the archer's familiar graceful robes, which made the form seem shadowy as it elegantly glided through the woods like a ghost. Halting high up in the thick of a bulky tree, not too far from where Maldwyn was standing, the archer crouched and fired another shot at the soldiers. Maldwyn smiled as he noticed more dark archers swinging through the woods, letting out a relieved breath as arrows blazed down on the guards.

Maldwyn rubbed his forehead, watching the king's guards hit the ground hard. The snow was spoiled from the spattered blotches of blood, bruising the pure white covering on the ground. When the last guard was shot down, attempting to flee the area, the archers sprung out of the trees with swift charm and poise.

They wore fine, dark, chestnut-coloured robes, hoods hiding their faces. A dash of red silk was visible beneath their thick leather belts which were wrapped around their waists.

Maldwyn recognised the beautiful robes of the skilful Erendil rangers.

Trudging over to where Maldwyn stood, slightly bent over as he tried to catch his breath from the sprint, one of the taller archers stepped to the front of the group. Holding their bow clasped in their hands, the man said, 'Well, well, what do we have here?' The voice was low and carried the singsong accent of the Erendil.

The man pushed his hood back revealing his brown eyes, which glinted with amber tones reflecting off the sun's light. Having not seen Jaecen's face in full quite like this before, Maldwyn noticed that he had a rather square face and cropped ginger hair. He also had a slight build that was perfect for moving swiftly through the tree canopy as a sentry.

The last time he had seen Jaecen was in the dungeons of the hidden city that was carved into the Anhalt Mountains, and Maldwyn had been drugged. He felt bad that he had been in such an unpleasant mood when he first met Jaecen, but Maldwyn had been their prisoner at the time.

He still recalled the strong, earthy, damp smell in the air the deeper Anton and Maldwyn had descended into the heart of the mountain, and the dungeons themselves were dimly lit by the distant torches on the tunnel walls. When they arrived, Jaecen greeted both Anton and Maldwyn from behind a desk.

Standing proudly in front of Maldwyn now, Jaecen grinned and bowed his head respectfully. 'Eminence! It is good to see you.' The other archers grouped behind Jaecen joined in with the formal gesture, each lowering their heads.

To Maldwyn, it was strange to be greeted in such a reverent manner. He smiled a little awkwardly to one side.

'Jaecen! Your timing is impeccable!' Maldwyn offered in response to the ranger who had anchored one end of his bow in the ground, ankle-deep snow hiding its tip. Placing his hands on his hips, Maldwyn took in a deep breath, steadying himself from the sprint. 'How's your family?' Maldwyn asked, gesturing one hand toward Jaecen as he remembered that the ranger's wife had been pregnant when they had met.

'Things are great, although it's best to stay out of Inara's way right now,' he joked, laughing at his little jest while the other archers shared side-eyed expressions. Maldwyn laughed along with him, supposing that Inara was Jaecen's wife. 'She may be carrying my child inside her, but that hasn't calmed her temper.' Amused by Jaecen's remark, Maldwyn let his smile climb higher up his cheeks, showing the whites of his teeth. He thought of how the Erendil were a people of enormous poise and grace and wondered what might constitute a temper among these people. 'Tell me, Eminence, what are you doing out here? You were supposed to be back in the palace with the prince.'

Maldwyn touched the side of his head and looked to the ground wondering how he could best answer the question, which was both sad and complicated to explain.

'That's a long story,' he said in a sombre voice, supposing it was the most honest answer he could give at this moment in time. Realising that he might be able to work out where he was for the first time in days, Maldwyn stared straight up at Jaecen and asked, 'Where exactly are we?'

'At the northern foot of the Anhalt Mountains, near the entrance to the mine.'

'The mine is around here?'

Maldwyn stepped nearer the group of rangers, recalling that a substance known as draconite had been found in the mine. Anton had told Maldwyn that draconite was a gemstone that formed from the scales of dragons' corpses and that it could be used as a potent magical ingredient that was most often used in curses. Considering Morloch Brandt's notes, Maldwyn wondered whether there was more history behind the iron mine than he had previously thought and whether this place was an ancient, buried prison holding the creature known as the Bringer of Oblivion.

'Has anything other than draconite been found there?'

Jaecen cocked his head as if confused by the question. 'The remains of what appears to be three dragons have been uncovered there, if that is what you mean, Eminence. Anton has recovered more gemstones as well.'

Maldwyn scratched his neck with the tips of his fingers. His nails were broken from his travels, which kept them short. 'There aren't any signs of the place being a prison?'

Jaecen shook his head and looked to the group behind him, who all responded with a similar look of bewilderment. 'To tell you the truth, most of us have never entered the mine. The sovereign controls access into that place, keeping it secure.'

Surprised by this remark, Maldwyn frowned. 'You've never so much as stepped a foot inside?'

'No, Eminence. We liberated the mine from Lord Darius on the sovereign's orders. I believe only the sovereign himself and the sorcerer, Anton, have entered the place since we secured the mine a few months back. You might do better to ask them.'

Growing impatient, the archers behind Jaecen began to look around, one of them kicking their boot into the snow creating a momentary, powdery puff that resembled a light and fluffy cloud. Looking at the bloodied bodies behind him, arrows sticking out of their frozen corpses, Maldwyn turned his face to the ground, saddened that it had come to this. Not wanting to keep them from burying the bodies for much longer, Maldwyn scratched the stubble along his jaw, which pricked the tips of his fingers.

'How do I get to the mine from here, or back to Dresden?'

'If you want to enter the mine, then I am afraid you will need to speak to the sovereign.' Jaecen stepped forward and placed a hand on Maldwyn's shoulder, which he found reassuring given he had been lost for days and was beyond exhausted. Turning back to the others with a flat voice despite his songlike lilt, Jaecen said, 'Bury the bodies and stay on alert. There may be more of them out there.' Each of the archers moved quickly to remove any evidence of the scuffle. Their chestnut-coloured robes glided through the air like dark, silky spectres. 'I will take you to see the sovereign, Eminence.'

A knot formed in Maldwyn's stomach at the notion of being so close to the mine and having to hike for hours up the mount to seek approval to enter. The idea that no one had stepped foot in the mine except for Anton and Jerrik for months, and that the Erendil were uncomfortable telling Maldwyn the location of the mine, was concerning.

He wondered what the sovereign was hiding, and this was not the first time he had felt this way about this man. Unable to argue with Jaecen, who was simply following orders, Maldwyn accepted his offer to help and followed him toward the place that had once been his prison.

CHAPTER NINE

The Handmaiden

'THIS IS AILAYA we are talking about, sire!' Theodor shouted, pushing himself off the sandstone wall that he had been leaning against with his foot.

Harlan stepped away and turned his back on the knight to look out over the ocean. For the most part, the black, glittery sand was hidden below a thick layer of powdered snow, but there was a thin line of burned, yellow sand where the tide had washed away the ice and snow. He sighed, something was comforting about the waves lapping against the shore.

'There has to be another way,' Theodor pleaded to his back.

Prince Harlan leaned on the stone half-wall, watching the gentle whitecaps form on the tips of the short waves. The skies were clear and the sun was high over the horizon, shimmering on the water. It was a trick on the eyes that almost made him forget that it was winter, but the biting wind whisking off the cold seas wouldn't allow him such pleasure.

'She's a maidservant,' Harlan uttered as steam gushed out of his mouth. He brushed the side of his face with his glove. He was growing weary from discussing the matter with Theodor. 'Do you have any better ideas?'

Theodor came up by Harlan's side and propped his forearms on the wall, leather vambraces grinding the sandstone. The knight's dark brown leather body armour squeaked as he pushed his shoulders back. His thick fur coat made the knight appear broader than usual. There was a hopelessness in Theodor's eyes that told Harlan he knew the prince was right.

'Your Grace, what about Master Damyan?'

Harlan admired his resolve. 'Master Damyan is the head of staff; he won't have time to get close enough to the woman.' Readjusting his black, woollen-lined, leather gloves, Harlan chewed his cheek. 'We need someone who will be able to be in Moya's presence if we want to get her to talk.' Theodor hung his head, staring toward the large docks in the distance, on the far side of the city.

From where they stood, at the top of the seaside palace mount, in the vast snow-covered castle gardens, Harlan could see most of the city. In the summer, this vantage would look over the terracotta roofs of the rich and the simple, thatched cottages of the working peoples alike. The brilliant green ivy vines that grew throughout the kingdom, much like a weed, would gleam against the capital's buildings which were an array of warmer colours, and the long, dark wooden dock would stand out against the vividly blue sea. However, it was winter now, and everything was grey and white as far as he could see.

Harlan glanced at Theodor, seeing the worry on his face. 'Look,' he started, wetting his lips with the tip of his tongue, 'I know you're worried, and if she refuses, then we will ask another one of the maidservants. It's just that—'

'We can trust her,' Theodor mumbled, finishing the prince's sentence.

'Yes, we can.'

'I understand it, Your Grace. I just don't like it.' The knight rubbed his clean-shaven chin with his hand, deep in thought. 'Fine, I will talk to her about approaching Moya.'

'Thank you,' Harlan said, leaning closer and offering Theodor a sincere, reassuring expression. Looking back out over the water, he studied the sails of the ships on the horizon, standing proud as they reached up and touched the sparse clouds. A small, lone rowboat was sailing out toward one of the larger ships, ferrying supplies.

'There's something else we need to talk about, Your Grace.' Still bent over the half wall, Theodor locked his hands together, weaving his fingers. 'I've had my people looking into the mine since it was mentioned the other evening.'

Bleary-eyed from the cold, Harlan squinted a fraction as he puckered his brows to better his vision. 'Have you found something?'

'The miners are missing, sire, and it seems as though there are a great many rumours related to the mine.' Forearms resting on the wall, Theodor flicked his hands in the air, as if he were shrugging with his wrists.

'What sort of rumours?'

Theodor took in a large breath of air. 'It's difficult to separate the truth from the lies, but there are stories among the common folk that suggest there may be more than iron in the mine.' Harlan thrust himself off the wall to better see Theodor through the wind which was making him wince. 'The mine has long been disputed between the capital and the mountain dwellers, hopping from one person's control to the next. Before your father lost control of the mine, people began to tell a fable about a rock that had been found there. Some people believe the missing miners became greedy, running away with masses of this mysterious rock, never to be seen again.'

'A rock?' Harlan asked, sounding unimpressed as he crossed his arms and lowered his head.

'I know it sounds ridiculous, sire,' Theodor started, putting up a hand defensively, 'but this stone is said to have been like looking into the stars themselves. The fables say it was of the deepest shade of black, darker than onyx, yet it shone with the brightness of a million stars as if the gods were beaming at them from the cosmos itself.'

'If,' Harlan began, seeing a puff of steam burst from his mouth, 'for the sake of argument, there was such a stone, do you have any ideas what it might be?'

'None, Your Grace, but, if it's true, then it's probably priceless and, according to Lord Darius, worth risking a civil war over.'

Harlan stroked his smooth jaw, mulling over the news. 'Your people are looking into these stories?'

'Yes, sire.'

'Keep me updated.'

'Of course, Your Grace.'

'We should head back to the castle,' Harlan put on a firm tone as he took in a final look at the stunning, bright horizon, glittering from the light of the gleaming sun. 'I've kept my father waiting long enough.'

*   *   *   *   *

The council meeting went for longer than usual, working through the missed shipment of supplies from Haradnor. It appeared as though their neighbour had been hit harder than expected by the winter, and Aberdeen was not the only village that had been unable to provide supplies sufficient to meet the demands of Dresden. A large number of towns from their allied neighbour had been impacted and were not capable of trading in the usually agreed wares. Harlan was concerned about what it would mean for his country.

Though Dresden had many skilled labourers, there wasn't a lot that could be done about a lack of provisions, other than to seek a new trade agreement quickly. The council was hesitant to embrace this option, however, knowing that it could potentially damage relations with Haradnor by angering King Sebulon. Trading with another kingdom would essentially leave Haradnor without a source of income or supplies, which would make the situation far graver for its people. Despite discussing many options at great length, the lords on the council had concluded that there may be no other option. Their priority was, after all, to protect the citizens of Dresden first and foremost.

Harlan raised the point that seeking a new agreement would have its difficulties due to winter being a tough time to barter new trade deals, but the council had been convinced that this was the best path to take. The keeper of the king's archives,

Gorlois, an older gentleman with a long, grey beard and a face that was a map of wrinkles, suggested sending aid to Haradnor as a means of maintaining good relations with their neighbour. While a worthy suggestion, Dresden did not have enough stores for both charity and trade. It was an unfortunate state of affairs to be in, and it would be quite tricky to navigate the political fallout this would cause. Troubled after the adjournment of the council meeting, Harlan walked in contemplative silence as he followed Theodor to the undercroft where Ailaya would be waiting.

The corridors of the servant halls were confined, and the light was dim. An unusual, cold draught plagued every corner of these halls, making them much colder than the imperial areas that the staff waited upon, unseen and unheard. In an attempt to avoid his father's spies, Harlan and Theodor had opted to slip through the servant door in Harlan's bed chambers.

Even though Harlan was wearing a hooded cloak, the few staff they passed stepped out of Harlan's way, staring at the floor, clasping their hands and pressing their backs to the wall, making way for the prince. It worried him that they had been noticed in the corridors, but he was reassured by the fact that the servant reports would be filtered through Master Damyan. At least his father would not learn of his movements in these halls.

Ahead of him, Theodor turned down a narrow, steep set of twisting steps. There was a strange sort of smell in the air, Harlan tried to put his finger on what it was and wanted to snap his fingers when he recognised that the odour was of mould growing on the damp, mildewed stone. Having descended the many flights of stairs, Harlan paused at the edge of the final step where the stone floor met with the dirt ground of the undercroft. He hadn't wanted to muddy his boots, but it appeared he had no choice.

Crossing the threshold into the arched cellar, Harlan glanced up at the vaulted, stone ceiling, which was a patchwork of stone bricks and thick mortar, decorating the roof in an assortment of greys. Although it was dark, it was quite a spectacle hidden beneath the castle.

Deeper into the undercroft, Harlan saw Ailaya waiting for them by one of the thick, square pillars supporting the weight of the castle above them. Her long red hair was pushed back over her shoulders, and she was wearing a moss-coloured linen dress. A grey wool shawl was wrapped around her shoulders, adding a layer of warmth. She kept her head down and curtsied as the prince approached, pressing the flat palm of one hand to the back of her other hand, holding them low. One foot locked behind the other, she kept her knees bent until permitted to rise before the prince.

'Your Royal Highness.' She addressed Harlan softly with a honeyed voice, as a slight cloud of steam escaped her lips. Harlan glanced at Theodor, who was doing his best to hide the distress on his face, and signalled for Ailaya to rise with a flick of the wrist. 'Ser Theodor tells me you wish for assistance in regards to a particularly sensitive matter relating to Lady Adria's handmaiden, Moya.'

Harlan could tell she was nervous about how formally she addressed him. Theodor scrunched his forehead tight. It was clear the knight didn't like watching the woman he loved being made to feel inferior.

'Please, no need for formalities.' Harlan told her, hoping to ease the discomfort. Lowering his hood, he caught the half-smile on Theodor's face.

Ailaya checked with her lover that this was okay before listening to Harlan's request. With a simple nod from the knight, she relaxed her stiffened stance, beaming at Theodor with a flash of joy in her eyes. She had a lovely, cheeky smile, forming sweet pinches in her cheeks as the corners of her lips curled up her face.

'Alright, Your Grace,' she said, speaking with a surprisingly confident tone as she looked him dead in the eyes, something that was usually not permitted for a woman of her stature. 'What is it you want me to do?'

Harlan smirked and tilted his head, impressed by her directness when she wasn't placating a member of the royal family. Theodor shrugged when Harlan looked at him as if saying that he had no control over her behaviour. Harlan momentarily regretted permitting the informality.

'I believe Theodor already spoke to you, while I was in the council meeting, about Lord Darius.' Ailaya gave a single nod of her head as she bit her cheeks. 'Well, Moya is Lady Adria's most trusted servant; she knows all of her lady's secrets.' Harlan quickly scanned the area, double-checking that none of his father's spies was in the undercroft listening in to their conversation. 'What I want is for you to befriend this woman and find out whether she knows anything about Darius's activities.'

'Is there anything, in particular, you want me to try to learn, sire?'

Harlan creased his lips together in thought. 'Don't ask anything obvious, just pay attention to anything you think sounds out of the ordinary. Try to focus on anything related to life in the downs, or working for the lord and lady.' Glancing over Ailaya's shoulder, Harlan noticed a brick missing from the wide pillar behind her head. 'I don't want you asking anything that will put you in harm's way. Just see what you can learn and report back to us.'

'I can do that, Your Grace.'

Harlan was pleased. Theodor scratched his forehead, as though something was bothering him. His body armour groaned. Angling his head to one side, Harlan waited for him to speak.

Eventually, Theodor stepped forward, took her hand, and keeping his voice low, he said, 'If you can, see if you can find out anything about the mine in the disputed regions, or listen out for any mention of missing miners.' Harlan was astonished by Theodor's suggestion. It was likely the most obvious, and thus dangerous, line of questioning he wanted her to ask. 'You have to be very careful. This is very dangerous, but I think we will all be worse off if you don't try to find out if she knows anything about that place.'

Ailaya stroked Theodor's hands, which were clutching hers tightly. Harlan smiled to himself, pleased to know they felt comfortable showing their affection for one another within his presence.

'I'll be careful,' she whispered, looking up into his eyes. Facing back to Harlan, Ailaya let go of Theodor's hand. 'There is something I can already offer you about Moya, sire.'

Harlan crinkled his forehead, noticing that Theodor had done the same. 'What is it?' Harlan asked, tilting his head towards Ailaya out of interest.

Ailaya arched a brow. 'Well, sire, I've had the opportunity to speak with her over the past few days since they arrived.'

'What has she told you?'

'Well, so far, Your Grace, Moya has mentioned that she has a brother who lives here in the capital. When I asked her about her brother and whether she was going to see him, she became a little cagey.' Pinching her mouth to the side, she let out a heavy breath, which released a rising mist of steam. 'For whatever reason, she didn't want to talk about it, so I let her change the topic.'

Theodor placed a soft hand on her shoulder. 'Did she give you any more information about this brother?'

Biting her cheek, Ailaya rubbed her long, thin fingers over her mouth and chin. 'She only gave me his name.' Shrugging with a helpless look on her face, she continued, 'She said his name was Sebastian.'

Studying the dirt, Harlan removed one of his gloves to rake his fingers through his thick hair. Theodor stepped back and placed a hand on his chin, cradling the elbow of his right arm with his left hand.

'Why do you seem bothered by that?' Harlan mumbled as if muttering to himself.

Theodor shook his head. 'There is a Sebastian on the staff, Your Grace. His full name is Sebastian Voigt. He is one of the hunters.'

'There must be many people by that name in the capital, mustn't there? Surely it can't be him?' Frustrated that he had hit another information blockade, Harlan scratched along the furrows of his brows before pulling his glove back on. Footsteps on the winding stairs behind them echoed throughout the cavernous undercroft. Harlan drew his hood back over his head to hide his face and looked at Theodor. 'We can't be seen meeting down here,' Harlan exclaimed, fearing that it may not be a member of the servant staff coming down the steps. If it was one of the guards completing their rounds, then Master Damyan would have no control over the meeting being reported to the king.

'Quick, sire! Hide behind the pillar!' Ailaya told them in a hushed voice. 'I'll lead them back up the stairs so you can make your way out.'

Harlan and Theodor sprinted to the other side of the wide, square column at Ailaya's back, and were able to obscure themselves in the dim light behind the bulky, stone pillar. Pressing his back to the massive support, Harlan pushed the flat of his hands against the surface of the pillar, feeling the deep grooves in between the bricks through his leather gloves. The footsteps grew louder, clicking on the stairs. He held his breath, anxious.

'Master Damyan!' Ailaya shouted, moving closer to the stairs.

Breathing a sigh of relief, Harlan and Theodor exchanged pleasing looks and slipped out from behind the pillar. 'It's alright, Ailaya,' Theodor told her.

'He's with us,' Harlan reassured.

'Oh,' she uttered, looking Master Damyan up and down for a moment. Damyan's silver streaks shone despite the darkness of the undercroft. He was wearing a black, suede doublet over his long-sleeved, navy-coloured shirt. His black pants were well fitted to the older gentleman. From the look Damyan was giving Harlan, he wasn't impressed that there appeared to be some sort of meeting going ahead without his knowledge. 'I didn't realise, sire.'

'This is what happens when you don't tell me about your movements, Your Grace.' Master Damyan scolded, wagging a finger at Harlan. 'If you had told me you needed a private place to meet, I could have given you the schedules of the guards and directed the staff away from the undercroft.' He folded his arms. 'Imagine if it hadn't been me coming down those stairs.'

Awkwardly, Ailaya looked from Damyan to Harlan and back again. Theodor itched behind his ear, like an apologetic child caught in a scheme. Holding his hands out, Harlan agreed with Damyan, grinning all the while.

'I'm sorry Damyan,' Harlan told him, walking further away from the pillar and, once again, pulling back the hood from his head. 'It was sort of a last-minute meeting after the council gathered. As you can see, we planned it poorly.'

'Would you like to tell me what is going on here?' Master Damyan gestured to the three of them as though they had been up to no good.

'Ailaya was just telling us that Moya has a brother here, in the city,' Harlan started, returning the master's intense stare as Theodor scuffed his shoe into the dirt. 'His name is Sebastian.'

'Sebastian Voigt,' Theodor joined in, holding his hand out, 'do you know if he has a sister?'

'No, I have no idea,' Master Damyan muttered. 'He's never mentioned his family, to be frank.'

Running her long, clean fingernails along her chin, Ailaya looked over to Harlan, frowning. 'Sire, is there no one in Karana Downs you can trust to infiltrate Lord Darius's keep and investigate things?'

Unable to think, Harlan shook his head and crossed his arms, hugging them tight over his chest. 'Not that I can think of... at least not for the moment.'

'That's not true, Your Grace,' Damyan stated flatly. Pleats formed in the corners of his eyes as he looked up with a serious face, giving Harlan the impression that he had been struck by a risky idea. 'There's your contact in the mountains.'

Harlan pulled a face, knowing that Master Damyan was referring to Jerrik. He was undecided as to whether he could trust the sovereign. Still, he thought, Jerrik had offered to help him wherever possible concerning proving Darius's betrayal.

'The mountains?' Ailaya gazed between Theodor and Harlan.

Shooting her a warning look, Theodor urged her not to ask anything further. It was clear he didn't want to place her at greater risk. Understanding his concern, Ailaya held his hand and dipped her head, as if trying to convince him with her eyes that she was willing to take the risk.

'It is best that you don't know,' Harlan said, backing up Theodor's concern. 'It will be safer for you.'

'It's someone among the Erendil, isn't it?' Rolling her eyes, she shot a look at Damyan. 'Someone released the prince and Maldwyn from captivity.' Master Damyan bowed his head, holding his hands together behind his back.

Theodor hung his head low, his arms limp at his sides. 'Go on, Your Grace,' Theodor told Harlan, sounding defeated.

'I made a deal with the sovereign and he let us go. Since returning to the palace, he has offered to help with investigating Lord Darius, but he can't get anyone into the keep where the lord resides.'

Putting her hands on her hips, Ailaya turned to Damyan. 'So then, how does that help us?'

'Your Grace, he might not be able to get someone into the keep, but his people are sleuths and have proven great at gathering information.' Pushing his shoulders back, looking proud, Master Damyan spoke in a very flat tone. 'We may not be able to learn anything from Moya or her brother, but the sovereign may be able to get information from the townspeople that may at least give us other leads.'

'It can't hurt to ask him, sire,' Theodor agreed.

Harlan hesitated as he considered his options. He wasn't sure how far he could push things with Jerrik, especially since he hadn't admitted to having found Kristian's ring. There was a feeling in the pit of his stomach that told him not to give up the ring quite yet. For now, he could keep up the deception while he looked into things.

'Alright,' Harlan gave in, supposing that he could at least send word to Jerrik. The sovereign would help as agreed, for a time. 'I'll draft a letter. Can you get him another message?' Harlan asked Damyan.

Full of pride, Master Damyan straightened his thick, well-fitted doublet, flattening the creasing from where it had bunched up on the sides. 'Of course, sire.'

'Excellent!' Ailaya clapped her hands and rubbed her palms together.

A quiet settled over them. The smell of mould on the bricks caught on the slight draught, reminding Harlan that it was there. Cold, he pulled his sleeves tight about his wrists as a cloud of steam escaped his breath.

'Before you go anywhere, sire, I was about to come looking for you,' Master Damyan declared. A sombre glint fled his control as he looked from Harlan to Ailaya. 'The prisoners from Alander are being processed in the dungeon.'

Theodor fired a worried look at Harlan. Ailaya clutched at her chest, terrified of what this meant for her best friend. Holding his breath, Harlan did his best to hide his fear from the others, but it seemed to be taking him over.

'What news do you have?' Theodor asked, sparing both Ailaya and Harlan from having to ask the question.

'I'm not sure. I haven't been able to see the list of prisoners, nor get into the dungeons while they're being secured. They have only just arrived in the dungeons, Your Grace.' Master Damyan looked to the floor. 'I thought it best to let you know as soon as they arrived.'

'Thank you,' Harlan managed.

The others kept speaking, but their voices faded away into nothingness as Harlan's mind became consumed with fear. He had a bad feeling that Maldwyn wasn't among the prisoners.

CHAPTER TEN

The Dying Flame

H E USUALLY AVOIDED coming here. Harlan hated the dungeons. The place reeked of human excrement seeping forth from the freezing, stone prison cells. The floor was poorly laid in this part of the castle with uneven bricks sticking out at odd angles, striving to catch a person by their boots. The hay strands and clumps of muck spread irregularly across the ground reminded Harlan of the stables. The corridor which led through the prison chambers was dark and cramped. Heavy timber doors, several feet apart, lined the corridor, marking the entrance to each holding cell.

The guard guiding Harlan and Theodor through the dungeons cleared his throat and stopped by a door, unhooking the large metal ring attached to his belt, which was overflowing with keys, each varying in size and length. He was a muscular man with beady brown eyes, who spoke as if he were conserving words and wore the lightweight brown and blue leather armour of the city's soldiers. His heavy, woollen coat had fur bunched up around his neck.

Harlan felt his heart slamming inside his chest, anxious to see if Maldwyn was among the survivors of Alander. From the way Theodor stared at the door, forehead crenulated, forming little ridges, Harlan could tell the knight was worried to find what lay beyond the door, or rather, who waited inside the cell.

The guard fumbled the key in the lock, nervous to be in the prince's presence. Harlan kept his expression blank, ignoring the man's incompetence. There was only one thing that mattered to him right now, and that was behind the solid, wooden door. As the lock turned, the guard pushed the door inward, hinges whining at being bothered.

The cell was packed with people huddling on the floor, hands cuffed. Beaten and broken, the men, women and children's faces were covered with filth. Bags beneath their eyes showed how little they had been allowed to sleep. Their clothes were tattered and torn, stained with dark patches, making them nestle together as tight as possible to conserve warmth.

Harlan signalled for the guard to leave, indicating for him to hand the keys to Theodor. Reluctant, the man glared at Theodor, annoyed that he was being dismissed. He placed the bundle of keys in Theodor's open palm, metal jingling like bells. Harlan waited for the guard to reach the end of the corridor, returning to sit by the sentries' station at the main entrance to the dungeons.

Drawing in a large breath, Harlan readied himself to walk into the chamber. His feet felt heavy as he crossed the threshold, moving a few paces inside. Theodor stayed in the doorway. Scanning the faces, Harlan searched the group of survivors for the face he knew so well, skipping over the women and children.

There was a man who appeared to be the right height and build, with dark, walnut-coloured hair, of about the same length and thickness as Maldwyn's, but, as Harlan lowered his head to better see the man's face, he realised it wasn't the one he was searching for. Where this man had a square face and brown eyes, Maldwyn's face was more of an oblong shape and his eyes were green, an almost ethereal sort of seafoam shade, with bright green flecks around the iris.

Pausing again on the face of a sleeping man, head turned to one side and resting against the brick wall, Harlan noticed a scar on the cheek facing forward. Maldwyn didn't have any scars; his face was unmarred.

Taking a few more steps into the huddle of shivering villagers, Harlan struggled to breathe, losing hope as his eyes jumped from face to face. He didn't care that they were watching him as he carefully manoeuvred through the crouching bunch. He just kept searching the faces of all the men, no longer caring for hair colour or height, wishing for the impossible.

'Excuse me,' muttered a man with grey hair, seated in the far, right-hand corner of the cell, head lowered. As the man lifted his head, Harlan noticed that he had amber eyes and dry, aged skin. His jaw was square, and his mouth was a thin, flat line. 'Are you looking for someone?'

Afraid to ask, Harlan's stomach turned. He glanced over his shoulder to Theodor, seeking his counsel. With a pained expression, Theodor dipped his head, telling Harlan to respond and ask the man the question he was dying to know.

Tightening the muscles in his face, Harlan held a stern, yet empty look as he zeroed in on the grey-haired man sitting in the corner of the cell. 'Who are you?'

'I'm Dimitri,' the man replied informally, clearly not versed in addressing royals. A young boy with brown hair, seated in front of Dimitri, shifted to stare at the man who was brave enough to speak with the Crown Prince.

'I am looking for a man from your village. He worked in the palace as a servant.' A mother, with honey hair and brown eyes, clutched her daughter tight, pulling her in closer to her chest. 'His name is Maldwyn. He's from your town.'

Dimitri bowed his head, hiding his eyes from the prince's view. 'I knew Maldwyn well. I'm sorry.' His voice lowered, sounding croaky. 'He was murdered in the attack. I saw it myself.'

Harlan's heart jumped into his throat. He lost his breath. Eyebrows tightening, hands stiffening, and standing frozen in place, Harlan strained to relax. 'How?' Hearing Theodor take a few steps into the cell, Harlan regretted the question as soon as it escaped his lips.

'When the fighting broke out, Maldwyn was in the street.' Dimitri looked up. His face was unreadable. There was no reason for Harlan not to believe what he was saying. 'He was chased down by the soldiers. I saw him get thrown into a burning building.' Harlan clenched his jaw. 'One of the guards pursued him into the ruins. Neither one of them came out of the building.'

Mute, Harlan became as still as a statue. An infant, cradled in its mother's arms, began to cry, sounding the broken screams of the prince's spirit. Theodor's boots clicked as he moved closer to where Harlan was standing. The people on the floor shuffled out of the knight's way.

'There are reports among the guards that brought you to the city, which mention the presence of a sorcerer in the village.' Harlan turned his ear toward Theodor's voice, keeping his stare on Dimitri. The man twisted his head to gaze at the wall, seeming to study the stone bricks. 'Do you know anything about that?'

'I'm sorry,' Dimitri said, locking eyes with Theodor. The look in his eyes was suspect. 'I can't say I know anything about that.'

Wheeling his head enough to see Theodor, Harlan saw him smirk. 'Thank you,' Theodor said as one of the prisoners sneezed. Harlan had a sinking feeling that there was something he was missing. 'Your Grace, we should get going.'

Harlan glanced from Dimitri to Theodor. After a moment, he thanked the people in the cell and apologised, genuinely saddened for their loss, as he felt he shared their pain. Together Harlan and Theodor left the cell. The knight was sure to lock the door behind them, spinning the bundle of keys around his fingers as they walked back to the guards' station. Harlan chose not to ask about the knight's final remarks until they were in a more private part of the castle.

*   *   *   *   *

Maldwyn kneeled before Jerrik, lowering the hood of his simple, yet warm, woollen travelling cloak. Seated on the plush throne, which was more like a divan on a tall, wide dais, at the top of a long set of steps, Jerrik reclined in his great chair.

An impressive timber structure was built around the throne with sheer fabric hanging down, shrouding the space. A window in the structure where the fabric was pinned to the posts revealed Jerrik wearing his white hooded robes with gold brocade embellishments, reminding Maldwyn of the sovereign's elegance and self-indulgence.

Smiling at the grandeur of the Imperial Hall, Maldwyn looked up at the domed ceiling which was crafted out of a stunning pattern of glazed tiles, arranged in swirling designs that created the illusion the roof was higher above Maldwyn than it was in truth. The walls were white and had blue and gold paint bespattered like glittering stars on the pristine background. The floor was laid out of large marble tiles with grey veins webbing through the glistening surface. He thought of how the last time he had been in this hall, he and the prince had been prisoners.

Jaecen, armed with bows, arrows and a variety of knives, stood proudly beside the kneeling Maldwyn. The visible line of red silk on either side of his leather belt shone from his dark brown robes, which glided through the air as he moved.

'Eminence,' the sovereign began, speaking with his beautiful lilting accent. His voice was like a calming birdsong. 'Welcome back to our stronghold. I must admit, you have returned to us sooner than I expected, but, as I told you, you are always welcome in the Anhalt Mountains. Please rise! There is no need for such formalities.' Jerrik got up from his seat and floated down the stairs.

Maldwyn stood weakly, exhausted from the hike, and locked his thumb under the strap of his heavy backpack. His wounded hand ached. 'Thank you, sovereign—'

'Please, call me Jerrik,' he said, holding up a hand to soothe things, helping Maldwyn relax. Maldwyn was a little nervous to be standing in front of Jerrik again, having once been his captive.

'Sovereign,' Jaecen began, smoothing his robes. 'We found him near the mine. He was being pursued by the king's guards.'

'The king's guards, you say?' The sovereign looked curiously at Maldwyn, eyeing him up and down from beneath his hood. The massive, oak doors to the hall grumbled as Tolamin and Tiana entered, each charming Maldwyn as they sailed up the length of the great hall.

Tiana, head of the sovereign's concubines, wore heavy make-up that accentuated the length of her eyelashes and helped to enchant onlookers with her startling grey-blue eyes. Her long, dark hair was curled and pulled back from her face. In a fitted, silk, navy dress with lace sleeves, she strolled with a perfectly straight back, displaying her tremendous confidence.

Heavily robed in pastel shades of blue, which was broken by the silver and white sash wrapped around his waist, Tolamin's eyes were shaded by his low hood. The holy man had several golden rings on each of his fingers with different sparkling gemstones embedded in their swirling designs. As a priest dedicated to the worship of Uller, the bowman god of winter and the hunt, Tolamin also wore a ring bearing Uller's symbol on a long chain around his neck.

'You sent for us, sovereign.' Tiana's voice was deep and raspy despite her singsong accent.

She stopped a short way back from where Maldwyn was standing. She had the elegance of the Erendil, yet she was far more relaxed than Tolamin and Jaecen appeared when standing in the presence of their sovereign. Maldwyn supposed it was because she knew his tender hesitancies and his dangerous cravings from between the sheets.

'I did.' The sovereign looked to Tiana with a soft face despite his dark, expressionless eyes. 'His Eminence has returned to us.' Tiana and Tolamin both bowed to Maldwyn, making him uncomfortable. 'Please, you were about to tell us about how you wound up in the woods being chased by the king's guards.'

Seeing each of their puzzled faces staring at him unnerved Maldwyn, and he wished he could be as invisible as his life as a servant. Guilt at having escaped the attack in his hometown tangled around his abdomen and squeezed. He wanted to sink into the background and disappear from their sight but was stuck with four pairs of eyes on him, waiting to tell them why the king's soldiers were chasing him.

'I was in Alander—my mother was ill—when there was an attack.' Tiana tied her brows together, making a fine dimple at the top of her nose. 'The king has ordered searches to be carried out around the kingdom so that he can find and execute sorcerers, but they weren't conducting raids… they were fighting and killing people and burning buildings to the ground.'

Placing a hand on his shoulder, Tiana offered him a tender look. 'I'm so sorry,' she whispered, as Tolamin grabbed the sacred ring hanging around his neck and uttered a discreet prayer.

'Alander is on the northeastern side of Karana Downs,' Jerrik pronounced, as Jaecen glanced sideways at his sovereign. 'You would have had to travel for a few days, moving north, around the downs, before turning south-west to make it into the mountains. Why would the guards chase you this far?'

'In the attack, I used my power to save a young girl in the village,' Maldwyn admitted, knowing that he was among people who held great respect for sorcery. 'I barely escaped after that and I was running so much that most of the time I couldn't tell what direction I was going.'

'Did any of the guards see your face, Eminence?' Tolamin asked, sounding worried.

'No,' Maldwyn answered, shaking his head.

'In any case,' Jaecen folded his arms as he spoke, 'the guards chasing him have been dealt with. We killed them when we spotted His Eminence in danger and buried their bodies out of sight.'

'You must be exhausted,' declared Jerrik, turning around and making his way back up the steps to his throne. 'You look gaunt. We will have plenty of time to discuss everything that has happened since you left the Anhalt Mountains with Prince Harlan.' Spinning around, Jerrik flicked the skirt of his robes back as he sat on the massive chair, ensuring that it didn't gather into a lump under his weight. 'Tiana, why don't you take Maldwyn to the baths and have him cleaned up?'

'Of course, sovereign,' Tiana agreed.

'Actually,' Maldwyn started as he took a few paces towards the steps which led up to the sheltered throne. 'There was something I wanted to discuss with you.'

'We will have time to talk later.' Leaning one elbow on the arm of his seat, Jerrik rested the side of his head on his knuckles, waving them off with his other hand. 'Tolamin, Jaecen, stay here, I need you to do something.'

'Come on,' urged Tiana. Her dress floated through the air as she moved, gliding elegantly. Having been dismissed, Maldwyn thanked Jerrik and reluctantly followed Tiana through the huge doors, into the long winding corridors.

Though there were no windows within the underground city, the bright colours from the mosaic floors, the enormously high ceilings, the smooth, woven rugs, and the chiffon draperies made up for the lack of natural light. Finely detailed swirling designs were painted on the golden walls. Reminded of the magnificence of the city of tunnels, Maldwyn smiled, feeling humbled by the architecture as he listened to the beat of their steps reverberate off the tiled floor.

Everyone they passed in the tunnels wore robes that varied in colour and detail. Hoods were drawn over their faces, keeping them shadowed. They appeared to walk like ghosts, drifting through the corridors as their robes fluttered behind them.

Reaching a wide, solid timber door that Maldwyn recognised, he stopped, noting the large, iron knocker, which was shaped like the head of an aggressive, fiery dragon.

'Will I get my privacy this time?' Maldwyn asked in a mocking tone, recalling the way he had been manhandled and washed like a dog by the concubines the last time he was taken to the baths as a captive.

Chuckling, Tiana opened the door and stepped inside. The floors, the walls and the ceiling were all fashioned out of white marble. Gold and turquoise glazed tiles were fixed to the walls in a symmetrical leafy pattern, breaking the blankness of the marble. Geometric motifs outlined the tiled leaf design.

The floors were wet and extended as far as the edge of a deep pool, which shimmered from the glassy, teal mosaics that made the water appear to have a crystalline texture.

There was no one in the baths, which made Maldwyn breathe a sigh of relief. Tiana went over to the benches along the wall opposite the pool, satin pillows artfully arranged upon them, and checked that there were plenty of towels.

Moving toward the pool, Maldwyn slipped his fingers under the straps of his pack to relieve the pressure from them digging into his shoulders. As he neared the water, he caught a whiff of the gentle, pleasing floral perfume of the scented pool.

'Here is a towel for you and some soap,' Tiana told him, handing Maldwyn a thick, plush towel that had a small, folded washrag and bar of soap on top. She watched him, with worried eyes, sucking in her bottom lip as he placed his backpack on the ground near the pool. 'Maldwyn, it seems like you've been through a lot since you were here last. Are you alright?'

'I'll be fine,' he said, untying his thick cloak and drawing it back off his shoulders.

It was warm inside the mountain. Beneath his makeshift bandage, his cut palm throbbed. By the look on Tiana's face, she didn't seem to believe him.

'You mentioned your mother was sick.'

'Yes,' Maldwyn said in a faraway voice. Tiana stared at the poorly bandaged gouge across his palm but said nothing. He thought about how he had not yet had the time to process the news of his adoption, nor mourn his mother's passing. 'She died.'

'Maldwyn… I'm sorry.'

'It's okay, you didn't know,' he reassured her, turning his gaze to the floor, noting the grey veins marking the marble tiles. Walking over to the bench, Maldwyn sat down, pushing the satin cushions to the side. He let out a pained breath and stared at the condensation on the floor. 'I feel like there is no way home.'

Tiana, still standing nearer to the pool, leaned her head to the side. 'What do you mean by that?'

'Ever since I left the city, it's been one thing after the other. I wasn't on the best terms with my mother when she passed, and now she's gone… my whole village is gone.' His stomach tensed. He felt ashamed to be standing in the safety of the mountains when so many others had suffered or died. 'I feel like I woke up and everything I knew and everyone I cared about slipped through my fingers… and now I have nothing.'

Tiana clicked her tongue on the roof of her mouth. 'There must be people left in the city that you care about.'

Closing his eyes for longer than a blink, Maldwyn turned his face down. 'I don't know whether I should return to the city.'

Tiana didn't say anything, she just stood quietly, watching him and giving him the space to unburden himself in his own time.

'I have a power that places everyone around me in danger.' Knowing that Tiana was perhaps the most honest person among the Erendil, he lifted his head and asked her, 'How can I go back there knowing that I'm returning to a life where I lie every day and that the people I care about would be executed if I lose control just once?'

'I understand… you're afraid for them.' Tiana looked away and tucked her hair behind her ear. 'Maybe you're right though, and perhaps, for the time being, you should stay here.' Tiana fiddled with her lace sleeves. 'You've been on the road for a while and you should know that there is danger in the capital. Prince Harlan sent word to the sovereign, informing him that King Viktor refused to believe his friend, Lord Darius, was a traitor. The prince is trying to prove that the lord has committed treason.'

Maldwyn scratched his head, scrunching together the muscles in his forehead. 'His father didn't believe him?'

'No. King Viktor is a stubborn man. The fact that the information about Lord Darius aiding Mikel came from the sovereign was enough for the king to refuse to believe the warnings. He considers us as the enemy.' Tiana ran her tongue along her teeth as though she were considering telling him something more.

'What is it? There's something else, isn't there?'

'Harlan is trying to protect his sister from King Viktor's sentence. He wants to free her from Mikel's clutches and get her out of the kingdom.' She crossed her arms over her chest, popping her hip out to one side. 'We believe that the princess is in the lord's keep. But we can't get close enough to Darius's stronghold to be certain. All we have are the few rumours circling among the townsfolk.'

Leaning forward and resting his forearms on his knees, Maldwyn swallowed. 'Have you told Prince Harlan this?'

'Jerrik sent word to the prince a while ago.' Staring at Maldwyn with her intense grey eyes. 'You were a servant in the palace and can blend in well with common folk in Karana Downs. Maybe you can help us get closer to the keep.'

Maldwyn did not respond to her suggestion. He had no control over his gifts and had never considered himself as much of a sleuth before. Eventually, Tiana told him to have his wound attended to by Anton and then made her way out of the baths.

Alone, Maldwyn sat on the bench as he thought about his mother's passing, the destruction of his hometown, and the news of Prince Harlan. The warm, moist air clung to his clothing, beckoning him to the water. Wanting to free himself from his worries, Maldwyn stripped off his clothes and slipped into the cleansing bathwater.

PART TWO

CHAPTER ELEVEN

An Unexpected Return

THE SHIMMERING TINCTURES stored in the timber stand seemed to glow with greater vibrancy than Maldwyn remembered, and the round bottle of dried yarrow leaves was full to the brim. It had been only half full when he was last in this room. The small phial of bilberry extract and the pastel lavender tincture of valerian root were at minutely lower levels. The difference was so slight that Maldwyn was sure it was imperceptible to Anton, who checked these supplies daily. Had Maldwyn not left the Anhalt Mountains, he was sure he would not have noticed the difference himself. Picking up a large container of bulbous, yellow flowers, Maldwyn turned it over until he saw the label "*Bitter Buttons*".

Carefully he placed it back down on the smooth countertop. A whiff of sandalwood incense in the Halls of Healing crept through the open door. He shifted toward the pleasing smell, feeling calmer than he had before entering this hall. The ghost of his captivity still haunted him, making this sanctuary among the mountains a strange graveyard of sorts.

Reaching out with a soft touch, Maldwyn stroked the sheer orange and red draperies hanging all around the single, overly cushioned, high-standing bed. He recalled how frustrated these delicate pieces of fabric made him feel back then, constantly getting in his way. He let out a laugh at the memory under his breath.

Looking back to the countertop, the glazed pottery bowls were stacked higher than he remembered, and he was sure there had been more than one amphora the last time he was here. It was strange to look around the place he had spent so much time in and see it with new eyes.

Behind him, steps shuffled through the open door. 'Maldwyn,' Anton's baritone voice reverberated around the small space. 'I had heard that you had returned and, I must admit, I hadn't expected you to be here.' As Maldwyn turned to face the healer, he straightened at Anton's massive figure by the door, a tad intimidated by his former keeper. His long-sleeved, golden shirt shone against his tanned skin and gleamed in stark contrast with his black trousers. The raven mark on his wrist, marking him as a descendant of the Raven Clan, was hidden beneath the fitted cuff of his shirt. Anton was a fair amount older than Maldwyn, which was evidenced by his laugh lines stretching out from his crooked nose. 'I mean… I wouldn't have thought you would be eager to return to the place that was once your prison.'

He wasn't, but he had come here in search of Anton. 'I was looking for you.'

'Oh?'

'Tiana suggested that I should come here and have you re-dress my wound.' Maldwyn, having left the gouge bandaged and kept it above the bathwater as much as possible, held his hand forward for Anton to see. 'I'm a little worried it might be infected. The skin was quite red the last time I checked it.'

Anton stepped forward to grab Maldwyn's hand, and carefully began stripping back the makeshift bandage which had been made from cutting apart a spare shirt in his pack. Beneath the fabric, which stuck to his skin, the wound had regained much of its creamy surface layer, and there was a clear red border outlining the gash. 'How did you get this wound?'

'I was running, trying to escape the king's guards when I was thrown and fell into a burning building, and I reached out to break my fall. My hand landed on a broken piece of timber.' Maldwyn winced as Anton peeled the fabric away from where it had glued itself to the palm of his hand. 'I didn't have time to dress it for a while and then I couldn't tell if there were splinters.' Anton placed his thumb and forefinger on either side of the cut and pulled the wound apart to better inspect the gouge beyond the buttery surface. 'There were a few times where I think I accidentally reopened the wound and made it worse while running.'

'Well, it's infected, but not beyond my healing.'

Anton grabbed one of the deep, pottery bowls and poured in some water from the tall amphora. He closed his eyes, placed a hand over the water and begin to chant some sort of incantation. Steam began to emanate through the gaps between his fingers and bubbling sounds rumbled inside the bowl. As Anton pulled his hand away, Maldwyn was amazed to see the rapidly boiling water.

'It's much faster than waiting for it to boil over a fire,' Anton told him, realising that Maldwyn was not used to seeing magic be used so freely.

The water continued to bubble away as Anton bent down and pulled out a granite mortar and pestle from beneath the counter. Into the mortar, Anton added some pale, dried yarrow leaves, stems of rosemary, yellow calendula flowers and bitter buttons, and some sort of long, sage-coloured leaves and roots from a small, wide jar labelled "*Comfrey*". Anton's hands moved swiftly as he continued to pull together an assortment of other herbs. Once finished, he began to grind the herbs together, using his elbow to push with as much force as possible.

'Have you found *The Power of Divinity* be of much use to you in learning to control your power?'

'To be honest, I don't understand how the book is supposed to help me.' Maldwyn folded his arms over his chest. 'The early parts of the book are mostly about the birth of the gods, the divine wars that led to their departure from this realm, and the relics they left behind, but I don't see what their power has to do with me.'

Adding more pressure from his shoulder through his elbow, Anton crushed the comfrey root. 'There is a rawness to your power that is unlike any we have ever known. Do you know who your father was?'

The question hit Maldwyn harder than expected. The truth of the matter was that he did not know who either of his parents was, and all he had was a swaddle and a cryptic note as clues. 'I don't know who my parents were. My mother told me—just before she passed—that I was adopted.'

'Oh, I didn't realise,' Anton paused and glanced up from the mortar with a considerate face. A shadow from his crooked nose shaded his cheek as he looked over at Maldwyn. 'Do you have any idea who they could have been?' Anton asked, adding a touch of the boiling water and a few droplets of some sort of pale orange tincture to the powered mixture to form a paste.

'I only have a swaddle and a meaningless note. There is nothing that I can follow.'

Anton raised his brows as he brought the paste together. 'That's a shame,' he offered, turning away to pull out a pair of scissors and a ream of muslin cloth bandages from a drawer underneath the countertop. Unwinding the first layer, Anton cut the cloth with the scissors and laid the piece flat on the counter. 'Have you heard of the Delarusian Prophecy?'

There was something familiar about the name, as though Maldwyn had heard it somewhere before, but he couldn't remember where. He shook his head.

Anton was methodical about the way he spread the warm poultice on the muslin, pushing it as close to the edge as he dared before folding them in and wrapping up the mixture.

'It's a peculiar prophecy, one that is believed by many to have already passed,' Anton told him as he cut another piece of muslin and gathered it into a clump. He dipped it into the cooled boiled water and gestured for Maldwyn to give over his hand. 'It says:

'*When the Valkyrie's tears fall from a purple sky, the Eagle will fall and the heavens will rain red. Darkness will follow, and day becomes night.*'

Anton began cleaning the wound with the warm cloth, pressing just hard enough to pull off the creamy surface and remove any dirt beneath the forming scab. The palm of Maldwyn's hand seared, throbbing with pain.

'Why is it believed to have already occurred?' Maldwyn asked as a means to keep his mind off the pain.

'On a particular night, about twenty-three or twenty-four years ago,' Maldwyn thought how he would have barely been born, 'back when I was about eleven-twelve years old, there were clouds that had this unmistakable purple hue, as if it was about to storm, but they were more vibrant somehow.' Once Anton was satisfied that the first clean was sufficient, he tossed the muslin into a bucket on the floor for burning. Grabbing a different tincture from the one he added to the poultice, he poured a few drops into the bowl of water. 'Then, the world was swallowed by darkness as the moon god's—Máni's—chariot overtook his sister's—Sól, the sun goddess—blocking her light from reaching our world. Thunder rumbled and rain poured in the dark,' Anton continued as he cut another piece of muslin, using it to mix the tincture into the warm water. 'Everyone was terrified, but there was nothing more horrifying than the red droplets on our hands when the sun returned to brighten the world; it was as though everyone had blood on their hands,' Anton began giving Maldwyn's palm a second cleansing.

'The rain was red? What did it mean?'

'Such phenomena are the result of divine disturbance.' Anton pulled Maldwyn's hand closer to his face, examining whether the wound was sufficiently cleaned. 'Though I can't be sure, I believe it suggests that something terrible occurred and something divine was lost or taken, but what that was and how that happened… who knows.'

'Do you suppose it was Iluvitar, Wayland's flaming sword?'

'No. That has always been on this realm.'

'Right, and it is connected to the Valuwan Prophecy.' Maldwyn scratched his head with his other hand in thought as he considered that he still didn't know the wording of the Valuwan Prophecy. 'Can you tell me what the Valuwan Prophecy is and what it has to do with the royal family in Dresden?'

'*At the dawn of the darkest day, Illuvitar will shine and sweep through the hordes of shadows. Only with the grace of the Lynx as his divine guardian, will Firebird deliver the realms into the light.*'

'The Lynx?' Anton tossed the second cloth into the bucket. 'Is it the same lynx mentioned in the Awakening of Firebird?'

'I believe that is highly likely.'

Anton picked up the poultice and muttered a few chants. 'Is it Prince Harlan?'

Holding up the poultice, Anton said, 'I have spelled this to stay warm and fresh for a few days. You shouldn't need a second one.' Anton placed the poultice over the wound and wrapped the remaining ream of muslin bandage around Maldwyn's hand. 'I believe that Prince Harlan might be the person referred to as the Lynx in the prophecies, however, I have no idea why the prophecies refer to him in this way.'

'What exactly are prophecies?'

'Divinations from the rulers of destiny: the Norns.'

Maldwyn threw his head back and stared at the ceiling. 'I know that, but I don't understand the difference. Are all prophecies left here from the Norns before they departed with the rest of divinity, or do they come from seers?'

'Ah, I see!' Anton knotted the bandage in place. 'Some prophecies were left here by the Norns; however, seers can intercept divinations. Time exists in all realms.' Maldwyn thought that was very confusing, and, by the look on Anton's face, his confusion was obvious. 'It is quite simple really. Time has always existed, as have the Norns. Therefore, as you know, when the rest of divinity was birthed from the Yawning Void, there became two distinct strains of power. That which gave divinity power over creation and destruction, and that which already existed and gave the rulers of time control over fate and destiny.

'I believe you are aware that seers are the mortal descendants of the Norns and dream time, picking up on the Norns' decrees. You may not have read it yet in the book we gave you, but when seers dream visions, they are seeing the most likely possible futures from the well of time. When seers dream in words, they are intercepting a prophecy, a destined moment whereby all rivers of time converge.'

'Right, so a seer could dream a vision of a possible future or a prophecy.'

'Yes,' Anton said with a matter-of-fact tone. 'But prophecies are rare. The Norns see themselves as caretakers of the well of time. They don't make things happen, so much as they guide events by warning gods with their divinations. Events unfold naturally within the well of time. A prophecy is a moment that all streams of time must pass through.' Anton rubbed his chin with his fingers, considering how best to put it. 'Essentially, as the Norns identify these unavoidable events, they transcribe them for the gods. These transcriptions are the words a seer may dream, should a new prophecy be identified in the well of time.'

'That makes sense.' Maldwyn pulled his hand back, noticing that it felt heavier with the dressing. 'What do these prophecies have to do with the prince and me?'

Anton sighed and rubbed his forehead. 'There is something about the two of you. There is you with your power, and Harlan… well, with something else.' Maldwyn leaned his hip against the counter as he watched Anton attempt to clarify his thoughts. 'When he was here in captivity, I could tell he doesn't have magic, like you, but there is something in his aura I couldn't quite put my finger on.'

'Could he be a seer too?'

Anton rubbed his eyes. 'That is very unlikely. The ability of a seer tends to favour the female bloodline. It's not impossible, but very unlikely. Besides, his dreams would have begun a few years ago, when he would have been the same age as Cassara.' Turning back to the counter, Anton began putting all the herb jars and tinctures back in their place. 'He is too much of his father's son to be keeping that secret.'

'Yes.' Maldwyn knew what Anton meant. The prince was not the most open-minded person when it came to sorcery. That had been an issue that troubled Maldwyn for some time. As Maldwyn turned to leave, he wondered why Anton had raised the subject of prophecy. 'Um, before I go, why did you mention the Delarusian Prophecy?'

Anton pursed his lips and hesitated to say anything further. 'This will sound strange to you Maldwyn, but I think even that prophecy has something to do with you.'

Maldwyn's stomach knotted at Anton's suggestion and he wondered if it were possible that the events of that day had something to do with his ending up abandoned in a field. Was it his fault these things had happened? Maldwyn wished his mother were still alive to ask whether his being found in a field aligned with the day that became night, but she wasn't.

Unsure what to say, Maldwyn held up his bandaged hand and mumbled his thanks. 'I'd best be going.'

Anton placed a hand on Maldwyn's shoulder. 'Remember, you always have a home among the mountains, Eminence.'

* * * * *

Some hours later, loud bangs against the door startled Maldwyn as he sat in the familiar guest chambers, waiting patiently on the massive bed. The last time he had been in this room, Maldwyn had not long been released from captivity; but now, as the sovereign's most honoured and esteemed guest, Maldwyn had been brought here as a sign of respect, showing him the renowned hospitality of the people among the mountains.

There were a variety of small, glistening vials of scented oils on the low-line dresser not far from the foot of the bed along the wall. A teal, glazed amphora with gold, geometric motifs painted along the rim of the jug, had been placed on top of the dresser near the glistening vials and was filled to the brim with water.

Next to the amphora was a fine, silvered goblet and a deep, pewter bowl that had a rag hanging over the side for washing. Toward the other end of the low-line dresser, was a smaller, metal bowl that was filled with small round desserts that had been made from dried fruits.

Though there were no windows in the city under the mountain and the air was thick with the balsam scent of the bursting baroque carved hearth, Maldwyn noted that the air was not stuffy. Pushing himself off the delicate, soft mattress to stand, a heap of silky pillows fell face down on the many layers of golden bedcovers.

The place where Maldwyn sat on the bed left behind ripples that distorted the gentle pattern of leaves and birds, which were stitched from a thin white thread. The white, chiffon curtains were gathered low and tied to each of the four posts that framed the humungous bed.

As Maldwyn strode by the hearth, he felt the warmth of the blazing fire radiating through the room and noticed that the light from the bursting flames gave the walls a saffron-coloured sheen. Maldwyn's new, leather boots, gifted to him by the sovereign, creaked with each step he took, having never been worn before. The ivory marble tiles had grey veins that webbed across the floor.

The door's handle was cool to touch as Maldwyn wrapped the fingers of his good hand around the metal knob. Moaning, the door opened, letting in a cool draught and revealing a tall man with a scar that ripped through his right eyebrow, which seemed to be pointing toward his hairline, who was standing quietly and patiently in the hall.

'Erik!' Maldwyn said, stunned to be met by the palace's former hunter.

Erik, who was not wearing the robes of the Erendil, but was dressed in black, plain pants and a well-fitted green shirt, didn't appear to look all that different. However, Maldwyn did note that there was a calm to his presence as if he had found the secret to inner peace within the Anhalt Mountains.

'I wasn't sure whether you would have come here.'

'Eminence, I believe it is, right?' Erik gave Maldwyn a reprehensive look, mouth slightly pursed.

Maldwyn felt bad for having lied to Erik about his powers for so long, despite knowing that the hunter was an esteemed sorcerer. Able to do little more than offer an apologetic expression, Maldwyn glanced down at the floor feeling a little sheepish.

'You were the one who told me I might find my kin hiding among the Erendil. You were right. Anton is a member of the Raven Clan.'

'I'm sorry that I wasn't more honest with you,' Maldwyn muttered as he gave Erik a half-smile. One of the logs on the fire burst suddenly in the background. 'I didn't want to place you in more danger than you were already in as a sorcerer.'

'I understand.' Erik shrugged, shaking his head he pulled the sleeve of his shirt tighter around his wrist, hiding the mark of his people. 'Perhaps better than most. I know what it was like in that palace.'

Scratching the side of his head, Maldwyn stepped back on his heels and held out an arm, making way for Erik to enter the room. Stepping through the doorway, Erik followed Maldwyn over to stand by the stone-carved hearth and looked impressed as he glanced around, appraising the room.

'You look well,' Maldwyn offered, trying to ease the tension between them.

Erik held his hands low, clasping them together. It was a habit that had stayed with him since working as a servant in the capital. 'For the first time in a long time, I feel that I have found a home.' His voice was a little wistful, clearly pleased with his life in the mountains.

'You deserve it,' Maldwyn muttered, closing the door to the corridor, shutting in the heat.

Maldwyn hooked his thumbs behind him in the belt of his pants, recalling the last time he stood in front of this fireplace with Prince Harlan. The memory of the prince saddened him as he wished he were able to be close to the prince, just to linger in his shadow.

Maldwyn thought how complicated things had been, the last time he was in the Anhalt Mountains, and considered that they had become even more so. Reminded of his conversation with Tiana, Maldwyn contemplated returning to the capital where he could return to the prince's aid.

Out of the corner of his eye, Maldwyn noticed Erik was watching him carefully as if he were trying to read his thoughts. 'You don't plan to stay, do you?'

'I'm not entirely sure,' Maldwyn answered, biting the inside of his cheek as he felt torn, being of two minds. Maldwyn knew he would find sanctuary with the Erendil, where he would be protected from King Viktor's wrath, but he felt he may be needed elsewhere.

Erik sighed, looking a little disappointed with his answer. 'I heard about your family.' Weighed down by the reminder of his loss, Maldwyn slouched and held his breath. He had to force himself to let in a deep gulp of air. The peppery smell of the burning logs caught at the back of his throat. Maldwyn resisted the urge to cough, as Erik went on to say, 'I am sorry for your loss.'

Wetting his lips with the tip of his tongue, Maldwyn glanced up toward the enchanting coffered ceiling. He took a moment to note how beautifully it was crafted as he gathered the strength to talk about what had happened in Alander.

'My mother was ill and had just passed away when the king's guards attacked.' Maldwyn touched the tips of his fingers to his forehead, rubbing along his tightened brows. 'They attacked everyone. I don't know if anyone survived.'

'Did you use your powers to escape?'

Maldwyn frowned and clicked his tongue against the roof of his mouth. 'I used my powers to protect a child, but when I reached for my magic again, it was gone.'

'The others—Anton and Tolamin, I mean—they told me you have no control over your abilities. Is it true?' Erik asked, as his stare dropped to Maldwyn's freshly dressed hand, corrugating his forehead. Small streaks webbed out from the corners of his eyes. Maldwyn moved his hand further from view to make the injury less obvious.

'None,' Maldwyn admitted to Erik, biting his lower lip and feeling deeply frustrated with himself. No matter his mother's warnings, Maldwyn wished he had at least some control over his abilities. 'I thought I was gaining control, but I'm not.' Maldwyn closed his eyes and crossed his arms over his chest as he recalled the swaddle and note his mother had given him, wondering what it all meant. 'I am afraid I will never control it,' Maldwyn mumbled.

Erik went quiet. The rip in his brow became more obvious as he crinkled his forehead. Maldwyn wondered what Erik was thinking as the man rubbed his chin. He contemplated whether Erik was disappointed in him, knowing the extent of his ineptitude.

Running the tips of his fingers along his jaw, Erik made a sort of upside-down smile. 'Well, sounds like we have our work cut out for us.'

'We?' Maldwyn shuffled his footing, unsure if he was understanding Erik's remark correctly.

'You trusted me to train the princess, but not yourself?' Erik grinned at Maldwyn with a mischievous look on his face.

Maldwyn drew his brows closer together, struggling to process the unexpected kindness. He was not accustomed to people treating him with such warmth.

'My peoples were known as the librarians of magic before the king forbade sorcery and massacred anyone associated with it.' Sadness washed over Erik's face as he recalled the loss of his people. 'Of course, it's not as though I have ever trained anyone like you before, but, to the best of my knowledge, no one ever has.'

Maldwyn's mother's words played in his mind, scolding him for using his powers and reminding him of the danger. Right up until the moment of her death, she was warning him to never use his powers, fearing it would get him killed.

His throat clogged at the reminder of his mother's passing. Pushing the thought from his mind, he tried to forget the grief that choked him.

'You can control it,' Erik reassured, slackening his shoulders. 'You just need to figure out how to harness it. Don't bury it anymore.'

Maldwyn didn't know what to say. There were times he believed he could control his abilities, but perhaps he was merely deluded, and, the truth was his powers controlled him. Maldwyn looked over to a small plate of burning incense by the bed's side and watched the way the thin line of smoke from the incense coiled through the air, its sandalwood fragrance mixing with the smoky scent of the fire. The white chiffon hanging from the frame of the bed swayed a little from the heat radiating from the fireplace.

The scene reminded Maldwyn of the mysterious temple in the woods, the place that left him deeply unsettled and where he had encountered a spectre, which taunted him with the voice of the love he had lost. He stiffened at the memory and turned his thoughts to the priest's notes.

Realising that Erik was new to the mountains, Maldwyn guessed he might be more forthcoming about the mine than anyone else, given that the peoples of the Anhalt Mountains could be quite secretive, despite their open-minded nature. 'Do you know anything about the mine?'

'I've never been there, but it's just a mine as far as I know,' Erik said, clearly confused by this question. 'Why?'

'I'm not sure yet,' Maldwyn replied, turning his head away. 'It's just a feeling.' As Maldwyn went on to ask about the temple in the woods, a knock sounded on the door. Holding up a hand to Erik, signalling that the conversation wasn't yet over, Maldwyn walked over to the door. As he opened it, he was greeted by Tolamin.

'Eminence,' Tolamin started, his accent sounding as if it sang the word from his lips. He was wearing his usual silvery-blue robes. 'The sovereign wishes for you to join him at dinner.'

Coming up behind Maldwyn, Erik's feet scuffed along the marble floor. 'It's alright, Mal. We can talk more later.' Maldwyn looked back at Erik, who was smiling at his friend. 'I'm glad you're here,' the hunter offered.

Maldwyn grinned at him as he slipped out the door and made his way down the corridor. Looking to Tolamin, Maldwyn nodded, before he moved over toward the bed where a dark, brown-coloured leather jacket was draped over the foot. Slipping his arms through the sleeves, he pulled on the jacket and followed Tolamin through the underground city, to the dining hall.

* * * * *

There was not a single surface in the dining hall that had been left untouched. The smooth, gently flowing fabrics splayed over the long oak table were a range of brilliant colours, refusing to be concealed by the copious platters, which were stacked high.

Sitting at the long table, between Anton and Tolamin, a strong waft of spices and citrus grabbed Maldwyn's attention. Anton leaned over, partially coming to a stand, to pile his plate with an assortment of zesty vegetables, warmed salads and spiced meat. Maldwyn smiled, noticing that the sorcerer had an impressive appetite.

Glancing up to the sheer, teal draperies hanging from the roof, Maldwyn felt soothed by the sort of mysticism of the dining hall. Provocative, string music filled the room.

Slow and silent, teasing the waiting audience, the doors opened to reveal Tiana, dressed in a jewelled, black corset and sheer, loose-fitting pants. A gold headdress was woven through her updo and a large, ruby hung over her forehead, dangling elegantly as she twirled into the hall. The other concubines, wearing similar, but slightly less extravagant, clothing danced around her, bracelets jangling to the beat of the music.

Tolamin, hood drawn over his face, straightened his back and turned to watch the dance. Maldwyn noted that the priest was captivated by Tiana's tantalising steps as if longing for something out of reach. Scanning the rest of the room, Maldwyn noted the expressionless faces of the sovereign's guests, which conflicted with the arresting glimmer of wanting and awe in their eyes.

Continuing around the room, Maldwyn glimpsed Jerrik at the near end of the great table, seated next to Anton. His dark eyes were fixed on Tiana as he rested his chin in the nook of his index finger and thumb. The look in the sovereign's eyes was not one of longing, as with Tolamin, but perhaps, Maldwyn thought, better termed as a look of wanting. To Jerrik's side, Anton looked bothered by the display. Maldwyn figured the sorcerer didn't approve of gawking at the sovereign's concubines.

Moving through the room, the concubines spun around and between the sovereign's guests. Pulling out thin veils from their garments, they smirked, lifting the shrouds through the air and bouncing them elegantly to the tune of the song in the background. The guests' faces were awash with wonder at the elegance of the dance, applauding loudly when the first dance ended, drowning out the soft melody still playing in the background.

Eventually, the music died down to a soft tune and the dancing ended. Tiana led the sovereign's harem of concubines over to a couch with plush, silky cushions where she sprawled out and lit a pipe, looking pleased with her performance.

'Sovereign,' Maldwyn said, turning to lock eyes with Jerrik. 'I am grateful for your hospitality, but I was hoping I might be able to access the mine.' Anton sat forward, stiffening his back, and stared over at Jerrik.

'The mine?' Jerrik's slick, singsong voice was laced with curiosity and the dark glint of his eyes fixed with Maldwyn's. 'What could you possibly want from that place?'

'I have a strange feeling that I can't quite explain—a hunch if you will—and I wonder whether there may be more than draconite within the mine.'

'Oh?' Signalling to one of the concubines meandering around the room, carrying a platter of sweet treats on the far side of the hall, Jerrik broke his fierce stare with Maldwyn. 'Well, I can't say there is anything we have come across that would be of specific interest to you, but it can be arranged.'

There was a slight change in the intonations of his accent that made Maldwyn question whether Jerrik was telling him the whole truth.

'Speaking of the draconite,' leaning over the arm of his chair, the sovereign plucked a marzipan tart from the concubine's plate as she came up to his side. 'Lord Darius has become increasingly fixated on reclaiming the mine. I understand that you were unable to capture Mikel and that he and the princess, Cassara, have fled to Karana Downs and sought shelter from Lord Darius. I fear Mikel has shared the knowledge of this gemstone with the lord of the downs.'

'It's worse than that, by the time the prince and I returned to the city, the draconite had already been used to curse Queen Sonia's pendant.' Hanging his head low, Maldwyn smoothed the tablecloth with the flat of his hands as he recalled what had happened. 'I managed to retrieve the pendant but can't be certain that the king wasn't already cursed.' Scratching his neck in thought, Maldwyn turned his head to the left a fraction where he noticed Tolamin watching Tiana laying back on the sofa, inhaling the grassy smoke through her long pipe. 'I didn't—I don't—know whether a curse can be broken, so I cast the pendant into the ocean, where it would be far away from the king's grasp.'

'I suppose it couldn't be helped,' Jerrik stated. As he bit into the tart he was holding, the flaky base collapsed in his hands, settling crumbs in the corners of his mouth.

'You were right to cast the queen's pendant into the ocean,' Anton reassured in a kind tone, leaning forward in his seat and placing a hand on the table, palm face down on the smooth tablecloth. 'Curses cannot be broken, Eminence.'

'Agreed,' Tolamin chimed in, his silvery-blue robes seemed to shimmer in the warmly lit hall as he shifted to face Maldwyn a little more squarely. 'Even the gods fall prey to curses, Eminence.'

As Jerrik pushed his shoulders back into the high-back of his seat, he sucked marzipan from his fingers and cleared his throat. 'Anton and Tolamin are correct, Eminence. There was nothing more you could have done.' Feeling more at ease, Maldwyn relaxed into his chair, rounding his shoulders. 'There was something I asked of the prince as well… before I released you both. I asked him to find a ring that belongs to my people. Would you happen to know if the prince found this before you travelled north to Alander?'

Filling his cheeks with air, Maldwyn shook his head. He didn't want to contradict anything Prince Harlan had told the sovereign. In truth, he knew that the prince had found Kristian's ring, but, for some reason, the prince seemed to have not mentioned this to Jerrik.

'Thank you, Eminence,' Jerrik replied, sounding disappointed despite his melodic accent.

'In the meantime, Eminence,' Tolamin began, seeming to sing as his words were spoken with beautiful rising and falling intonations, 'do you have any more control over your abilities?' The priest reached over the table and picked up a spiced pear tart from the platter in front of him.

A whiff of ginger cake stole Maldwyn's attention momentarily as one of the concubines passed with a platter of sweet treats. It reminded Maldwyn of the sort of cake his mother used to make. A tightness pulling in his chest bothered him. Grabbing the goblet on the table in front of him, Maldwyn sipped the plummy, red wine, letting go of the reminder.

'Unfortunately, not.'

'We believe we may be able to help you with that.' A sly smile crept up Jerrik's cheeks, making the shadows from the hood of his robes grow darker. 'I have talked at length with Anton, Jaecen and Tolamin about your abilities, and we believe that your lack of control comes from a lack of focus.'

Maldwyn frowned, trying not to take offence to the well-meant criticism, and looked over to Anton. 'We think you may be overthinking matters.' The sorcerer said in a matter-of-fact tone. 'When you're trying too hard to hold your power in, or to will your power to the surface, you aren't transcending the limitations of this realm. The moment you become absorbed within your mind is the moment you trap yourself and lose any control you have.' Anton sipped wine from his tall, pewter goblet. 'You need to learn to be completely present, within the moment, to gain control.'

'Our god, Uller,' Tolamin's words sang from his lips as he clutched the ring hanging low over his chest, 'is a formidable hunter, and his teachings say: to wield more than mere strength by brandishing true power, one must conquer one's mind, achieving complete presence in the here and now, and become more than their will.' Tolamin let go of the sacred ring, resting his hands on his lap. 'This teaching is the foundation of our belief system and the most important rule followed by our rangers.'

'For this reason,' Jerrik started as he wiped crumbs from the corners of his mouth with his thumb, 'I have asked Jaecen to spend some time with you, teaching you the ways of our peoples and how to defend yourself. At the very least, should you choose to leave the Anhalt Mountains, you may find yourself in danger, and knowing how to defend yourself may save your life. Erik and Anton will also teach you what they know about magic. Hopefully, between the two you will not only find control but peace of mind as well.'

Their kindness in wanting to help him, as no one else in his life ever had, humbled Maldwyn. 'I don't know what to say. Thank you seems too small.'

'You're too important, and I fear we are nearing the days of prophecy.'

'Which prophecy?' Maldwyn pressed, fearing the one that called for his death.

'All of them,' Jerrik replied.

With that, Maldwyn quietened, allowing the conversation to continue to unfold around him as he became stuck in his thoughts and worries about what it all meant. After Maldwyn had consumed quite a few more goblets of wine, he finally relaxed into the evening, no longer so concerned with matters.

He shared a few laughs with Tolamin, surprised to learn the priest had quite a quick wit despite his quiet, sacerdotal nature, and listened closely to Anton's stories recalling the ways of his people before they were slaughtered. Eventually, the banquet ended, and Maldwyn was guided back to his chambers by Anton. Each of them stumbled in the corridors, tripping a little on the grand staircase. Maldwyn was looking forward to resting as he lay on the massive bed. It didn't take long for him to drift off.

CHAPTER TWELVE

The Moon Sorceress

HARLAN PAUSED TO APPRECIATE the watercolour sky, which was tinted with dusky pinks and gentle, orange hues that marked the setting sun. As he glanced around, he noticed the way snow caked itself into the recesses of the adjoined timber and stucco mansions and that the once glossy, green vines were now crystallised and hung lifelessly from the tall buildings.

'We are almost there, Your Grace,' Theodor said to Harlan's back, standing a few paces behind where the prince stood, looking around his beloved city.

As he breathed in a deep breath, Harlan noted that the air was thick with the smell of wood fires burning from the buildings all around. It was seasoned with a peppery touch from the scorching coal bursting skyward from a nearby smithy. Tilting his head to glance back at Theodor, Harlan let out his breath, steam rising from his mouth before continuing along the slippery, cobbled path banked on either side by snow.

The streets were mostly empty as Harlan and Theodor made their way through the wealthy districts, situated close to the palace. The few noble men and women that were out paused to bow or curtsey as they recognised the Crown Prince passing by, each of them wearing layers of beautifully patterned silk clothing and thick furs which were wrapped about their shoulders.

Paying them little attention, Harlan kept his expression neutral and strode by with his head held high, walking mostly in silence toward the House of Yearning, a place renowned for its luxurious services to entertain the wealthy. Master Damyan and Theodor had arranged a meeting with the courtesan, Lorelei, who, according to their accounts, was a sorceress.

Harlan had kept his reasons for wanting to consult with a sorceress to himself, much to the dismay of his loyal comrades. He had promised to ensure the safety of any sorcerer, or sorceress, willing to take such a risk by revealing themselves to him.

As they arrived outside the manor, Harlan noted that it was striking, rising above the neighbouring buildings with a sort of sombre grey exterior. The entire place was structured around a square courtyard that had a huge, frosted tree in the centre of ice-covered, crisp shrubs.

Shimmering vines hung off the roof of the building, lining the courtyard like a set of crystal curtains. The gable roof was sloped and had exquisite carvings of crouching wolves in each of the corners of the eaves. A rounded set of steps led up out of the courtyard to the main entrance of the House of Yearning.

As Harlan reached the carved, mahogany doors, he heard the ice path behind him cracking under Theodor's feet and paused with his fingers resting on the handle lever, hesitant to meet the mysterious sorceress. Though Harlan had been inside the House of Yearning many times, hosting diplomats and royal guests with the entertainment services offered by the courtesans, he couldn't recall being personally hosted by Lorelei, the woman who owned and ran the place.

As Theodor stepped up to the prince's side, Harlan pushed on the lever, opening the door. He cringed as the hinges creaked. Inside was a wide, open parlour room that had dark stained, polished, wooden floors.

The walls glowed with the warm light of the beautiful lanterns, which hung over the timber-framed, red cushioned settees. Courtesans, dressed in sleek, floor-length gowns with draping sleeves, rushed to surround the prince and his guard as they entered the lavish parlour room, pulling off their outer coats to hang away.

'Your Royal Highness.' Came a saccharine voice from the archway to the main parlour room, leading beyond the entryway.

A woman with brown skin, amber-coloured eyes and jet-black hair, wearing a gold, flowing dress, glided forth through the other courtesans. She stopped to curtsey before him, keeping her eyes low. A waft of her rose-scented perfume filled Harlan's nostrils.

'I have been waiting for you. My name is Lorelei.' She looked up, turned to Theodor standing behind the prince and smiled softly. 'It's good to see you, Ser Theodor.'

'You too,' Theodor offered gently, stepping forward to the prince's right. One of the pouting courtesans slipped away from the prince to clutch onto the tall and strong-looking knight.

'Please come with me,' Lorelei instructed, leading into the expansive mansion.

The men and women that worked in this place were all well-dressed in fine, flowing garments, presenting themselves as respectable service providers. There were delicate, harmonious instruments being played from cushioned nooks to cover the muted conversations.

Mingling guests, waiting to be guided to the private rooms upstairs, relished the attention of the courtesans, sometimes daring to reach out and touch them. When they noticed the prince and his guard, the guests paused to bow their heads.

On either side of the main room, was a grand, rosewood staircase that wrapped around the walls, meeting at a flat landing a few steps below the first storey. As Harlan followed the line of the timber and wrought iron balustrade with his eyes, he noticed that the place was bustling.

The floorboards creaked on the upper landing as Harlan and Theodor followed Lorelei upstairs, leaving the other courtesans behind. Lorelei led them through the corridors toward the more extravagant rooms in the House of Yearning, designed for hosting their most distinguished guests.

The chambers they were brought to had a wide reception area with stunning, stained-glass windows that were shaded by heavy, crimson curtains. Gold motifs edged the timber framing of the two scarlet settees facing a short, weighty rosewood table. A huge candelabrum hung from the roof, bathing the space with a dim light.

To the left, double doors were open, leading to a lavish room that had a large, four-post bed which was surrounded by velvety, cherry drapes. The sand-coloured bed sheets were silky, and the rosy bed covers matched the red, buttoned cushions, which were carefully placed on the bed. A hint of cinnamon in the air was pleasing to Harlan and masked the smell of the burning candles.

'Ser Theodor,' Lorelei started, holding her hands together, interlocking her fingers. 'It might be best for you to wait here while the prince and I discuss matters in the other room.' Theodor looked awkwardly at the plush chairs before walking over and taking a seat. 'Your Grace,' Lorelei held out one of her arms, indicating for Harlan to step into the next room, 'if you would please step inside.'

As Harlan walked toward the bed, not pausing to look back, he heard Lorelei shut the doors to the reception area.

'Are you sure I can't interest you in any of our services, Your Grace?' Lorelei asked, running the tips of her fingers from his shoulders down his back.

Harlan moved away and turned to face the courtesan, shaking his head.

'Sorry,' he told her, putting more space between them with a few back steps. 'I'm just here for your help.'

'Of course, sire,' Lorelei replied, giving him a curious look. Walking around him she sat on the bed, leaning back on her hands which were stretched out behind her. The draping sleeves of her golden dress were swept over the side of the bed, reaching for the hardwood floors. 'Theodor mentioned that I would be granted your protection in exchange for helping you with something.'

'True,' Harlan uttered, glancing out the stained-glass windows above the low line set of drawers to his right, 'but I want to be clear that what we discuss here is sensitive to me and is not to be mentioned to anyone, not even Theodor.'

'I am a courtesan,' Lorelei began, brushing her smooth, black hair back and turning her head to reveal a crescent moon-shaped mark behind her ear, 'and a sorceress. I can be discrete, Your Grace.'

'Good.' Harlan walked over and sat on the soft mattress, beside Lorelei. Reaching into the pocket of his fitted, royal-blue shirt, the prince pulled out a small, scrunched-up piece of paper and handed it to Lorelei. 'I was hoping you might be able to help me with this.'

Bringing her brows together, Lorelei leaned forward and took the note, carefully peeling back the edges. Her eyes moved from one side to the other as she read the cursive script Harlan had come to memorise.

'Was this written by the late queen… your mother?' Lorelei gazed up at Harlan with a curious, yet troubled expression.

'Yes, it was.' Clearing his throat, Harlan steeled himself for the many questions that were sure to be swirling about her head. 'Some of what is written in that letter appears to be true.'

'So, the reason the princess was sentenced to die was that she is a seer?'

'Yes, it is.' Harlan swallowed the ball at the back of his throat. 'She was caught practising sorcery in an attempt to control her dreams.'

'Was your mother a seer too?'

Harlan shook his head and puckered his brows.

'I only mean that a seer's power typically follows the female bloodline.' Lorelei tucked a loose lock of hair behind her ear. 'If your sister, the princess, is a seer, then it's possible your mother was too.'

'I wouldn't know about that.' Harlan wetted his lips and pinched his mouth to one side. 'A few months back, I learned that my mother was executed for having an affair with Kristian Sadler, the then Magical Advisor.'

'So, this note is from before magic was outlawed,' Lorelei interrupted, pulling a face as she worked out the timeline in her head.

Harlan guessed that Lorelei knew about Queen Sonia's execution and the rumours of her affair from the unsurprised look on her face. From what Master Damyan had said, only Harlan and Cassara had been kept in the dark about their mother's death. Ignorant civilians may not have known the truth, but Lorelei certainly wasn't ignorant.

'Yes. My best guess is that this note is from a few days before Kristian was executed, followed by my mother's death.' Harlan rubbed his hands together nervously, noticing a cool bite in the air coming through the glass. 'I need to know if you can tell me whether my mother completed that ritual mentioned in her letter. I need to know if they did something to me.'

Sighing, Lorelei stared over at the set of drawers. 'I might be able to convene with the gods and seek the truth through a sign.'

Standing up, she went over to the unit of drawers and pulled out enough thick, votive candles to place them in a large circle on the floor. Walking over to the window, Lorelei studied the moon through the coloured glass, fiddling with her long sleeves.

'Since I didn't know what you needed from me, I prepared some things in advance. It's not the perfect conditions to be calling on Máni, the moon god. If I appeal to the goddess Nótt as well, we are more likely to get an answer.'

Pulling out a piece of paper from another drawer, a small pot of ink and a fine paintbrush, Lorelei leaned over the unit of drawers, spread out the parchment and painted some symbols. Harlan recognised that her calligraphy was in the ancient Naedarian language, belonging to the mythical era when the gods were rumoured to have walked the realm. Next, she took out a silver bowl with beautiful engravings around the outside and added some cinnamon sticks, sage and cedarwood incense.

'Okay, I need you to sit in the middle of the candles.' Lorelei pointed to the circle on the floor as she continued to add items into the bowl from a small pouch.

Harlan pushed himself off the bed and walked over to the candles, shooting a strange look back at Lorelei before kneeling on the floor, unsure of what she was going to do. He had never been around much sorcery in his life and was uncomfortable with the situation, despite needing to know the truth of his mother's letter.

Holding the bowl steady in her hand, Lorelei entered the circle and came to her knees opposite Harlan, who bunched a few inches back, making sure there was plenty of space for them both. Muttering some words under her breath, the candles came to life, flames dancing around the wicks.

Lorelei pulled out the parchment, lit it in the flames and tossed it in the bowl with the herbs, spices and incense, and she began to chant inaudibly. Knowing better than to interrupt a ritual such as this, Harlan sat in silence, waiting for her direction.

After what felt like a long while, listening to the chanting as he sat in silence, Lorelei opened her eyes and poured the contents of the bowl on the floor. Her eyes glowed a warmer amber colour and the ashen mixture from the bowl moved about the space between them as if having a life of its own, forming into a Naedarian word that Harlan did not recognise upside-down.

'What is it?' Harlan pressed, watching as Lorelei frowned and turned her head to the side. 'What does it say?'

'It means that you were given a gift… a sort of blessing.' Lorelei swished her hands through the air and shrugged as though she was trying to understand the meaning of the message. 'However, this part here,' she pointed to the section where the script flicked upwards, 'tells me this word is "siwyon", which has a dual meaning. The first meaning is "a gift", and the other is "a guard". Yes, I would say your mother completed a blessing ritual, but I can't be certain what blessing she cast.'

Harlan clenched his jaw, mulling over what he had just been told. Lorelei was staring at him with her glowing eyes.

'Is there a way to find out more about the spell?'

'Without knowing the exact spell, I can't offer you more.' Lorelei stared at the script between them. 'I can only read the signs from the gods, and this is what they are telling me about the spell your mother cast.'

'Gift or guard, that's not a lot to go on.'

'It's all there is.' Lorelei blew out some of the candles and stood, stepping out of the circle. When she turned back to the prince, her eyes were no longer glowing. 'My resources are finite, especially with the laws being as they are. Without more information, I can't give you any more answers.' Placing her hands on her hips she pressed her shoulders back. 'Find the spell, then I might be able to offer you something more.'

Harlan felt his heart racing as he worried about whatever ritual his mother had performed. He wondered why she would have done something to him and what his mother had meant by his destiny having a heavy burden. The thought crossed the prince's mind that his mother had dreamed of his future, learning the course his life was likely to take when he was barely old enough to talk.

*   *   *   *   *

As the prince entered the palace grounds, catching the eye of a guard he passed, Harlan felt the weight of the man's stare. He was afraid the man might somehow see the spell in the air around him. Everywhere he went, Harlan felt his father's spies watching him as if they knew.

Did they know? Was his father's anger not about Harlan's defiance, but based on the king's suspicions about the events that occurred the night of the queen's arrest?

The prince tried to silence his mind, but each attempt spiralled into a train of thoughts that led back to what he had learned. Frustrated, Harlan picked up his pace once he entered the palace corridors, heading straight for his chambers. He was barely aware of Theodor following him, only hearing his steps every so often as a reminder that he wasn't alone. He loathed being followed everywhere he went.

Though he had grown up around an entourage of servants and guards, he yearned to be away from it all. He ignored Gorlois, cradling an array of scrolls for archiving, as he passed by him in the hall, rushing to his residential wing.

The grand parlour to the prince's rooms had tall windows that were covered by deep, sapphire-blue curtains and a great door that led to a balcony overlooking the wide, square courtyard a few floors below. Large lounge chairs faced a low table with a beautiful display of glowing candles, arranged on a round silver tray.

Making his way through the room to the long corridor beyond, Harlan headed toward his private bed chambers, passing the expansive formal dining and study areas on the way, both of which had much larger tables than were in his bed chambers.

Thrusting the doors to his private quarters open, Harlan glanced around, checking everything was in its place. As expected, the bed had fresh linen and the curtains had been drawn over the glass windows, hiding the glistening stars and moonlight. The table centred in the massive room was clear and the papers on his desk were undisturbed. The fireplace popped to greet him, and the lounge cushions had been plumped.

'I'm retiring for the evening,' Harlan said over his shoulder to Theodor.

'Of course, Your Grace,' Theodor replied to the prince's back. 'Sire, if you don't mind me asking, did you find the answers you were after?' Bothered, Harlan looked back at Theodor who blinked a little nervously. 'It's just that you seem… unsettled.'

Harlan let out an exasperated breath, wanting to shut the door and be alone with his thoughts. As he went to speak, a few knocks sounded on the small servant door. 'Can it wait?' He called, sounding quite curt.

'Your Grace,' Master Damyan's smooth voice bellowed through the door. 'I have a report you will want to hear.'

He didn't. At least, not right now.

'Come in,' he called, knowing Damyan would be concerned if he turned him away a second time. He pulled off his coat and hung it over the back of one of the chairs around the table.

The servant door cracked open. Head hung low, Ailaya entered and curtsied, wearing a simple, charcoal-coloured dress with long sleeves as she seemed weighed down with sadness. Seeing her was a reminder of the news of Maldwyn's death.

Master Damyan followed her into the room in his usual black servant attire. His silver streaks were darkened by the shadows being thrown by the fire. Still, his presence was as commanding as ever as he bowed with a perfect posture.

'You said you have a report,' Harlan said, hurrying them to get to the point so he could dismiss them.

'Yes, sire,' Master Damyan replied, bowing his head. 'The first report is regarding Ser Gerard.'

Harlan had never much liked Ser Gerard. The prince thought he was a sort of smarmy type, false with a touch of arrogance. His opinion of the man plummeted after learning Gerard supported the kidnapping of Prince Ilarion Xylan, the Third Prince of Valdemar, when he was a child. The kidnapping had taken place during the war with Mordiallok and remained a controversial tactic.

'The knight was seen by my servants speaking with Lord Darius's sentries. The man that saw them said their behaviour seemed off, sneaky even. There may not have been anything nefarious to the matter, but it remains unusual for them to have been speaking.'

'Monitor Gerard,' Harlan ordered, keeping a neutral veneer. 'I've never trusted him anyway. Let's be sure of what he's up to.'

'Of course, sire.' Master Damyan moved closer toward where Harlan was standing and glanced over at Ailaya. 'We also have news about Moya's brother.'

The sword at Theodor's hip jostled as the knight walked up to Harlan's side. 'Is it the hunter on the staff?'

'It is indeed Sebastian Voigt,' Ailaya replied, lifting her gaze from the floorboards to glance at Theodor. Harlan noticed her eyes were puffy and her face was a little flushed. It was clear she had been crying. 'Moya told me her brother left the palace, and that he now works as a carpenter in the lower districts of the city.'

'Based on his name and occupation, I sent some of my trusted servants out on a few errands around those parts of the city.' Master Damyan cleared his throat and pushed his shoulders back. 'The man now runs a shop not far from the markets.'

Harlan scratched his forehead as he considered his options. He wondered how this information would help him gain Moya's loyalty.

'Maybe she will tell us something if we use him as leverage,' Theodor said, as any true soldier would.

'No,' Ailaya said in a firm tone. 'He's done nothing wrong and doesn't deserve to be pulled into this any more than he needs to.'

'I only meant that if Moya believes we may harm him, she may be more likely to speak about the lord's plans.' Theodor shifted, resting his hand on the hilt of his sword as he looked a little hurt that she might think badly of him.

'We can work out what to do with that information later,' Master Damyan said, easing tensions in the room. 'Your Grace, I have been thinking long and hard about the situation with your mother's pendant. Mikel was considered missing at the time and the person that cursed her pendant must have had access to your father's chambers. I'm sad to say it, but, as far as I see things, there must be another sorcerer in the palace.'

Prince Harlan cocked his head to the side and folded his arms over his chest. 'What do you mean another?'

Ailaya creased her forehead, looking confused as she glanced between Theodor and Damyan as they each shared a knowing look. 'Your Grace, there was a sorcerer on the staff who may no longer be with us.'

'There was a sorcerer on the staff and you knew about it!' Harlan felt his jaw drop as he tried not to shout. Heading over to the fireplace, he rubbed his temples, feeling more annoyed.

'It's the man that I helped remove your mother's pendant from the castle, sire.' Theodor said, sounding as though Harlan should have been aware of this.

The prince whipped around to face him, forming fists. 'You only mentioned that you had helped a sorcerer. You said nothing about him working in the palace.' Ailaya was frowning at Theodor, seeming disappointed that he and Damyan hadn't shared everything with her either. 'How can you be certain this man wasn't the one that cursed the pendant in the first place?'

'Your Grace, I trust this man implicitly,' Theodor said, trying to diffuse the situation. 'I believe you would too.'

'As do I,' Damyan agreed, clasping his hands. Harlan thought for the first time he was seeing the man's perfect servant veneer crack from the glimmer of discomfort in his face.

Harlan pinched his lips together and clicked his tongue, 'Explain what you mean when you say he may no longer be with us.'

'He's missing. We're not sure what happened to him, sire, but we believe he may not be coming back.' Theodor sighed, and Harlan could tell he was considering his words carefully. The heat of the fire warmed the back of the prince's legs. It was soothing. 'There are reports that he may be dead.'

Harlan sucked his lower lip in thought. Catching eye contact with Ailaya, he could tell Theodor's words reminded her of Maldwyn's death.

'I'm sorry,' he offered to the room, unsure whether he should say more. 'Do we have any leads as to who this other sorcerer might be? Is he one of my father's guards, or is he a servant?'

'I have reviewed my people as closely as possible, sire.' Master Damyan composed himself, hiding the worry that had touched his face. 'I am confident there are no sorcerers on my staff, which makes me think he is a soldier. Given the proximity he must have to your father, it is someone he trusts.'

It was a night of bad news. 'I've heard enough for now,' Harlan told them, staring up at the stone ceiling.

'Of course, sire,' Ailaya mumbled as she tucked her hair behind her ear. 'We will leave you to your evening.'

As she and Theodor went to leave through the servant door, hand in hand, they paused when Master Damyan did not follow.

'Go ahead,' he said in a soft voice. 'I need to speak with the prince for a moment.'

Harlan glowered at Master Damyan as the others left the room. The door clicked closed behind them.

'Do you wish to speak about whatever's troubling you, sire?'

Damyan went over and picked up the wine jug and goblet, from the small table by the lounge. He filled the cup with the rich, red liquid as Harlan turned to face the flames. Heat emanated from the fireplace and embers sparked around the dancing blaze.

'Nothing's troubling me,' Harlan lied, studying the inferno.

'Of course not, Your Grace.' Master Damyan smiled and passed the goblet to Harlan with one hand as he placed his other comfortingly on the prince's shoulder. 'In all seriousness,' Master Damyan focussed his stare on Harlan, 'it worries me when you keep everything in all the time.'

'I don't have the luxury of letting everything out.' Harlan chewed his cheek, ignoring Master Damyan beside him. 'I'm being watched all the time. If it's not by my father, then it's by my people or my enemies.'

'Sire, I had a hand in raising you.' Harlan sensed a fatherly concern. 'I can see that you're suffering.'

'What do you want from me?' Harlan snapped, throwing his arms out such that wine sprang from the goblet and into the fireplace. The inferno burst into a short-lived firestorm. Rubbing the tips of his fingers along his forehead, Harlan apologised for losing his temper. 'I have a lot on my mind right now.'

'It's alright, Your Grace,' Damyan muttered under his breath. When Harlan glanced at him, Damyan was watching the fire.

'Ever since I learned about my mother's execution, it's been one thing after the other.' Harlan hung his head, wanting

Maldwyn's insight, and placed a hand on his chest to soothe his pain at the reminder of his death. 'I am stumbling from one lie, or one thing, to the next. I feel like I don't know what or who to trust, and the person I was beginning to trust… is gone.'

'I understand.'

Master Damyan went over to the prince and pulled him into a warm embrace. Harlan wondered how different things might have been if he had never pushed Master Damyan away as he grew older. Under his father's advice, the prince had stopped trusting those around him and distanced himself from those that helped to raise him.

'For what it's worth, sire, at least make time to mourn for Maldwyn.'

Staring at the mantelpiece, resting his chin on Damyan's shoulder, Harlan stifled his tears. He wondered if Damyan harboured suspicions about Harlan's fondness of the servant he would request to remain at his side, or whether Theodor had said something to the master of the staff.

The thought crossed his mind that he may have been referring to the news of his mother, or the loss of his sister. Though the princess was alive, she remained out of reach. Not knowing what Damyan was referring to bothered the prince, but he dared not to ask for clarification out of fear of what the master might say.

CHAPTER THIRTEEN

Rising Embers

THE SILKY, WHITE MOUNTAINS shone against the clear blue skies, and the tall trees dared to reach for the heavens so that they might stroke the face of the beaming sun goddess as she rode through the sky on her powerful chariot. Though the air itself was odourless, there somehow seemed to be a tasteless purity all around that could not be defined.

Damp, pine trees peppered the scentless air with their perfume. The hills were home to a haunting beauty as if they had been imbued with the essence of life itself, humming with a spiritual calm and filling Maldwyn with a sense of contentment he had rarely known. There seemed to be a memory among these rising and falling mounts, a story Maldwyn was sure had been lost to the rigours of time itself.

Every day for the last few weeks, Jaecen would lead Maldwyn in the early morning to the mountain's peak where they would commence his training, which lasted for hours. It began with various tasks designed to warm him for the arduous training.

There was a grace to the way Jaecen performed a variety of martial manoeuvres that made it appear as though he was dancing, waltzing with the invisible spirits that lived in the memory of these trees. Though Maldwyn admired Jaecen's effortless fluidity, captivating and demanding his complete attention, he had been unable to achieve the serenity required to master a fraction of the ranger's skill.

Maldwyn had been told that he would find focus in conquering his mind and being completely present, but something was holding him back from losing himself to the task and being in tune with his surroundings. Try as he might, Maldwyn could not easily find harmony within himself, making his training harder than he had expected.

After the many hours spent training with Jaecen, Maldwyn would return to the mountain city, where he would meet with Erik and Anton to spend his afternoon learning all that he could about magic. There was poetry to everything he learned, old romantic fables, and sorrowful ballads telling of the eternal pain the gods and goddesses suffered, all of which made Maldwyn question whether longevity was a gift or a curse.

Even the goddess of the damned, Hel, troubled him as he began to wonder whether her cruelty was a product of her role in punishing the wicked souls left for her domain, or of the torment that she had endured from her own, more beautiful family members, on account of her scarred face.

Had she suffered as much as her kin, or more? Maldwyn could not decide.

After his training would end, Maldwyn would retire to his chambers where he would read further chapters of *The Power of Divinity* or he would skim through more pages of the Priest of the Blood's notes. Having a broader understanding, Maldwyn read both texts with a more open mind, pondering the very abstract nature of the notion of morality.

Finally, before resting, he would practise meditation, seeking silence, but all he found was noise. Slowly, over the days and weeks that passed, Maldwyn was becoming convinced that his mind could not be conquered, and control over himself and his abilities would never be found.

On a particularly cold morning, Maldwyn woke to see a blue roof over him as steam escaped his lips. Hands burning, Maldwyn turned his head to glance about his chambers, only to find mountains and trees all around where he lay in the powdery, thick snow.

Pushing himself up off the floor, his damp clothes clung to his body, freezing him in the midwinter chill. Lost and confused as to how he had gotten outside, Maldwyn thought about how he had not sleepwalked since he was a child as he rose to stand, shivering. He wrapped his arms around his torso, trying to conserve his body heat as best he could.

Knowing his surroundings well by now, Maldwyn ran for the mountainous city, desperate for warmth. The near-invisible sentries in the trees did not seem to be surprised to see him return.

When Maldwyn made it back to his chambers, Jaecen was standing by the door, leaning his back against the wall with his arms folded over his chest. The dark-brown hood of Jaecen's robes hid the ranger's expression from Maldwyn's view.

He could tell from the way Jaecen swiftly unfolded his arms and pushed away from the wall that he was surprised to see Maldwyn was not inside. Worse yet, Maldwyn knew he looked cold and exhausted, which would only distress the ranger.

Worried for Maldwyn, Jaecen opened the door and ensured he was unharmed before leaving to get Maldwyn some tea while he changed out of his wet clothing. It was a relief to light the fireplace and pull on something warm and dry to wear. As Maldwyn sat in the armchair by the fire, listening to the flames interrupting the quiet, he soaked up the warmth, feeling his frozen limbs defrost.

Not too long after he had left, Jaecen returned with a tray that had a pot of tea beside a small, blue and gold ceramic cup and saucer. Placing the tray on the small table between the two armchairs opposite the fire, a soft, low sound of the tray landing caught Maldwyn's attention.

Jaecen poured the tea into the cup. The liquid swilled around the sides, making a hushed splashing sound. A whiff of steam coiled toward Maldwyn with the noticeable scent of orange and cinnamon tea soothing his concerned mind.

'I can't do this,' Maldwyn mumbled to the ranger.

Jaecen took a moment to pass Maldwyn the cup and take a seat on the vacant chair opposite him, crossing one leg over the other.

'What are you saying, Eminence?' Jaecen finally asked with the beautiful rising and falling intonations that came with his accent.

'This,' Maldwyn stated plainly, leaving his tea to cool. 'Focus and silence. I can't do it.' Glancing down at his tea, Maldwyn watched the way tiny ripples danced over the surface of the liquid as his hand tremored. He was not exhausted at this moment so much as he was defeated. 'How do I tune out everything around me and within me to be present and conquer my mind?'

Jaecen lowered his hood, revealing his ginger hair. It was rare for these people to ever lower their hoods. At times, Maldwyn wondered if there was a spiritual reason for their robes, but he had come to accept the cultural difference of the people who dwelled among the Anhalt Mountains and hadn't bothered to ask.

'Eminence, you must change what you're doing,' Jaecen told him with a firm voice. 'You're searching for silence, where you should be searching for peace.'

'What's the difference?'

'Silence itself is unattainable.' Jaecen leaned forward and indicated to the fire, crackling in the background. 'The world around you will make the noise for you even if it were possible for you to one day achieve the complete silencing of your mind, no matter how unlikely that is. Inner peace is the result of acceptance. Thoughts and emotions make us who we are, but they are not all we are. You are what you do, Eminence.'

Maldwyn frowned and sat up taller, looking Jaecen dead in the eye. 'Tiana once told me just as you have, but I don't think I understood it then either.'

'Thoughts and emotions cannot be removed,' Jaecen began, gesturing to indicate that Maldwyn was reaching for something impossible, 'but they can be accepted. Once you accept these things, the power they have over you lies in your ability to let them go. Think of them as clouds. Some are darker than others, but they always pass by.'

'How do I let thoughts and feelings go? And, how is that different from trying to silence them?'

'You can only let something go once you acknowledge that is there and choose to move beyond it. You have to heed things to let them go. Silencing your mind is burying your thoughts, and it cannot be done.' Jaecen scratched along his temple. 'Eminence, there is a man in Karana Downs I meet from time to time, gathering information on our enemy. He does not know I am Erendil, but he runs a local tavern the lord's guards frequent to gamble. They say plenty when they are drunk and socialising. This man says that there is both good and evil in everything around us, and that only in accepting that these things exist within us can we choose to be good or evil. I don't know how to help you exactly, but maybe this Leith's words can help you.'

The teacup wobbled on the saucer as Maldwyn was struck by the name uttered among Jaecen's words.

'Wait, what did you say?'

'That there is a balance in all existence and maybe this man's words can help you,' Jaecen repeated, weaving his brows together.

'No, not that… the man's name.'

'Leith?'

Looking down to the flames, Maldwyn pondered whether this could be his mother's long-lost husband. If so, then maybe this man knew something that could help Maldwyn work out who his birth parents were.

'Is something wrong, Eminence,' Jaecen asked, sounding quite concerned.

'My mother's husband's name was Leith.' Maldwyn shook his head, considering the chances that he would stumble upon the man who could have been his father.

For a moment, Maldwyn recalled the impression his mother had given of Leith, that he may have encouraged Maldwyn to use his abilities. In an instant, he saw how dissimilar his life could have been.

'He might be able to help point me in the direction of my birth parents. By understanding them, maybe I can understand myself.' Maldwyn pulled himself forward to the edge of his seat. 'If I can master your training and manage a fraction of control over my power, then the sovereign has told me he wants me to go to Karana Downs and infiltrate the keep, gathering evidence of the lord's betrayal. Can you tell me how I can find this man?'

Jaecen grinned as the fire burst suddenly. 'I can do you one better, Eminence. I have already spoken with the sovereign and requested that I be your guide around Karana Downs, and he has approved my proposal. In the lower town, I am well-versed and can help you get around and gather useful information. As for the keep itself, I have never been able to find a way inside, but I will do what I can.' Smiling, Jaecen pushed himself up to stand and pointed to the tea Maldwyn was holding. 'You had better not let that go cold. Take the day off, Eminence. You could use the rest and one day will hardly make a difference. You have much still to learn.'

'Thanks,' Maldwyn muttered as he watched Jaecen glide out of his chambers. Filled with a new purpose, Maldwyn relaxed into his seat and sipped at the soothing tea.

CHAPTER FOURTEEN

Solstice Light Dance

THE WAY THE FROSTED trees held glowering lanterns in their spindly fingers up to the night sky, keeping the blackness at bay, looked to Prince Harlan like a series of small groups of old, hunched men, searching for spectres in the twilight dim. In the vast, open royal gardens, which were covered in a thick layer of powdery snow, bonfires roared at the stars, spitting embers that spiced the air with a smoky bite. A cold, gentle breeze stung Harlan's cheeks as he scanned the bustling winter festival.

For as far as the prince could see, people clustered together, mesmerised by the many performances, gossiping about the royal festivities, spreading the standard rumours of affairs within the court, and devouring copious amounts of food and alcohol. Across the gardens, somewhere just out of sight, relaxing flutes accompanied by harmonious string instruments could be heard charming the crowds. In the gaps between the clusters of people, Harlan spied fire dancers twirling flaming staves in their trance-like state, creating glowing hoops that seemed to hover in the air.

A silver tray, carried by a palace servant, floated by the prince. The waft of ginger desserts and syrupy dumplings in the man's wake filled the prince's nostrils with the sweet perfume. Looking down to the pewter goblet Harlan held in his left hand, the prince brought the cup to his lips, taking a sip of the warm, mulled wine, letting it coat the roof of his mouth before he swallowed.

'It's incredible!' One of the ladies of the court said to the group where Harlan was standing. 'The entire city has music and performances on every corner. Your Royal Highness,' she said, turning to him, batting her lashes, 'the view from the royal balcony must have been spectacular.'

Every year, the royal family gathered on the balcony that overlooked the main courtyard at the front of the palace to watch the commencement of the festivities. The public raced to assemble in the main courtyard to catch a glimpse of the entertainment. This year, the tension between Prince Harlan and King Viktor had mostly gone unnoticed by the public, but the absence of Princess Cassara had sparked a wave of gossip to reignite.

'Yes, it was,' Harlan replied in short, uninterested in the shallow conversation as he waited for Theodor to return with an update. There was a moment of quiet before the conversation from the rest of the group carried on again.

The court officials around him were a pretentious group, however harmless, and Harlan was only in their company to blend in with the festivities for an appropriate amount of time. He couldn't risk raising the suspicion of Lord Darius. Besides, standing among this particular group had placed him in the perfect position to keep a watchful eye on Gorlois, the Keeper of the Archives.

Glancing to his right, Harlan smiled lopsidedly as he spotted a servant, wearing the formal staff attire, reminding the prince of the first time he set eyes upon Maldwyn. It had been at an outdoor banquet, much like this, except it was autumn. The single-breasted, wool overcoat had been beautifully tailored to fit Maldwyn, and the charcoal-coloured gloves had a slight silky sheen.

That night, Maldwyn had fumbled when serving the prince and looked Harlan dead in the eye; something someone of Maldwyn's standing was prohibited from doing. The prince had been unable to forget that moment, and the memory caught Harlan off guard, causing him to feel a little out of place in his present company.

Theodor's arrival, stepping up to the prince's right, was a welcome interruption.

'Is everything set?' Harlan mumbled to Theodor, speaking out the side of his mouth. Another sip of the mulled wine warmed the prince's cold, stinging cheeks.

'Yes, sire,' Theodor replied, clearing his throat.

'Good.' Harlan excused himself and turned to leave the group.

'You'll need this, sire,' Theodor said, handing Harlan a small pouch that had daisies embroidered on one side. 'I doubt he'll believe you without it.'

'Thank you.' Harlan stopped in his tracks to pass his half-drunk goblet of mulled wine to one of the servants that were cleaning empty platters from the buffet table. The servant bowed, keeping his gaze on the ground.

Harlan paused, listening to the group at the end of the buffet for a few moments.

'I don't know, Gorlois,' said a middle-aged man with hollow cheeks and a prominent Adam's apple. He and Gorlois appeared to be deep in conversation, debating council matters. The rest of the group ignored their discussion. 'The Queen of Ellinor, Yale, sends aid with strings attached. Mark my words, she wouldn't be helping with the situation in Haradnor if her kingdom wasn't going to benefit in some way.'

Gorlois, standing to the man's side, scratched his grey beard. 'We can't turn away any deal she offers. If it weren't for her, the lack of supplies coming from Aberdeen could have ruined both Haradnor and Dresden. I'm afraid we need her help.'

'Excuse me, Gorlois,' Harlan butted in, holding out an open hand. Both men bowed, showing their respect for the Crown Prince. 'Do you have a moment? There's something I'd like to discuss with you.'

'Of course, Your Grace,' Gorlois said softly.

As Harlan led Gorlois away from the crowds, with Theodor following close behind, the prince made small talk with the Keeper of the Archives. Eventually, they neared the frozen river that ran behind the castle grounds, towards the forest.

In the summer, this space was an open, grassy glade with a stone bench overlooking the water. In the winter, as it was now, the river groaned beneath the ice, and the hedges marking the glade were hidden under a blanket of snow. The pristine space was unmarred by footsteps.

Harlan motioned for Gorlois to join him on the iced bench, while Theodor remained a few paces behind them, keeping watch. 'I understand your niece has been taken from your care.'

Gorlois chewed the inside of his cheek. 'After my sister died, Elyse was orphaned. I took her into my care for a time, and graciously accepted your father's arrangements to have her sent away to a place where she would receive the best education.'

'You don't have to tell me my father's lies.' Harlan told him, staring at the grumbling ice as he hooked one foot behind the other. 'He took her to use as leverage against you, but what I don't understand is... why?'

'I'm sorry, Your Grace.' Gorlois pinched his lips together and shook his head. 'I can't tell you anything.'

'I doubt that,' Harlan said, pulling out the pouch Theodor had given him. Gorlois's eyes widened as he glimpsed the embroidered daisies. 'I've spent quite some time replacing the guards surrounding your niece with people I trust, people loyal to me.' As he reached for the pouch, Gorlois's bottom lip quivered and his left eye twitched. 'She's safe, and I can arrange for you to visit her.'

'Sire, working for the crown and upholding the integrity of the archives—of history—has been the honour of my life.' Tilting his head, Gorlois frowned. 'Your father has been ramping up his agenda against sorcery.' Opening the pouch,

Gorlois pulled out a fine, silver bracelet with oval links and a simple charm of the cosmic tree. 'My niece was taken by your father to force my hand and make me go against everything I believe in.'

Harlan drew his brows together, watching Gorlois as he turned the charm over in his fingers. 'What did my father make you do?'

Gorlois sighed, placing the bracelet back in the pouch. 'King Viktor has had me reviewing and rewriting the historical records, removing all references to sorcery which does not align with his notion of how magic should be perceived.' He carefully tied a loose knot, closing the bracelet inside the pouch, and scratched along his fluffy beard. 'He is ensuring that magic will be remembered as a scourge that needs to be eradicated.'

A sinking feeling overwhelmed the prince as he glanced over the expanse of ice. Tall, statuesque trees on the other side of the frozen river held their arms out wide as if worshipping the glimmering stars. Harlan quickly looked back to check where Theodor stood in the distance, back facing them as he kept a lookout.

'My father has already outlawed magic, what can he gain by rewriting history?'

'Your Grace, over the years, as you grew, King Viktor divided the people more and more, playing on their fears. He has gone from being a king for the people to a king that amasses personal power by pitting his citizens against one another. Once friendly neighbours now spy on one another and obsess over their differences.' Gorlois licked his dry lips. 'His ability to draw out people's fear and hatred to manipulate the public has proven so successful that Dresden's allies are following King Viktor's example, outlawing sorcery.' Bringing his hands up to his mouth, Harlan blew warm air into his hands to relieve the pins and needles sensation in his cheeks. 'Sire, rewriting history, in the way your father has me doing, I suspect, is to use it as evidence to sway the public opinion and commence war with any kingdom that opposes his worldview. Your father will win the minds of people and let regions tear themselves apart until he can sweep through the surrounding lands and claim them for himself.'

'So, that's how my father plans on uniting the lands. By using people's hatred to systematically execute the masses.'

'I'm afraid so, Your Grace.'

'Knowing that your niece is safe, can you restore the archives?'

Gorlois sniffed back the drip forming at the tip of his nose. 'Though your father doesn't know it, I maintained the original records once rewritten, by moving them somewhere they would be kept safe.'

'Where?'

'To the place that secrets are kept: at the House of Yearning.'

Harlan snorted, amused at the thought of history being protected by courtesans. 'Can I count on your support?'

'If you can continue to keep my niece safe, and permit me to see her, then you will have not only my support but my loyalty.'

'Thank you,' Harlan replied, noting the earnest expression on the keeper's face.

Gorlois stood and bowed, preparing to head back to the festivities. As Harlan looked up at the clear night sky, the stars shimmered like glistening gems, reminding the prince of the rumours of the stone found in the mine.

'One more thing,' Gorlois made a curious face, 'Lord Darius is intent on regaining the mine. There are rumours about the workers of the mine going missing and a special gemstone being discovered there. Have you ever come across any references to where the miners went or even the mention of such a stone?'

'Not that I am aware of, sire,' Gorlois tucked the pouch into the pocket of his coat, 'but I can do some research and get back to you.'

'I would appreciate that.' Harlan stood and placed a hand on the man's shoulder. 'My people will be in touch soon to arrange a meeting with Elyse.'

Gorlois nodded, bowed again, and left the snow-covered glade, pausing as he passed Theodor standing guard. In the distance, the flutes dulled the chatter, and the soft glow of the lanterns threw shadows around the stone palace walls. Taking in one last look at the naked woods across the groaning river, Harlan pushed himself up to stand and steeled himself for the next events of the evening.

The prince dawdled as he meandered over to Theodor, feeling no need to rush the evening along. Theodor, eyes fixated on the path and hand resting on the hilt of his sword, mumbled as he said, 'Shall we head over to meet Ailaya at the eastern tower?'

Harlan moistened his lips as he pulled the sleeve of his coat back over the wrist of his glove. 'Yes, we need to know if Moya will agree to help us.'

Theodor led the way along the path, cutting around the back of the festivities toward the eastern wing of the castle. Lord Darius, Lady Adria and King Viktor all appeared distracted as they remained deeply engaged with several court officials. Harlan was mindful that this evening was the final night before the lord and lady of the downs returned to the northern border.

As Harlan and Theodor cleared the festival, the prince noticed Master Damyan approaching King Viktor, right on schedule.

The path they walked along was lined on either side by mounds of snow and appeared almost striated, having been cleared away by shovels, the resultant patterning was highlighted by the orange hue from the hanging lanterns. Rounding the bend of the eastern tower, which was covered with a feathered patchwork of ice on the grey stonework, Theodor nodded in the direction of where Ailaya and Moya were waiting.

Flicking her long curls of auburn hair back over her shoulder, Ailaya smiled a sort of private smile as she noticed Theodor. Seeing the prince close behind, she quickly grabbed the skirt of her olive-coloured dress and curtsied. Moya, a portly woman with short, mouse-brown hair, high cheekbones and a dimpled chin, gathered up her black dress and curtsied to the prince. Harlan passed on his gratitude and signalled for them to stand.

'I'm sorry to have put this upon you, Moya,' Harlan said, looking back to check they hadn't been followed.

'Is it true?' Moya asked, eyes watering from the cold. 'Can you get my brother safely out of Dresden and away from the lord's reach?'

'Yes,' Harlan replied, flatly. 'After learning about his situation, I wanted to help.'

A few days ago, Ailaya had come to Harlan with an update on Moya's brother and the prince knew how he could win over her loyalty. Sebastian was a magic sympathiser. For quite some time, Lord Darius had used this knowledge to blackmail Moya, keeping her by his wife's side in a constant state of fear.

'I have reached out to one of the diplomats in Ellinor working on the current negotiations. Felix and his family have been trusted friends of mine for some time. With my recommendation, Felix would like to employ your brother. The wage and lodging he is offering are considerable.'

Biting her lip, Moya gazed out into the night, hesitant to speak. Harlan waited patiently, not wanting to rush the maidservant.

'Are you sure he'll be safe, Your Grace? Ellinor doesn't tolerate sorcery.' Holding up her hands, trying not to offend the prince, she continued, 'It's just… my brother has no other family, and he is…' She took in a deep breath and glanced at Ailaya for strength. 'Being around a lot of people can be difficult for him. It's why he chose to pursue carpentry. He spends his days' woodworking, crafting beautiful cabinets.'

'I understand,' Harlan told her in a soft voice. 'Felix and his family are good people and Ellinor doesn't execute sympathisers. Your brother will be able to continue to do what he loves with safety and security.' Checking over his shoulder, the prince lowered his voice, 'You would also be free of the lord's threats.'

'We will need to convince your brother to take the job though,' Theodor added, giving Moya a firm stare. 'We can provide the means, but we can't make him take the offer.'

Ailaya wrapped her arm around the woman's shoulder as Moya let out a breath, giving the woman extra support.

'Your Grace, how can I help?' Moya, looking worn, asked in a resigned tone as she leaned into Ailaya's embrace.

Harlan lifted his head to look at Moya more squarely. 'What do you know of Lord Darius's plans?'

'Not much, I'm afraid. Based on conversations I've overheard or the bits and pieces I have gathered from Lady Adria, I believe that Mikel's infiltration had a deeper purpose than cursing your father.'

'How so?' Harlan pressed, urging her to elaborate.

'It all goes back to your mother, Your Grace.' Moya moved to the side and Ailaya pulled her arm away. 'Her death led to a war that King Filip never accepted losing. Lord Darius provided the means for Mikel to infiltrate the capital in exchange for King Filip agreeing to fund a mercenary army for the lord.'

'Do you know what's in the mine?' Theodor let his hand fall from the hilt of his sword. 'Why does Darius want it so much?'

'I don't know. I only know that he wants it.' Small puffs of steam rose out from Moya's mouth as she spoke. 'Mikel had plenty of opportunities to assassinate your father and he never took them, Your Grace. He has operated in the palace for months on his grandfather's behalf, spying on your father and potentially steering him toward defeat before any battles are waged. King Filip has been planning for the long term, and he is not about to enter any wars that he isn't going to win again. Mikel cursing the pendant and being captured all seemed to be part of their plan. The intention was for Mikel to be executed.'

'But that doesn't make sense,' Harlan told her, stepping a little closer. Ailaya and Theodor both made similar expressions, knitting their brows together. 'Why would Mikel risk his life just to fail and be executed?'

Moya pulled a strange face. 'Mikel is sick.' Lowering her head, she looked at each of them. 'Didn't you know?'

'No,' Harlan said, shaking his head.

'He's dying from a lung sickness. He'll be dead come next autumn.' Moya seemed surprised that his illness had managed to go unnoticed in the palace. 'His execution would have meant that King Filip would have had cause to announce war… one he knew he would win.'

'The princess changed their plans when she escaped with Mikel,' Ailaya mumbled, touching a hand to her cheek.

'I'm sorry, Your Grace,' Moya started, looking to the ground, 'but, that's all I know.'

'Is it enough, sire?' Ailaya asked, looking up at the prince.

Harlan shook his head. 'It's hearsay at best. Unfortunately, my father won't believe the word of a servant when it comes to Lord Darius's betrayal. We need more, something solid.'

'Sire, I'm afraid the only way we will get the evidence we need is to travel to the keep in Karana Downs,' Theodor told him. The grave look on Theodor's face troubled him.

Harlan sighed. 'What about the miners that should have returned when the Erendil reclaimed the region?'

'I've heard what anyone in the downs has heard, which is that they are missing.' Moya shook her head, shrugging. 'Supposedly, on the outskirts of the downs, hunters sometimes report hearing cries that people believe belong to the miners, but nothing has ever been found.'

Harlan pulled his shoulders back and let out an exasperated breath. 'Let's hope Master Damyan has some success.' The music playing in the distance wasn't enough to soothe the prince's worry. 'Thank you, Moya. I appreciate everything you've told us. We won't trouble you anymore.'

'I'll speak to my brother tomorrow, Your Grace. I'll make sure he takes the offer.'

Ailaya led Moya back into the eastern tower by a nearby servant entryway. The door was small and tucked away, making it tough to notice at first glance. The hinges squeaked.

'We'd better get back before your father comes looking for you, sire.' Theodor turned and headed along the path, leading the way back to the festivities.

Harlan stopped to watch the fire dancers twirling their flaming staves as they made it back to the royal gardens, amazed by their skill. Behind him, he heard the flirtatious giggling of one of the ladies of the court.

'Damyan's on his way over, sire.'

Harlan turned to look where Theodor was indicating. Master Damyan, wearing similar, but more distinguished, serving attire, was heading toward them. His posture was perfect as always.

As one of the servants walked by with a tray of mulled wine, Harlan grabbed a goblet to drink, taking a sip to quell the information overload of the evening. The smell of the spices had a relaxing effect.

'Your Royal Highness,' Master Damyan formally addressed, bowing as was expected. 'Your father wants to speak with you.'

Harlan lowered his voice, 'Did he believe you?'

'I believe so, Your Grace,' Master Damyan confirmed, looking a little pleased with himself. The silver streaks in his hair gleamed under the light of the lanterns and fire dancers. 'He's waiting for you in the sacred grove.'

'Alone?' Harlan checked, hoping that Lord Darius wouldn't be in his father's shadow.

'Yes,' Master Damyan said. 'He wasn't happy though, sire. I wouldn't keep him waiting too long.'

Harlan grinned and looked over to Theodor. 'I think we should watch the show for a while. I'll head over once I finish my drink.'

Theodor shrugged at Master Damyan, resigning himself to the lack of control he had over Prince Harlan. After everything Harlan had learned, he was in no rush to appease his father. The king could wait, for a while.

* * * * *

It wasn't a long walk from the main gardens to the sacred grove. As Harlan walked into the clearing he passed a few guards, leaving Theodor behind at the edge of the trees. King Viktor was standing in front of the lone, evergreen ash tree, which stood wide and tall, limbs reaching out in every direction. The rippled surface marked its age, housing frost in the crevasses.

'You wanted to speak with me, father,' Harlan said to King Viktor's back.

The black streak in his father's hair was less obvious under the black sky. His broad shoulders were hidden by the fur mantle wrapped around him. 'I need you to lead the men being sent to Karana Downs in the spring.'

'Of course.' Harlan smiled to himself. 'May I ask why, father?'

Harlan knew why. He had manufactured the reason, having Damyan forge a report of rumours of a fabled sword, which had supposedly been found in the mine and was being kept hidden in the downs. Harlan had ensured the report would be worded in such a way that it would lead his father to believe the sword was Iluvitar, the very sword for which the king had sent the prince to the Anhalt Mountains to retrieve.

Harlan knew now, this had been a lie orchestrated by Mikel to ensure the prince was out of the palace while he sent reports from the capital, shared secret information and orchestrated events to ensure his execution. Harlan felt it was fitting to use the same lie to have his father send him where he wished to go. He had wondered whether his father would be suspicious of Harlan, but, thankfully, the king did not think clearly when it came to sorcery.

'We've received an interesting report that requires investigation.' King Viktor, not turning to face the prince, flicked Harlan the letter that had been forged by Damyan over his shoulder. The slant of Damyan's cursive letters ensured that the script in no way resembled the master's normal handwriting.

'Father, surely this isn't true,' the prince said, careful of his tone.

'Possibly not, but if there is any truth to the rumours, then we need to know.' King Viktor turned to face his son. After everything Harlan had learned this evening, it was difficult for him not to give away the lie and keep his expression neutral. 'That weapon is dangerous and needs to be destroyed.'

'Of course, father,' Harlan agreed, handing the letter back to the king. 'Why wait until the spring though? I could return with Lord Darius tomorrow.'

'We can't afford to raise suspicions.' The king pursed his lips and narrowed his eyes as if he were trying to better his focus in the darkness. 'I want you to lead the forces we are sending to minimise any legitimacy being afforded to these rumours. Once you are in the downs, you can investigate the reports in private and, should there be any truth to them, acquire the sword. Then, you will bring it here, where it will be safe until we know how to destroy it.'

Harlan was frustrated that he would need to wait until the spring, but, as long as his father was watching his movements closely, he wasn't confident that he would be able to get to Karana Downs without his father's approval. For now, he could be patient and focus on planning his next step without concern about Lord Darius's presence in the palace.

'I will see to it, father,' Harlan said, waiting to be dismissed.

'One more thing, if in the unlikely event you find Lord Darius is involved in treasonous matters, stop him at all costs.'

Harlan tilted his head, surprised by his father's final order. 'I thought you were on good terms with the lord.'

'Good, that means he does too.' King Viktor leaned forward and lowered his voice. 'Though he was once a trusted friend, I can no longer trust his sincerity.'

Gobsmacked, Harlan drew his brows together and smirked. 'Why?'

'He's grown more arrogant and bold than I remember. Besides,' King Viktor fiddled with the sleeves of his thick, woollen coat beneath his mantle, 'Lady Adria said something to me that I found interesting. She offhandedly said that if I took a closer look at her husband, I'd see that he's a changed man who is more brutal than I believe.'

'Did you ask her what she meant?'

'Of course,' King Viktor replied, making a face as though that was a given. 'She brushed it aside and said time changes everyone.'

'But you think there's more to it.'

'I'm not completely ignorant, my son.' Harlan hated being patronised by his father. 'I may not have had my focus on Lord Darius because of the border issues in the region, but I am fully aware that the downs are plagued with rumours of depravity. It's quite simple, I can no longer look the other way.'

'Send me now, I'll find out what he's up to and put an end to it.'

'I'd rather send the heir to the throne with a full escort when the weather is on your side.' There was a hint of worry in the king's voice. 'There's no rush, son. In spring, when the conditions are suitable, you will go there under the guise of providing reinforcements to secure the border. You will find out what he's up to and, if treasonous, stop him. If that sword happens to be there, you will return to the palace with it where we can keep it secure.'

Eventually, after a silence settled between them, the king waved him off and Harlan bowed before leaving the glade. Theodor was waiting for him near the king's escort of soldiers. The smoky spice in the air made him smile, especially knowing that the evening had gone better than according to plan. He was somewhat impressed with his father's orders and flattered that he had even appeared to care, though he supposed that was a result of him being the king's heir.

A part of him wondered whether King Viktor regretted his sentencing of Cassara or yearned for his wife, the queen, who he had executed. Although Harlan knew the king would never admit that he was fallible, the prince couldn't help speculating where the unexpected sincerity he had felt from the king had come from.

CHAPTER FIFTEEN

Let Sleeping Dogs Lie

WHEN MALDWYN WOKE to the buttery walls and the gold and ivory tiles of the coffered ceiling in his chambers, he felt exhausted, as if he had had too much sleep, if that were possible. Unmotivated, he lay in the soft bed, willing to waste the hours of the morning, hoping that he would eventually be struck with the desire to leave the warm comfort of his quarters among the Anhalt Mountains. In the last few weeks, his training had been going well and he knew he could rest for as long as he wished, taking the day to relax.

As Maldwyn lay in the bed, head resting on the cloudlike pillow, laying on his back with his arms sprawled out to each side beneath the disordered bedcovers over his body, he replayed the prior evening in his mind. For the first time, sitting alone and meditating in his quarters, Maldwyn had controlled the slowing of time around him, though he had not been able to stop it completely, as he had done before.

Opening his eyes to see the flames swaying from side to side filled him with a sense of pride, knowing he was learning to control his power. His fighting ability had come far as well, being able to best Jaecen in a fair sparring match.

Rolling over to his side, he reached his hand out over the surface of the wide, otherwise empty, bed and slid his hand up to the vacant pillow. Maldwyn had found a home among these mountains, but that hadn't curbed his yearning for connection.

There was a hollow sensation that was eating at him from the depths of his gut. He remembered the way that Dimitri had protected him back in Alander. He regretted running and leaving his people behind but had set himself the task of redemption by making Dimitri's choice worth his sacrifice.

Maldwyn had been raised by a woman that had taught him to be invisible, to go through life never being noticed, but now there were people, like Dimitri and the Erendil, that had all these ideas of what Maldwyn could achieve. The fear that he might never live up to these expectations haunted him, making his heart race a little faster, despite how tired he felt upon waking.

Rolling back to stare at the chiffon canopy of the four-post bed, Maldwyn let out a puff of air, as if it would release the anxiety that was trying to choke him as he rested. In an attempt to prevent himself from continuing on the downward spiral his mind was taking, Maldwyn thought of the notion that going to Karana Downs may, in some way, help Prince Harlan and comforted himself with the possibility of seeing the prince one more time. If that were possible, then maybe he would find something worth living for, against all odds.

Thinking back to the mention of the mine, Maldwyn noted how quick Jerrik had been quick to change the subject. As swiftly as Maldwyn had broached the topic, Jerrik had flicked it aside and moved on to the next matter to discuss. Blaming himself a little for his willingness to easily let the matter slide, Maldwyn scratched the side of his nose out of frustration as he considered other avenues he should have taken, which might have given him more answers sooner. Maldwyn couldn't help but wonder why the sovereign was so guarded about the mine.

Eventually, Maldwyn heard footsteps echo in the corridor outside. It must have been some passing Erendil official or other, so he hauled himself up from the comfort of the soft pillow he was resting his head against and wiped his hands over his eyes, as though it that would somehow clear the remaining tiredness from them. He stretched his arms out and yawned, but that didn't help to wake him either.

He began to make his way over to the low-line dresser, beyond the foot of the bed and over by the wall opposite the fireplace, with heavy steps. A slight headache throbbed in his temples at being upright. He paused as he walked, grabbed the delicate, timber post at the foot of the bed and waited for the pulsating to subside before taking the final steps toward the dresser. The air was a little peppered from the smoke of the dead fire.

As Maldwyn stood in front of the dresser, he poured some water from the teal amphora into the deep, pewter bowl, adding a few drops of the pleasant, flowery-scented oil that had a hint of cinnamon. Using the rag that hung over the side, he mixed the oil into the water and began to wash, cleaning away the evening muck that clung to him.

Once he was cleaned and dressed, Maldwyn pulled on the thick, neatly tailored, charcoal-coloured, wool coat that the Erendil had gifted him and left his room. He wandered through the corridors toward the outdoor space he knew was nearby, wanting to hear the morning song of the birds in the trees.

As he passed the marble staircase that descended deeper into the city's tunnels and the humungous, crystal candelabra that speckled the walls with an eerie light, Maldwyn smiled, feeling a little brighter for having left the false comfort of his bed. The light tricked his eyes into believing there were windows to the outside world, allowing beams of light to teem over the grand staircase. The velvety balustrade was sculpted of an almost colourless stone, carved into geometric patterns that repeated down the length of the staircase.

Standing before two massive doors with swirling patterns carved into their surface, Maldwyn placed a hand on one door and pushed it open. A freezing gust swept all around him, making Maldwyn wrap his arms tight around his body to try and stay warm. The insulation of the tunnelled city had managed to fool him into forgetting the frost that waited beyond its doors.

Outside, the sandstone paved platform was buried beneath a layer of snow, some of which had been shovelled to the sides already. There was no balustrade here, the edge of the platform fell away with the steep slope of the forested mountain.

Though the place was beautiful, as Maldwyn knew well, it was a different sort of charm in winter. The trees all around the area were little more than two-toned oversized sticks; one layer of white facing the sky, and a greying brown layer looking down at the ground below. The long arms of the immensely tall trees reached for the sun that was hidden behind the thin layer of fluffy cloud cover. The purple tint warned of another snowfall. The piles of autumn leaves were nowhere in sight for the pristine, white blanket that shrouded them. Birds sang happily from the trees, marking the start of a new day, ignorant to the bitter cold that chased mankind indoors.

As he stayed just beyond the doorway looking out, Maldwyn shivered and forced himself to suffer the frost, yearning for the calming sensation of the fresh, forest air. It was so crisp that Maldwyn could taste the sourness of the damp, naked wood.

'It's a most beautiful spot, isn't it?' The sovereign's calm voice seemed to sing from behind Maldwyn.

Turning to face Jerrik, Maldwyn lowered his head a little, still feeling unsure of the exact customs for showing his respect to the sovereign.

'Yes, it is,' he offered, noting that the sovereign was wearing black, linen robes with charcoal accents woven into the fabric.

An arctic blue, silk sash was wrapped around his waist and the base of the robes cascaded gracefully toward the floor. His dark hood was drawn over his face, keeping the sovereign as mysterious and difficult to read as ever he was.

'I was about to come looking for you.'

'No need, Eminence. I am here.'

Jerrik neared Maldwyn by a few paces, steam pouring from his lips. Something was captivating about the presence of the sovereign. He demanded awe, something that King Viktor was not able to do, at least not in the same way. Jerrik didn't need to lower himself to the violence and rage that the king needed to rule over his people, rather the sovereign did so with a certain sort of arrogance that seemed to distil over the minds of his followers, ruling them with his enigmatic confidence.

'Was there something you needed?'

'Umm… not really.' Shrugging, Maldwyn shook his head. 'I guess I just wanted to check if there was anything I needed to know before heading to Karana Downs with Jaecen and Erik.'

'Yes, according to the prince, Lord Darius has been in league with the King of Mordiallok for some time.' The sovereign seemed to pause, as though he had just noticed the crispness of the fresh air, and gazed out over the white woods. 'When you arrive in the downs, you will need to confirm whether the guests in the keep, rumoured to go by Imogen and Lance, are actually the princess and her cousin. If so, the princess may be able to provide evidence that may help Prince Harlan. Erik will be going with you, so he should be able to help convince her to aid her brother. You should know that Lord Darius is back in the downs, meaning the keep will be at full strength.'

It seemed simple enough, but there was a nagging feeling in the pit of his stomach that worried him. Convincing Princess Cassara would prove to be quite difficult, given she had remained in Karana Downs under asylum for some months now. Lord Darius had helped her when her family was trying to execute her. Maldwyn wondered whether she would see reason, even with the help of Erik. Not sure what to say, Maldwyn simply nodded.

'On another note, Jaecen tells me you still want to visit the mine.'

'Yes,' Maldwyn began, biting his cheek.

He hadn't expected that Jaecen would have shared that with the sovereign. There was a part of him that thought the ranger would have let the matter go, leaving it for Maldwyn to discuss with the sovereign directly, as Jaecen had instructed him to do on many occasions. That was not the case.

'The mine has been disputed for so long, I wanted to see it.'

'When I asked you, what could have been of interest to you in the mine, you suggested that there might be more than draconite in there. Why?'

Having been backed into a corner, Maldwyn decided to be honest with the sovereign. Though at times, he wasn't sure he trusted Jerrik, Maldwyn was sure that the sovereign wasn't working against him.

'Before Jaecen found me in the forest,' a cloud of steam escaped Maldwyn's mouth and wafted on the gentle wind, 'I had stumbled into a temple, not too far from the foot of the Anhalt Mountains. It was an abandoned temple. There, I found references that suggested the worshippers had been searching for a place in the mountains where there may be remnants from the divine wars. From the notes I read, I believe the mine could be the area that interested them.'

'Notes?' Jerrik asked, sounding unsurprised. 'How much have you managed to read of *The Power of Divinity*?'

Maldwyn decided to keep the knowledge of the priest's journal to himself for the time being. He wanted to see how forthcoming Jerrik would be with whatever was going on.

'I've read enough to know that Hel is an enemy of the gods, and Wayland was once imprisoned in this realm during those divine wars.'

'Hmm, yes.' Jerrik held out his gloved hands and Maldwyn thought his fingers seemed particularly long. He hadn't noticed that before now. 'Well, when the gods won the war against Hel, they separated the world of the living from that of the dead. They didn't however condemn her worshippers, known as Children of the Flesh. At least, not until they actively went against the gods and sought to free Hel's son who had—as you have said—been imprisoned in this realm. You may have noticed that the temple you happened upon was cursed by nightmares.'

Surprised by Jerrik's honesty, Maldwyn looked to the floor and tilted his head a fraction to the side, taking a moment to pay attention to the birds as he recalled the ghost of Will, beckoning for Maldwyn to join him in the afterlife.

'There were things I saw there,' he muttered.

'They were just visions, Maldwyn.' Jerrik placed a hand on his shoulder to comfort him. 'Whatever you saw, it wasn't real. I know that temple well and can assure you that the gods cursed the temple to keep worshippers away.' Pulling his hand back, Jerrik straightened his shoulders. 'When Anton and I discovered that there was draconite in the mine, we restricted entry to ensure the safety of all. There truly is nothing else in there, but if you wish to see it, then I will take you.'

Maldwyn was astounded, he had not thought Jerrik would be this forthcoming. He wondered if it were a trick, or an attempt to have Maldwyn leave the issue alone. Whatever the sovereign's reasoning, Maldwyn decided to take him up on the offer.

'Alright, when do we leave?'

'Now. Follow me,' Jerrik said, his accent made it more difficult for Maldwyn to gauge the tone in his voice.

Jerrik turned and led the way inside the mountain. The two descended the grand staircase that seemed to spiral downwards from the peak to the base of the mount.

Maldwyn followed the sovereign through the many wide corridors, walls gleaming and mosaic patterns shimmering from the ceilings and floors. Many of the side rooms were accessed through tall, wide archways and had colourful glazed tiles glistening from the floors. Gentle fabrics swayed at passers-by.

Maldwyn recognised the lavish Halls of Healing where he had first been held captive within its golden walls and the polished mosaic floors that were a collage of colours. The smell of the sandalwood incense here had a strange effect on him, reminding him of the time he spent locked away in the healing room behind the main hall, despite the sanctuary he had found in the underground city.

Over time, Maldwyn had come to respect the sorcerer, Anton, no longer seeing him as merely his captor, but as a man wrestling with the peaceful nature of his peoples and the forceful will of the sovereign to which he owed his livelihood.

Further along, they passed a place that was teeming with hooded figures, each seated around the room at several tables of varying sizes and lengths. There was a lot of chatter and the strong smell of what Maldwyn could only guess was tea. He supposed it was some sort of a tea house where people could gather and socialise.

The more they walked together through the halls, the more Maldwyn thought it was strange that the robed people weren't surprised by their sovereign walking amongst them, without any guards about him. In many ways their society was more liberal, freed from many of the restrictions that held Dresden back, but in others, it was quite repressed, as with the case of the concubines. He questioned how the rule of being sovereign worked, wondering whether it was a position to which the people elected a leader, or structured by birthright, as was typical with monarchs.

After passing through the better part of the underground structure, they made their way through the main gates and exited the concealed city. Together, they walked for what seemed to be hours before they made it through the woods, trekking up and down the mounts, to where the mine was waiting for them. Snow began to gently fall from high above them, wisping through the woods.

The entrance to the mine was a dark, gaping abyss, like a yawning mouth, which was cut into the side of a steep, rocky mountain that had been turned to pure white. The snow all around was untouched, making the blackness of the mine seem all the more foreboding.

Staring up through the twiggy trees, Maldwyn thought of how he had not glimpsed any rangers for the entirety of their hike, though he knew they would have been watching him. That thought gave him slight chills to fully realise their skill at concealment high up among the trees.

Maldwyn halted, waiting by the blackened entrance. All around was silent. There were no birds, no wolves, no deer, no moose, no foxes, not even squirrels in the woods. The unnatural silence worried him, as though there was something about this place that wasn't quite right. A strange sense of unease swept over him and he was afraid of what lay beyond.

Jerrik grabbed a torch that hung from the wall just inside the cave. It was a metal torch with a thin stem for gripping and a wide, round top for lighting. He ran his hand along the base of the torch in a very careful and specific manner. Maldwyn's eyes popped as flames came to life, lighting the area for what seemed to be miles inside the cave.

'I didn't know you were a sorcerer,' he said, amazed to see the flaming torch.

'I am not, but Anton has spelled the torch to ignite at a certain pattern drawn along the stem. Come on, you will see there is nothing to worry about.'

Deep down, something knotted as though his intuition didn't agree with Jerrik, but Maldwyn persevered and followed the sovereign inside. As they walked, Maldwyn noted the markings where tools had scarred the walls, which had a sort of red, dusty tinge, indicating the presence of iron. Large rocks had been stacked to the side as if waiting to be piled on a cart and transported to Karana Downs where they would be smelted into steel.

They passed by a wooden cart that had remnants of iron ore and heavy-handed hammers and chisels inside, and there was a shovel, laying over the cart, as though it had been left there while the miner had stepped aside for a short break. Pickaxes leaned on the walls every so often, leaving the illusion that at any moment the workers would return and this place would be full of life.

But it wasn't.

In the distance, there was an unnerving sound, water dripping at uneven intervals. Smaller tunnels diverted from the main path, searching for more iron as the main tunnel began to lose its red, dusty appearance. There had been no sign of dragon remnants, specifically draconite, as far as Maldwyn could tell.

After quite some time walking in silence through the unsettling quiet tunnels, the main pathway ended by the edge of a black pool. The water was perfectly still, and the cavern roof was a jagged mess of red rock and moss above the underground lake.

'See,' Jerrik said in a calm, strangely flat tone given his songlike accent. 'There is nothing here.'

Stepping closer to the water's edge Maldwyn searched for something he felt was here, but couldn't see with his eyes.

'What's on the other side of the water?' Maldwyn asked, pointing as he thought he saw some sort of writings on the far wall.

'It's just rock walls, Maldwyn.'

As Maldwyn focused more on that wall, he thought he saw a small, ring-like shape in the middle of the cursive text.

'You don't see that?'

'See what?'

'I could swear there is something written on that wall in the distance.'

'I don't see anything other than the jagged walls.'

Maldwyn couldn't read the expression on Jerrik's face for the hood and the shadows cast by the firelight. He supposed Jerrik was being sincere, why else would he have brought him here if there had been anything to be seen? Perhaps in searching for something, Maldwyn was just convincing himself that there was indeed something to be seen.

'You're right,' Maldwyn mumbled hesitantly, scratching along his jaw. 'We can go.'

Jerrik turned to leave, and, as Maldwyn went to do the same, he thought he caught sight of a tiny glimmering gemstone. He looked a little closer, but the light of the flame had moved further down the tunnel, and Maldwyn told himself it was just the light of the torch glimmering on the surface of the black water.

The two walked once more in silence as they passed the ghosts of history in the tunnels. When they reached the exit, Jerrik put the torch out and hung it back on the hook in the wall. Maldwyn was eager to leave, despite the nagging feeling telling him he should have insisted on looking a little more closely. Walking at a decent pace, the return journey seemed to take less time than it had for them to trek down the mountains toward the mine.

CHAPTER SIXTEEN

The Mists of Karana Downs

A S MALDWYN MEANDERED through the immense corridors of the underground city, pack hanging off one shoulder, he was mesmerised by a massive set of scalloped archways with a leafy pattern carved into the buttery walls, which climbed up toward the vaulted, white and gold, tiled ceiling. Peeking through the arches to the space beyond, Maldwyn stood in awe at the glimpse of a magnificent, life-size, stone sculpture of the bowman god, aiming at an invisible target.

Moving through the arch to take a better look, Maldwyn admired the way the sculpture's moulded robes seemed to be flowing in a gentle wind, and his hood was drawn high enough to keep his gaze mysterious. Rings were carved around each finger and the veins in the marble figure webbed along the surface of the statue, bringing it to life.

Standing still in the place of worship, Maldwyn glanced around the area and saw that it was lined with long, rounded pillars that concealed small alcoves with silky, purple, cushioned bench seats set into the niches. A hint of sweet musk perfume caught Maldwyn's attention as he heard muttering coming from one of the alcoves, concealed beyond the pillars.

'I'm worried about you, Tiana,' whispered Tolamin's familiar voice, carrying the singsong accent of the Erendil. 'Lately, you've been growing distant.'

'Do you remember what it was like before Jerrik became our leader?'

'Of course.' Tolamin said, in a calm and measured voice. 'Before him, we were skilled nomads, practically invisible among the mountains, we didn't even know this place existed. It was always a fight to maintain our claim over the mountains as Dresden grew larger. We lost so much in those turbulent years before we settled here.'

Maldwyn had assumed that the Erendil had created this underground city and that this had been the reason King Viktor had been unable to defeat them in the disputed territories. Learning that these people had lived as nomads, constantly running from King Viktor, and living in persistent fear before Jerrik's rule, surprised Maldwyn. He wondered how Jerrik came to power and whether the Erendil ever followed a leader before him.

'Without his guidance and leadership,' Tolamin continued, his voice reflective, 'I fear we'd have all died years ago. He united our people and brought us here where we wouldn't be found. He brought us a period of peaceful diplomacy with Dresden through Kristian. He gave us a home.'

'Do you ever doubt him?' Tiana fell quiet, and Maldwyn wasn't sure whether he should let them know he was nearby. He considered trying to slip away before they noticed.

'All the time,' Tolamin uttered, his singsong voice low and tender, 'you can trust me with whatever is weighing you down.'

'The ring that the sovereign is after… the one he demanded Prince Harlan return, in exchange for freedom.' Tiana's raspy voice was a little choked as if her worry was strangling her voice.

Hearing a reference to Kristian's ring put Maldwyn on edge. He decided to linger a while by the statue, to see if he could learn what Prince Harlan already suspected, which was that there may be something about the ring Jerrik hadn't shared.

'Kristian's ring?'

'Yes,' she said in a faint tone. 'I'm afraid he has motives for wanting that ring.'

Tolamin exhaled loudly. 'What could he want with the ring?'

Maldwyn moved his head toward the alcove where he heard their voices.

'I don't know.' Maldwyn heard one of them shift in their seat, feet scuffing on the mosaic floor. 'For years, he's built a following among our people. We follow him, to the point of blindness at times.'

'You can't blame people for that though. I mean, look at how we are today. We are safe and prospering.'

Tiana's lack of response made the halls fall silent. Maldwyn wished he could see the look on her face, but to move closer would give away that he was there eavesdropping. He held his breath, keeping as quiet as possible.

'Why shouldn't people follow him?'

'I overheard him talking to Anton, and he mentioned something about believing the ring to be a relic left in the mortal realm by the gods. He wants it for something, but he's secretive, and he heard me outside the door. I don't know what he wants with the ring.'

'I'm sure there's nothing to it,' Tolamin pressed, trying to ease Tiana. 'Perhaps he just wants to ensure it isn't found and destroyed by King Viktor. We've lost so much history these last few years.'

'You're probably right,' Tiana said.

There was a kindness to the way she spoke to the priest that told Maldwyn there was a closeness between them. Maldwyn heard her shoes on the floor, figuring she must have stood from the seat in the alcove.

'I should go.'

'Of course,' Tolamin said, a little sadly. Maldwyn caught sight of the priest's pastel blue robes, the silver and white silk sash seeming to shine, as his figure stood from a nearby alcove. Tolamin bowed to the sovereign's concubine, watching her slip out of the temple through a side door. After she was out of sight, the priest turned away and headed for the small, private room at the back of the temple.

Waiting for a while, by the statue, Maldwyn considered whether the sacred ring was created by the gods. If that was the case, then the ring may be dangerous and he needed to get word to Prince Harlan, but he had no idea how to send the prince a message, given he was no longer a part of the palace circle and wasn't sure who he could trust in the mountains. For now, he would have to keep the knowledge to himself.

* * * * *

As the weeks passed by, Maldwyn's control over his power grew and he was now able to summon forth fire at will, no longer sporadically conjuring flames. His ability to slow time was difficult to master, but he had been able to slow the world more than once. He still hadn't ceased time again but felt that command over his ability would come with more practise.

Having dedicated himself to learning Jaecen's tranquil, effortless fluidity as he manoeuvred, Maldwyn's skill improved at an exceptional rate. He committed himself to embodying the Erendil's principles, closely following Jaecen's guidance and being completely focused on his present surroundings.

The snow on the mountain's peak, where Maldwyn and Jaecen trained, had slowly melted into the forest floor, revealing blades of bright, green grass below. The naked trees were blossoming, covered in new shoots of leafy growth. The birds in the trees gathered in greater numbers to sing their morning tune earlier in the day, greeting the rising sun. Morning dew clung in droplets to the leaves, giving the fresh, crisp air a sweet scent.

Watching the winter months draw to a close as the forest returned to life had been serene. As spring came to full fruition, Jerrik gifted Maldwyn with a set of silky, hooded Erendil robes and decided that he was ready to head to Karana Downs.

Tiana and Tolamin hadn't been at the main gates to see them off, but Jerrik and Anton had made the effort to wish them luck on their journey. For the entirety of his stay in the mountains, like their esteemed guest, Maldwyn had withheld as much as he could, trying to maintain some privacy from the people that worshipped him. He didn't understand their devotion.

As Erik, Jaecen and Maldwyn trekked through the blooming woods, each carrying packs filled with supplies, they climbed over large fallen trees that blocked the way, jumped over bulbous root systems and trod carefully over the uneven ground. The forest floor was a patchwork of soft grasses, broken twigs and dying bulbs that had been shed to make way for the sweet blossoming flowers, honeying the air.

Before setting out, Maldwyn had been told that Karana Downs was just over a day's hike northeast of the mountains and that they would have to be careful not to be spotted by King Viktor or Lord Darius's men. For this reason, they trekked mostly in silence, making as little conversation as possible, and chose to camp in the misty evening forest without a fire.

As they sat there, snacking on the food from their packs, unable to see the blinking stars through the leafy canopy, Maldwyn turned to the silhouette of Jaecen supposing he may be able to answer some of the burning questions on his mind.

'I, um… recently learned that your people were nomads in the mountains before finding a home in the underground city. What was that like?'

Erik, leaning his back against the rock wall they were camping next to, paused as he took a bite of the bread roll that he was gnawing on, interested in the answer. Maldwyn, sitting against a tree, leaned forward, resting his forearms on his knees, having already finished eating for the evening.

Jaecen's silhouette looked up to the canopy, considering his answer. 'I was quite young then, but I remember it being difficult… never having a home, especially when King Viktor sent forces into the mountains.' Jaecen scratched along his jaw. 'But, moving around was normal to us.' Putting his hands behind his head, Jaecen reclined against his pack. 'We never knew of the tunnels beneath the mountains. If it weren't for Jerrick bringing us there, then we probably would have all been hunted to extinction.'

'How did Jerrik know of the place?' Erik asked, sounding quite confused.

'I don't know. I'm not sure which community he belonged to. We existed in pockets back then,' Jaecen whispered, being mindful of making too much noise. 'He must have happened upon it one day and told his people. Eventually, word spread of the migration to the citadel, and we all came together under Jerrik's rule.'

'Forgive my ignorance,' Maldwyn murmured in the quiet, squashing himself down on his bedroll, pressing his back against the tree. 'If your people were nomads, how come they had a representative on the council?'

Laughing, a low sort of rumble as he tried to stay quiet, Jaecen rubbed the underneath of his eyes. 'When the tensions between our people and the capital were at their lowest, under King Aleksander's rule, King Viktor's father, a role of magical advisor was created on the council as a means of solidifying peace. Although our people were nomadic, we harboured many skilled sorcerers and had a deep understanding of the gods, given our devout worship.' Jaecen's silhouette disappeared as a cloud of mist moved between them. 'That all ended with King Viktor though. His crusade put tensions on the rise again, long before Kristian's affair with the queen.'

Erik clicked his tongue against the roof of his mouth. 'Did you ever learn what began the tensions between your people and the capital?'

'Who knows really?' Jaecen sighed, sounding as though that was the hardest question of all, and one for which he was still seeking answers. 'What I was taught, is that it has always been territorial. As the capital expanded the kingdom's borders, clearing land for farming and building towns and villages, my people were marginalised as wanderers and pushed further into the mountains.'

'I'm sorry,' Maldwyn offered, even though it was something he had no power over. 'What about the mine? Both sides claim ownership over it.'

'Oof,' Erik murmured, surprised that Maldwyn would dare to ask about the possession of the iron mine.

'Well, no one really knows that either, do they?' Jaecen's shrug scraped the buckles on his pack. 'My people claim that they founded the mine, and sold this ore to the capital before its expansion pushed us further into the mountains. The capital claims that, since we were nomadic, the mine was founded and run by their people, even though it was within our lands at the time.'

'I don't think anyone will ever be able to answer that one, Mal,' Erik said, folding his arms over his chest. 'We should just be glad it is under your people's control, given the significance of finding draconite in there.'

'Why did Jerrik order an assault and for the rangers to retake the mine?' Maldwyn pulled his coat a little tighter over his chest. The evening air was quite cool, even though it was spring.

'There were rumours among miners in Karana Downs that a stone had been found. What they described sounded valuable. Jerrik wanted to know what they had discovered, so he ordered us to attack the mine.'

'I hate to think what Lord Darius would use the stone for,' Erik added, putting the remnants of his bread back into his pack. 'I'm going to rest for the night,' Erik told them, hopping into his bedroll.

Jaecen and Maldwyn stopped talking after that, eventually sliding into their bedrolls for some sleep. It had been a while since Maldwyn had slept outdoors and he couldn't get comfortable. Tossing and turning, he was unable to find a spot clear of rocks and twigs. Though it took him reaching the point of exhaustion, in the end, Maldwyn drifted off to sleep, dreaming of the lake in the mine.

CHAPTER SEVENTEEN

Destitute Downs

THE NEXT MORNING, Maldwyn awoke to the dappled light cascading through the leafy canopy and the sweet and soothing smell of morning dew, which was met by the damp bark perfume. His eyes were gritty, and he felt as though he had hardly slept. The warm, dense blanket over him seemed heavier than the evening prior as he pushed it back, hauling himself up to a seated position.

Jaecen, having already packed away his gear, was dressed in simple travelling clothes with a thick, beige, wool coat. It was strange to see him in anything other than his brown, smooth ranger robes with the leather belt over the red, silky sash. He seemed to be quietly muttering to himself in a different voice.

'What are you doing?' Maldwyn asked, looking over to see Erik was still sleeping.

'Practising a neutral accent,' Jaecen replied in his usual lilt. 'Can't have my accent giving us away when we get to Karana Downs.'

Covering his mouth, Maldwyn yawned. 'Sorry, I didn't sleep too well.'

'That's okay. We might have to wake Erik though,' Jaecen said, looking over at the mound where Erik had bundled himself under his blanket.

'You might be right,' Maldwyn agreed, surprised that Erik seemed to be sleeping so well.

Jaecen got up, walked over to Erik, and gently shook him awake. Erik opened his eyes, stirred in his bedroll, clicked his tongue on the roof of his mouth a few times, and rolled over, drifting back to sleep.

Giggling, mostly to himself, Maldwyn started rolling up his blankets to strap to the bottom of his pack. Sighing, Jaecen folded his arms and scratched his head, struggling to remain polite as he tried to wake his comrade.

'Here, try this,' Maldwyn said, pulling out his waterskin and handing it to Jaecen.

'Really?'

Maldwyn shrugged. 'It might help him wake.'

As Maldwyn turned his back to pull out some food to coax Erik out of his bedroll, he heard water trickling behind him. Looking back, he saw Jaecen standing, holding the waterskin over a soaked, groaning Erik, who looked startled.

Cupping a hand over his mouth, Maldwyn said, 'I meant for you to offer him a drink.'

'Oh!' Jaecen grimaced apologetically to Erik, who appeared quite offended as he sat up.

'Good morning, Jaecen,' Erik declared in a perturbed tone of voice.

'Sorry about that.' Jaecen offered the remaining water to Erik, who scowled up at him.

Maldwyn grinned to himself as he turned away and pulled out some bread and cheese from his pack. He worked hard not to burst out laughing, letting out a few giggles under his breath.

'Erm… if you're hungry, I have some food here for us,' Maldwyn mumbled, offering some breakfast to break the tension as Erik patted his face dry with his thick blankets.

After they had eaten, and Erik had pulled on his simple travelling clothes and his olive-coloured fleece jacket, which was buttoned up to his collar, they finished packing up their camp and set out for the final part of their trek to Karana Downs.

*   *   *   *   *

The rest of their hike was easier than the day before, the ground flattened out as they reached the end of the mountain ranges. More and more grass carpeted the forest floor as they neared the edge of the woods, and the trees stood further apart, splaying their arms with ease.

Every so often, the large oaks would rustle their leaves in the soft breeze. Butterflies would sweep through the air to dance around the travellers' faces, showing off their beating, brightly coloured wings. Squirrels squeaked as they raced up the wrinkled branches.

Spring had always been Maldwyn's favourite season. He liked the perfect, temperate weather and the way everything blossomed and came to life. Creatures that had migrated north, chasing the sun's warmth, or tucked themselves away to sleep for the winter, returned in abundance, celebrating the arrival of warmer weather.

In the distance, Maldwyn heard the idle laughter of children. 'We're coming up on the farmlands on the outskirts of the town around the main keep.' Jaecen advised, leading the way through the thinning crowds of trees. 'Our people have only ever gotten as far as the town itself.'

Wide, open pastures with roaming cattle were visible beyond the tree line. Amid the gentle, rolling hills, Maldwyn spotted three young children racing each other across the fields. A small, humble dwelling with fencing around the crops poking through the soil, nestled into the base of the hill.

'This way, Eminence,' Jaecen told them over his shoulder, steering Maldwyn and Erik toward the north, in the opposite direction to the simple home.

Pulling the straps of his pack back up his shoulders, Maldwyn put his head down and followed Jaecen, watching his own feet as he walked. After the lack of sleep that he had the evening prior, Maldwyn was looking forward to resting when they reached the town. Erik was looking exhausted too from hiking up and down mountains, despite that he had slept well and was quite alert.

Along the way, the former hunter hadn't been able to resist a few jests about being thirsty, which Jaecen had been able to laugh about. It had been a long time since Maldwyn had travelled with anyone and he had forgotten the simple merriment that ensued.

The closer they got to the keep, the more timber-clad farmhouses they passed, which appeared to be shrinking in size. Some must have been no larger than a few rooms. The people in the area seemed dirty and wore haggard, shaggy clothes they kept to themselves, barely taking notice of the three passing travellers. Maldwyn pondered how many of these people had lost income when the mine was taken from them, or how many had witnessed firsthand the disputes between the mountain folk and the king's forces.

There was a strong steely, ash smell coming from the town's forges. Taking the back streets into the downs, Maldwyn was struck by the piles of muck and broken pottery on the footpath, cutting into the barefooted beggars, as they reached the main streets of the town.

The buildings had few windows and were a little worse for wear. People slept on torn rags in the alleys shooting off the main paths, between the tightly packed buildings. Their pallid complexion and tattered clothes made Maldwyn feel guilty. Hordes of people swarmed the streets, ignoring the paupers grabbing at their clothes.

A small-framed, elderly man, sitting against the wall of a shop, wheezing as he breathed, grabbed at Maldwyn's neatly tailored, charcoal coat. Maldwyn paused to acknowledge him, noticing his horseshoe hair, deep wrinkles from spending days on end under the sun and missing teeth. As Maldwyn considered giving him some spare coin, Jaecen grabbed him, pulling him along.

'Neither of you should give them anything,' Jaecen instructed, putting on his neutral accent. Erik glanced at

Maldwyn, sharing a distressed expression. 'It's hard to tell the poor from the very poor around here and you can't save them all.'

'I didn't know things were this bad,' Erik uttered.

'All the money is hoarded inside the keep.' Jaecen indicated toward the black stone wall rising from the ground. Guards could be seen manning the wall between the parapets. 'We need to get through this district to the safer areas. The crime is too high in these parts.'

Maldwyn and Erik trusted Jaecen's judgement, following him through the mobs, and skirting the walls of the keep. There was a marked difference as they twisted around a corner, heading toward what Jaecen told them was the main entrance to the keep.

Soldiers were patrolling these streets in greater numbers, wearing the deep blue leather armour of the king's guards. Seeing the number of soldiers from the capital that was stationed in Karana Downs made Maldwyn wonder how many guards had been positioned here by the king over the years.

Crossing a broad street, wide enough to fit horse-drawn wagons, Maldwyn noticed that these buildings were better maintained and had windows watching over the well-guarded street. There were vines, creeping up the walls of the timber and stucco shops and blooming bushes sprouted by the covered entryways.

These people's clothes weren't stained and torn, as they were in the slums. However, they weren't exactly good quality either, when compared to the people in the capital, or the folk in the mountains.

'We need to make a stop before heading to the inn,' Jaecen said, stopping to let a man, pulling a cart full of supplies, go by them.

'What for?' Maldwyn asked, gathering by the blank expression on Erik's face that he didn't know either.

'We have some spies nearby. They're the ones that have been sending Jerrik reports.' Jaecen itched the tip of his nose. 'We'll want to know if they have any news for us.'

'Lead the way,' Maldwyn replied, gesturing to the crushed, dirt path ahead of them as the overloaded cart was wheeled out of their way, leaving a trail up the street.

The three of them pressed on, sticking close together. There was a powdery residue in the air, coming from the steel furnaces on the edge of town. Looking to the sky, Maldwyn noted that it was well after midday from the way the sun hung lazily over the downs.

Guiding them toward a quaint shopfront that had a modest, stall window and a closed sign hanging from the door, Jaecen glanced back.

'This is the place.'

As Maldwyn got closer, he saw that there were petite, ceramic ramekins, which were filled with small mounds of crystalline salts, dried herbs and colourful spices, lined along the stall counter.

Stepping inside, Maldwyn was overwhelmed by the strong, tangy smell. Pails of herbs and spices lined the shop shelves, with large metal scoops dug into the containers. Metal bowls, containing samples, were haphazardly arranged on the counter, around a set of large, metal scales.

An older woman with squinty, brown eyes, leathery skin and thin lips was seated behind the counter. She seemed not to notice them until they stood a few paces from her.

'Uller's blessing, Jaecen!' She spoke in a hoarse voice, masking her minute accent as she looked at the ranger down the bridge of her nose. 'We expected you earlier in the day.'

'Sorry, Ines, we had a later start than expected.' Jaecen put his hands on his hips, eyeing Erik. 'Is your husband, Bayard, here?'

'He's waiting in the back,' she told them, pointing with her thumb over her shoulder to the lightweight curtain hanging over a doorway.

'Thank you, Ines.'

Jaecen ducked through the curtain, leading Erik and Maldwyn into a neat office that had extra stores on shelves. There was a simple desk topped with accounting papers that were bound together with sturdy twine and a thin-tipped writing brush next to a little inkwell by the records. A gentleman reclined in a basic timber chair behind the table.

'It's about time you showed up!' The elderly man said in a gruff voice, standing up from the chair. He had milky eyes and pockmarked cheeks. 'Did you run into some trouble on the way?'

Jaecen shook his head.

'Just a late start on our end.' Maldwyn had a feeling Erik's oversleeping wasn't going to be forgotten for the rest of their stay in the downs, and longer, probably. 'This is His Eminence, Maldwyn,' Jaecen announced, making Maldwyn uncomfortable as the man bowed.

He heard Ines rise from her seat and pull the curtain back to take a peek. As Maldwyn looked over at her, she lowered her head respectfully.

'This here, is Erik, the Raven Clan sorcerer that has been given refuge from the palace.' Stepping more to the side to let Maldwyn and Erik move further in, Jaecen signalled for Ines to join them. 'Maldwyn, Erik, this is Ines and Bayard, the most cunning spies we have in the area.'

'You flatter us,' Ines said, batting a hand at him. 'We're nothing more than a couple of spice traders from the mountains, keeping a listen out wherever we go.'

Bayard smiled, clasping his hands behind his back. 'We used to be rangers back in the day,' he told them, beaming with pride. 'Ines and I are just happy we can still be useful in our ripe age.'

'You'll always be useful and have a home with your people,' Jaecen said, slapping a hand to the man's shoulder. 'We're about to head over to the inn to find a place to rest, do you have any updates for us?'

'We do,' Bayard declared, sounding a little concerned. 'We didn't have anything until a customer came in recently, just a few days ago.'

'It was the wife of one of the soldiers around here,' Ines added.

Erik frowned and stepped back on his heel. 'What did she tell you?'

'Well, she came in to buy her usual amount of dried sage,' Ines began, rubbing along her jaw with her nails and scrunching her face together around her nose, reflecting on the morning's events, 'and she was talking about her husband, and their newborn… Nathan… no, Ethan. I can't remember,' she mumbled, making a funny expression.

'Just get to the point,' Bayard told her, shaking his head.

She scowled. 'If you know it so well, then why don't you tell them.'

Bayard sighed and rubbed his forehead, frustrated.

'Anyway,' Ines continued, turning back to lock eyes with Maldwyn. 'She was telling me about extra forces being sent from the capital to reclaim the mine.'

'King Viktor is sending more men for the mine?' Maldwyn blurted. He had thought, or rather hoped, that the king would let the mine stay under the Erendil's control.

'Why yes, Eminence.' Ines blinked as she stared at him, perhaps unbelieving that he was who her people believed him to be; Maldwyn couldn't be sure.

Bayard folded his arms over his chest. 'Apparently, they are being led by Prince Harlan.'

'Would the prince betray us?' Jaecen asked as all eyes shot to Maldwyn. 'We did imprison him for a time.'

'I remember,' Maldwyn scolded, putting them in place. Jaecen's guilty expression suggested that he had forgotten Maldwyn had been held captive too. It had been a long day, and Maldwyn didn't mean to make everyone ill at ease. 'No, I don't believe he would betray your people. He needs you.'

'I agree with Maldwyn,' Erik chimed in, alleviating the tension. 'Prince Harlan is many things, but I have a hard time believing he would use the mountain peoples in such a way as this.'

'It has to be a ruse of some kind… perhaps to get into the keep.' Jaecen touched his hand to his cheek in thought.

'He has been looking for evidence against Lord Darius for a few months now. As far as we know, he only has hearsay.' Ines ran her finger along the underneath of her eye.

'Not to mention, he is still looking for his sister,' Bayard mumbled. 'I feel we could have avoided this if we had been able to get one of our people into that blasted keep.'

'That's not your fault,' Maldwyn offered, feeling bad for them blaming themselves.

'Does this change your plans?' Bayard turned to the three of them, asking broadly.

'Not our part of it,' Jaecen said. 'We are here to infiltrate the keep. If anything, the news may be good for us.'

'How so?' Bayard looked puzzled as he glanced over to Jaecen.

'Because,' Jaecen answered. 'Prince Harlan may be able to get us inside. At the very least, his presence may create a distraction that we can use to our advantage.'

'We can't count on that alone. Things may not work out the way we hope and we need a contingency plan,' Bayard muttered and let out a laugh under his breath. 'In some way, I suppose… thanks to the prince, we have an option on the table. There's something I never thought I'd hear myself say.'

'I never thought I'd hear it either.' Ines cleared her throat.

'Okay, great! We'll do some networking and see if we can find other options, in case we need them,' Jaecen said, sounding very pleased with the news. 'Is there anything else we need to know before we leave?'

'Not that I can think of.' Bayard said, looking over to his wife for confirmation. Erik sneezed into his elbow and apologised to the room.

'No, I think that is all we have today.' Ines turned to the three of them and smiled in a sort of grandmotherly way. 'You three should get to the inn. We can talk more tomorrow if we think of anything we have missed.'

'Thank you. Your help is always appreciated.' Jaecen smiled and began to head for the curtain.

Ines waved them all through, following close behind Maldwyn. As Jaecen and Erik left the shop, Ines grabbed Maldwyn by the arm.

'I was very sorry to hear about your capture. Your ability to forgive our people for what we did says a lot about what an incredible person you are. It has been an honour to finally meet you, Eminence.'

Maldwyn thanked her as she bowed and then followed the others out of the shop. As they walked through the streets, Maldwyn thought about her words. He had accepted their help when he needed it and had been flattered by their hospitality, but forgiveness felt like more than that, and he wasn't sure he had given it.

The inn Jaecen led them to was like any other. It was a large, two-storey building on the corner of a crossroads with a gabled roof and a veranda that wrapped around the building facing the streets. Inside, beyond the dining hall, was a working kitchen near the storage area which was above the cellar. There were a few private function areas, which could be hired for events, but they were currently empty and the doors to the rooms were closed. Out the back of the inn, Jaecen told them, was the chamber room and the stables. Upstairs, Maldwyn assumed, was the accommodation.

'Riley!' Shouted a rotund man with a deep voice, wiry, steel-coloured hair, and a long beard. 'I hadn't expected you back in town until the summer!'

'I am scouting for wares to trade,' Jaecen replied, keeping his accent undetectable. 'The harsh winter has my stores running thin. These men work for me. We'll need a few rooms and a tab for the duration of our stay.'

The man rustled around in some drawers beneath the counter he was standing behind, pulling out some keys and handing them to Jaecen. 'You know how it works around here. Rooms upstairs and make sure you stop by this counter to pay before you leave.'

'Thank you,' Jaecen offered, handing Maldwyn and Erik each a key. Locking eyes with Maldwyn, he looked as though he had been struck with a thought. He turned back to the man. 'Quick question, do you know if Leith will be at the tavern today?'

Jaecen had mentioned, back in the mountains, that the man who ran the inn was a personal friend of Leith's. The tavern was on the same street and the two looked out for each other's establishments from time to time, warning each other about unsavoury customers and keeping an eye out for trouble when the other was away.

'Not at the moment. He's away getting supplies. He should be back in a couple of days though.' The man leaned forward, resting his forearms on the counter. 'Should I take a message for him?'

'No,' Jaecen quickly looked over to Maldwyn and made a face, checking that this was correct. 'I'll catch him when he comes back. Thanks again!'

The three wound their way up the creaky, wooden stairs to their respective rooms. Maldwyn was pleased to see the room was neat. Directly in front of Maldwyn, in the centre of the far wall, there was a wide, simple bed with a straw mattress, ivory cotton sheets and a reasonably thick, beige bedcover.

To the bed's right was a bedside table with a cupboard underneath. The short, fat, buttery candle placed on a metal dish on the table's top was fresh. At the foot of the bed was a deep trunk that had bulky leather straps and large, sturdy buckles. To the left of the bed, was a blank space before an open, leaded, colourless glass window patterned with a series of perfectly stacked diamonds.

On the left-hand wall, was a clean fireplace, which was like a little cave burrowing into the stone exterior wall with no mantlepiece over the top. The grey stone of the left and far walls were in stark contrast to the beige stucco interior wall to the right of where Maldwyn stood in the doorway.

Relieved to be able to sit for a while, Maldwyn peeled his pack off his shoulders, placed it on top of the flat-topped trunk, and lay on the mattress on his back, stretching his arms out to his sides. As he lay there, Maldwyn thought to himself that he would have to get up before he fell asleep, but allowed himself a few minutes to indulge in the comfort of a bed.

As time went by, Maldwyn hardly noticed the drop in temperature. Turning his head to gaze out the window, Maldwyn thought of how the sun would stay in the clear blue sky for a while longer, even though it was almost time to eat and retire for the evening.

That was one thing Maldwyn loved about the winter months. The sun would set earlier, making it easier to go to sleep. Rubbing his head, soothing the headache settling in from the lack of sleep he had had the prior evening, Maldwyn pulled himself up and headed for the dining hall downstairs, where he supposed Jaecen and Erik would be waiting.

As expected, Jaecen and Erik were seated at one of the beaten tables, looking as weary as Maldwyn felt. Erik was already snacking on a slice of buttered bread, which had been plucked from the dish in the centre of the table.

The dining hall was half empty, with people spread out, sitting at every second table or so, making Maldwyn speculate whether many travellers came through Karana Downs. The hall felt much warmer than his room as heat radiated out from the kitchens. When Maldwyn moved to sit at the table where his comrades were waiting, the man that had been at the front counter came over.

'We'll bring some stew over for each of you,' he told them. 'Riley, you should know Oliver was pleased to hear you were in town. He's just feeding the horses out the back, but he's going to stop by your table soon after.'

'Great, thank you,' Jaecen replied.

As the man walked away, Erik turned to Jaecen, leaning his elbow on the table. 'Riley?'

'Sorry, I forgot to tell you both about that,' Jaecen replied, quietly. 'It's the identity I go by in these parts. Riley Lindholm, a travelling merchant. It's best that Jaecen of the Erendil, ranger and murderer of the king's men, not be associated with a person frequenting inns and taverns in the downs.'

'That makes sense,' Maldwyn chimed in, reclining back into his seat. 'Who's Oliver?'

'He's the stableman.' Jaecen looked around checking no one was listening. 'He's also a member of the resistance here.'

'Resistance?' Erik crossed his arms, lowered his voice and leaned closer to Jaecen. 'Against Lord Darius?'

'Against the king.' Jaecen made a serious face, dimpling between his brows. The warm glow of the candles made his ginger hair appear darker. 'Not all of us can abide the displacement caused to so many, nor executions of people like you. Oliver's parents were renowned in the downs. They owned a store selling wares to sorcerers. When he and his brother were adolescents, their parents were executed under the king's new law.'

Maldwyn sat taller and stared at the rough table, thinking about the king's decrees, mulling over the thought of how many people must have died under King Viktor's rule.

'Oliver and his brother, Loris, both joined the resistance. Loris went so far as to join the guard a few months ago, but he is stationed in the town and never gets close to the keep. He does, however, receive a lot of information from reports or casual gossip among the guards, which he shares with his brother. Oliver, on the other hand, is limited by a severe limp, so he is unable to join the guard or a number of trades. Working here, he can eavesdrop on travellers and report back to the resistance with news from the inn or his brother.'

'I hadn't realised there was such a movement,' Maldwyn confessed, feeling a little strange about the idea. He wanted the king's rule to end as much as anyone, but he wasn't sure he supported a violent uprising. 'Are these resistance people dangerous?'

Erik may have been a hunter, but his people were mostly pacifists, and he looked worried too. Picking at the skin around his fingernails, Erik avoided eye contact, clearly uncomfortable with the idea.

Jaecen let out a breath. 'Angry people are always dangerous.' Holding up a hand, he signalled for the conversation to end.

As Maldwyn looked over to where Jaecen's eyes darted, he saw the man who owned the inn heading for their table, carrying a tray. The tip of his long beard rested on the edge of the salver as he placed it down on the table.

Carefully, the rotund man unpacked the tray, serving them each with a bowl of stew, spoons sticking out of the bowls, and a mug of ale. The subtle earthy smell of the turnip, mushroom and leek pottage reminded Maldwyn of home. For a mere moment, he acknowledged the loss he felt deep in his core, yearning for his former life, then he let it go and thanked the man as he turned to leave.

The broth was a perfect consistency; not too watery, and not too gluggy. The vegetables were tender and tasted fresh, and the ale was sweet and almost fruity. All in all, it was a decent meal, better than Maldwyn expected.

As they were eating, Maldwyn heard a door thud and noticed a skinny man with a square jaw, wheat hair and a limp coming toward them. He had kind eyes, despite the nervous expression on his face.

'Riley!' The man Maldwyn presumed to be Oliver held his hands out, indicating that he was surprised by his visit. Jaecen smiled and glanced up at the man. 'How's the life of a travelling merchant these days?'

'Same as usual,' Jaecen replied, shrugging. 'Oliver, these are my associates, Maldwyn and Erik.'

'Pleased to meet you,' Oliver said, looking at them a little awkwardly. 'I have some things to discuss with you when you're finished eating.'

Jaecen held the back of his hand over his mouth and lowered his voice. 'Feel free to take a seat. You can speak freely in front of them.'

Oliver surveyed Maldwyn and Erik before taking a seat at their table. 'Are they your real names,' Oliver asked, flicking a sly expression at Jaecen.

Erik's brows arched. 'You know he's from the mountains?'

'And that his real name is Jaecen,' Oliver confirmed, grinning.

'Oliver and his brother have been informants of ours for a while.' Jaecen ran his fingertips along his jawline. 'Yes, they are their real names. What do you have for us?'

'It's about Prince Harlan.' Maldwyn shot his head up from his stew, interested in what the man was about to say, given what Bayard and Ines had already told them.

'We already know he's on his way here with the king's forces,' Jaecen stated, sounding unimpressed.

'Maybe… but did you know he's in danger?' Oliver smirked, full of hubris. 'My brother heard reports earlier today that the prince and his regiment will be taking a short rest at Valondale Castle, about a day's ride south of here.

'No one from the palace has stepped near that place since Queen Sonia was executed.' Maldwyn wrinkled his forehead. 'The lord has been in contact with traitors among the prince's guard to organise a plot to assassinate the prince on his march north. The prince is to be lured into a trap not far from the castle.

'He'll be brought to the waterfall in the woods where he will be ambushed. He must have gotten under Lord Darius's skin back in the palace. I wish I could have been there. Who knew the king's son might turn out to be an ally—no matter how temporary that may be?'

Trying to remember his training and maintain his focus, Maldwyn struggled against the tightness tugging at his chest as his stomach knotted.

'When is this set to take place?' Maldwyn asked in a distant tone.

'The prince is set to arrive at the castle tomorrow afternoon,' Oliver answered, tucking one of his feet under his chair. 'My best guess would be tomorrow night. The forces will set up camp outside the castle. So, probably midnight, when the moon is high.'

'How will he be lured to the waterfall at that time of night?' Erik asked before taking in a heaped spoonful of his pottage.

'I don't know,' Oliver said in a flat tone.

'We can't make it in time to help him,' Jaecen rubbed his temples seeming stressed. 'We don't have horses. We couldn't even get him a message if we tried.'

'I can lend you a horse, but only one.' Oliver checked the area and made a face, shrugging. 'Any more and it wouldn't go unnoticed.'

Erik clicked his fingers and pointed toward Maldwyn. 'You are the only one the prince knows and trusts of the three of us. You should go to warn him. We need him on our side if we're to someday overthrow King Viktor.'

'He's right,' Jaecen muttered, locking eyes with Maldwyn. 'You should go to his aid.'

The thought of reuniting with the prince knotted Maldwyn's stomach further. He had yearned to return to his life in the palace, but that life had come to feel more and more like a distant memory.

'We don't have time to send messages.' Turning back to the stableman, Jaecen asked, 'Do you have any more details, anything that could help?'

'There aren't guards at Valondale Castle anymore as it has been all but abandoned. It operates on a skeleton staff. My brother's understanding was that the lord has mercenaries to frame your people for the prince's murder.' Drawing his mouth over to one side, Oliver bit his cheek. 'You should have time to rest here for the night,' Oliver said, turning to Maldwyn as he rose from his seat. 'I'll have a horse ready for you at dawn. If the rebellion is to succeed someday, we need someone like Prince Harlan to lead it. We need a person that can unite those of us calling for an uprising and take charge. Without him, I worry we will never be rid of that filth on the throne.'

'You're right, Oliver.' Jaecen sounded just as disheartened as Oliver appeared. Once the man had limped away, the ranger faced Maldwyn and said, 'You will need to trust your training, Eminence. We won't be by your side. Now is the time for you to focus.'

Erik placed a hand on Maldwyn's shoulder, 'Trust your power. When you return, we will be waiting for you. Hopefully, we'll have secured a way into the keep by then.'

Maldwyn took in a deep breath and stared at his stew, having lost his appetite. Together, the three of them mumbled through the rest of their evening. It was clear they all had other things on their mind and everything was resting on Maldwyn's ability to not fail, as he had done many times before.

When they finished eating and retired to their rooms for the night, Maldwyn sat on his bed for a time, meditating, focusing his mind on the task at hand. When his worries had eased, and Maldwyn felt he would be able to sleep, he stripped off his clothes and slipped into the bed.

CHAPTER EIGHTEEN

Dancing in Time

THE MORNING MIST clouded the way toward Valondale Castle as Maldwyn rode south, following the directions Jaecen and Oliver had given him. The horse's hooves pounded into the ground, tearing up the grassy fields as they raced the sun toward the rise of the moon, signalling the day's end and, possibly, Maldwyn's failure. The grey rock of the river's edge had been buffed by the raging flood as the river rushed south, searching for a gap leading to the ocean where the water would find its home in the sea.

Skirting the base of the Anhalt Mountains, Maldwyn passed into the forest once more and was struck by the pungent smell of the damp wood and the sweet, perfumed flowers blossoming on the shrubs, padding the forest floor. New leaves were shooting out from the rippled arms of the trees like tiny growths. Chaotic, gnarly roots clutched the dirt in their claw-like grip as though they were anchors, securing the tree to which they were stemmed to the ground, making Maldwyn's horse leap over the misshapen hurdles.

Maldwyn stopped once to let the horse rest, hoping he was making good time. The reigns to which he gripped too tight had reddened his palms as he shadowed the sun's light, speeding through the endless, enduring memory that existed in these woods to where fate awaited him at the waterfall's edge.

The sounds of the rapid water, rustling leaves and chirping wildlife were like an orchestra of nature, spurring his horse to gallop faster into the waning day. Guided by the river, darkness did not slow them. His horse charged through the dappled starlit wood.

As he heard the splashing falls, Maldwyn looked up. He spotted the prince, back facing the river. Prince Harlan was encircled by several dark figures. From this distance, Maldwyn could not be sure how many mercenaries the prince faced.

Tuning out his loud thoughts, Maldwyn focused on the harmonious melodies of the world around him. He heard water droplets dripping from the low leaves into the rippling river's surface. He heard the perfect chanting of a hooting owl in the trees overhead. The pounding of his horse's hooves matched the rhythm of his beating heart.

Closing his eyes and taking an almighty breath, finding his quiet centre, Maldwyn pulled his horse to a stop a few feet from the prince. He somersaulted from the saddle, holding his arms crossed to his chest, and twirled through the air.

Time felt meaningless in his spinning bubble, listening to his surroundings as his robes fluttered through the air. Hood drawn over his face, Maldwyn wore the clothes he had been gifted by the mountain folk.

Knowing he may need to erupt with the flurry of power that burned within him, Maldwyn wanted to not be recognised. The hood would hide his face, and the robes themselves would indicate that the prince's saviour was one of the many among the Erendil.

Landing between the prince and his assailants, Maldwyn held his hands up, ready for the sounds of war to guide him, unarmed, through the twilight battle. Half a dozen roughened warriors held swords, edging forward.

'What's this?' One of the mercenaries mocked. 'One guard! You think you're enough to protect the prince!'

A man, wearing the royal blue leather armour of the king's forces stepped forward from the black shadows. As the light of the moon touched his face, Maldwyn recognised the knight by the large mole on his jaw. It was Ser Gerard.

'That's not his guard.' Gerard retorted, sounding a little offended. 'No matter. Kill them both.'

Releasing a fraction of his power, Maldwyn slowed time around him just enough to give himself an edge, but not so much as to be thought of as unnatural. Though he had come to better control his gift, Maldwyn felt it best to hold it in reserve as a last resort, hoping to be able to face the prince. A moment, where they could reunite without Maldwyn needing to fear execution orders.

Catching the wrist of one of the fighters swinging a sword toward his head, Maldwyn yanked the man's hand around, causing him to drop his sword. Knocking his feet out from under him, Maldwyn spun, forming fists.

Another swinging arm came in from the other side. Ducking in time to dodge the slice, Maldwyn calmly thrust a powerful fist into the man's chest, forcing the air from his lungs.

As the man lying prone on the ground struggled to his feet, and the other caught his breath, the rest of the band of soldiers rushed into action. Being one with the air around him, Maldwyn danced with time.

He deflected blows with fluidity, delivered furious kicks with graceful precision, and pirouetted to the prince's defence, whirling him out of danger. The fabric of time connecting each moment yielded to his power.

In constant motion, his flow was endless as he duelled the shadowy figures wielding swords. One of the mercenaries went for his heels. Maldwyn served a flying kick to the side of the man's head, making him crash to the ground, unconscious. The sound of the sword landing on the rock stilled the spiritual orchestra of the trees.

The prince had tried a few times to jump in and help, but Maldwyn had been quick to thrust him out of harm's way. The gauntlet for Prince Harlan's life had begun and Maldwyn could not allow him to risk his life.

Maldwyn's oneness with his surroundings was unmatched as he somersaulted off a tree, carrying himself on the breeze. He thwarted an incoming blast, swiping it aside.

One by one, each of the attackers fell.

Until a fist, connecting with his jaw, sent Maldwyn staggering back into a tree by the waterfall's edge, making him lose his grip over the current of time. Unleashing a torrent of blows into Maldwyn's stomach and head, Ser Gerard battered him as his goons slept, cradling wounds. Unable to bring the dance back, or to break free from the fists bashing him, Maldwyn brought his arms up defensively, covering as much of his head, chest and stomach as possible.

In the background, he heard movement as a shadow grabbed a sword, which had been laying alone on the grey rock by the water's edge. Trying to regain his breath and control, Maldwyn attempted to break free only to open himself to more strikes.

The shadow moved.

Blood spurted on Maldwyn's face as the sword plunged into the knight's back, poking through his chest. Grabbing Maldwyn by his robes, Ser Gerard stumbled as he staggered away. Slipping on the wet rock, he fell to the ground defeated, tossing Maldwyn backwards into the falls.

Maldwyn stopped time as he went over the edge, but even this could not break his fall as he smashed into the foaming surface of the water.

Powerless against the strength of the falls, unable to swim, Maldwyn sank beneath the force of the tumbling river, which pressed him deeper into the pool at the waterfall's base. There was no way to save himself. No simple flame could burn through this amount of water before he drowned, and stopping time wouldn't bring him to the surface. It would only serve to prolong this painful moment.

He felt as though the water had come alive and hands were pulling him down. Having not taken a breath before falling, Maldwyn was desperate for air and couldn't stop the gasp from escaping his mouth.

Spattering and convulsing beneath the water, Maldwyn felt the torture of drowning. Then, in complete silence, as his gasping ended, he stared up to see the moon's light glistening on the surface of the water above him, like drowning pearls, only he was the one beneath the crashing river.

* * * * *

When Harlan saw the hooded man, clearly one of Jerrik's men, go over the edge of the waterfall, he ran forward and searched the surface of the water, fifty or sixty feet below him. The misty spray at the base of the fall obscured his view, but so far as he could see, the man had not come up for air.

Quiet, he waited, watching for any sign of movement breaking free from the flowing river, knowing that he owed the man his life. The wind shifted. An owl hooted. The water splattered over the rocky ledge. The final breath of the dying knight stirred around him, yet there was no sign of his saviour.

Looking over at the glazed eyes of the knight, Harlan pondered how long Gerard had been in league with Lord Darius. As the empty eyes stared back at him, Harlan wondered whether more of the soldiers camping on the other side of the castle grounds might be compromised.

As the moonlit water endured unaffected, Harlan looked back down, still seeing no sign of Jerrik's man. Shaking his head, indebted to the drowning man, Harlan knew he had to do something.

Taking a few paces back, the prince stripped off his buckled jacket, tossed it on the ground, and pulled off his boots. Drawing in a few large breaths, he sprinted and dove over the edge of the falls, plunging into the water below.

The weight of the water crashing over him helped to push him deeper, but he struggled to see anything in the hazy, blackness of the water. Feeling around with his hands out in front of him, Harlan swam through the flowing river, unable to get a grip on anything that seemed like it didn't belong in the water.

Needing another breath of air, Harlan swam back through the soft, flowing current of water, lifting his head above the surface of the river. The fragrant aroma of the woods filled his nostrils as he drew in another great breath before submerging himself back beneath the waterline. Following the light of the moon, he swam through the murky river, until he saw the gentle swaying of fabric.

Wrapping his arms around the back of the man's torso, Harlan kicked and felt that the man's boots were stuck on a submerged log. Swimming down, the prince freed the man's laces from where they had gotten caught on a protruding branch attached to the log and propelled them up to the surface of the water. The back of the man's hooded head flopped lifelessly against the prince's chest as Harlan swam them away from the mossy rock wall of the waterfall, where the river plunged over them.

Dragging the man's limp body up onto the grassy area by the river's side, Harlan collapsed on the ground beside the man. Glancing over to the body to his left, the prince noted that his chest was not moving and he appeared to not be breathing.

Rolling over to check whether the man's breath was too shallow to be noticed, he reached out to feel whether there was air passing out from his nose. As he turned the man's head under the moonlight, the prince recognised the lifeless face staring at him.

'No,' he muttered, cupping a hand to Maldwyn's smooth, bruised cheek. 'No… no,' he continued to mumble to himself as he pushed Maldwyn over to lie on his side and cleared the grit clogging his airway. As there appeared to be no change, Harlan jabbed him a few times in the back between his shoulder blades, trying to induce coughing. 'Don't you dare die now!'

As Maldwyn coughed, spurting out a gush of water, he began to shake. Holding his hand, Harlan clung to him, tucking himself in behind Maldwyn, holding him as he struggled to breathe.

The woods were quiet and the honeyed air calmed the prince as he wondered how it was Maldwyn was alive. Although he was curious, Harlan didn't say or ask anything of Maldwyn, because he didn't care how he had come to be here, he only cared that he was by his side.

Letting Maldwyn rest, normalising his breath, Harlan nuzzled into the silky hood over his head. As Maldwyn calmed, the prince let go of his hand and ran the tips of his fingers along Maldwyn's arm to his shoulder, coaxing him to roll over to his back.

In the full light of the moon, Harlan gazed into Maldwyn's green, seafoam-coloured eyes. Running his hand along Maldwyn's smooth jaw, the prince touched his forehead to Maldwyn's, hardly believing that he was lying right before him. Tracing the air around Maldwyn's mouth with his own, Harlan lingered in his warmth, feeling the space between them.

Swept up in his presence, Harlan pressed his lips against Maldwyn's, as he had done once before when Maldwyn was weakened from a poisoned arrow. Slow and gentle, he longed to live in this moment.

Pulling away, Harlan stared into Maldwyn's eyes, mesmerised by the lime flecks that caught the moon's light.

'I thought you were dead,' he murmured.

As Maldwyn knitted his brows together, he lifted his head slightly toward the prince. Harlan closed his eyes for a moment, relieved that Maldwyn was alive and breathing. Maldwyn lifted his hand, running his fingers along the nape of the prince's neck. Harlan's breath caught in his throat.

Slow and uncertain, Harlan thought, Maldwyn raised his head from the grass and returned the prince's kiss. Lost in the sensation of Maldwyn's affection, Harlan relaxed his shoulders and ran his fingers back into Maldwyn's wet, walnut-coloured hair as he sank into the rhythm of his soft, smooth lips.

Slipping his hand down to the leather belt around the waist of Maldwyn's robes, Harlan unbuckled it and untied the silk sash beneath the belt. Sliding the saturated robes back off Maldwyn's shoulders, Harlan kissed his bare neck. When Maldwyn pulled at the prince's shirt, Harlan helped tug it up over his head. Running his hands up the prince's back, Maldwyn rolled him over and placed soft kisses all over his chest.

Losing himself to his passion, Harlan fumbled as he tore off Maldwyn's shirt. Together, under the light of the moon, they wrapped themselves up in each other's warmth, enjoying the pure delight of their reunion.

PART THREE

CHAPTER NINETEEN

Welcome to Valondale Castle, Where Memories Reside

'WHAT HAPPENED TO YOU?' The prince muttered as he lay on his back on the grass, staring up at the sky with one hand behind his head.

Maldwyn lay with his hands resting on his stomach, bruised from having been pummelled by Ser Gerard, he glanced over to glimpse the prince and was captivated by the way his stone-blue eyes shone up at the stars.

Looking up at the crescent moon through the gap in the trees where the river split the forest in two, Maldwyn hung onto the question for a while, letting the sound of the soothing, flowing river's current fill the space between them. He wondered what he could say that could answer the prince's question and sum up the last few months.

Should he mention the death of his mother, the destruction of his home, the way he had been hunted like a dog by the king's guards, or the haunting he experienced within the ruined temple? How could he explain everything he had learned in the mountains?

'I lived,' Maldwyn mumbled, hearing a touch of remorse in his own voice. The guilt and shame he felt for surviving the king's attack crippled him from time to time. 'Life went on.'

'I'm sorry about your mother… and your village,' Prince Harlan offered, seeming to pick up on Maldwyn's internal pain.

Maldwyn kept watching the bright, shimmering moon, despite that the prince turned his head to gaze over at him. Eventually, Maldwyn guessed that Prince Harlan sensed he didn't want to talk about matters as the prince twisted his head back up to the sky.

'I never told the sovereign I was headed to the downs, but why didn't he tell me you were alive?'

'I'm not sure.' Breathing in the sweet, night air, Maldwyn watched the silhouette of the tree canopy, waving their bushy limbs in front of the stars. 'I suppose, he thought he was keeping me safe, and it seemed unimportant after a while.'

'I doubt that.'

'He and his people saved my life.' Maldwyn clenched his wounded jaw, struggling with his feelings concerning the mountain folk. First, they were his captors, seeing him as the prince's lowly servant, then, they were his saviours, worshipping him for the person they believed he would one day become. 'I owe them more than my thanks.'

'Will you return to them, go back to the Anhalt Mountains?'

Maldwyn smirked as he became very aware of the space between them, lying side by side, watching the stars. 'Not exactly.' Forgetting the pain in his jaw, Maldwyn pursed his lips, trying to hide the smile creeping up his face. 'I wasn't in the mountains, I was in Karana Downs, trying to help you. The keep has been difficult for the sovereign to breach, but a few of us were sent to try and get past the gate.'

'A few of you? So, others are waiting in the downs,' the prince licked his lips and smiled, obviously pleased to hear they were headed to the same place, 'and you plan on staying for a while.'

'I guess,' Maldwyn said, smiling and turning his head on the grass to look at the prince. The ring on the chain around his neck glinted at the blinking stars, seeming to hum throughout the fibre of Maldwyn's being as he stared at it and recalled Tiana's suspicions that it might be some sort of magical relic. 'Why haven't you told the sovereign yet about finding that ring?'

Prince Harlan let out a large breath of air. 'No reason in particular. It's more of a feeling.' Maldwyn watched as the prince furrowed his brow. 'When the sovereign first asked for the ring, he made out as though he wanted it to put Kristian's spirit to rest, but the longer I go without giving it to him, the more I see how insistent he is upon getting his hands on it, and the less his reasons make sense to me.'

'You may be right,' Maldwyn told him, running his fingers through the soft blades of grass at his sides.

'Do you know something?'

'Only that he wants it.' Maldwyn wasn't sure whether to mention Tiana's concerns. He wasn't certain that there was anything significant about the ring, nor whether it posed any danger. If things were as Tolamin suggested, and Jerrik wanted to preserve the relic, if it were indeed some sort of divine artefact, then he didn't want to see the prince destroy the ring unnecessarily.

Lying still, thinking about the secrets between them, Maldwyn pressed his head back into the soft ground, rubbed his aching torso, and listened to the sound of the rushing falls, splashing against the rocky wall. The scent of moss was mostly masked by the sweet, tiny, star-shaped, white flowers blooming between the blades of grass. He knew Prince Harlan was staring at him, making him feel exposed, as though the prince could read his thoughts and knew the truth behind Maldwyn's lies.

A knot formed in his stomach and Maldwyn felt awfully guilty. The prince rolled over, propped his head upon his hand, and ran his fingers down the inside of Maldwyn's arm, making him shudder. He leaned closer, in a comforting manner, and Maldwyn felt his warm breath on his neck. Staying quiet, he couldn't help himself from speculating what the prince might be thinking.

'Mal, you weren't the only one to survive your hometown the night it was attacked,' Prince Harlan told him. Maldwyn frowned up at him and studied the prince's face. 'There were others.'

'Your Royal Highness!' Shouted desperate voices from the woods above, coming from the top of the waterfall.

'Sounds like Theodor brought a few men out to look for me!' The prince sat up and began pulling on his wet clothes. 'It was only a matter of time before he'd come looking!'

Tossing Maldwyn his shirt, and whipping him in the mouth, Prince Harlan checked whether anyone was looking down from the top of the waterfall as he wriggled into his pants.

'Prince Harlan!'

Following the prince's lead, Maldwyn pulled his sodden shirt over his head, being careful not to trouble his tender chest, tugged his pants up and over his hips, fastened his pant belt, and drew his saturated robes over his shoulders. Bootless and jacketless, the prince stole a quick kiss before throwing Maldwyn his leather waistbelt and shoes.

When Maldwyn finished lacing his boots, the prince helped him up to stand and led the way back through the trees up the side of the mountain, stepping gingerly through the brush with his bare feet.

The shouts grew louder as they went up the steep mount, around the cascading falls, drowning out a nearby hooting owl. Large, moss-covered boulders got in their way, but the roots of the trees created an uneven staircase to help them along their path.

As they made their way to the top, Maldwyn saw that the mercenaries' bodies had been lined up along the rocky river's edge. Two guards, holding flaming torches, were moving Ser Gerard's body over with the other's and Ser Theodor, wearing his leather armour, was standing, looking down the waterfall, holding the prince's jacket in his right hand.

'Theodor,' the knight turned, bearing the torch he held toward them, 'would you mind giving me that back,' the prince asked, pointing to his jacket.

'Your Grace, what happened here and who's this?'

Maldwyn lowered his hood and bowed his head respectfully to the knight, reminding himself not to look upon the prince in the presence of others, despite the intimacy they had shared.

'Ser Theodor, it is good to see you again.'

'Maldwyn!' The knight's eyes went wide, but the tone of his voice told Maldwyn the knight wasn't completely surprised to see him again, alive. Handing the prince his jacket, he directed his stare to Maldwyn. 'Didn't I tell you I thought the man was lying, sire?'

Pulling his jacket over his shoulders, the prince left the buckles undone as he looked around for his boots. The two guards bowed to the prince after they laid Ser Gerard on the ground, then turned to gather the weapons. Ser Theodor walked along the rocks, keeping his torch out in front of him, realising what Prince Harlan was looking for, the knight grabbed the prince's leather boots from behind a tree.

'What man?' Maldwyn asked, holding his mouth in a lopsided way to alleviate the slight throbbing of his jaw, as he fought the urge to look between the prince and the knight.

'It's what I was about to tell you,' the prince mumbled under his breath. Ser Theodor's cheekbones seemed more prominent in the shadowy night as he shifted on his feet. 'There were survivors from your hometown that were gathered and brought to the palace dungeons.' Maldwyn felt himself frown as he forced himself to study the rocks by the river's edge. 'There was a man—he said his name was Dimitri—and he told us that you had died. He said he saw you crash into a burning building, and you never came back out.'

'Dimitri's alive!'

'Yes,' Ser Theodor confirmed, passing the prince his boots. In the background, the two guards piled the weapons besides the bodies. 'As are others from your town. But, they are still in the dungeons. The king doesn't know what to do with them.'

'Why?' Maldwyn asked, still at war with the desire to look up. 'They haven't committed any crimes!'

'No,' Prince Harlan said, pushing his foot into one of his shoes. 'The situation is a mess. The reports say there was confusion and fighting broke out. Once that happened, my father's men gathered the survivors and, not knowing what to do to manage the state of affairs, they marched the survivors to the capital.' Placing his hand on the tree beside him to stabilise himself, the prince drove his other foot into his boot. 'The tragedy of what happened in your hometown is a problem for my father, and he can't massacre the remaining survivors now that they have been marched through the city streets.'

'For now, they are safe,' the knight added, trying to reassure Maldwyn. Weapons clanged together as the two guards tossed more swords on the pile.

'But they are in the dungeons?'

'Maldwyn,' the prince placed a hand on his arm. It was distinctly less romantic than it had been by the river's side. 'They are alive.' Maldwyn rubbed his eyes, struggling with where to look and how to respond to this news. 'Why did this man tell us you were dead?'

'He helped me escape,' Maldwyn admitted, letting out a weighted breath. 'I did get thrown into a building, and a guard did follow me into the wreckage. If Dimitri hadn't snuck up behind the man and stopped the guard, then he would have killed me for sure. He saved my life and made sure I escaped.'

'He must have been a good friend to you and your family to protect you like that.' Ser Theodor's voice hinted that he was speculating about something. Maldwyn remembered that the knight had caught him using his gift in the palace.

'He was the father of a friend of mine, and like family,' Maldwyn said in such a way as to confirm Theodor's unspoken suspicions.

'I'm sorry for your loss, but rest assured that Dimitri is alive,' the knight said in a kind voice. The two guards paused, checking the surroundings before wandering along the water's edge to where Maldwyn noticed his horse's form in the distance, drinking from the river. He was glad to see it hadn't wandered too far. 'Sire, what happened here?'

The prince kneeled beside Maldwyn and began lacing up his boots. 'Gerard was a traitor. After I sent you to check on the regiment's encampment, beyond the castle grounds, he came and told me that there was something by the river that needed my attention.' The prince shrugged. 'It was a trap. These men were waiting to kill me.'

'Your Grace, you should have waited for me to return before heading into the woods at night unarmed,' Theodor scolded, shaking his head.

'I know, but I didn't see any reason for there to be any trouble. Gerard is a lot of things, and although I was suspicious about him meeting with Lord Darius's guards, he always seemed loyal to my father.

'Besides, he said that the area had been secured, but that there was something unexpected that had been found by the waterfall. I didn't see it coming that he was leading me to my intended death.' Standing back on his feet, Prince Harlan sighed. 'Seems the sovereign kept Maldwyn safe and taught him some new things.' Maldwyn could hear that the prince was smiling. 'It was lucky that Maldwyn arrived in time. How did you know I was in danger, by the way? The sovereign didn't know I'd be here.'

Keeping his gaze to the ground, Maldwyn said, 'We received a warning that such an attempt was going to be made from an informant in Karana Downs.' Maldwyn's horse's hooves clip-clopped along the slippery rocks as the two guards led it back toward where the bodies had been gathered. 'Sire, we believe the order was given by Lord Darius.'

'Lord Darius? That can't be right,' Harlan responded, sounding doubtful as his voice deepened.

'Sire, you did get under his skin back in the capital.' Theodor reasoned in a dull voice, standing stiff.

'Think about it though,' The prince cautioned the knight. 'Darius isn't a fool. When you're trying to manipulate someone, like my father, would you attempt to assassinate his son, and the heir to the throne, when no evidence of your betrayal has even been gathered?' Maldwyn shot his gaze up to see Theodor's face darken. 'It's too bold a step. My father wouldn't ignore my murder. Darius is too smart for something like this.'

Maldwyn dropped his eyes to scrutinise the twigs and dried leaves littering the forest floor just as Theodor turned to him. 'Why do you think Lord Darius gave the order?'

Running through the details in his mind, Maldwyn frowned. 'The order came from someone in the keep and the rumours among the guards said the order was given with the lord's seal.'

'Do you think someone in the keep would impersonate the lord?' Theodor asked the prince in a grave tone. Maldwyn didn't catch the prince's response. 'One thing's for sure, Your Grace, we'll have to be careful. Things will only get more dangerous, especially once we arrive in the downs.' Theodor looked Maldwyn and the prince up and down, 'How did the both of you end up sodding wet and, in your case, sire, half-dressed?'

'Well,' the prince started, scratching behind his ear, 'after fighting off my attackers, Maldwyn was set upon by Gerard, who had him pinned. I took up a sword and stabbed Gerard, but, as he staggered away, he pushed Maldwyn over the edge of the waterfall.' The prince swallowed, shifting his stance, as Maldwyn glanced up and pursed his lips. 'I waited at the top to see if Maldwyn would come up for air, but he didn't.' As the prince paused, Maldwyn wondered whether Prince Harlan realised he couldn't swim. It occurred to Maldwyn that, after the pummelling Ser Gerard had given him, the prince may have thought that Maldwyn had been unconscious by the time he hit the water. 'So, I took off the clothes that would weigh me down, and dove in to pull him out.'

'I am in your debt, Your Grace,' Maldwyn mumbled quietly as he bowed. After so long away from these formalities, Maldwyn had almost forgotten the way it made him feel insignificant.

'I'll have these men call off the search for you, and then I'll personally escort you both back to the castle, sire.' Theodor spoke in a firm voice, putting his hands on his hips as he stared at the prince. Maldwyn wanted to look up, and as he lifted his gaze from the slippery rocks along the river's edge, he glimpsed the knight eyeing Maldwyn's horse. Theodor's face fell and he parted his lips in thought. 'There should be room in the castle stables.'

Theodor stepped away, heading for the two guards by Maldwyn's horse, issuing orders to have the search called off and resecure the castle perimeter. Maldwyn stole a moment to peek over and catch the prince's gaze while the others were distracted. The prince grinned at him.

As Theodor led the horse over to them, handing Maldwyn the reins, the prince turned and began heading into the woods, away from the river. The dried twigs crunched beneath his feet. Maldwyn stroked the coarse mane of the charcoal silhouette of his stallion, which nuzzled into his face before turning to follow Prince Harlan and Ser Theodor.

In the background, the rushing falls teemed over the edge and the owl, hidden in the trees, hooted farewell. A gentle, cool evening breeze swept over him, making the sopping-wet Maldwyn shiver.

Making their way through the forest, the three of them trod along the uneven and unfamiliar path. In places, the light from the moon was completely hidden and the world beyond the torch's glowing radiance was lost to black.

It wasn't a long walk from the waterfall to the castle, which rose out of the soil like an ancient monument to the crown. The smooth, stone walls were pristine, unblemished by age, and the serene castle seemed to weave through the low, peaceful hillside.

Approaching the back entrance, Maldwyn paused in awe as a stunning courtyard appeared before him through the trees. The space was longer than it was wide and was shaped like a kite. Lanterns, hanging from decorative, tall timber posts lit the space, revealing a blooming garden with shrubs that were shaped like a series of small hills that were huddled close together.

The smell of jasmine blossoming in the courtyard took Maldwyn back to the capital's streets where jasmine flowered out the front of people's houses. A timber boardwalk, fashioned from thin oak planks, wrapped around the edge of the courtyard and followed the lines of the castle walls. A long and wide step, not far from where Maldwyn stood at the tree line, led up onto the pointed tip of the courtyard boardwalk.

Maldwyn was swept away by the majesty of the place as he left the woods behind and stepped onto the small grassy space before the step, following the prince to the edge of the raised boardwalk. A well-dressed servant, wearing black, fitted clothes, stepped out from around the corner of the castle walls and waited by the edge of the walkway. The servant bowed to the prince.

'Your Royal Highness, welcome back to Valondale Castle!'

'Thank you,' Prince Harlan said, stepping onto the walkway. 'I need you to take this horse to the stables and see that it is looked after.'

'Of course, Your Grace,' the man bowed again and made his way over to take the reins. Maldwyn grabbed the saddlebag, into which he had packed his things before the man led the horse around the side of the castle.

Inside, was beautiful, like the sort of place he would have imagined as a child when his mother would tell him old fables designed to keep him in line. Low, plush settees were placed around the open rooms and tall, fleur-de-lis hall stands rested against the walls beneath large paintings of detailed landscapes. Massive rugs were spread out over the wooden floors as Prince

Harlan and Ser Theodor led Maldwyn through the stunning, old castle.

When they reached the residential wing, Theodor slowed and grabbed Maldwyn's arm to bring him to a stop. 'Your Grace,' the knight began, letting his hand fall loosely at his side, 'Why don't you settle into your quarters for the night, and I'll help find somewhere for Maldwyn to sleep?'

Prince Harlan stopped to look back at them, lifting his head by his chin and weaving his brows together. Standing behind the knight, Maldwyn didn't bother to direct his stare to the floor. The orange hue of the many lanterns hanging from the walls made the prince's usually bright blue eyes gleam a sort of muted apricot colour.

'Sire, you should get some rest after the ordeal in the woods,' Theodor pressed in a kind voice, placing a hand on the prince's shoulder to urge him to retire for the evening.

Hesitating, Prince Harlan opened his mouth as if to protest, but eventually lowered his head, giving in to what was expected of him.

'See to it that he is looked after,' the prince instructed before turning and continuing toward his chambers.

'I don't think I need to guess why you wanted me alone,' Maldwyn whispered, making sure his voice wouldn't carry in the vast open spaces of the charming castle, 'but couldn't this wait until I've had a chance to change out of these soaking robes?'

'Well, I think I am well and truly overdue an explanation, and I am sure a bit of water and some wet clothes won't hurt you,' Theodor said, rubbing along his jaw and chin.

Placing a hand on Maldwyn's arm, the knight turned and led Maldwyn back the way they had come, toward a small parlour room that had high ceilings, deep, mahogany shelves lining the walls, and two armchairs facing an open fireplace.

Above the fireplace, mounted on the wall, was a double-edged sword, its blade tapered such that it subtly resembled a leaf, bringing the centre of balance toward the grip. Though the fire had not been lit, the small candles bundled together on the petite, ornate table between the chairs were gleaming with dancing flames.

'I'm not sure what to say,' Maldwyn replied, following Ser Theodor over to the seats.

'Why don't you start at the beginning?'

The knight gestured for Maldwyn to take a seat as he relaxed back into one of the chairs, undoing the belt to which his sheathed sword was attached. Ser Theodor stood it to rest against the arm of his chair.

'There's not much to say,' Maldwyn said, wondering what to tell the knight. His robes squelched a little as he sat in the fabric armchair. 'I don't know why I have powers, but I know I was adopted. As far as I see things, I'm just a man. I was raised on a farm, and I lived a simple life.'

'But you're not like everyone else.' Theodor leaned forward and rested his forearms on his knees. 'You have your own power. You're destined for greatness. There are prophecies about you.' Taking in a deep breath, Maldwyn struggled with the bewildered look of admiration the knight was giving him. It was as though he wasn't looking at a mere mortal, but rather as if he were staring at something—someone—deserving of worship. 'I take it Ailaya doesn't know about you.'

'No,' Maldwyn exhaled, making the candles between them flicker. 'Telling her would have put her in harm's way, which I never wanted to do. Before being captured by the folk in the Anhalt Mountains, and then you, I could count the number of people who knew about my magic on one hand.'

'Dimitri, he was one of them.'

'Yes, though I hadn't always realised that.' Maldwyn watched as the knight tried to unravel the mystery of his life. 'His son, Will, and I were… close, and Dimitri came to think of me as his other son. It's the reason Dimitri lied and told you I was dead. He was protecting me.'

'Then, the sorcerer that was rumoured to have escaped the attack on your village, that was you?'

Maldwyn was conscious not to lean back into the seat too much, given his robes were saturated.

'Yes.' Scratching the side of his face, Maldwyn remembered the moment his power failed him. 'I used my power to protect a young girl, but then it was gone.' Shifting forward, Theodor pinched his brows together, forming a dimple above his nose. 'I've never had a lot of control. It's something the Erendil has been helping me with since I found my way to the mountains.'

Staring up at the sword, Maldwyn was fascinated by the ornate detailing along of cross-guard. The pommel on the other side of the sword's grip was shaped like a swirling knot.

'That sword has been in the royal family's possession for generations. It was King Dietrich I's sword. Prince Harlan's great-great-great-grandfather and the first King of Dresden. Back then, the kingdom's borders expanded as far as the city itself, which was much smaller in those days.' Ser Theodor looked up at the sword with admiration. 'The sword was passed down as an heirloom before being hung here. The stories say the blade is perfectly balanced, able to cut through its opponents like butter, and, to this day, remains undefeated.'

As Maldwyn smiled at the legend and glanced down to the mantlepiece, he noticed a round carving, which, in the centre of a circle, had a finely detailed eagle perching on a branch beside a falcon. There was something familiar about it, and, after a moment studying the carving, Maldwyn recognised that it was very similar to the embroidery on the swaddle his mother had given him.

'What's that?' Maldwyn asked, pointing to the carving above the cold, dark fireplace. A cool, evening draught swept down the chimney.

'The carving?'

'Yes,' Maldwyn frowned and shot his stare to the knight. 'What does that mean?'

'It's an old symbol,' Theodor said as he shrugged. 'It represents divinity, specifically the Vanir.' Tilting his head, the knight watched Maldwyn a moment. Maldwyn wished he knew what he was thinking. 'Freya, the goddess of love and the queen of the golden fields of the afterlife, is said to have the most spectacular feathered cloak, which trails on the ground behind her as she walks the fields. It is rumoured that the goddess has a love of birds, so strong that she morphs into a falcon to feel the freedom of soaring through the skies. That symbol is as old as the gods.'

Remembering the eagle borne on the note his mother had kept inside the swaddle, Maldwyn tightened his forehead. 'If a falcon represents Freya, then what about the eagle?'

'Well, the falcon represents both Freya and her twin brother. Both of them have similar stories, but many forget the eagle, which is their younger brother, Alerion.' Theodor stared at the carving and made a face as he tried to remember something. 'Alerion, the god of desire, identified more closely with the eagles, admiring their strength. So, when his siblings take flight as falcons, it is said he soars above them, out of sight, flying in the form of an eagle.' Theodor pressed his shoulders back. 'Is there some reason that symbol means something to you?'

'I'm not sure yet,' Maldwyn answered, wondering what it all meant.

As the knight let the matter go, he continued to question Maldwyn on his powers, the cursed pendant, the events around and after the king's men attacked Alander, and what he knew of the prince's plans to uncover the lord's duplicity. Maldwyn was very forthcoming, explaining everything as best he could, even explaining the encounter in the ruined temple, only filtering out the unnecessary details. It was cathartic to speak as openly and frankly as they were, without the pressures of the mountain folk's expectations, nor the usual fear of danger.

As they both grew weary, and the conversation came to a natural close, Ser Theodor stood, signalling for Maldwyn to follow, and led him through the alluring castle. Through the occasional window, Maldwyn spied the shimmering stars and caught the whiff of the blossoming jasmine. Stopping by a door in the residential wing, the knight held up a hand, as though he had one more thing to say.

'I've kept your secret, as promised, but, for what it's worth, you need to be careful.' Maldwyn's stomach twisted at the thought of all the secrets he had kept. 'You can sleep here for tonight.'

'Thank you, for everything. Not many people in your position would choose to keep my power secret.'

Ser Theodor smiled, nodded knowingly and walked away, disappearing into the castle.

CHAPTER TWENTY

The Divine Guardians

THE AFTERNOON BREEZE was seasoned with the pungent, sweet scent of blossoming flowers. Beneath the glistening surface of the large pond that wove through the castle gardens, was a small, dark fish whose fins were like smooth shadows that wrapped around its shimmering deep-blue scales. Bushy shrubs, bespattered with tiny, colourful flowers, crowded around the edges of the water, shaded by the young, thin trees and their rugged arms which were splayed wide.

Reaching up, Maldwyn felt the silky leaves between the tips of his fingers. It was quiet and peaceful. The sort of day that made him think of his childhood. A song his mother used to hum came to mind as he glanced up at the clear skies overhead.

Slipping his fingers into the pocket of his pants, Maldwyn pulled out the cryptic note that had been left with him when he was abandoned as an infant. He had brought it from Alander, packing it in a small, leather saddlebag. He unfolded the paper and studied the eagle symbol as he considered Theodor's words.

Staring at the emblem, he yearned to know what it meant and how it was connected to Alerion. The air wrapped him up in its relaxing warmth as he flipped the parchment over and traced the black wings above the cursive writing with his fingers. *Keep him safe.*

'What does it mean, mother?' Maldwyn mumbled and looked around, checking he was alone. He rubbed his chest, which was still a little sore from the fight with the prince's attackers. Above him, resting on the branch was a small squirrel with beady eyes, reddish-brown fur, and a bushy tail.

Sharing a momentary inquisitive gaze with the little creature, Maldwyn smiled to one side and reached out a greeting hand. The squirrel squeaked, scurried along the branch, and ran down his arm to sit on his shoulder.

'Well, hello there,' Maldwyn muttered, folding the note back over as he glanced at the fluffy animal on his shoulder. 'You're a friendly little one, aren't you?'

Maldwyn giggled as it ran around the back of his neck, tickling him with its coarse fur and luxurious tail. Leaning forward to help the squirrel keep its steady footing as it manoeuvred around his neck and the collar of his clothing,

Maldwyn flinched as the soft and fuzzy tail whipped him in the eye. Jumping off his shoulder, the squirrel ran down his arm, snatched the note and took off back up the tree.

'Hey!' Maldwyn shouted after it, chasing the squirrel as it bounded from branch-to-branch and tree-to-tree around the garden.

Frustrated at being unable to catch the critter, Maldwyn slowed, took in a breath, summoned forth his ever-flowing power, and closed his eyes. He focused and let go of his constant grip as he brought the world to a halt.

When he opened his eyes, the butterfly moving across his path had stopped, wings no longer beating. The water's surface was perfectly still and the few fish were motionless. The small, blue finch sitting in the leafy apple tree was no longer singing.

Maldwyn moved forward, toward the squirrel, which was sitting on a low branch a few paces from where he stood. He shook his head and stretched up to grab the note.

Just as the tips of Maldwyn's fingers touched the parchment, the squirrel moved. Maldwyn stood paralysed for a moment, stunned as it raced away with the note in its mouth.

'What are you?' he whispered to no one as he made sure the rest of the world around him was unmoving.

Out of options, Maldwyn rushed after it, running through the gardens, across the grass that wrapped around the pristine stone walls of the castle and further over the grounds toward an old building, detached from the main castle. The squirrel darted through a crack in the coarse, beige stones of the outer walls of the two-storey house. The upper story was set on a peaked roof.

Not far from the gap in the wall was a clouded, glass window with bird droppings speckled along the outside ledge, which was a fraction ajar. Maldwyn drew his brows together and made his way over to peek inside the building, wondering whether he should follow.

Inside, Maldwyn saw a modest room with a simple green and beige patterned rug in front of a quaint hearth. A rough box of kindling, which was poking out the top, sat to the side of the fireplace next to a set of iron pokers hanging from a stand.

Spying the squirrel in the centre of the rug with his note, Maldwyn searched for anyone inside. If Jaecen were here, Maldwyn knew the ranger would caution him from rushing into anything blindly. But Jaecen wasn't here, and Maldwyn wanted to get back the only connection he had to his mother, his hometown and his origins more than he wanted to be careful.

Besides, Maldwyn didn't want to lose sight of the squirrel clutching the only sign he had, pointing him to his true family. Unable to see anyone inside, he pulled the window fully open, noticing a cushioned bench seat just beyond the ledge, built into the window frame, and climbed inside, checking that there was no one around.

To his left, he noticed a shelf fixed to the wall that had yellow, uneven candles that were grouped on one end next to a pair of secateurs. At the other end was a small, clay pot with tiny leaves cascading out the top, down the side and over the edge of the shelf. The leaves had a slight silvery sheen, and the plant gave off a mild grassy scent. To his right, Maldwyn saw a doorway that led to the rest of the house. As far as Maldwyn could see, the door was open, but there was no one in sight.

Slow and careful, Maldwyn made his way over to the rug, crouching. The squirrel ignored him and began nibbling the edge of the paper. Maldwyn kneeled and offered his hand to distract it from eating. The squirrel sniffed his fingers and turned away, dropping the note.

'Hey there, do you mind if I take that back?' Maldwyn mumbled as he stretched over the squirrel.

Someone coughed from the doorway behind him.

Maldwyn jumped.

'Sorry,' offered a gravelly voice.

Maldwyn turned to see a bald, stocky man with a wide nose, wearing basic tan-coloured clothes.

'I didn't mean to spook you.'

Feeling on edge, Maldwyn's power sparked, trying to escape. Just able to keep it contained, Maldwyn decided to plead ignorance while he determined who this man was, and what he was after.

'I'm so sorry, I didn't think anyone was home,' Maldwyn said as he rubbed behind his ear. The pressure of the hard floors on Maldwyn's knees made him want to stand. 'This squirrel took something of mine and I was just trying to get it back.'

'Squirrel?'

Maldwyn frowned and stared at where the creature should be, but it was gone. The note, Maldwyn's only clue to his origins, was lying on the ground. Leaning forward on his knees, Maldwyn picked up the folded piece of paper, frowning as he noticed nibble marks in the corner of the parchment. The only thing that could explain what had happened in the gardens, and where the squirrel had disappeared to, was magic.

'You'll have to forgive my little friend,' said the man with the gravelly voice as Maldwyn stared at the blank space where the squirrel should have been. 'He was only conjured as a means of bringing you here.' Maldwyn pushed himself up to stand tall and face the man as he walked into the room, head low and arms hanging loose at his sides. 'Please, I didn't mean to manipulate you.' Outside the window, Maldwyn heard the distinct buzzing of a bee. 'I was afraid of approaching you in person and being seen together. You never know who may be watching.' There was a fearful glint in the man's eyes and Maldwyn supposed he was being honest. He knew what it was like to constantly be fearful or apprehensive. 'As it is, I have taken a risk, but I recognised the robes you wore the other night and know that your kind is allied with my people.'

Maldwyn lifted his head, trying to work out what this man wanted from him. Putting the note back into the pocket of his trousers, Maldwyn broke the man's stare and looked around the room.

Hanging on the wall above the fireplace was a stunning painting of the castle gardens, capturing its harmonious grace as if it were a divine oasis. The detail of the jasmine vines creeping up the bodies of the trees was so stunning he practically smelled the sweet flowers. Sitting by the pond was a woman wearing a flowing black dress with long, raven-coloured hair that was pulled over one shoulder. With one hand, she clutched the winged pendant hanging below the line of her neck. Her other hand was reaching up to the eagle, soaring above her. Maldwyn's power began prickling as he stared at the painting.

'Who are you?' Maldwyn whispered. Mesmerised, he wasn't sure whether he was asking the man or the painting.

'My name is Rhys.' Maldwyn looked back to see the stocky man watching him with arms folded. 'I'm a sorcerer and I need your help.'

The window hinges groaned at the slight wind. Turning his head away and stepping forward, Maldwyn lowered his voice. 'How could you need my help?'

Unfolding his arms, Rhys fidgeted with the cuff of his plain, linen shirt. 'My father used to be the gardener here, back when the queen was alive. He was a sorcerer. His rhythmic chanting gave these gardens their majesty. He wanted to recapture the beauty of that painting in real life.' Staring at the woman by the pond, Maldwyn listened to Rhys's raspy voice as he studied the winged pendant. It was silver with faint detailing that resembled filigree latticework in the wings. There seemed to be a stone in the centre, but it was mostly covered by her fingers holding it close to her chest. 'It's beautiful, isn't it?'

'Who is she?'

'My father never really told me who the maiden was meant to portray. I don't think he knew.' Rhys walked over to stand beside Maldwyn and studied the brushwork. 'But there is something about her.'

'Yes, there is.' Maldwyn sighed, feeling close to answers that, as always, seemed just out of reach. 'You were telling me how you need my help.'

'Yes. Well, before my father went on the run and was executed, he taught me everything he knew, including passing on a secret to me.'

Maldwyn moved closer to the man, seeing the sincerity of the look on his face. 'What secret?'

'Years ago, a short time before Queen Sonia and her lover, Kristian, was executed, they came here, to Valondale Castle, with Prince Harlan and Princess Cassara. Though I was a boy, I remember it clearly since the king didn't accompany them on this trip. Kristian was a friend of my father's, and he came with the queen seeking this.' Rhys held out a cerulean, radiant gemstone, the shape of a teardrop in his hand, passing it to Maldwyn. 'It's called sea glass, an incredibly rare and potent gemstone. It's an ingredient for a spell they were trying to cast.'

'A spell?' Maldwyn shook his head and tightened the muscles in his face, confused. 'What spell? What were their intentions?'

Rhys tilted his head toward the door. The light through the window seemed to shine from the top of his bald head. 'Follow me.'

'Why should I trust you?'

'I showed you that I am a sorcerer. I think I am the one who is in more danger of trusting you.'

Maldwyn followed Rhys, accepting the point he had made. Just beyond the doorway, was a thin, stuffy corridor with a few other doors leading to adjoining rooms, and a set of worn, timber stairs.

The place had a rustic charm, reminding Maldwyn of his hometown, and there was a sweet, zesty flavour to the fresh spring air. The stairs creaked beneath their weight as they walked up to them to a small area with a bookcase tucked into a nook in the wall. It was warmer in this part of the house, and the airflow was lacking compared to downstairs.

Rhys stared at Maldwyn for a moment, as if questioning whether he should hand over the secret he had kept for years on behalf of his father. After the momentary pause, he pulled out a botany book, flicking through the pages until he pulled out a yellowing, crinkled piece of parchment.

'This was what they were planning.' Maldwyn held the spell in his hands and studied the ingredients, noticing sea glass on the list. Holding the stone in his other hand, Maldwyn noted it was cool to the touch. 'It's known as the Invocation of the Divine Guardians.'

'What does it do?'

'This is an ancient spell—more like a ritual—which has rarely been cast successfully due to the difficulty of gathering some of the ingredients on that list, the sea glass being the hardest.' Rhys held his hands forward as if he were holding an invisible ball. 'The spell calls on the goddess Freya, for a blessing. In most cases, even where the ritual was completed properly, Freya has refused the blessing.' Maldwyn frowned as he glanced down at the spell. 'A long time ago, when I was a boy, my father told me that Freya had two loves: birds, for the untethered freedom she saw in them, and cats, for their mysterious nature.

'Even in art, this has spilt over where birds are often used to symbolise divinity and love, whereas cats are depicted as mysterious guardians. The stories say that the goddess not only morphs into a falcon to soar through the clouds, but that she travels throughout the celestial realms on a chariot drawn by massive wildcats.'

Smiling to one side with a dreamy look on his face, Rhys looked to the ground as if trying to hide his wavering hope that he might see such exquisite pleasures in his next life. 'When this spell is cast, it calls on the goddess to share the gift of being a divine guardian, a protector of the gods. Rumours say, that these protectors were granted certain… qualities… and that some could transform into large wildcats.'

'The Lynx,' Maldwyn mumbled inaudibly. Interested, Maldwyn creased his forehead, feeling the tightness in his muscles. 'What sort of qualities?'

'I'm not sure,' Rhys said, shrugging. 'This spell hasn't been successfully cast for generations. My father only mentioned that it was possible.'

'Why did the queen want this?'

'According to my father, she seemed burdened, as though she knew something we didn't about her children.' Rhys closed the book and held it between his arms over his chest. 'The queen never told my father why she wanted to complete this ritual, but my father believed it was for her son, the Crown Prince.'

Maldwyn cleared his throat, confused about what the queen could have known. 'Do you know if they completed the ritual—if they cast this spell?'

'No, but I know that they intended to try.'

Maldwyn considered how many atrocities Queen Sonia must have witnessed in the palace, and all the warning signs she would have seen before the king led his quest to exterminate all sorcerers, but he couldn't understand the desire or need for this spell. Biting his lower lip, Maldwyn recalled how learning about Queen Sonia's execution had been the spark for Prince Harlan to question his father's actions. Perhaps, Maldwyn thought, knowing the queen's acceptance of magic, as well as his sister being a seer, would be enough to help the prince see sorcery in a different light.

'Why come to me and not go to Prince Harlan with this?'

Rhys made a bitter expression. 'Unfortunately, the prince has been raised by his father and has followed the king's directions with very few questions over the years. Those soldiers out there are being marched to the northern border to defeat your people. Though, I suppose your being here, means there is more to that than I know.' An uncomfortable feeling in his gut made Maldwyn stand taller and push his shoulders back. 'He may not be the king, but I can't take the chance to tell him without risking my own execution.'

'You said you needed my help.' Maldwyn rubbed his nose with the back of his hand. 'What must I do?'

'The spell needs to be triggered to work.' Rhys's raspy voice softened as he spoke, hugging the book. 'It can be cast and remain inactive for years, never manifesting in any meaningful way. You see, it needs a catalyst, something that signals danger.' Licking his lips, Rhys looked up to the roof.

'So, what triggers it?'

'Pain, but not regular sadness or simple physical pain.' Pinching his forefinger to his thumb as he held the book with one arm, Rhys gestured that he was making a specific point. 'It must be spiritual anguish. That is why sea glass, which is also known as the tears of the sea god, Ran, is used. Only when the subject feels true undeniable and spiritual pain does the spell manifest.'

Maldwyn stared at the aged parchment. Inky blots bled in places as if the spell itself was crying from the flowing script.

'What I need your help with is finding out whether the spell was ever cast,' Rhys said, looking very worried as he stared at Maldwyn with a serious expression. 'If the queen and her lover succeeded and this was used on Prince Harlan, then the prince may one day be caught off guard should the spell ever become triggered. He may also be swayed to our side for fears of his father's reaction.'

'How would I be able to tell?'

'With this,' Rhys indicated to the sea glass in Maldwyn's other hand. 'Sea glass has a faint glow that grows stronger in the presence of more sea glass. It is so rare that finding more than one at a time is very difficult. However, as this was a component of the spell, this gemstone will sense its presence in the prince and should have a faint glow whenever it is near him. There's no reason for me to be close enough to the prince, but you can be. You'll help me, won't you?'

'I will help you.'

Maldwyn smiled as he looked up. He contemplated whether this was why the prince had come to this castle after all these years. He hadn't had a chance to ask the prince and had been left wondering about the purpose of his visit here. The only way he would learn how much the prince knew was for Maldwyn to confront Prince Harlan.

'Do you mind if I keep this as well?' Maldwyn asked, holding the spell up in his fingers.

'I suppose not. It doesn't do any good being hidden on these shelves.' Rhys tucked the book into the gap and pushed it into place. 'I can trust you, can't I?'

'Yes. I want what you want: freedom.'

'You should get going before anyone finds you here and people begin to ask questions.' Rhys's wide nose shadowed his upper lip as he turned back toward the stairs.

Maldwyn followed Rhys back down the creaking stairs to where the fresh breeze wafted through the place with the honeyed smell of the spring air. 'You can take the door this time.' Maldwyn smiled awkwardly and Rhys took him through the corridor to the entrance. 'We need to be careful, but if you need an ally, then don't hesitate to come by.'

'Thank you,' Maldwyn said, slipping the gemstone and spell into his pocket with his note, which he was glad to have back. 'Take care of yourself,' Maldwyn offered as he walked out the door and headed back to the castle.

* * * * *

Waiting for the prince to return from his royal duties, Maldwyn stood in Prince Harlan's drawing room. The dark, smooth hardwood floors were almost black, but the afternoon glow brought out the burgundy grain running through the floorboards. Two dark, mustard settees with gold leafy patterning embroidered into the fabric faced a low-line, black and gold table.

On either side of the room, behind each of the lounges, were huge windows looking over the garden. Lightweight curtains that were an off-white colour framed the bright emerald shades of the garden and the mauve afternoon sky. Hanging from the ceiling were black candelabras with gold swirls twisting around the black arms and cupping the candles in place. The room smelled of cinnamon, but Maldwyn couldn't tell from where the scent was coming.

Behind Maldwyn was the door to the main castle, and on the other side of the room, directly in front of him, was a hallway leading further into the prince's private chambers. Maldwyn pulled out the sea glass and looked at the way it gleamed softly. It was a beautiful stone and unlike any gem that he had seen before. The divinity emanated from it, and the longer he was in its presence, the more he felt its sorrow.

The door opened, hardly making a sound. Maldwyn turned around and bowed, tucking the teardrop-shaped stone into his palm, holding it in place with his thumb as he clasped his hands. He glimpsed a second pair of boots in the doorway behind the prince and supposed it was Theodor.

'I'll need you to have the servants address the issue in the western wing as soon as possible and make sure the soldiers in the camp are prepared for a morning review.'

Keeping himself bowed, Maldwyn remained quiet, knowing better than to speak or move in the prince's presence while the knight was still around.

'Yes, Your Grace,' Theodor said flatly, feet facing the prince just inside the drawing room.

'You may go,' Prince Harlan ordered in his smooth, deep voice as his shadow waved the knight away.

Ser Theodor's shadow bowed and took a back step before turning and walking out the door, closing it behind him. Maldwyn heard the latch click into place.

'I'm sorry I haven't come to see you,' Harlan offered in a soft tone as he ran his fingers along Maldwyn's jaw, guiding him to stand tall.

Maldwyn leaned into his touch. Prince Harlan was wearing black trousers and a black, densely threaded, silky cotton shirt, with a large circular lace pattern sewn over his chest in a fine golden fibre. The sharp lines of the shirt accentuated his broad shoulders.

'I understand,' Maldwyn told him, being somewhat familiar with the innumerable demands on the prince as heir to the throne. 'And, I have to admit, I have come here for other purposes.'

'Oh?' Prince Harlan tilted his head and folded his arms over his chest. 'I'm intrigued.'

'Well,' Maldwyn started, feeling torn about how much to share about his encounter with Rhys, 'it's just that someone on your staff approached me about something and I think you need to know about it.'

The prince stepped closer and cupped Maldwyn's face with one hand. 'What happened?' Harlan's blue eyes studied his own. The setting sun seemed to brighten the gold hues in the room behind the prince. 'Are you okay?'

'I'm fine.' Reaching up to hold the prince's hand, Maldwyn smiled. 'This man gave me something because he was afraid of coming to you with it.' Harlan wrinkled the space between his brows, pulling them together. 'But I want an honest answer as to why you came to this castle because I have a feeling it is related.' Prince Harlan pulled back and looked away. 'Look, I'm not stupid. No one has visited this place since your mother's passing and it isn't exactly on the way to Karana Downs.'

'You're right, I do have my purposes for being here,' Prince Harlan shrugged, 'but I don't want to endanger you more than I have.'

'Well, I'm fairly certain that I am already at risk, having endangered myself by sharing what we've shared. Not being informed of whatever is going on might make it more dangerous for me, not less.' The prince put on his royal veneer, something he didn't often do around Maldwyn. 'Does this have something to do with the prophecies?'

'Prophecies?' Harlan's genuine confusion convinced Maldwyn that he wasn't here searching for Firebird or the fabled sword. 'Why would you think that?'

'The man I met gave me this.' Maldwyn sighed as he pulled the spell out of his pocket, being careful not to grab the other piece of parchment he kept there. 'It's a spell that calls upon Freya for a gift. The person who gave this to me said that it would grant the subject certain qualities, as a protector of a sort, and that they may even be able to change their form into a wildcat. When I heard that, I thought of the figure termed as the Lynx in the prophecies.'

The prince took the spell and studied it closely. He kept his worry hidden well, but Maldwyn was able to see through his mask.

'You once told me that some people believed Firebird was alive. Is it hard to believe this man might be too?'

As much as Maldwyn wanted the truth from the prince, what he was gauging at this very moment was whether he could trust the prince in the way he wanted. Maldwyn stepped closer to the prince and leaned his head forward, waiting for Harlan to say something, but he said nothing. The prince rested his forehead against Maldwyn's.

'It was your mother, Queen Sonia, and Kristian who wanted this spell. They intended to use it on you. So, Your Grace, is this what you were searching for?' Maldwyn whispered in a soft and tender tone, letting the prince know he could be trusted. 'Tell me, is it you in the prophecies?'

With his eyes focused on the floor, Maldwyn saw the blue glimmer of the stone he was still clutching. It was brighter than before, just as Rhys had said it would be.

'Who told you this?' The prince tried to shift the conversation. Maldwyn felt him tilt his head slightly.

'That doesn't matter right now. I promised I wouldn't let him be executed.'

Staring back into the prince's eyes, he noticed how intense his stare was, like the way a cat fixed its eyes on its target and watched without blinking. He thought about how Harlan could sometimes seem aloof and recluse, while at others he was intense, curious and overly protective. For a long time, Maldwyn had assumed much of that was due to his royal title, but now he considered that there was more to the prince than meets the eye.

'Is this the reason you came here? Did your mother use this on you?'

The prince looked like he'd never been put on the spot quite like this before, staying silent as if he were afraid to admit the truth. It must have been difficult for him, learning that he was under a spell, but one that had been cast by a mother's love.

King Viktor had raised the prince to see magic as evil, something profane to be feared. Queen Sonia had disagreed. When she was alone and afraid, she had turned to sorcery, the gift of divinity, for guidance. Maldwyn wondered why she had been so burdened and what she may have known, as he watched the prince struggle with what he was hearing.

'You can trust me,' Maldwyn offered, hoping to ease the prince into opening up about the truth he was loathed to admit.

'I came here, retracing my mother's steps, hoping it wasn't true.' The prince seemed a little shaky. Maldwyn caressed along his jawline and rested his other hand with the glimmering stone on the prince's waist. 'I found evidence that she had wanted to use magic on me, but I couldn't be sure whether anything had been done until I met a sorceress who confirmed it for me.' Prince Harlan pulled his head back. Maldwyn could see the uneasiness through his stoic expression. 'I needed to know what she did, so I came here searching for answers. Now I know,' he mumbled in a faraway voice.

'Now you know,' Maldwyn echoed, running his fingers through the prince's thick, blonde hair.

The prince pinched his mouth together and shook his head, looking down at the spell in his hands. 'Why would she do this to me?'

Maldwyn slipped the sea glass into his pocket while the prince was distracted with his thoughts. Holding both of his hands to the prince's cheeks, Maldwyn brought his gaze up, the way Harlan always did for him.

'I don't know, but, I think, it doesn't change anything. You're remarkable.' Maldwyn told him, plain and simple. 'Your father couldn't be more wrong about things.' Maldwyn leaned in, tenderly kissed him on the lips and wrapped him up in his embrace.

The prince relaxed into him and held him tight, as though he were afraid to lose him. If Prince Harlan wasn't so good at hiding his emotions, Maldwyn thought he would cry. The cinnamon air was comforting and Maldwyn felt time passing as he kept the prince safe and warm in his arms. He wanted to share everything with the prince, but felt now was not the time.

CHAPTER TWENTY-ONE

Wildflowers

S LOW AND RELUCTANT, the prince rolled over and checked Maldwyn was sleeping. His idle breath was deep and measured, and his expression seemed wistful. Heat radiated from his body between the soft sheets. The smell of him lingered on the prince's pillow as Harlan shifted to check the height of the moon through the window behind Maldwyn's sleeping form.

The stars were twinkling brightly, and the subtle wind rustled the leaves of the trees outside. Prince Harlan knew he was going to be late, but he wanted to stay by Maldwyn's warmth a little while longer.

Grudgingly, the prince pushed the covers back and got up to stand, being as quiet as possible so as not to disturb Maldwyn. Tired, Harlan stumbled a little as he pulled on his clothing, but Maldwyn remained peaceful, barely stirring.

Taking a moment to indulge himself, the prince kneeled beside the bed and leaned on the comfortable, springy mattress, watching Maldwyn sleep. Harlan reached out to touch him, but stopped short and brought the sheets back up over his bare shoulders.

When the prince left his chambers, he was careful to make sure he wasn't spotted as he went over to the stables. The smell of hay and muck smacked the prince out of his sleepy daze as he headed over to his black stallion, stamping the ground, ready to be freed from confinement. Harlan went over and stroked the side of its long face.

It didn't take him long to saddle the horse and sneak away from the castle grounds. Knowing that the area was operating with a skeleton team and having familiarised himself with the patrol routes of the guards, it was easy for the prince to slip away unnoticed. Riding along the hillside, the prince paused to take in the glowing fires of the troops camped by the castle before kicking his steed into a steady gallop.

It was not a far ride to the meeting place, set in a field of yellow wildflowers which, at this time of night, appeared a lighter shade of grey in the monochromatic landscape. The sweet floral scent made him want to sneeze, but the prince managed to suppress it by rubbing the side of his nose. The memory of being brought here and running through these fields after the death of his mother, free from palace pressures, entered his mind. He dismounted when he spotted someone waiting in the blossoming field, further in the distance, and left the horse to wander behind him.

'Hello brother,' his sister offered in a sweet voice, turning around to face him, smiling. The blades of grass and tiny wildflowers brushed along his boots as he moved closer. Her lightweight, pastel blue, satin weave dress was covered in tiny white flowers and it flowed around her as she moved. Under the moonlight, her long, black, and wavy hair shone, and her highlighted cheekbones seemed more prominent than he remembered. 'I'm glad you understood my message.'

'Cassara, you seem well.' The prince pressed his shoulders back and kept his distance, wary of his sister, given how long she had avoided his attempts to make contact. 'The flower was unmistakable, and a good call back to our childhood.'

'Peyton loved taking us to this place,' Cassara sounded pensive as she looked around the twilight, rolling hills.

Harlan thought about the past for a moment, recalling the woman that had raised them after their mother passed. She was a kind woman who kept herself at a distance. Back then, he didn't understand why, but now he was familiar with the lonely burden of royalty.

'I knew you would remember it if I could get the flower to you.'

'How did you manage to get it into the castle?'

'I have my ways.' Cassara flicked him a shy smile, as though she was assessing how much to tell her brother. 'As a seer, I dreamed you would be in Valondale Castle, so it was easy to use a spell and send the flower to you. If I hadn't known where you were, then I could never have sent that to you.'

Harlan felt his pulse quicken as he thought about magic, worrying that she could sense a spell in the air around him.

Cassara's face fell and she took a step back, making the prince wonder what his expression showed.

'I thought you didn't agree with our father hunting me.' Afraid that she was pulling away, Harlan tilted his head and contemplated all the ways he could reach out to the sister that, in many ways, was now a stranger to him. 'Being hunted, like a dog, takes a toll you know.'

'I don't agree with what he's doing,' Harlan moved forward and held a hand out, gesturing as he spoke, 'and, for what it's worth, I'm sorry.' Pausing, trying to find the words, he looked to the side and watched the way the breeze created waves in the field of grey flowers. 'I tried to contact you… so many times— to help—but you were always out of reach.'

'I'm well aware of your efforts.' Cassara replied in a low and soft voice as she folded her arms, and stared up at the stars. 'In my dream, you seemed happy in Valondale Castle,' she mumbled at the sky. Harlan thought there was a glimmer of sadness in her eyes the way the moonlight made them glisten. Her hair framed her face as she sighed. 'I have very few memories of that place.'

'As do I.'

'Hmm,' Cassara sighed and fixed a stern gaze on the prince, 'I suppose so. I'm glad you came and that you're not worried about meeting me out here, alone.'

'Well, you are my sister.' Harlan put his hands on his hips, standing tall. 'Although, I expected you would have Mikel with you.'

'He's not quite up to it at the moment.' Harlan waited, having learned that Mikel was suffering from a sickness. A glimmering dragonfly flew between them, reflecting the brightness of the moon off its wings. Reflective, Cassara watched it fly off. 'I dreamed he could help me, but I never dreamed that he was suffering.'

'I heard about his illness.'

'We've already lost so many people Harlan. You may not see him as family, but for me, he's more like a brother than a cousin. He shared truths with me, empowered me and protected me these past few months.'

Harlan felt guilty that he hadn't been able to be that person in her life; that he wasn't able to be the person she turned to and leaned on for safety and support. As he dwelled on the feeling it morphed, changing into anger.

She had pushed him away when he had wanted to do all those things for her, and Harlan couldn't help himself from wondering why.

'Cassara, we may have never been close, but we grew up together and blood still binds us.'

She scoffed.

'It's a pity blood doesn't matter to our father,' she replied with a biting tone.

'You were caught practising magic.' Harlan tried to justify the king's actions, trying to sound as though he still believed the words he had been raised to repeat.

Throughout his childhood, magic was something to be feared and the laws were designed to ensure magic could not harm people. However, now that he knew of his mother's faith in the craft and that she had turned to it for some unknown reason, he had begun to question everything he had been raised to accept as true.

'That's more than using your gifts of a seer,' he continued to attempt to reason. 'You broke the law, and that means someone trained you in sorcery.'

'Yes, someone did, but it was only to help me understand who and what I was, and how to control the nightmares. He wasn't a seer, so the only way he could teach me was by using sorcery.' The horse nickered behind him and the grassy flower field rustled as it meandered. 'It was only a matter of time until father found out what I was, and by learning about the craft, I was able to keep my secret a little longer as I came into my gifts. Although, I didn't think I would be discovered so soon.'

'Who helped you?' Harlan relaxed his arms and took a few steps forward. 'Was it the same person that tried to curse our father using our mother's pendant?'

'How rich!' Cassara's expression grew angry and she shook her head. 'You're accusing me of conspiring with the person that tried to curse our father... our family.' Cassara flicked her hair back off her face and slammed her hands to her hips. 'Unlike him, I'm not full of hate... at least, I never used to be.'

'You saved Mikel, a traitor to the crown. Do you have any idea how many people he must have harmed, how many deals he would have made to get where he did?' Harlan took a moment to stop himself from lecturing her and telling her she should have turned to him, her actual brother, instead of Mikel. 'If you were not working with him, then why did you save him instead of coming to me for help?'

'It's as I said, I had a dream that he could help me escape and bring me home to our mother's people.' Cassara sounded sad and brushed her hands on the skirt of her dress, which swayed with the wind. 'I was desperate and, in my dream, you weren't there. Mikel was, and he was leading me toward Mordiallok. It's difficult for me to tell the difference between real dreams and my visions, but this... this felt real.' Her eyes glistened as she stared back up at the stars. 'So, I went to him for help and safety, not to you.'

'Your cell in the dungeons should have been locked,' Harlan tightened the muscles in his face as he pointed to the ground, bothered by their frosty meeting, 'and you were wearing the chains that would suppress any ability to draw on magic.'

'You're right,' Cassara shrugged and the corner of her mouth twitched as though she may cry, 'but the dream I had came to me the night before I was arrested. Then, someone, I can't be sure who it was, saved me. This person freed me from the chains and left my cell unlocked.'

'Who?'

'I have my suspicions,' Cassara smirked and looked at him with a smug expression, 'but there's no way for me to know for certain.'

'You're a seer.' The wind swirled, whipping Cassara's hair into her face. Harlan checked where his stallion was behind him. 'Are you telling me you can't see who it was?'

'My gift isn't something I can just use at will, but, for the most part, that's right. When I dreamed of the night I escaped, I could almost see it all, but the face of the man who did free me… it's missing.' The slight wince was enough to give away how much it troubled her. 'So far as I know, there is only one person I have come across that I cannot see, that I seem to be blinded to, and he was in my cell before I escaped. He's even responsible for helping me meet the person who taught me about magic.'

'Who is it?'

'That's my little secret to keep.' A sly look crept over her face as Cassara tilted her head to the side. The sweet smell of the wildflowers moved around them as the breeze swirled, slightly changing direction. 'Tell me, why did you never tell me the truth about our mother's death?'

Harlan tensed and shook his head. 'I was trying to protect you by preserving the notion that our father was benevolent.'

She clicked her tongue on the roof of her mouth. 'You did well. You kept me ignorant.' The guilt of failing her overwhelmed him and he saw tears welling in her eyes. 'I never wanted your protection. What I needed was for my brother to be honest with me.'

'I'm sorry,' he offered, hoping she could see how much it pained him. 'I don't know how to make the hurt I caused you feel better. I thought I was doing the right thing.'

'I know, but your apology isn't enough now.' She sounded as though she may cry. Harlan wanted to hug her, but they had never been close as siblings. As royals, they were raised to rarely show affection and to maintain an aura of power by remaining ever impassive. 'Maybe if I had known how deep our father's vendetta went, I would have known the true danger and would have fled sooner. Instead, I tried to control things and suppress who I was.'

'I know, and that's why I want to help you.' The aching he felt for not being someone she felt she could approach choked him. 'I want to make amends.'

Turning cold, she gave him a blank, almost cruel look, hardening herself for whatever she was about to say. 'I'm willing to make a deal with you.'

'You want to make a deal.' The flippant way she suggested a transactional exchange to secure his aid, when he was offering it without strings attached, irked him, putting him more on edge. Behind him, Harlan heard his horse snacking on the flowers, sneezing as the flowers filled its nostrils. 'What deal?'

'You and your entourage help Mikel and I cross the border,' Cassara grinned, pleased with whatever she was about to say, 'and I won't go after the man who's lying in your bed right now.'

Harlan felt his heart pound in his chest as he formed fists with his hands. His stomach knotted and he felt nauseated. 'I don't know what you're talking about.'

'Oh Harlan,' the princess lowered her voice, 'we grew up together, I know when you're lying. Besides, I don't need my power to see what's going on. I have my ways.'

'You have an informant,' Harlan whispered into the night, closing his eyes as he took a breath.

'Technically, I don't, but Mikel does… and he's a sorcerer. The man cursed a certain pendant at Mikel's request, though that turned out to be a pointless feat. You should beware of the man with the scar on his neck.' She looked at him with a remorseful face. 'I don't want to see Maldwyn harmed, but if you force us to protect ourselves, he won't be safe.'

'You're threatening him?'

'I don't want to, but, if I have to, I will.'

Harlan, once again, went from pained to angry as he scowled at her. 'You come to me for help to cross the northern border, and, though I would have given it freely, you threaten Maldwyn's life.' Harlan stepped forward, close enough to stand taller than her, intimidating her and making her look away. 'If you so much as even try to harm him, I will kill you. I will kill you all.' Tilting his head as he glared at her, the prince tightened his fists. 'Lord Darius is a traitor, who has been bold enough to order an assassination attempt on my life. Not to mention, he was the arresting officer that brought our mother to our father for execution… he will die at my hand.' A glimmer of surprise twinkled in her eyes as she stared at him. 'As for you and Mikel, I think the mountain folk will be glad to lend me a hand and put you both in chains.'

'My, my,' she sounded callous, 'I hadn't realised.'

'Realised what?'

'That he was more than a fascination for you.' Harlan swallowed, trying to maintain his intimidating stance. 'You're in love with him.' Pulling a lock of hair back from her face, she gazed at him, astonished by the depths of his affection for Maldwyn. 'Does he know how you feel?'

'You quit being my sister when you threatened his life.' The horse whinnied to his back as if beckoning him to leave. 'I guess we were never that close after all.'

'Fine,' Cassara stepped back a few paces and plucked a flower from the ground, 'but how much do you know about him really?' She waved the flower at him, trying to get under his skin. Harlan stayed firm. 'How many secrets is he keeping from you, I wonder?'

Interest piqued, the prince folded his arms and took in a deep breath of the fresh, sweet air. 'What are you saying? What have you seen?'

'I thought we weren't that close.' The princess stalked around him, the way their father sometimes did, making his skin crawl. 'Truth be told, I haven't seen anything about Maldwyn.'

Uneasy, Harlan turned to her as she stopped circling him. 'I won't fall for your manipulation. So, how about this? I'll spare you and Mikel if you help me stop Lord Darius.' Her shoulders slackened. 'Come on Cassara, he had a part to play in our mother's death.'

'Tempting, but that was the past.' Her voice was flat and cold. 'Why would I help you harm the person who's keeping me safe now?'

'Because he's a traitor. It's in his nature to look out for himself. Having you there with him is simply a means to an end and he is using you.'

'You make a fair point, but there is a problem.' A sad look overtook her. 'I'm not sure I can trust you anymore. And I can't afford to be wrong.'

'You think you can trust him?'

'No.' Cassara smiled at him and her glistening eyes sparkled. 'Perhaps it is I who is using him.'

'What are you up to Cassara?'

'Give me time and I'll be in touch about your offer.' She turned and started walking away through the fields. 'Be on your guard,' she shouted, 'life always has consequences, I should know.'

'One more thing,' the prince called to her back, 'why did you flee to the northern border? It's one of the more dangerous paths to take.'

The princess stopped and sighed. 'Going south of the Anhalt Mountains,' she said over her shoulder, 'along the coastline, toward the western border would have placed us on a path that is well patrolled. Going west, over the Anhalt Mountains, would have taken us to the Erendil who have been chasing after Mikel for some time since he stole something that belonged to them. We couldn't be sure of the reception we would get there. East, by sea, would have been the better choice. I see that now, but it would have taken me farther away from where I wanted to go.' Twisting her head, a bit more over her shoulder, Cassara smiled at him and shrugged. 'I wanted to meet our mother's family. I wanted to go somewhere I could belong. So, we went north to where we could seek shelter with Lord Darius, but he won't permit us to cross the border.'

There was a moment of silence and neither of them moved. A nightingale twittered and swirled in the sky overhead, turning with the wind, gliding across the stars on its splayed wings. The prince's stallion snorted behind him, excited by something in the grass.

'If you mean well,' Cassara continued. Her voice wavered as she stared back at the horizon ahead of her. 'Then you should know you're right. There is something in the mine, though I have not seen it. Lord Darius wants it for himself, and it's quite powerful. Despite that he is sheltering us, the lord is an ambitious man and should never be allowed to reclaim the mine. Protect it from him and our father.'

Cassara muttered a goodbye and made her way into the night. Harlan never saw a horse but assumed she had one nearby, somewhere out of sight. For a while, Harlan watched her walking away, feeling more troubled now than before their meeting. Worried about Maldwyn he made his way back to the silhouette of his stallion, mounted its back and raced toward the castle.

CHAPTER TWENTY-TWO

The Hills of Yearning

I T WAS A PERFECT sort of evening, Maldwyn thought. The mottled orange and purple-hued sky had a calming radiance and the crescent moon blushed across the waking stars at the blazing sun. There were sounds of chatter coming from the campfires in the distance behind Maldwyn and there was a hint of roasting meat that wafted through the air.

Climbing the soft rolling hills, away from the encampment, Maldwyn paused to take in Harlan's silhouette in front of him, staring out at the shadowed forms of Karana Downs on the horizon, his back toward Maldwyn. Harlan's broad shoulders were pressed back, proud.

The burden of their complicated relationship weighed on Maldwyn as he wondered what plans fate had in store for them. Wanting to remember the simplicity of this moment, no matter what paths they were destined to follow, Maldwyn traced the lines of the prince in his mind.

The darkening sky had given Harlan's blonde hair a sandy brown tint. The sharp lines of his charcoal trousers and his grey-blue shirt woven with a gold dragon brocade gave the prince a refined presence that demanded attention. For an instant, Maldwyn felt sad, knowing that their time together would come to an end, and he hoped Harlan wasn't fraught with the same feeling of sorrow.

The last few days, as the prince wrapped up his royal engagements at Valondale Castle, and then set out with the king's regiment, had been like a dream. Maldwyn had come to ponder when he might awaken and find himself back in reality. No matter how much he wanted to hold onto the way things were, he worried how it would feel as it inevitably slipped through his fingers. Having lost so much in his life, Maldwyn wasn't sure he could withstand the pain, but he knew that nothing lasted forever.

For this reason, he lingered atop the hill, standing a few paces behind the prince, painting the image into his memory forever. When the moment passed, Maldwyn steeled himself and wandered over to the prince's side.

'It's a pretty view,' Maldwyn said as he looked out and studied the rolling hills. The shadows settled in the valleys, growing as the sun sank further beneath the skyline. Harlan didn't respond, nor did he move. 'Theodor is no longer with us and the number of soldiers in your company is smaller than it was at Valondale Castle.'

'You've been paying attention,' the prince praised, smirking as he inhaled deeply. 'It's peaceful here. I just stepped away to clear my mind.'

Maldwyn knew Harlan had been concerned about the news from Master Damyan regarding the formation of the Triple Covenant, the finalised security and trade agreement between Dresden, Haradnor and Ellinor. On the surface, it was good news for the kingdom, however, the prince feared this signalled the mobilisation of King Viktor's anti-magic agenda.

Damyan's message had also warned that the king had begun questioning staff directly about the theft of Queen Sonia's pendant, which meant he had begun to go around Master Damyan. The information being shared with the king was no longer able to be controlled, and that troubled Harlan.

The news had stirred the guilt within Maldwyn for all the truths he kept hidden, and he had wanted to come clean to Harlan, but the timing always seemed wrong. Recently, since confessing that his mother had used a spell to protect the prince, Harlan had been somewhat reserved. Come what may, this time Maldwyn planned to get things right, but felt that the prince wanted to be alone at this very moment.

'Do you want me to leave?'

Prince Harlan smiled in a way that said Maldwyn couldn't be more wrong. 'Not at all,' he said in a deep voice as he wrapped his hand around Maldwyn's, staring out at the distant shapes of the buildings in the downs. Maldwyn felt a fluttering sensation in his chest. 'I sent Theodor away with some men for a few days to complete an errand for me.'

'Is that wise to send your most trusted guard away?' Maldwyn was careful to mask the worry in his voice. 'Lord Darius is trying to have you assassinated.'

'I'm sure I am safe with you by my side. You've saved my life a few times now.' Harlan's hand was warm and comfortable in his grip. 'I sent Theodor to secure the disputed territories around the mine.'

'Are you betraying Jerrik?' Maldwyn asked, surprised by the prince's boldness.

Harlan shook his head, looking offended. 'He and a select few soldiers under his command, those that I trust, are securing the area on behalf of the Erendil. I owe Jerrik for helping me these past few months, and for keeping you safe when I couldn't.'

'I see.' Maldwyn was both flattered by the prince and embarrassed to have assumed the worst. 'Are you not afraid of the fallout with your father?'

'No,' Harlan sounded confident. 'They won't be wearing the palace armour that makes them identifiable. Lord Darius is more likely to suspect either mountain folk or forces from the Kingdom of Valdemar, just west of the mountains.' The prince was calm, yet his face fell into sadness as he let go of Maldwyn's hand. 'There's something you need to know.' The setting sun highlighted the prince's strong jawline and cheekbones. Maldwyn searched his face for clues, waiting for the prince to go on. 'It's about the survivors from your hometown.'

'What is it?'

'I received word that, in my absence, my father has decided to send your friends along the southern coastline.'

'Why?' Maldwyn put his hands on his hips. 'What's there to send them to?'

'There's a place where people are sent to work as labourers. My father forces them to lay roads between cities and towns.' Maldwyn pulled back a step, hooking his thumbs into the belt of his casual travelling attire. 'This particular group of labourers are laying a new roadway along the coastline to secure a route into Valdemar that goes south of the Anhalt Mountains, avoiding the dangers therein.' Harlan rubbed his forehead and eyes. 'The conditions they will be under are poor, and, in some ways, they will be worse than the palace dungeons.'

Maldwyn held his hands over his face and turned away frustrated. He wondered whether this was the beginning of the end.

'I'm so sorry,' Harlan murmured, placing his hands on Maldwyn's shoulders.

Dropping his hands from his hips, Maldwyn took a few steps toward the camp and halted. The thought of making things worse by rescuing his people with his abilities troubled Maldwyn. He didn't know what the right thing to do was. In the downs, Jaecen and Erik were waiting; to the south, his people were in trouble; and here, the prince wanted him to stay.

The prince breathed in deeply and pulled Maldwyn into a warm, strong embrace that made him feel assured. Relaxing in his strong arms, Maldwyn wished that time would stop. He let go of his power and lived a while in the prince's arms until the world returned to its usual rhythm.

Maldwyn leaned back from Harlan's firm hold.

'We'll save them,' the prince reassured him, smiling, and stroking along Maldwyn's hairline. 'I promise to do what it takes to free them, but it is going to take some patience.'

Gazing over to Karana Downs, Maldwyn studied the jagged, black shapes of the town in the distance outlined by the glowing sky. By now, Erik and Jaecen would be worried. The thought occurred to him that Leith may have returned to the downs by now and Maldwyn wanted to meet him while he had the chance. Besides, he owed it to everyone to return to Karana Downs and finish what had been started.

'There's something I must do… over there… in the city.'

Puzzled, Harlan shifted his stance, wincing a tad in the corner of his left eye. 'You're coming back though, right?'

The question wasn't unexpected, what was, however, was the touch of sadness in the prince's voice. The sounds of the crickets chirping in the grass seemed to grow, filling the quiet space between them.

'I'm not sure when,' Maldwyn answered with a heavy heart and mind. The prince was the only person that could tear him away from the places where he had obligations. The Erendil had set Maldwyn on a new path, one that meant he was ever-present, ignoring the woes of his past and setting aside his concerns about the future. For Maldwyn, this was not an easy task, and the prince made it more difficult.

Having set aside the truths he wanted to share with the prince, seeing that now was not the right moment, Maldwyn felt tormented by the weight of the secrets he was keeping.

'Okay,' Harlan started and cleared his throat. 'But, stay safe and never let me hear rumours of your death again.'

In the background, the hushed sounds coming from the camp drew Maldwyn's mind away. The prophecy of his impending death entered his thoughts. Erik had told him not to fear death; that all creatures are fated to die someday, and to bear in mind that knowing it was coming could be thought of as a gift. Few people have the chance to live their life as though every day could be their last. Despite what Erik had told him, Maldwyn was struck by the desire to live. He wanted to know what kind of king the prince would make and to see how he would age.

The memory he painted of the prince standing on this very hill, came to the forefront, and Maldwyn intended to take it with him, until the end. 'I wouldn't dream of it,' he lied, smiling.

Maldwyn turned his back and walked away, back down the hill toward the encampment settled over the grassy hills and valleys. The large canvas tents were huddled around the rising ground, like wintry snow caps, and smoke from the fires coiled upward to the deepening purple skies. The laughter around him, as Maldwyn passed by the fires where the soldiers ate, seemed far away. Sentries remained on guard and patrols made their rounds, checking the security of the camp. No one paid much attention to him, knowing that he had been brought from Valondale Castle at the prince's command.

Maldwyn felt sure rumours were swirling through the troop about him, but, for the most part, these were just curious murmurs. Luckily, he had not been recognised, which was something Erik and Jaecen had both feared.

Once Maldwyn collected the few things that he had brought with him from Karana Downs, he headed to where the horses were being kept, on the other side of the camp. The makeshift area that the horses were confined in was bigger than he expected, with a rope fence, that was supported by thin spiked posts, marking the area. The horse he had borrowed was easy to spot, standing in a section roped off on its own. The golden-palomino horse shone as the setting sun kissed its coat and its white mane twinkled at the moon behind.

When Maldwyn finished saddling the horse, he mounted and set off over the hillside toward Karana Downs. Glancing back, he spotted the prince, standing alone as though he were an island.

The wide-open pastures on the outskirts of Karana Downs were quieter than he remembered, with only the cows occasional mooing filling the air. The humble dwellings were surrounded by crops poking through the ground and could be seen dotted about the fields. The orange candlelight from inside gleamed through the windows.

Reaching the town, Maldwyn was welcomed by the strong smell of steel and ash, which was still pouring out of the town's forges. The horse was good at navigating around the broken pottery and piles of muck that marked the streets. The window shutters of the smaller cottages, two-storey houses and shops were closed and the alleyways, between the buildings, were empty, if not for the few homeless people laying on the ground.

As Maldwyn rode by a small alley that led to nowhere, he heard a young girl's voice singing. There was something about the words of the song, which seemed to be about the life of a starving orphan, that tore into his gut.

He wanted to offer her money or a meal, but was cautious of Jaecen's warning. As much as he wished it to be otherwise, Maldwyn could not help all the people suffering in this place.

When Maldwyn reached the crossroads where the inn was located on the corner, he rode by the veranda that wrapped around the building, toward the stables at the back. Oliver was there, limping as he tended to the horses. The relief on his face to see the horse returned was evident. After learning that Jaecen and Erik were at the tavern a few doors down, not at the inn, Maldwyn left and made his way down the street.

The tavern was a smaller building than the inn, not in height, but in width from the street. An alley ran between it and the closed store on its left. It was loud in the tavern, Maldwyn could hear the laughter, talking, shouting, and crying from the street. Two men, arm in arm, left the tavern singing and stumbling down the path. Maldwyn doubted they would make it home.

Recalling that this was the place Leith was rumoured to work, Maldwyn hesitated, unsure if he was ready to meet the man that had abandoned him and his mother. He considered leaving and waiting by the entrance to the inn, but sooner or later Maldwyn would have to face the answers he was avoiding. Maybe by hearing what had happened, from someone other than his mother, he could learn who his parents were and leave things where they belonged, in the past.

Pulling the door open, the smell of spirits and body odour coated the inside of Maldwyn's nose. It was busy and loud. Drunk people staggered around the room, hanging onto chairs and tables for support. A woman was crying against the wall on the far side of the tavern, beside a blazing fire, her face buried in her hands. People seemed to be ignoring that she was upset. The counter in the back right-hand corner of the tavern was lined with people shouting their orders to the man and woman serving drinks.

Scanning the faces of the tavern for Erik and Jaecen, Maldwyn slowly walked through the room, toward the counter, until he saw them gambling with a group of soldiers. Managing to lock eyes with Erik, who seemed happy to see him alive, but signalled that he and Jaecen couldn't leave the table at that moment, Maldwyn walked up to the serving counter. He managed to spot a free stool as someone stumbled away, hands clutching several mugs. Mildly impressed that he didn't spill any of the mugs as he hobbled back to his table, Maldwyn shook his head and sat down at the end of the counter, tucked against the wall.

Behind the counter were barrels with stained corks stopping the wine from pouring out all over the floor. Above the barrels were shelves with ceramic bottles of what Maldwyn expected were more expensive spirits.

The man bartending was tall and scruffy looking, with greying hair and a short, well-trimmed beard that distracted from the subtle wrinkles stretching out from the corners of his eyes. He was wearing a light-tan-coloured shirt and dark brown pants that were tucked into his black boots.

Based on what Maldwyn knew, the man seemed the right age to be his mother's husband. He watched as the woman went into a room out the back and the man Maldwyn assumed was Leith served drinks. The man seemed friendly from the way he laughed with his patrons. It was a deep sort of dirty-sounding belly laugh that he bellowed. The sort to make anyone smile. Waiting patiently, Maldwyn wondered what he would say when he came over.

Then, the moment happened, and the man stood in front of Maldwyn, staring at him from behind his chestnut-coloured eyes. 'What can I get for you?'

'Erm, just an ale,' Maldwyn replied, buying himself more time.

As the man spun around and moved behind the counter, filling a simple wooden mug with ale from a barrel, Maldwyn reached into his pocket and pulled out the note that had been left with him in the field. A ball formed in his throat as he saw the man coming back over.

'Here you go,' the man said, plonking the cup down on the beaten countertop. 'That'll be five copper pieces.'

'Are you the owner of this tavern,' Maldwyn checked as he reached into the coin pouch hanging from his belt and placed five copper coins on the counter.

'Aye, I sure am!' The man watched him carefully with a suspicious look on his face. 'What's it to you?'

'My friend told me your name is Leith,' Maldwyn placed the note he held in his other hand on the counter, with his coins, 'and I hoped you might be able to help me with this.' Wary, Leith picked up the note and peeled it open. 'My name is Maldwyn, please help me.'

The man's mouth parted slightly and the muscles in his forehead tensed as he examined the drawing and words on the parchment. It was clear he had seen it before, and never expected to set eyes on it again.

'My mother died,' Maldwyn went on as he removed his hands from the counter, hiding that they were tremoring from the surge of emotions. 'She left me with that, and I hoped you could point me toward my birth parents… to understand who I am.'

Leith folded the parchment back up and slid the note across the counter to Maldwyn. 'I'm sorry about Renate, she was a tough woman.'

'She was,' Maldwyn agreed, remembering how independent she had been compared to other women in his hometown, but, he supposed, that had never been her choice.

'I'm not sure there is anything I can tell you.'

'Please, I have come a long way.'

Shrugging Leith turned to walk away, leaving Maldwyn without answers. The memory of the impression his mother had given, that Leith may have encouraged his powers, came to the fore of his thoughts. Quickly checking that no one else was looking at them, Maldwyn cupped one hand over his other, hiding it from view.

'Look,' Maldwyn told him, releasing his power, and conjuring a tiny flame between the thumb and forefinger of the hand he was concealing. Leith's mouth went agape, and his eyes widened. Maldwyn quickly shook his hands, letting the flame go out as he drew his power back. 'Please, don't say anything,' he said, looking over his shoulder to check none of the guards in the tavern was suspicious. Most were too busy gambling to notice. 'I don't need much from you. I just want to know anything you can tell me about the day I was found.'

'I don't think anything I can tell you could explain…'

From the other end of the counter, the woman that had been serving drinks with Leith shouted for his attention. Leith momentarily waved her off and told her he was busy.

'I'm sorry,' Maldwyn said, shaking his head and shoving the note back into his pocket. 'I shouldn't have come. Please, forget I said or did anything.'

'No, wait.' Leith reached over and grabbed Maldwyn's wrist to stop him from leaving. His hands were aged, and his skin was dry. 'Give me some time to do a few things around here, then meet me outside in the alley once you've finished your drink.'

'Alright.' Maldwyn bowed his head and pressed himself back down into the hard stool.

Leith pushed the coins back to Maldwyn. 'You can keep your coins. I won't accept them.'

As Leith disappeared into the backroom, Maldwyn placed the coins back in his pouch and hid his face in his hands. He took a few breaths there to calm himself, wishing Harlan or his best friend, Ailaya, were by his side. The ale was warming and helped a wave of emotions pass by.

Sitting by the counter, sipping his drink, Maldwyn thought of how different his life might have been had Leith stayed by his mother's side. He imagined what they would have been like together, as a couple. Would Leith have been the type to open doors for her, or make her smile when she was sad?

Maldwyn let himself picture the sort of father he might have been. He envisaged that he would have been supportive and kind, exactly the sort of person he could have benefitted from growing up. So many possible opportunities were missed, and a whole world of potential realities was lost because he didn't stay.

After he finished his drink, he sat still on the stool, quietly waiting with his hands on his lap, like a child expecting his parent to come and get him. Glancing over every so often to see that Erik and Jaecen were still seated at the table, gambling, Maldwyn felt utterly alone.

People at another table cheered for the dice to land the way they wanted and erupted into a joyous uproar, singing when they won the bet. At another table, deafening laughter broke out. The more Maldwyn tried to ignore the cacophony of merriment, the more it burned his ears, irritating him to no end.

Finally, he saw Leith emerge from the backroom, slip out from behind the counter and gesture for Maldwyn to meet him outside. Jumping out of his seat, Maldwyn left the tavern, eager to leave the noisy establishment.

The alley was dark and cramped. There was an overturned crate next to an empty barrel, leaning against the tavern wall. Leith was standing with his back against the wall, one foot resting on the crate, arms folded. Maldwyn stopped a few paces from him and stared at the muck-covered ground.

'What did your mother tell you about things back then?'

Annoyed that he was straight to the point, Maldwyn frowned at the ground. He got the impression Leith wanted to get things over and done with so Maldwyn would leave. It wasn't that he expected the man to care about him, but his apparent disinterest bothered Maldwyn more than he anticipated.

'Not much, I'm afraid. She didn't tell me anything until she was dying.' Maldwyn stared up at him to gauge a reaction, but Leith didn't seem surprised by that fact. 'She said that you had both been trying to have a child of your own and couldn't. That one day, she found me abandoned as an infant, wrapped in a blanket with that note I showed you. She convinced you to keep me as your own.'

'Is that all she said?' Leith seemed bothered when Maldwyn nodded his reply. 'Figures she'd only tell you the part she could stomach.'

'What do you mean?'

Leith drew in a large breath of air and moved away from the wall, knocking the crate as he placed his foot back on the ground. Maldwyn began to dread whatever he was about to be told and considered leaving to preserve his memory of his mother.

'Renate and I split because we didn't see eye-to-eye when it came to you. At first, we didn't know who you belonged to, which was why we decided to keep you and raise you as our own. I knew how much it meant to her to be a mother.'

The tavern door in the street banged as it was thrust open and a man paused by the alley to catch himself on the wall. They waited until he was gone.

'I hadn't wanted children, so, being unable to conceive felt like a blessing in some ways.' The words cut Maldwyn deeply. 'Naturally, when she brought you home, I had not been impressed. One day, when I was out working in the fields, a woman visited our home, looking for you. Renate wanted to keep you. So, she told the woman that an infant had been found, but that it had been taken by a priest for its safety. She sent the woman through Haradnor, to sail northeast, beyond the Isle of Wight to a place known as the Evermires, where she had said the priest was headed.' Leith cleared his throat, and his face was ashamed. 'If the woman didn't die from the journey, or bandits along the way, then she was probably captured by raiders and sold into slavery somewhere over the ocean.'

Maldwyn felt something in him shatter at the prospect of his last connection being dead or enslaved. 'Who was she?'

'Renate said her name was Eretrya. There had been some sort of a tragedy and you were lost. What that was, or her relation to you, or even how you ended up in the field, I don't know. And, because of Renate, we will never know.' Maldwyn chewed his cheek, wishing he could forget what he'd learned. 'After that, Renate and I fought… we fought a lot. In the end, I couldn't stop wondering about what might have happened to the mysterious woman, nor live with Renate's lie and what it meant she was capable of, so I left.'

Leith let his arms fall loose at his sides. Maldwyn stared back at the ground, avoiding eye contact, angry that it hadn't crossed Leith's mind to take the infant he had been responsible for with him. Yet then, Maldwyn supposed Leith had never wanted him.

'Was she a good mother at least? She wanted it more than anything.'

Maldwyn sniffed, holding together his broken pieces. 'I don't remember much before I was about three or four and we learned of my abilities. She believed in the law and that made things complicated... difficult.'

Maldwyn hesitated. His earliest memories still pained him to reflect on, and he carried the self-hatred she gave him everywhere.

'When she would lock me away in the broom cupboard, as punishment for not controlling my power, I used to stare into the darkness and count, holding everything in and wishing you would open the door and rescue me. That you would realise you had left me behind.'

The darkness of the cramped alley reminded him of the cupboard, and, just like when he was a child, Maldwyn stared at the ground and counted, keeping his sadness to himself.

'You never came.' Mustering all his strength, Maldwyn swallowed his emotions and forced himself to look up at the man that could have been his father. 'She was a strong woman, and a hard mother. Cold and, at times, cruel, but, for all her faults, she did her best and there was one thing she did just right.'

Leith frowned and crossed his arms back over his chest. It was clear he was uncomfortable with the turn the conversation had taken.

CHAPTER TWENTY-TWO

'What was that?'

The pain of more than twenty years rose inside Maldwyn as he stared at Leith's aged face. 'She was there.'

'You don't know how sorry I am about that.' Maldwyn no longer cared. It was too late for an apology that wasn't given out freely. 'I don't know anything else to help you, but I promise that I will keep your secret safe.'

'You had better,' Maldwyn told him, not wanting to let Leith off the hook for abandoning him. 'Thank you for being honest,' Maldwyn said, feeling his emotions rise back to the surface. He turned and walked away, heading back to the inn where he would wait for Erik and Jaecen.

Angry and alone, Maldwyn stopped by the downstairs kitchen at the inn and bought a bottle of wine. He ignored his training, knowing Jaecen would be disappointed, nevertheless, just this once, he was going to indulge himself and make the pain of being unwanted by his father, hated by his mother, and remaining without answers go away.

He sat on the floor in his room, back against the bed and poured the wine into a cup, which he drank. Then, he drank another and another and another, continuing to drink until he felt his mind change, his eyes unable to focus and his tongue heavy. He told himself the pain was less, but that wasn't quite true.

CHAPTER TWENTY-THREE

The Debt

WHEN MALDWYN WOKE, he was lying on his side, sprawled out on the floor. The empty wine bottle had been knocked over, red droplets forming around the unsealed lip, and the cup from which he had been drinking was upside down. His eyelids were heavy and his head pounded as he looked around the room. A rotten sensation in his gut left him nauseated. He tried to swallow the ball forming in his throat, but his mouth was too dry.

Pushing himself up to sit with his back against the bed, Maldwyn noticed another bottle by his feet that he didn't remember purchasing and regretted how much he had drunk the night before. He broke into a sweat and wanted to be sick, feeling the burning sensation creeping up into his mouth, making him gag. He was quick to cup his hand to his mouth and force himself to swallow, refusing to be sick on the floor.

It didn't help that the air in his room was stale and smelled of red wine and port. After taking a moment to collect himself, Maldwyn stood from the floor and went over to open the window, hoping the fresh air would help take the edge off.

But when he opened the leaded, glass pane, he was greeted by the thick odour of molten iron and coal. He yearned for the freshness of the hills and pondered what the prince might be doing.

Maldwyn hated himself. He had been so hopeless and pitiable, self-destructing after meeting someone he had never really known. Before last night, Leith had been nothing more than an idea in his head.

Ashamed, knowing how disappointed others would be in him, Maldwyn let his head fall. The streets outside were quiet and the sun hadn't yet risen fully, washing them in dusky hues. A few mounted guards headed north through the streets, toward the rich district that surrounded the main entrance to the keep. The horses looked prestigious.

When he had wasted enough time and felt able to take a breath without needing to wretch, Maldwyn turned to see the state of the room. The door to the cupboard beneath the bedside table was ajar and the fat candle on the tabletop had burned down to a stub.

At the foot of the bed, which had its bedcovers lumped over the side as though Maldwyn had reached for them during the night, was the other bottle of wine beside the deep trunk. The upside-down cup was in front of the dead fireplace and there were red wine stains on the floorboards where they had dripped from the fallen bottle.

Seeing the result of his downfall only made him feel worse as the shame overwhelmed him. Maldwyn picked up the bottle, not far from where he stood by the window, and placed it on top of the bedside table, next to what remained of the candle.

Angry with himself, Maldwyn began to tidy the room, fixing the covers on the bed and scrubbing the wine from the floor. Something was comforting to Maldwyn about cleaning. He supposed it was because he had grown up working hard in a village, and went on to work as a palace servant for long enough that it had become somewhat of a routine means of distraction for him.

He felt mildly better when everything appeared in order, and paused to have a drink of water, wetting his swollen tongue. He grabbed an apple from his pack and sat on the bed, being careful not to make a mess of the covers. Stretching his neck, and turning his head from side to side, he noted that he felt a strain in his neck muscles from sleeping on the floor. The apple was sweet and crisp when he bit into it.

Once he had finally dressed and the sun smiled at him through the window, Maldwyn left his room and made his way down the creaking stairs to the dining room. The place was quiet with only a few people seated at the tables eating breakfast. There, he spotted Erik and Jaecen waiting for him, seated by a table in the far corner. Both of them had a bowl of porridge for breakfast. Jaecen saw Maldwyn first and waved him over, looking pleased to see him.

The owner of the inn scratched his wiry beard and cast Maldwyn a pitiful gaze as he cleared some bowls from one of the tables in the dining area. He paused as he went by Maldwyn and offered to bring him a bowl of porridge for breakfast. Smiling, Maldwyn nodded.

'I hope you're feeling better,' the owner added, slapping Maldwyn on the shoulder with his free hand.

His queasiness had subsided for the most part and Maldwyn wished he could remember coming back down here for more wine. Maldwyn looked at the innkeeper awkwardly as the man continued to the kitchen with a pile of bowls, cradled in one arm.

Sitting at the table to join his comrades, and trying to suppress his remaining headache, Maldwyn glossed over as many of their questions as he could, making sure to apologise for not returning sooner. The steam off the porridge that was brought to him had a gentle whiff of cinnamon, and there were dried fruits stirred into the mix. A few nuts were sprinkled over the top.

'Those guards we were gambling with had some interesting insights, Eminence,' Jaecen said in a hushed voice before pushing a spoonful of porridge into his mouth. Though he was masking his accent while in the downs, there was a polished edge to the way he spoke that reminded Maldwyn of his usual lilt. 'Apparently, Lady Adria has been meeting with mercenaries in secret.'

'Mercenaries?' Maldwyn looked from Jaecen to Erik, as he picked up the wooden spoon, which he poked into the mushy porridge. 'Why would she be meeting with mercenaries?'

'Morale is low among the king's men here.' Erik leaned forward, lowering his voice. The scar tearing through his right brow was more noticeable in the light of day. 'They are torn between their king and their lord.'

'Eminence, it seems as though the mercenaries belong to her husband and she is attempting to buy their allegiance to assure her security.' Jaecen ran his tongue over his front teeth, sucking out the piece of oat that had settled along his gums. 'Whatever her reasoning, it seems clear that she doesn't trust her husband's ambition any longer and has plans of her own.'

'On another note,' Erik started as Jaecen went quiet, taking in another mouthful of oatmeal, 'You've arrived just in time.' Erik checked around to see whether the owner of the inn was within earshot. He was not. 'We have a way into the keep.'

'What?' Maldwyn asked, surprised by the news. Jerrik had been trying to find a way into the keep for months, and now it seemed there may finally be a path inside the impenetrable walls. 'How?'

'Oliver's brother has been moved to the company manning the entry gates to the keep,' Jaecen answered, with a sly expression. 'We're meeting him tonight.'

When they had eaten their meals and finished briefing each other on the time lost, Maldwyn left the inn to wander the streets, waiting for nightfall to come. By late afternoon, the clouds rolled in, blackening the ashen air. Maldwyn could smell the rain in the atmosphere, despite the stench bursting from the forges on the outskirts of town. A heavy droplet fell from the sky, landing on the back of Maldwyn's hand, warning of a brewing storm.

After heading back to the inn for shelter, the rain developed into a persistent downpour, hammering on the roof above his room. He closed the window, shutting out the rain which was falling at a sharp angle. The shutters on the outside of the building banged.

Wasting time, Maldwyn pulled out Morloch's diary, reading more of the priest's notes and learning about the initiation ritual whereby Hel's followers burned a two-faced skull into their forearms. When he had read enough, Maldwyn spent the final hours with Jaecen meditating, until he felt as calm and centred as he had within the Anhalt Mountains.

As the afternoon passed into evening, the downpour continued, with occasional cracks of thunder which roared at lightning strikes. It was as though the gods had come to warn them about what lay inside the keep.

Dressed in black from head to toe, they moved like shadows through the empty, greyscale streets, streams of water channelled on either side of the paths. It was dark and the rain was cold. The moon was hidden behind the dense cloud cover, making it difficult to be certain of the time.

Oliver's brother, Loris, was a short fellow, smaller than Maldwyn expected, with a kind smile and prominent brows, and waited for them by the battlements, not far from the main gate. The brown and deep blue, leather armour he wore looked a little long in the torso.

The plan was for them to be waved through by Loris and do some investigating. At dawn, they were set to be smuggled out in a supply wagon. A servant had already been bribed to help them escape the next morning. Despite the rain, the plan was set and things needed to go according to plan if they were ever going to pass through the gate to the keep.

'Someone is going to need to distract the other guard on this side of the gate,' Loris told them in a softly spoken, modulated voice. The black walls behind him merged with the starless night sky. 'Lead him away and waving you through won't be an issue.'

'I can do it,' Maldwyn volunteered, standing tall.

'Mal, we need you in there,' Erik replied, sounding worried. The black cloth covering the lower half of his face, below his hooded jacket, made it difficult to discern his expression.

'I know and, thanks to your guidance, I'm sure I can lead him away and meet you inside the gate.' Erik seemed unsure, however, he didn't argue with Maldwyn.

'I believe in you, Eminence.' Jaecen sang in his normal accent, slapping a wet hand to Maldwyn's shoulder. 'Before we split up, we need an idea of the layout of what lies within these walls.'

'I've already drawn up a rough layout for you, but with the rain, I fear it won't be much help,' Loris said, pulling out a rolled-up piece of cloth from the neckline of his leather chest armour. 'Basically, there are five main buildings. The stables, are on your left as you enter the grounds. The servant quarters, kitchen and laundry are all kept in the same building opposite the well, just up from the stables. There is a guesthouse on the right, which is next to the temple of Forseti, the god of justice. Finally, there is the main hall of the keep, where the lord and lady reside.' Taking the time to look at each of them, Loris grinned. 'Give me some time to return to my post before approaching the gate. Good luck!'

The three of them waited against the tall, stone walls surrounding the keep, trying to stay as dry as possible. Maldwyn went first, jogging toward the main gate, splashing through the puddles along the dirt footpath. He paused, nearing the entrance to the keep.

The gates to the keep were monumental, crafted from the same black stones of the fortifications. Carved into the gates, around the lowered portcullis, was a long, zigzagging serpent that wound through a leafy ribbon. Through the teeming rain, Maldwyn discerned that the guard closest to him was staring down the main street. Beside him, was Loris who glanced the other way when he spotted Maldwyn sneaking toward the other guard on duty.

Swift and silent, Maldwyn crept up on the guard. He grabbed the money pouch hanging from the guard's belt, before shoving him and running up the main street away from the gates.

'That prick just stole my money!' The guard shouted to Maldwyn's back, regaining his footing.

'Are you going to just stand there? Go after him!' Loris shouted to the other guard.

When Maldwyn heard the other guard chasing him, racing up the drenched, slippery paths, he turned down a side street toward the poor district, leading him further from the gate. He dodged a group of saturated paupers shivering on the streets and jumped over a pile of wood stacked by a workshop. A drunk man staggered in his path. Maldwyn ducked down an alleyway, slowing to a jog.

Reaching a dead-end, Maldwyn waited until he heard the splashing of the guard hurrying up the alley behind him. Releasing his grip over his power, Maldwyn watched as the rain stopped falling, drops hanging in the air like falling stars, glimmering at the frozen crack of lightning above. Turning around, he came face to face with the guard.

His face was filled with anger. Moving closer, walking in the frozen rain, Maldwyn noted the way the droplets hit him with no force and clung to the surface of his clothes. The air smelled sweeter with the rain, and the night was unusually bright from the whitening bolt suspended between the clouds.

Maldwyn placed the money pouch in the guard's hand and smiled, hoping the man wouldn't hold a grudge.

Running back to the main gate, Maldwyn hoped he could rejoin his comrades before time returned to the world. He felt relieved when he saw Loris in the distance, waving Jaecen and Erik through the open portcullis.

Racing time itself, Maldwyn sprinted, seeing that the rain was starting to fall in slow motion. As Maldwyn passed through the gate, he heard the lattice gateway click into place.

Reaching the other side, thunder boomed as the world returned to life and he rushed to hide by a large oak tree in the middle of the grounds. Bent over, Maldwyn pulled the cloth covering his nose and mouth down, taking a moment to catch his breath.

Upon the first impression, the keep was pristine, despite the muddy pools from the pouring rain, and the architecture reminded Maldwyn of the capital. Buildings were wrapped in vines that hung like drapes in some areas. From where he hid, Maldwyn saw the stables, servant quarters and the guesthouse. He also noted that there was a patrol heading toward where he guessed the main hall was located.

'All clear!' Loris shouted back by the gatehouse. 'Shut the gate!'

'Nicely done,' Erik muttered, looking down at him from the path a few paces away from where Maldwyn was crouching. Jaecen's face was hidden by the hood over his head and cloth covered the lower half of his face. 'You've gained a lot of control.'

'I had good teachers,' Maldwyn said, pushing himself up to stand.

His saturated clothes felt heavy, and the hood did nothing to keep him dry. Pulling up the mask from around his neck, Maldwyn stepped out from behind the tree, following them toward the stables.

The stables were big and smelled mostly of hay. Maldwyn could tell they had been cleaned before nightfall. The horses stamped their feet and neighed every so often. A large, empty, two-wheeled cart was kept at the far end of the stables, arms resting on the ground. Waiting under the cover of the stables, they hoped for the rain to ease up while they studied the patrol routes as best as possible through the blanket of rain.

'I think we should split up,' Jaecen suggested, standing near the cart with his arms folded. 'We can cover more ground if we do.'

'Won't that be more dangerous?' Erik was sitting on the ground, against the wall with one leg extended.

'I don't like it,' Maldwyn started, feeling a little warmer having stayed out of the wind and rain for a while, 'but I agree with Jaecen. There are too many buildings to search together. It would take us too long.'

'Okay,' Erik scratched his chin, deep in thought as he pressed his head back up to the wall. 'Well, I used to be a servant. I am familiar with the layout of these areas and know where we might find information.'

'You're right,' Jaecen said, picking at some dirt beneath his nails. 'You should scout around the servant quarters.'

'I'll take the main hall,' Maldwyn volunteered. The looks on each of their faces said what they didn't dare to utter. 'To get in there, someone is going to have to cross the grounds in direct view of the patrol. Not to mention, we have no idea what is inside that place. With my abilities, I am in the best position to do what needs to be done.'

'Be careful,' Jaecen warned. 'I suppose that leaves the temple and guesthouse to me.'

'There seems to be a bit of activity around the guesthouse.' Erik nodded his head toward the stable door as if he could see the outside from where he sat, which he could not. 'It can't be Princess Cassara, or we would have known from reports sooner. Wherever the lord is keeping her, it must be in the main building.'

'Don't worry, I'll be careful,' Jaecen said, making a troubled face. The horse behind Maldwyn poked its nose over the enclosure and exhaled beside his face. Maldwyn noticed that there was an insignia on the saddle blanket he didn't recognise, hanging over the stall door. 'We should meet back here before dawn so that we are ready to leave with the supply wagon.'

After a short while longer, the rain had eased to a drizzle and they headed out to explore the keep. The main building was lit up by torches on the other side of the open courtyard. Maldwyn crossed the grounds with ease, remaining unnoticed, and entered the main house through the service entrance on the side of the building.

The door was small and plain, tucked away, out of clear view. Maldwyn was relieved that it wasn't locked as he opened it, entering the lord's residence.

Beyond the door was a long corridor with glowing, framed lanterns hanging from the walls between the evenly spaced archways. A gaudy hallstand with painted gold legs stood between two arches. The stone floors were polished and the high ceilings made the corridor feel bigger. Maldwyn was surprised that, although this was a service entrance, there didn't appear to be designated areas separating the staff from nobility, and he was pleased that there was no one lurking in this part of the keep.

As Maldwyn crept through the main house within the keep, he saw that the furnishings were richly decorated with gold tones on almost every surface, to the point of being tacky. Even the creamy candles had been tinted with a gold fleck. It was obvious that Lord Darius had been pocketing a large portion of the king's funds, and had no issue putting that fact on display inside the keep, for all to see.

Passing through several parlour rooms, storage areas and dining halls, avoiding detection with the aid of his gift whenever he heard footsteps approaching, Maldwyn came across a spiralling, narrow staircase beyond a short, stone archway. The rain could be heard pelting against the windows further up the stairs in the growing gusts of wind. He waited and listened to check there was no one at the top. Hearing no signs of activity, Maldwyn climbed the stairs.

At the top was a small alcove with an arched, leaded window and a hallway that extended to the right. The corridor was long and dark despite the gleaming lanterns. Walking slowly and carefully, Maldwyn smelled burning wood thickening the air and coating his nostrils. Following the scent, Maldwyn came upon a door that was slightly ajar. Inside he heard hushed voices.

'Did you mean it?' A familiar voice asked from inside the room.

Maldwyn warily stepped nearer, keeping as close to the stone wall as possible, and peered through the gap. Inside the room, he saw Princess Cassara, looking regal in her silver, long-sleeved, beaded dress, sitting in an armchair.

Opposite the princess was Mikel, resting back in his seat. His slick, black hair was combed back and his usual sneer was gloomier than Maldwyn remembered. He was pale and it was as if it was difficult for him to show any expression.

'No,' the princess replied quietly, staring at a popping fireplace. 'Without him, I'd have never met Erik.'

Maldwyn leaned a little closer, remembering that he had been the person that brought Erik to help the princess. He wondered what she was talking about with Mikel.

'They connected me to something I didn't know I needed and Erik helped me to see the world in a new light.' Princess Cassara bowed her head sadly as she reflected on her mentor. 'One very different than my father would have had me believe. The world is terrible, but he and Erik helped me to see that it is also beautiful and full of extraordinary people.'

She smiled to one side and tucked a lock of her glossy, black hair behind her ear. Though Maldwyn had never noticed it before, he saw a familial similarity as the two cousins sat side-by-side.

'And, I know in my heart that it was he who freed me from my cell, even though he appears in my dreams as nothing more than a blur. Without Maldwyn, I'd be dead, and I'd have never gotten the opportunity to learn all the things you've shared with me. To learn about my mother and a whole half of my family I barely knew existed.' The princess grinned and leaned over to hold Mikel's hand, which was resting on the arm of his chair. 'Though, I wish I had seen how much pain you were in.'

'I've been honoured to know you, princess.'

Mikel coughed, holding his other hand over his mouth. It was a deep phlegmy cough. Cassara let his hand go, giving him space to have a fit.

'I guess, I owe him my life, my very essence, for setting me free from my father's tyranny, which was somehow more than the literal chains around my wrists. It's a debt I don't know that I'll ever repay. I only threatened Harlan with it because I didn't know how sincere he was. He's always been the Crown Prince and we've never been close enough for me to know how he truly feels about my being a seer. I needed to know Harlan would help us.'

'You make me wish I had been nicer to him,' Mikel muttered, letting his hand fall from his mouth. For a long time, Maldwyn hated Mikel, but seeing the sick knight now, he pitied him. 'I just assumed all the servants in the palace were puppets to the king.'

'Maybe you'll get your chance to make amends before the end.'

Mikel laughed, weakly. 'Maybe you will get the revenge your mother deserves. We are family after all.'

'Getting my father will be difficult,' Cassara rested back into the cushioned seat, 'but there is one way we can avenge my late mother.' Mikel frowned. 'Harlan said Lord Darius was her arresting officer.' Maldwyn wondered when the prince had been in contact with his sister. Harlan hadn't mentioned anything to him. 'We both know the lord hasn't been a good host and that the moment we become useless to him he will set us aside. It's why he won't allow us to cross the border. He wants to use us against Harlan.'

'Your dream, the one you've been having for months… it's the servant, isn't it?'

The princess nodded with a faraway look in her eyes. 'I'm walking in these corridors, and Lord Darius is leading me to a room, but inside is a forest. It's lush and full of life, yet still, for some reason, I feel haunted. He points to a beautiful, white lynx that is lying dead on the ground, in a pool of its blood.

'When I move closer, the lynx morphs into Harlan. Behind me, someone is weeping. I look over and see a valkyrie crying, kneeling on the ground. Her face is buried in her hands.'

Princess Cassara cleared her throat. Maldwyn looked around to check his surroundings as he listened in by the door.

'I pull her hands from her face and she tells me that she lost *Him* and stares at a blurred man. An eagle flies over and she smiles, takes my hand and tells me, "You can't save *Him*". I don't know if she means the faceless man or my brother. Finally, Lord Darius kills me and I wake up.' Cassara looked up to the roof as if searching for meaning in the air around her. 'Every time I dream it, he kills me.'

'I think it's time we put an end to this nightmare of yours and save the people we can. You know what you have to do.'

'Yes,' Cassara said, her face turned dark. 'I do. We're out of options.'

As they returned to silence, Maldwyn snuck away and turned down a passageway leading to another door that faced a window, striated by the rain. Thunder boomed outside, but he saw no lightning marking the skies. Maldwyn let his power free, watching the rain outside cease to fall, and opened the door to the lord's office.

The room was wider than it was long and there were two windows on the other side of the room. An angled writing desk with a bench seat was in front of another door to the left of a bulky, oak table. A blank piece of parchment lay on the table beside an ink bottle and a feathered quill. To the right was a short, long shelving unit with scrolls and books aplenty. A round, low-hanging candelabra with dead candles hung in the middle of the room.

Closing his eyes, Maldwyn focused on one thought: burn. The candles flamed, coming to life, and the rain fell into action again. Maldwyn stepped inside the well-lit room, sure that there was no one inside, and closed the door behind him.

He pulled the cloth mask over his mouth down around his neck, made his way over to the lord's desk and sat in the high-backed chair. On either side of the table was a set of built-in drawers. The bottom drawer on both sides had a small keyhole. Maldwyn tried to open them, but they were locked.

He searched the other drawers, hoping to find something to indicate the lord's treason. Mostly, all Maldwyn found were useless items, such as extra bottles of ink, a timber-framed hourglass, a selection of wooden rulers, varying in length, letters from King Viktor and spare sheets of parchment.

When Maldwyn rummaged through the final drawer, second down on the right-hand side of the desk, he noticed the end of a thin piece of black ribbon, poking up from the inside. He emptied the contents of the drawer and pulled on the tab, lifting its base to find a hidden compartment. There he found a flat, plain key, which looked as though it would fit the lock on the bottom drawers.

Starting with the right side of the desk, Maldwyn slipped the key in the lock and turned it over. A fat book with a brown leather cover filled the space. Maldwyn reached in and pulled out the heavy book, placing it on the desk.

Flicking through the pages, Maldwyn realised he had found the lord's ledger and smiled when he saw references detailing funds being received by both King Viktor and King Filip. According to the ledger, the numbers of mercenaries on the lord's armed forces were greater than suspected among the king's guards that had gambled with Jaecen and Erik back at the tavern. Maldwyn wondered where the extra forces were being reserved.

The figures also detailed payments referring to the maintenance of a place termed "*The Pit*". Unable to find any specific details about the mercenaries, or the mysterious pit, Maldwyn closed the ledger and unlocked the remaining drawer.

There he found a series of letters and maps. Feeling on edge, Maldwyn rubbed the back of his neck as he sorted through the papers. He thought he heard a sound, but ignored it, assuming it was the rumbling sky outside. A massive crack of lightning and thunder made the windows shake. The rain slammed into the glass as the wind picked up.

Unfolding one of the aged-looking letters, Maldwyn skimmed the contents, noting citations made to a deal between Lord Darius and King Filip dating as far back as the Battle of the Shadow Plains. Pausing at the end of a sentence, Maldwyn was stunned to learn that the deal was a part of the conditions of the surrender of Lord Darius's forces.

It didn't make sense. The victory of the Shadow Plains was the lord's greatest military achievement and the reason he had been awarded the lordship of the downs. If this was true, then his entire status was based on a lie.

Shocked, Maldwyn sat back, feeling his heart race from nerves. His skin crawled when he glanced down to the drawer and spotted a black rock with brilliant, colourful flecks. Staring at the rock was like staring into the cosmos. Recognising the stone as a piece of draconite, Maldwyn reached down and grabbed the potent gemstone, considering how long the lord had known of its existence.

Knowing the danger of draconite, Maldwyn pocketed the gem, hoping that this was the only piece in the lord's possession. As Maldwyn began putting what he could back in the drawers, he stopped when he heard a creaking sound coming from behind him.

A sudden and painful searing in his head overwhelmed him, blurring his vision. A soft, whispering chant could be heard over the pouring rain, and someone's fingers pressing into his temples made him cringe.

Unable to breathe, Maldwyn choked and twitched from the pain boring into his brain. Flashes of his memories came to the surface and he envisioned his mother's face. He tried to turn away and fight the mental probing, only to feel the pain intensify.

Letting go, Maldwyn's powers abandoned him. Foam filled his mouth. Sweat beaded on his forehead. He stiffened, feeling the veins in his neck bulge as he tried to keep his memories to himself. The door in front of him opened, but he could not see who had entered through his watery vision.

'What do you think you're doing?' He heard the princess ask in a firm voice.

'Help… Cassara,' Maldwyn managed to mumble, bleary-eyed and struggling for breath. He hoped she would spare him, knowing that she felt indebted to him.

'Get away from him!' She said sharply.

The fingers fell from Maldwyn's temples. As he blinked, he saw the man lean on the desk beside him. His sleeves were rolled up and Maldwyn noticed a two-faced skull burned into the man's forearm.

'You've overstepped… again.'

The rain sounded louder and their voices seemed muted. He couldn't tell if it was the aftereffect of whatever was being done to him, or whether the rain had gotten heavier.

'He's not supposed to be here,' the man said.

'Neither are you,' the princess replied. 'Now get out of here.'

The man pushed himself back up and dawdled over to stand in front of her. Maldwyn couldn't make out either of their faces.

'Yes, Your Grace,' the man said. As he went to leave, passing by the princess, the man dropped his shoulder, deliberately bumping into her.

Still trembling and convulsing as he gasped for breath, Maldwyn stayed where he was seated. The door closed and the princess came over to crouch beside him.

'Maldwyn, look at me.' Maldwyn tried to turn his head. It was difficult. 'He works for Mikel. He's useful, but can't be trusted and we need to get you out of here.'

'I need to get these to Harlan,' he argued, a little delirious. The sweat began to make him feel cold, causing him to shiver.

The princess stood and flicked through the letters and ledger. 'This is great Maldwyn, but you need to listen to me. You're not safe here.' She piled up the letters with the ledger and stuffed everything back into the drawers, locking them tight.

'No, you can't. We need these,' Maldwyn tried to tell her.

'Maldwyn, I have the key,' she said, holding up the key for him to see. 'All of this, I can deal with it.'

She grabbed his arm and wrapped it around her shoulder, helping him up to stand. He stumbled, trying to use the desk to hold some of his weight.

'Let go, okay. I am going to walk you right out of here.'

Weak, Maldwyn leaned on the princess, following her lead through the halls and down the stairs toward the service entrance, struggling to stay on his feet. His feet felt heavy and the glowing lanterns burned his eyes, making him squint.

'Are you alone here?' she asked, letting him hold himself up on the hallstand while she opened the door and checked the grounds outside.

'I need to get to the stables,' he mumbled in reply.

'It's clear outside as far as I can see.' Princess Cassara told him, coming back to help him keep moving. 'The stables, you say. Are there people meeting you there?'

'Yes.' Maldwyn swallowed as he allowed the princess to support him. 'It's Erik.' He could tell from the silence that she was surprised to know her mentor was close. 'And a ranger from the mountains.'

Though he couldn't see the details of her face, he saw her raise her brows. 'You're quite the surprise today, Maldwyn.'

His knees almost gave way several times as she led him across the grounds, heading toward the stables. The rain felt like heavy pellets, shooting down from the sky.

'Where are the guards?' He asked, noticing that he hadn't seen any on patrol.

'They will be changing shifts about now, so we have a window of time to get you out of here.'

Maldwyn slipped in a bit of mud, unable to see ahead of him in the black night, which was made worse by the rain. Cassara, caught him by his belt, helping him to stay on his feet.

He was relieved to reach the shelter of the stables, collapsing to the ground when she let him go.

'Your Grace!' Erik sounded surprised. Maldwyn was able to make out his form bowing, but couldn't see much else. 'What happened to him?' His voice dropped as he looked at Maldwyn, shaking on the ground.

'We don't have time to catch up,' the princess warned, holding a hand up. Her voice sounded strange and Maldwyn felt he was starting to pass out.

'I think I'm going to faint,' Maldwyn muttered, leaning back into the stall he was resting against.

'You need to get him out of here.'

'We can't leave until the morning.' Erik looked around, desperate for a way out. 'We're still waiting for Jaecen to return.'

'Where is he?' Princess Cassara pulled something out of her pocket. Vision darkening, Maldwyn closed his eyes and tried to count his breaths.

'He was searching the temple and the guest house.'

'I'll go get him. Take this.' She handed something small and round to Erik. 'It's the lord's seal. With it, you will be able to leave without question.' Princess Cassara came and crouched beside Maldwyn. She grabbed his hand and felt his forehead with the back of her hand. 'He has a slight fever. You need to get him to Harlan's encampment where he'll be safe and can be treated.' She spoke over her shoulder to Erik. 'Maldwyn, hang on there. You'll be alright.'

'Wait, what happened?!' Erik shouted as the princess ran back into the stormy night.

Maldwyn's eyelids became heavy and the world darkened. He felt as though he was falling. The world left him and he fell into dreams.

CHAPTER TWENTY-FOUR

Burying the Hatchet

'WE'RE KEEPING THEM in the supply tents on the north-western side of the encampment, Your Royal Highness,' said Markus, the soldier who was serving as his guard and reporting to the king in place of Theodor.

The firelight behind Markus shadowed his face, accentuating his five o'clock shadow and thick brows. His curly hair was drenched, emphasising how disorganised he appeared for an officer of his rank. Harlan felt sure that he could be trusted not to report too much detail to his father, given he had been handpicked by Theodor.

'Is there any reason to believe they are assassins?'

Harlan crossed his arms, tired and unsettled by the wind whipping around his tent. The pouring rain had gotten heavier. He had woken to the news that some suspected assassins had been caught trying to enter the camp. It wasn't yet dawn from what he could tell, though the storm made it difficult to be sure.

'We're not certain, sire.' Harlan heard voices in the camp, shouting about some mud causing issues near the horses. 'We thought it best to hold them and wait for your orders.'

Harlan rubbed his gritty eyes, standing by his travel trunk, and looked over at the tea-coloured sleeping pallet, wanting to go back to the warmth between the sheets. The heat from the iron brazier was a relief, given how cold the storm was for spring.

'Have you interrogated them?'

'Not me personally, sire. The weather has caused several issues around the camp that have kept me busy liaising with the other officers to rectify.' Markus pressed his lips together and made a serious expression. 'Given the nature of the suspicions, I thought it best to advise you, especially since this isn't the first attempt.'

'What did the patrol that found them tell the other officers, before coming to you?'

'Your Grace, they mentioned that they were asking for you by name and one of them seemed ill, but that could be a tactic to get close to you and make a move.'

Harlan didn't want to deal with the matter at this time in the morning, yet was somewhat intrigued with the circumstances that had been put to him. The report stated that three people, masked and dressed in black had approached the camp on the north-western outskirts of the settlement on horseback. They hadn't put up a fight when the soldiers approached them and went with them willingly to the supply tents.

'Alright,' Harlan said under his breath, submitting himself to the situation, 'give me a moment to prepare myself, then take me to where they are being held.'

'Yes, sire!' Markus bowed, stepped back a few paces and left the tent, walking out into the teeming rain.

The prince changed out of his sleeping garments, into warmer and more presentable clothing. Grabbing his leather jacket, and slipping his arms into his sleeves, Harlan stood by the fire, taking a moment to properly wake before marching out of his warm and dry tent. The smoky air was soothing.

'This way, sire,' Markus said when the prince emerged from his tent, leading the way across the muddy encampment. Harlan's boots squelched into the sodden ground.

The air was sour, despite the rain, and the mud was worse than he expected, given they were on the raised ground of the hilly landscape. The soldiers rushing around the site looked exhausted, lacking in sleep as they fought the elements.

Most of the officers remained sheltered in their tents. Infantry was patrolling the campsite, securing the ropes of sagging tents, and wedging planks of timber under the wheels of flooding wagons in an attempt to stop them from sinking further into the muddy ground. The fires and torches around the campground struggled to burn, withering down to thin erratic flames.

The two soldiers by the oblong pavilion where the supplies were kept were standing at attention, despite the heavy rain. The blades of their spears pointed up at the black heavens as they bowed when Markus and Harlan approached.

Relieved to step out of the rain, the prince shook his head and wiped the excess water off his face. Markus did the same beside him.

There were barrels, chests and cartons of supplies and equipment set out in rows around the tent. Several guards waited further down by a row of barrels. Their shadows crept around the walls of the canvas pavilion like formless ghosts.

'Your Royal Highness,' one of the soldiers said approaching the prince and bowing. 'The prisoners are just down here.'

'Were they armed?' Markus checked, glancing at the guards at the other end of the tent.

'One of them had a knife and some basic weapons on their horse,' the guard said, looking over his shoulder and scratching his nose, 'but they weren't carrying anything else worth mentioning. We've yet to inspect the packs they were carrying.'

'If they were assassins, why weren't they better armed?' Harlan asked, wiping his boots on the grassy ground that remained somewhat dry.

'I don't believe they are assassins, Your Grace. Nothing indicates this to be the case. They may be here to pass on a message,' the guard shrugged and made a doubtful expression, 'but they are insisting on seeing you, sire.'

Harlan nodded and waved a hand forward for the guard to lead them over to where the prisoners were being kept. He couldn't see much through the men standing on guard at first. At best, he could see two people kneeling and a third laying lifeless between them.

As the guards each bowed and stepped aside, Harlan didn't recognise either of the men kneeling, dressed in black with hoods pushed back and cloth face coverings bunched around their necks. There was something familiar about the man with red hair, but Harlan couldn't quite place where he had seen him before.

Turning his attention to the man on the ground, head laying in the lap of the man with a scar ripping through his right eyebrow, Harlan felt a tightening in his chest when he recognised Maldwyn. Eyes closed, he looked as though he had fallen into a peaceful, yet mournful, rest. He was soaking wet and his left arm hung dead on the ground. Fighting the urge to rush to his side, Harlan slowly walked over and crouched beside them.

'Did Jerrik send you?' He asked as quiet as possible.

'Yes,' said the man with ginger hair, looking wary of the prince. 'He sent us to infiltrate the downs and bring you what you needed to stop the lord.' His voice rose and fell with the accent of the mountain dwellers.

Harlan bit his lip and pushed Maldwyn's wet hair back off his face. 'What happened?'

'Your Grace, we were inside the keep,' the man with the scar began, bowing to address royalty.

Harlan thought this was odd. The Erendil had never shown him any respect as the Crown Prince.

'We were searching for evidence of the lord's corruption and the extent of his treason. We separated to cover more ground. Sire, we don't know what happened to him.' The man looked nervous and leaned forward, holding Maldwyn close in his lap. 'I can help him, but there are too many people watching, Your Grace.'

Harlan glared at him, guessing that he was suggesting the use of sorcery. The man lifted the sleeve of his black, leather jacket to reveal the mark of a raven. Beside him, the man with red hair, crinkled his forehead staring at the guards behind the prince.

Taking a moment to resist his knee-jerk reaction, Harlan considered trusting in sorcery. Maldwyn's blank face was worrying. Pushing himself up to stand, Harlan headed over to where Markus waited behind him.

'Dismiss the men inside the tent. Keep the guards that have been posted outside by the entrance.' As Harlan turned away, he remembered one final order and quickly spun back to Markus. 'See if you can find somewhere for these men to be housed, discreetly.'

'You want them sheltered when so many of our men are struggling in the storm, Your Grace?' The tone of his voice was disapproving.

Harlan looked back at Maldwyn, remembering their time together in Valondale Castle. He smiled, yearning to hold him once more.

'Yes,' he told Markus in a firm voice. 'These men are informants and the fewer people who know they are here, the better.'

'I understand, Your Royal Highness.' Markus bowed and walked over to the other guards in the tent, delegating orders.

Turning back to the man with the scar as Markus left with the other guards, Harlan crouched once more and lowered his voice. 'What do you need to help him?'

The man sat taller, surprised. 'Sire, he has a fever that we need to break, he's been unconscious since we left the keep, and he has had a few seizures on our way here.' The man with the scar turned Maldwyn's head to show marks burned into his temples. 'My best guess is someone used a spell to delve into his mind like they were searching for something.'

'For what?' The man with red hair puckered his brows. The firelight brought out the amber tones in the man's eyes. The wind outside stirred and Harlan noticed the roof of the tent was sagging above them.

'I don't know,' the man with the scar answered, sounding frustrated. 'I know as much as you do. Someone hurt him and the princess brought him to the stables where we were waiting.'

'Wait, my sister was there?' Harlan asked, worried that Cassara had been the one to hurt Maldwyn. 'Did she do this?'

The man with the scar looked at him, concerned. 'No, Your Grace.'

'But she knows magic.' Harlan argued, suggesting that she could have done this. Outside, he heard Markus talking to the guards. 'She's threatened him before.'

'Your Royal Highness, I don't know what she's said to you, but she doesn't have this kind of skill.' The man with the scar swallowed and stared at him with a cautious gaze.

Harlan had the feeling there was something the man wasn't saying. The prince glanced at the red-haired man, who looked away.

'How can you know that?'

The man with the scar looked down and hesitated as if he were afraid to lock eyes with the prince. Harlan thought he might even be ashamed. 'Your Grace, I was a servant in the palace. I was also the princess's mentor. I fled the palace after her capture.'

Harlan stewed on that information for a moment as he stared at the man who put his sister on an execution path. Ignoring the anger that he felt brewing deep down, Harlan cleared his throat and turned his attention back to Maldwyn.

'Okay, so someone else did this and we don't know what happened.' Harlan wetted his lips and placed a hand on his cheek, raindrops soaking his skin. Maldwyn's blank face dropped a little as the scarred man shifted his weight on his knees. 'You said you can help him. How?'

'Well, we need to get him dry and warm, but first, we need to ease his psychic pain. We could wait for him to wake, however, I fear that it would take too long and we wouldn't learn what happened to him for quite a while.'

The man with red hair nodded and loosened the cloth mask bunched around his neck. 'I agree. We need to do something for him.'

As Harlan looked at him, he wondered why he seemed so familiar and tried to place who he was during his time in the Anhalt Mountains, but he couldn't.

'If you have the right herbs, I can ease his pain which should bring him around faster. I'll need to make tea since we haven't the time to make an effective tincture. I'll need boiling water, fenugreek, tartar root and sage.'

'You should check the boxes over there where the physician supplies are kept,' Harlan told him, pointing to the wooden boxes a few rows up. 'I don't know that we'll have everything, but you should find most of the herbs, an iron kettle and a cup.'

'That's fine, I won't need a kettle. As for the herbs, there may be other options that I can use as substitutes.' Frowning and accentuating his scar, the man looked down at Maldwyn. 'I need to lay him down to check the supplies.'

'I can take him,' Harlan offered, reaching out to slide Maldwyn over to his lap, not caring how they both watched him with curious faces. The prince stroked his smooth face, laying Maldwyn carefully over his legs. Harlan thought he seemed so lifeless, yet perfect, like a doll.

'Come on, give me a hand,' the man with the scar said to his comrade.

Getting up to his feet, the red-haired man paused, watching as the other man went toward the boxes. 'You must not recognise me.'

Harlan felt uneasy when he locked eyes with the man. Despite his singsong accent, there was a nervousness in the man's voice. There was something about this angle that reminded him of the man that had been his gaoler in the mountains.

'My name is Jaecen, and I want you to know that I am sorry for the part I played in your captivity.'

Tense, Harlan clicked his tongue. 'I recognise you.' Holding his breath as he tautened his stomach, the prince tried to offer a smile. It was the best he could do. 'We're on the same side now, right?'

'Yes, we are,' Jaecen said, staring over at the other man with the scar, searching through the boxes.

'What about him?' Harlan pointed to the other man with his chin. 'Who is he exactly?'

'Erik?' Jaecen laughed awkwardly. 'He was one of the servants as he said. A hunter, specifically. It's how he got the scar.'

'And the mark on his wrist?'

'It's the mark of his people. He's a sorcerer, born into the Raven Clan. They're pacifists and healers.' A low rumble of thunder outside caught Harlan's attention. 'Your father massacred his people.' The guilt of his father's actions choked Harlan and a knot formed in the pit of his stomach. 'We're only aware of two living descendants. Erik and Anton.' Jaecen patted his jaw and sniffed. 'I should go and help him.'

Gazing back down to Maldwyn as Jaecen walked away, Harlan stroked his hair. 'Everything's going to be okay,' he reassured, more for himself, and leaned down and kissed his forehead. The marks on his temples were dark, reddish-brown and looked sore.

Erik took his time with Jaecen, lifting lids and carefully sifting through the supplies. Every so often he would shake his head, disappointed that he couldn't find the ingredients he needed. Thunder continued to rumble outside, but it was softening to a low grumble. The rain was easing, and the commotion of soldiers running about the camp had quietened down.

Mumbling an incantation, Erik brought the water to a boil in a shallow bowl and added the mixture of dried herbs and spices in a plain, metal strainer. They waited for the concoction to steep, letting it cool so as not to scald Maldwyn's throat.

Keeping his voice low, Erik placed his hands over the marks on Maldwyn's temples and began to chant a rhythmic, melodic invocation. Harlan felt the full force of Maldwyn seizing in his lap, body twitching as his head turned from side to side. Panicking, Harlan tried to hold him as he jerked.

'Sorry, Your Grace.' Erik pulled his hands away from Maldwyn's temples and peeled his eyelids apart, checking his eyes. 'I didn't expect his reaction to this to be so strong.'

'What did you do?'

'Imagine that the mind is a web of rivers with an infinite number of smaller streams flowing into them.' Erik sat back on his heels, turning to the bowl of tea on the ground next to him. Jaecen pulled out the strainer, shaking off the excess drips. 'Our will guides us along these streams through our thoughts and memories, but, if you overwhelm the mind, flooding them, our will becomes lost inside. Trapped for lack of a better explanation.' Erik dipped the tip of his finger in the bowl, checking the temperature. Harlan watched the sorcerer closely, intrigued by what he was saying. 'I have just calmed the rushing in his head, returning the streams to their normal flow to help bring him back to himself. This tea will help to ease the residual pain. His seizing means it was worse than I expected. He must have fought against whoever did this.'

Seeing that Erik was ready to administer the tea, Harlan lifted Maldwyn by the back of his head, just enough to ensure the concoction wouldn't spill all over him, missing his mouth completely. Erik pried his mouth open while Harlan kept his head raised and rested the edge of the bowl against his lower lip, tipping it slowly to pour the tea into his mouth. A small amount of liquid ran down either side of Maldwyn's mouth. Sitting on his feet, Jaecen remained silent, keeping out of the way.

'The tea will be less potent than a tincture, sire, but it will work to also help to break his fever,' Erik told the prince, pulling the bowl away from Maldwyn's lips. 'He probably won't wake for a few hours. Is there somewhere dry and warm we can take him? He's been cold and wet for too long.'

Harlan rubbed his forehead with the back of his hand as he thought of the best course of action. In truth, the warmest and driest place in the camp would be Harlan's tent, although, how he would get Maldwyn there without drawing attention or raising suspicion was a concern.

'I could have him brought to my tent, which will be the safest place for him, but we'll have to wait for Markus to return. The last thing we need is to raise suspicion with my father's men.'

'Of course, sire,' Erik said, sitting back on his heels again and wiping his forehead with his forearm.

Jaecen scratched his chin and began piling up the remaining supplies to put back in the boxes. 'There was something I learned in the temple, but we left in such a hurry I haven't had a chance to mention it.'

'What is it?' Harlan asked.

'The priest of the temple had received word that there had been a concerning shift of faith in Aberdeen.' Leaning into his elbow, Jaecen sneezed. 'Apparently, by the time the Queen of Ellinor stepped in to offer aid to Haradnor, it was already too late for the people of that town. Many died in the freezing winter months, lacking basic supplies from their usual trade. According to the priest's diary, the suffering has caused a large number of people to turn to an old religion.'

'An old religion.' Erik muttered as he helped Jaecen gather the ingredients. 'What religion would they possibly turn to?'

'Supposedly, they have shown signs of worshipping Hel.'

Harlan looked from one worried face to the other. 'That's not ideal for obvious reasons, but what's the main concern with it?'

'Sire,' Erik started, pausing as he picked up a large jar filled with bulbous tartar root, 'Hel is an enemy of the traditional gods. She rules over the souls of the damned, and her bloody battle with the gods is the reason for the barrier between the spiritual realm and our mortal realm being raised during the divine wars.' Erik placed the thick hessian cloth over the jar and began tying a thin rope around it to seal it. 'She saw cruelty in the natural world, and became convinced that the only option to rectify creation was to destroy all life and start the world anew.'

'The people of Aberdeen aren't sorcerers,' Jaecen told the prince as Erik carried the tartar root and the smaller jars of herbs back to the supply boxes. 'However, her followers historically were, and they were known as the Children of the Flesh. They were dangerous and cruel, seeking to further her plans. They naively believe she will spare their souls and bring about a better, fairer world.'

'But,' Erik argued as he came back to kneel on the ground once more, 'in order to find such a perfect world every living thing must die. Innocent and good people, plants, animals, everything without exception. Could you sacrifice it all, Your Grace?'

Taking in a deep breath as he held Maldwyn in his arms, Harlan looked over to the entrance, checking for Markus' return. 'So, what do we do?'

'What can we do, sire?' Erik folded his arms as he stared at Jaecen. 'They're just people.'

'Uller, save us,' Jaecen mumbled through his soft accent and pressed the ring he was wearing on his middle finger to his lips. 'The hope is that this is nothing more than a phase for the town. Until they show any signs of planning to exterminate mankind, the propagation of her worship can be nothing more than a situation to monitor.'

The three of them quietened down after that and Harlan left the other two to their small talk as they waited. It seemed to be taking a while, but Harlan knew there was a lot Markus was managing on his behalf. Having diverted patrols, Markus returned and snuck them across the encampment toward the officer's tents. Markus carried Maldwyn to the prince's tent, as

Harlan had directed, before taking Erik and Jaecen to sleep in his pavilion, where Markus could keep an eye on them.

*   *   *   *   *

'Why did you do that?' Harlan asked from behind his sad, blue eyes.

The orange glow from the fire behind where he stood made his hair look more golden than it was in daylight. Maldwyn pushed himself up to sit in the prince's warm, dry bed. He noted that someone had changed him out of his black clothing and into basic sleepwear. The shirt was loose and creamy in colour.

'What you did was incredibly stupid.' Tired, but feeling strangely well, Maldwyn offered a shaky smile. 'I could have walked you right in there, no questions asked and kept the lord's people distracted. Any number of things that would have been safer.'

'I'm sorry.' Maldwyn swallowed. His mouth was dry. He desperately wanted some water but felt it was the wrong time to ask. 'When I left you the other day, I didn't know that Erik and Jaecen had already formulated a plan to infiltrate the keep.' Outside the rain was lightly falling on the roof of the tent. 'I went back to the downs without you because I had to tell them what had happened and that I was alright. There was also someone I needed to meet.' Harlan frowned and glanced to the side. 'I thought that if I went with them, we'd all be able to cover more ground inside the keep and that things would be safe enough. I didn't expect a sorcerer,' Maldwyn said in a pleading voice, hoping for the prince to forgive him.

'You didn't think there would be sorcerers!' Harlan raised his voice, except it was not so loud that the guards would hear them. Pinching his mouth together, he held his hands behind his neck for a moment and stared at the floor. 'What about my sister,' the prince asked, dropping his hands to his side and stepping closer, 'or Mikel's informant that cursed my father?'

'I just…' Maldwyn searched for somewhere to look but ended up staring at his lap. 'I didn't think…'

'No, you didn't,' Harlan agreed, lowering his voice and shaking his head. Maldwyn thought he seemed very angry with him. 'I asked you to do one thing, which was to be safe… to stay alive.' The prince looked to his left tightening all of the muscles in his face.

'I'm sorry, Harlan.' Maldwyn hung his head lower, feeling guilty that he had caused the prince to worry this much.

The recollection of the mental pain inflicted upon him made Maldwyn shudder. He couldn't understand why his attacker had searched his memories the way he had and he hoped that the man hadn't seen his powers. Though he felt minimal pain, he felt drained.

'It was really hard for me to wake up right now.'

Harlan softened and exhaled. He walked over to sit on the bed beside Maldwyn and pulled him into a strong, warm hug. The prince's leather jacket creaked as he held him tight. Maldwyn noted that the prince smelled of a hint of cedarwood and relaxed, feeling at home in his arms as he closed his eyes.

Pulling back, Harlan turned his head closer and kissed him softly, mouth slightly parted. As he drew away, the prince pressed his forehead to Maldwyn's.

'What about the person you met?'

'What do you mean?' Maldwyn asked, worried that the prince might think worse of him if he learned that Maldwyn was adopted. He knew it was a silly way to think, but Maldwyn had never been wholly accepted before, and his adoption felt like another flaw.

'Who were they? What happened?' Maldwyn pulled his head away from Harlan's and licked his lips, avoiding the prince's stare. The fire in the background popped. 'Are you hiding things from me?' Harlan asked, sounding a little hurt.

Maldwyn thought of all the things he hadn't yet shared with the prince. Although they had known each other for over a year, Maldwyn had spoken little of himself. His mother had always taught him to keep everything hidden, thus trusting others with his deepest truths was difficult for Maldwyn. Worried about how to answer that question, he chose to ignore it, and answer the prince's initial question.

'I met with the man that should have been my father. He left my mother when I was a child.' Maldwyn avoided looking at the prince. He didn't want to see if Harlan pitied him. 'Before my mother died, she told me that I wasn't her child. She told me I was abandoned in a field and that she and her then-husband, Leith, the man I met, took me in to care for me. I thought he could help me find out how I ended up in the field, or help me find my parents, but he couldn't.' Maldwyn shrugged hearing his voice waver. 'The best he could tell me was that a woman, Eretrya, came looking for me, but my mother hid me and sent the woman northeast, to the Evermires, almost as far east as one could sail.'

Harlan cupped the side of his face and Maldwyn leaned into his touch. His hands were smooth and warm.

'Why didn't you say anything?'

'I couldn't. I didn't want to burden you.'

'I know it's hard to trust people, I really do. Royal families have subordinates, but rarely have friends.'

Some soldiers outside on patrol marched around the tent. The beat of their steps caught Maldwyn's attention.

'You never need to hide anything from me.'

Maldwyn wanted so much to believe him and show the prince what he could do. He considered that the prince had proven himself to be more open-minded than Maldwyn ever thought.

'Erm, well,' Maldwyn uttered, wavering on whether to commit to sharing his powers with Harlan. 'There's something… I mean, I want to tell you…' Maldwyn laughed awkwardly when he saw the way Harlan was looking at him. 'It's just that…'

'It's just me, Mal.' Harlan grabbed his hand and stared at him with his intense crystal blue eyes. 'Whatever it is, just take a breath and I'm sure you'll find the words.'

'Your Royal Highness,' came a voice from outside the tent. 'We have news from Theodor.'

'But just hold that thought,' Harlan said holding a finger up and heading over to the entrance.

Maldwyn ran his fingers through his hair, frustrated with himself and considering that this was a sign for him to keep his powers secret a while longer. Maybe his mother had been right.

Harlan mumbled through the cover hanging over the entrance to his tent, holding it back to peer through the gap. It sounded like things had gone well and that the disputed areas in the woods had been successfully secured. The prince would be happy with the report, even if he didn't show it through his aloof veneer.

When Harlan came back over to sit on the bed, the chain around his neck caught the firelight and glinted. 'You were going to tell me something.'

Maldwyn lifted the chain around Harlan's neck, pulling it out from under his shirt to see the ring and smiled. 'Are you ever going to give this to the sovereign?'

'I gave him my word, so I suppose I have to. Besides, his people brought you back to me, protecting you twice at my request now.'

Harlan smiled as Maldwyn turned the ring in his hands. The dark, red jewels were the colour of blood and were set into a wide silver band with swirling motifs. He noticed a small engraving on the inside of the band as he thought of Tiana's suspicions.

'I'll give it to Jaecen and tell him to bring it to Jerrik. I owe the sovereign; a lot more than I want to admit.' Maldwyn angled the ring a little more toward the light as Harlan spoke, and noticed that the marking was of a swan. 'He came through as an ally these last few months.'

'Harlan, did you know this marking was here?'

Maldwyn stared up at him, as he tried to remember why it seemed familiar. He felt like he had read about items marked with an engraving of a swan. For some reason, Maldwyn recalled having come across this before his village was attacked.

'Oh, yeah… it's just some engraving of a swan. Meaningless, I think.'

Maldwyn thought about it harder, watching the low flames of the fire dance in the iron brazier a few feet from the sleeping pallet. Then, it came to him.

He had read about it in *The Power of Divinity*. Wayland, the smithy god, had crafted many items while in captivity, most of which were marked with a swan in dedication to his wife. The etching not only meant it was crafted by a god, but that it was imbued with their divinity, making this a relic of the gods.

'Harlan, I don't know how to tell you this, but that marking isn't meaningless.' Snatching the ring, Harlan examined it more closely. 'I've read a lot,' Maldwyn started, feeling that now wasn't the right moment to share his gifts with the prince, 'and this insignia is a marking left on creations by Wayland, the smithy god.' Maldwyn recalled that Tiana had overheard Jerrik speaking with Anton about Kristian's ring. She had been under the impression that Jerrik knew this ring was divine and she feared the sovereign's reasons for wanting it. 'I think it's a relic of the gods.'

'What?' Harlan squinted as he stared at the marking. 'Is it dangerous? Why wouldn't Jerrik tell me what it was?'

'He's a believer in preserving the gifts divinity bestowed upon the world,' Maldwyn told the prince, remembering that Tolamin had suggested as much to Tiana. 'He welcomes sorcery and everything that divinity brings.' Maldwyn shrugged and raised his brows. 'I don't think it's dangerous or you would know by now. I suppose he didn't tell you what it was because he was worried you might destroy it.'

'But if it's a relic of the gods, then it must do something.'

'I guess so,' Maldwyn said, hearing sounds in the camp beyond the tent. The rain drizzled, hardly audible. 'I think you would have to wear it as a ring to know what it does.' Harlan pulled the chain over his head and began sliding the ring off the chain, making a move to put it over his finger. Maldwyn grabbed his hand. 'What are you doing?'

'You just said I would have to wear it to know what it does?'

'But you don't know what will happen! Maybe it makes you invulnerable, or it could be cursed. Maybe it was designed to slowly kill the wearer. Maybe it will make you have hallucinations and drive you insane, or any number of things.'

'Fine, then what do we do?'

Maldwyn shifted closer, feeling a strand of straw sticking up from the mattress into his leg. 'I know you don't want to hear this, but you should give it to Jerrik. He has people there who can research the ring and understand it without doing anything rash and dangerous like putting it on.' Harlan smirked and turned away. 'I don't want you to get hurt. Weren't you just lecturing me for not thinking things through?'

'Fine. You're right. I'll give it to Jaecen and he can take it back to the mountains and my debt will be paid.' Playing with the sleeve of his jacket, Harlan seemed on edge. 'You were going to tell me something, what was it?'

Maldwyn worried that Harlan seemed to be in the wrong mood for a heart-to-heart. He feared that the prince would become more agitated, and would reject Maldwyn as a thoughtless reaction to learning about the secrets he was keeping, to learning about his abilities.

'Ah, it's not important. It can wait. You probably have things you need to do.'

'Whenever you're ready, Mal.' Harlan put the ring back on the chain and pulled it over his head. 'For as long as it takes for you to trust me, I'll wait.' Harlan stood and left the tent, stepping into the rain.

Annoyed, Maldwyn threw himself back onto the bed and slammed his hands to his face. Wishing he had said nothing at all, he closed his eyes. The thought that Harlan felt he was hiding things and didn't trust him made Maldwyn feel horrible. He hated that he was hurting the prince.

CHAPTER TWENTY-FIVE

Wildcat

'I S MALDWYN ALRIGHT?' Cassara asked, standing alone at the top of the bright green, grassy hill, looking over the knolls and valleys below. The clouds had parted for the morning sun, letting through warm beams of light. The air was sweet and there was a soft breeze that was neither warm nor cool. Her dark wavy hair whipped around in the wind and her burgundy dress flowed effortlessly.

'He will be,' Harlan told her as he climbed the hill to stand on her left, hand resting on the pommel of the sword hanging by his hip. 'Erik tells me I have you to thank for that.'

'The threat I made, to hurt him so that you would help me, I never meant it. But, please understand,' Cassara gave the prince a stern expression, 'my caution toward you comes from the fact that I don't know if I can trust you. You've always stood by our father, silent as he executed people who simply sympathised with sorcerers.'

The truth hurt.

'I wish things were different. That I could show you I can be trusted.'

Cassara softened and looked down at a large bag, hidden in the long blades of grass on her right. It was a pale blue bag, reinforced with brown leather. It looked heavy.

'Maldwyn left these in my care last night. Seems he found the evidence you've been searching for. I'm choosing to trust you now, please don't prove me wrong.' Cassara smirked, staring into the distance. 'He didn't read through all of this, but I have. It's quite the read.'

'How bad is it?'

'Well, for starters, Lord Darius's celebrated victory is a farce. King Filip won the Battle of the Shadow Plains. Darius surrendered to spare the lives of his men, but King Filip knew that he would ultimately lose the war. He was outnumbered, unfamiliar with the terrain, and lost almost every other battle against our father. So, King Filip offered Darius a deal.' Cassara looked up at the clouds as they moved across the sun, throwing the hills into a moment of shadow.

Harlan turned to face her, tilting his head, interested to hear what she had to say. 'What was the deal?'

'In exchange for his loyalty, King Filip told Darius he would spare him and his men, agreeing to falsify the events of the battle. Darius has been reporting to King Filip and accepting payments from him for years.' Cassara folded her arms and turned to face him. As the sun reappeared in the sky, beaming down on her face, she squinted. The shadows moved over the hills like formless creatures swimming over the emerald grassy hillocks. 'He's been a traitor longer than he's been an ally for our father.'

'Okay.' Harlan reached into his pocket and pulled out the black, shimmering stone he had found in Maldwyn's clothes. 'Maldwyn had this on him, and I've heard rumours about such a stone being found in the mine. What is it?'

Cassara smiled and reached her hand up to grab the stone. 'This is what he wants from the mine.' She studied it, mesmerised by the way it glimmered in the sunlight. There didn't appear to be a single blemish on its surface. 'It's quite beautiful for something so dangerous. It's called draconite and while it has many uses, it's mainly used for harmful purposes, such as an ingredient in curses.'

'Why would Maldwyn take this? Would he know what this is?' Cassara turned back to stare out over the hills, holding the stone up to the sun ignoring him. 'You said he's hiding something, what is it?'

'Last night, I had a dream.'

'I'm serious Cass. Is it bad?'

Cassara smiled. 'I know you are, so listen. Last night, after I found Maldwyn and all of this, I had a dream of the past, the evening our mother was arrested.' Harlan held his breath and went quiet. 'Before she went to the grove where she and her lover were arrested, our mother learned about a place she believed the mine had tunnelled into.

'Back then, although there were tensions, there was peace between the mountain folk and the city folk. The mine was temporarily gifted to the people of the mountains and they made some discoveries. Kristian had been concerned for some reason, so together with our mother, he researched the mine for months. Whatever they learned, they feared.' She took in a deep breath and pushed her shoulders back, holding the stone in her hands.

'In my dream, Darius was the officer that brought the news of our mother's affair to our father. I wonder whether he knew then that these stones could be found in the mine.' Cassara handed the piece of draconite back to Harlan. 'I believe he organised their deaths so that he could have control of the mine. I think he wanted our mother out of the way to get to whatever's in there, and I'm certain it's more than these rocks.' Harlan took the stone. It was cold to the touch. 'I am certain King Filip didn't know of the lord's involvement in his daughter's death, but I promise you, he will as soon as I make it to Mordiallok.'

'Does this mean you're agreeing to help me?'

'Yes, Harlan.' A lock of hair blew over her mouth. She hooked her nail behind the lock and pulled it away. 'There's more though. He's been hiring mercenaries, and stationing them at a place referred to in his ledger as "*The Pit*". I believe he has been doing experiments there with more of those stones.'

'Experiments, what sort of experiments?'

'I'm not sure,' Cassara replied, sounding troubled. 'It has Lady Adria afraid, to the point that she forged the orders to assassinate you.' Smiling, Cassara held her hands together below her hips. 'She came to me for advice. She's very smart. She pays attention to everything, meets with her husband's mercenaries, and is always listening. She figured you'd survive and take care of her husband for her, but you haven't made any rash movements and the lady is getting skittish.'

Harlan slipped the cold, glittering gemstone back into his pocket, put his hands on his hips and studied the blades of grass as he thought. A gust swept over them, making the grass dance, as a breeze swirled around them.

'So, whose side is Lady Adria on?'

'Her own.' Running his hands through his hair, Harlan walked away, putting some space between them as he processed what he had been told. 'If we kill him, we can end all of this.'

'I know!' Harlan threw his hands up. 'I just need a moment to think.'

They stood quiet for a while as the breeze swirled. Scanning the hills, Harlan spied a wildcat with black tufts on its ears watching him in the distance. A strange sensation overwhelmed him. It was as though he was being called to by the lynx watching him.

'I'm glad Maldwyn's alright,' she offered, changing the subject. 'Is he awake yet?'

'He is,' Harlan mumbled entranced by the cat watching him. 'Erik helped bring him around, but I guess you knew he might.'

'So, you know who Erik is to me.' The lynx stood and began pacing in the distance. Harlan thought it was an odd place for a wildcat to venture. It had come quite far beyond the woods. 'I'm surprised you let him help.'

'Yeah, I couldn't sit by and do nothing.' Cassara moved over to where he was standing, following his gaze. The lynx took off, racing out of sight.

'Lynxes, they're such mysterious creatures.'

'Hmm.'

Tired from the horrible storm that had kept him awake most of the night, and the early morning to meet his would-be assassins, Harlan rubbed his gritty eyes. The thought of fighting with Maldwyn earlier that morning bothered him. He looked over to his sister. The last time they had spoken, things had been on edge and full of mistrust. After all this time, could they ever really be siblings?

'Harlan, is something wrong?'

'Do you ever worry about the traits we got from our parents?' She shook her head and frowned at him. 'It's just,' Harlan scratched the back of his head, 'I got angry with Maldwyn when he woke up. When he was in pain and need of comfort, I got mad. The more I think about it, the more I wonder, what if I'm just like our father?'

Her brows shot up, surprised by his question. 'Why did you get angry with him?'

'He promised not to get hurt, and then he almost died... again.'

Scratching the top of her head, Cassara let out a breathy laugh. 'Do you have any plans for genocide? Did you not choose to protect me when our father chose to kill me? Do you not have friends in the Anhalt Mountains?' Smiling, she folded her arms. Harlan nodded, seeing her point. 'Sounds to me like you were just worried about him.'

'Thanks,' he muttered, feeling at ease.

'I bet he's sitting wherever he is, feeling just as bad. You can make peace with him.' Harlan was gazing at the horizon and Cassara moved her head until she locked eyes with him. 'Whatever Maldwyn hasn't told you, I'm sure he has his reasons, but you can trust him. Just be patient and show him that he can trust you.' Cassara looked over her shoulder in the direction of the keep, hidden by the hills. 'I should get back. There's a detailed map in the bag. Lord Darius is heading to the mentioned pit in five days. He's very angry about losing ground in the disputed territories, though he doesn't know—what I suspect is—that this is because of you. He wants to send mercenaries into those parts that have just been taken from him. At nightfall, in five days, be there. It'll be the best chance to not only remove him from power but destroy his forces and see what he's been up to.'

'I'll be there.' Grinning, he rested his right hand on the spiral pommel. 'Cassara,' he shouted when she was halfway down the hill, 'Erik and Jaecen mentioned there had been activity in the guesthouse of the lord's keep.' She stopped in her tracks and turned back to him. Her glossy, black hair shone under the warm, glowing sunlight and her burgundy dress seemed more of a scarlet colour as shadows were banished from the hills. 'Do you know who's there?'

'It was some representatives from Haradnor. They left early this morning. The new trade agreement between the three kingdoms means that Karana Downs needs to contribute. I'm not sure what the lord has agreed to trade.' As she turned back to continue down the hill, Cassara held a hand up and shouted, 'Be there in five days, brother! Don't be late!'

* * * * *

When Harlan returned to the camp, he went to the royal blue canvas command tent and began unpacking the bag Cassara had given him on the long table. Two braziers on either side of a small, round table filled with refreshments were lit inside the tent, brightening the space.

Harlan flicked through the letters, disturbed by the numerous layers of the lord's lies, and skimmed the entries in the ledger, seeing the reference to "*The Pit*" that his sister had mentioned. As he found the maps and splayed them out across the table, Harlan unbelted his sword and leaned it against the leg of the desk. He took a seat and studied the surrounding lands.

He spent hours working through strategic scenarios, attempting to predict the lord's counter manoeuvres. When the prince was sure he had devised an almost flawless plan of attack to lure the lord's mercenaries out of the pit and into an ambush, he rose from his seat to look outside. From the setting sun, Harlan could tell the hour was getting late.

Tucking his fingers beneath the collar of his lightweight leather armour, Harlan pulled out the chain he kept Kristian's ring on and left the tent, making sure to grab his sword before he left. Markus was standing outside the pavilion with reports on the status of the settlement. Harlan listened to Markus's updates as he wove through the camp toward the officer's sleeping tents where Erik and Jaecen would be resting.

The officer's tents were uniform in size and had navy blue banners hanging around the top of the pavilions. Markus's tent was at the end of the line, nearest the prince's. If Theodor were still travelling with the battalion, Markus's tent would have been his, but Theodor was deep in the disputed lands.

'Stay here,' Harlan ordered, pausing when he heard Jaecen talking in a lowered, worried voice.

'How much can we trust the prince? You used to work for him.'

'I worked for the palace,' Erik corrected the ranger, 'not the prince. Although, I am sure we both have our suspicions about his association with Maldwyn, which means he can be trusted.'

Harlan swallowed, hoping that Markus wasn't listening from where he stood, a few paces away. 'I assume Anton told you his beliefs about the prince and why he's important.'

'Yes, he's the wildcat for our little bird.' Harlan turned his head a little to better hear what Erik was saying. 'Maldwyn needs to be careful; the awakening is creeping closer. I can sense it around him as he grows stronger. There's nothing more we can do to prepare him.'

'Shouldn't we tell him it's approaching,' Jaecen asked in a careful tone.

'He already knows about the prophecy. What difference would it make telling him it's nearing?'

'I suppose you're right,' Jaecen conceded.

As the conversation faded, Harlan lifted the flap and slipped into the tent. There were three sleeping pallets lined along the walls of the space. Jaecen and Erik were seated on either side of a table in the middle of the area, sipping away at the pot of tea between them. They had changed out of their black clothing and into basic travelling gear. Harlan noted that Jaecen wasn't wearing his usual robes.

'I see you both look comfortable,' the prince said, stepping into the tent. 'It looks as though Markus was able to get your things back from the guards.'

'Yes, Your Grace,' Erik replied and bowed his head. 'We carried Maldwyn from the keep to the inn where we had been staying. There we gathered our things and a friend gave us some horses to leave.'

'Apparently, the palomino horse Maldwyn had borrowed previously had been searching for him since it was returned,'

Jaecen added, grinning at the prince. 'Owen, our friend, said he would tell the owner that the horses he gave us got spooked in the storm and escaped.'

Harlan pulled out the third seat at the table and sat between them. His sword caught on the edge of the seat. He knew they weren't likely to answer any of his questions about what he'd overheard, so he chose to cut to the chase.

'I'm going to take the lord down and I have a plan set for nightfall in five days.' Pulling the chain over his head, the prince slipped the ring off the end and held it up to Jaecen and Erik. 'Your sovereign wants this ring. I'll give it to him and he can keep possession of the mine, but I need one more thing from him for my plan to succeed.'

Jaecen sat back and folded his arms, kicking his feet out under the table. 'What do you need from us?'

'Some rangers to strike a weak point and lure the lord's mercenaries into a trap.' Harlan looked over to Erik who had remained silent, sipping his tea. 'I want you to stay with me until the battle is almost won. I need you to help take Cassara and Mikel to the border.'

'Of course, sire,' Erik agreed, bowing.

'Whether you choose to return to the Anhalt Mountains,' Harlan began, placing his elbows on the tabletop, 'or stay by her side through the Shadow Plains to Mordiallok, is up to you.'

'I understand, Your Grace.'

Turning back to Jaecen, Harlan placed the ring on the table and pulled a small note out from his belt. 'This has everything Jerrik will need to know for us to succeed.'

Cautious, Jaecen reached out and picked up the note and ring. 'When do I leave?'

'I'll have Markus bring you to the disputed lands tonight when it's dark.' When Harlan stood to leave, he spied three packs together, near the foot of one of the small sleeping pallets. 'Is one of those Maldwyn's?' he asked in a flat voice. 'I can bring him his things.'

Jaecon looked uncomfortable entrusting Maldwyn's belongings with the prince, but Erik went over to the packs and grabbed a bag. 'Did he wake okay this morning, sire?'

'He seemed better,' Harlan answered, taking the heavy bag from Erik.

As Harlan left holding the bag, he was tempted to take it back to the command tent and search for answers to the puzzle he felt Maldwyn had become. Standing where the prince had left him, Markus was slouching.

'Markus, I need you to get someone to take a message to Theodor.' He pulled out another note from his belt and handed it to the soldier. 'I'll also need you to take Jaecen to the disputed lands after nightfall.'

'Yes, sire.' Markus bowed, taking the note. 'Before you leave, I've been looking into that person you wanted me to find. There was a foot soldier with a long scar on the back of his neck. He hasn't been seen since we set up camp here.'

'Good,' Harlan said, mildly worried. 'If he's gone then it means he doesn't know what I am planning and can't inform the lord. I'll be in my tent if you need me.'

It was a relief that the camp had recovered from the chaos of the prior evening. As Harlan walked toward his tent, he ignored the few officers he passed. The weight he felt as he headed back to Maldwyn seemed heavier than the pack he carried in his left hand, but he couldn't put things off any longer. It was time he returned to apologise.

When he entered the tent, Maldwyn was sitting on the ground with his legs crossed, hands resting on his knees with his palms facing the roof of the tent.

'What are you doing?' Harlan asked as he kneeled beside him. The hilt of his sword pressed into his hip.

Maldwyn opened his eyes, striking Harlan with how green they were before the firelight. Lime flecks veined through his irises around his pupils.

'Just trying to clear my mind,' Maldwyn replied in a smooth, low voice.

'I, uh,' Harlan uttered, feeling unsure of the best way to reach out to Maldwyn after their disagreement earlier, 'brought you your pack.' The prince put the pack on the ground in front of Maldwyn. 'Jaecen and Erik had it with them.' Maldwyn grinned and looked over at Harlan. 'I thought you might want to be closer to your things. You spent so long without them while you were at my side.' Looking straight into Maldwyn's gaze, Harlan sat taller. His leather body armour, which was tailored like a high-collared jacket, creaked. 'I want you to feel safe because I don't think you have felt that for some time.'

'I'm sorry for this morning,' Maldwyn offered.

'No,' Harlan told him, shaking his head and letting out a heavy breath. 'I am sorry. I didn't mean to bite your head off.' Studying Maldwyn's face, Harlan struggled to see how he was feeling. 'This is my peace offering.' Smiling, Harlan pushed the bag closer to Maldwyn until he saw a crack in his stern expression. Maldwyn let out a slight chuckle and pulled his pack over. 'What do you keep in there, by the way? That's one heavy bag.'

'Well not all of us have a palace,' Maldwyn said in a brazen tone, 'or a house. Some of us carry everything we own in a small, yet heavy, pack.'

Harlan felt bad that there was a lot of truth to Maldwyn's statement and pressed his weight back into the heel of his boots. Maldwyn eyed him for a moment and opened the bag, pulling out rolled-up clothes. He grinned lopsidedly as he pulled out a small blanket of some sort.

'You studied a lot as the Crown Prince. How much did you learn about the old ways, the times before your father?'

Harlan pinched his lips together, took in a deep breath and sighed. 'Honestly, I'm questioning everything I learned.'

Maldwyn pulled out a small piece of parchment that looked to have been folded as many times as possible and handed it to Harlan. Prying open the parchment by the corner of the crinkled note, Harlan was confused when he saw the familiar symbol of an eagle, wings spread wide and its head angled to the side with its beak open. He turned the page over and saw a pair of black wings above cursive script that read: *Keep him safe.*

'I don't understand,' Harlan admitted, frowning at Maldwyn.

Turning away, Maldwyn picked up the blanket and handed it to Harlan. The prince unrolled the petite, rectangular blanket made of the finest silk. It was a pale, chartreuse colour with leaves embroidered around the border. Yellow flowers were sewn into the leafy pattern. In one corner, was a falcon and an eagle perching on a set of branches. In the opposite corner, was a black, winged horse, rearing on its hind hooves.

'Do you recognise the symbols?' Maldwyn asked as though he was desperate for an answer.

Harlan tilted his head and stared at the two items. 'Well, the eagle and the falcon on the blanket are the symbols for Alerion and his sister Freya. Alerion is the god of desire and Freya is the goddess of love. The winged horse doesn't typically feature in this type of work as it symbolises the valkyrie, who are the divine warriors and defenders of the gods.

'They're fierce and represent everything the fertility gods, the Vanir branch of divinity, don't.' Harlan turned to the letter and quickly glanced at both sides again. 'Based on that, I'd guess this is meant to represent Alerion and an unnamed valkyrie, but I don't know what it means.' Studying the words beneath the wings, Harlan glared at Maldwyn, 'Why?'

'I told you I was found abandoned in a field.' Maldwyn swallowed and looked to the floor. 'My mother told me she found those with me before she died.'

'Keep him safe,' Harlan read aloud, watching Maldwyn for a reaction as he thought of how Erik had mentioned a "little bird". 'What does it mean?'

Looking Harlan dead in the eye, Maldwyn shrugged. Harlan felt there was something otherworldly about his seafoam-coloured eyes.

'I don't know, but I think it can help lead me to my parents, or the woman that searched for me, Eretrya.' Maldwyn looked like there was more he wanted to say, however, wasn't sure whether it was safe.

'I'll help you find the answers you need,' Harlan offered, placing the blanket and note on the ground and grabbing Maldwyn's hands.

'I want to believe you,' Maldwyn said, voice a little shaky with nerves, 'but you may not like where that leads.'

Looking up to the dying flames in the brazier, Harlan smiled. 'It's not about me if it's what you need.'

'Do you mean that?' Maldwyn checked, bringing his brows together.

Nodding, Harlan slipped a hand along his jawline, caressing the nape of his neck. 'Whatever you need, Mal. I'm here.' The prince leaned in and placed a gentle kiss on Maldwyn's mouth. 'For now, though, you should know that I am sending Jaecen back to Jerrik with the ring tonight. If you need to see him before he's gone, you should tell me so I can have you brought to him.'

'Tonight?' Maldwyn rubbed the space between his brows. 'That's quick.'

'I need him to get a message to Jerrik. I have a plan for nightfall in five days, but I need the sovereign's help.'

'Okay,' Maldwyn said under his breath. 'You're right, I should see him, even just to say goodbye. Jaecen and Erik are the reason I'm here now.'

'Consider it done,' Harlan said, pushing himself up to stand.

'Where are you going?'

'I need to visit some officers around the camp and put some plans in motion. I'll send Markus over to bring you to the others and I'll be back in time to eat dinner.'

Maldwyn smiled and nodded, running his hands through his chestnut-coloured hair. Maldwyn seemed surprised that Harlan hadn't pried beyond what he had been comfortable telling the prince. Harlan grinned in return, curious about Maldwyn's parentage, wondering whether he might be the little bird he needed by his side according to prophecy. Was it possible that he was enamoured with and was staring at the prophesied man that his father had been paranoid about existing... that his father wanted dead? Still, Harlan thought as he stepped out of the tent, he was pleased that he had begun to chip away at Maldwyn's defensive walls.

CHAPTER TWENTY-SIX

The Moonlit Gauntlet

THE DENSE MIST IN THE WOODS was like death's trap as Harlan sat back in his saddle, waiting for the sound of steel to signal the battle had begun. It was dark and the air carried the bitter scent of tree bark. The horses of his mounted forces were quiet, holding formation in a straight line overlooking a murky valley, well away from his infantry.

A bird squawked suddenly and loudly, fluttering away through the arms of the fat trees. A moment of silence was followed by the squeals of death calling from the pit, northeast of his position among the hills in the woods at the foot of the Anhalt Mountains.

Though not the typical conditions for a battle, Harlan was planning on luring the lord into something unexpected. The impulsive attack from the mountain folk placed at the weakest point of the pit would infuriate Lord Darius, and the poor conditions would lull the lord into a false sense of security when the rangers feigned retreat.

If Harlan was right, and he knew the lord as well as he thought, Lord Darius would send his mercenaries after the rangers to keep the location of the pit secret. He would not anticipate the prince's forces materialising from the fog.

A calm soon settled as the cries died out. Harlan guessed the rangers were staging their retreat, taking off into the trees as smooth and formless as mist, leading the mercenaries into the ambush.

They waited.

The night air was torn with the sounds of terror as Harlan heard the lord's forces batter against the shield wall of his infantry to the northwest of the valley below. The horse he sat on stamped its foot into the ground. Hysteria broke out among the mercenaries who suffered defeat. A lone man, clutching his sword, turned and ran back in the direction of the pit, passing into the prince's view.

Markus notched an arrow, drawing his bowstring and aiming at the runner. Harlan held out his right hand and placed it on the soldier's forearm.

'No, don't!' Harlan locked eyes with Markus. He could make out the soldier's glare beneath his thick brows. 'Hold the line!'

'Sire, he'll raise the alarm!' Markus argued.

'I know… I want him to,' Harlan said, watching the man run out of range.

'How many men will the lord send as reinforcements, sire?' Maldwyn asked as his golden horse shifted impatiently.

His silky robes from the Erendil gave him a mysterious presence as he sat tall on his shining steed. Harlan had wanted him to stay behind, but Maldwyn insisted on joining the battle. At least, Harlan thought, he could keep Maldwyn safe with him by his side.

'He won't send all of his forces,' Harlan said, fixing the buckle of his leather vambrace which dug into his wrist. 'The man will only report the encounter with the infantry in the valley. He'll send enough of his forces in the pit to decimate the infantry, which is the better part of a thousand men based on Cassara's information.' Steel chimed below them as a cloud of mist rolled over the valley, blocking the battle from sight. 'Given the secrecy around whatever the lord has been doing here, he only brought a few selected guards with him from the keep. The rest of my father's men are still in the downs. With our mounted force here and Theodor's men on the other side of the valley, we outnumber them.'

'Will the lord send a message to the keep for reinforcements, Your Grace?' Erik called from the other side of Maldwyn.

Harlan shook his head. 'I doubt it. They're my father's men, which means they answer to me as the Crown Prince.' The steel fangs of death in the valley stabbed into the lord's barbarians. 'Are you certain Theodor received the message?' Harlan checked with Markus.

'Yes, Your Highness,' Markus replied, keeping his bow at the ready. 'His men won't move on the other side of the valley until we have started the charge.'

'All we need to do is wait,' Harlan reassured, watching as the fog parted to reveal the moonlit slaughter of unsuspecting mercenaries. He hardened himself to the guilt creeping in as he heard their cries. 'Our men down there can handle the situation for the time being.'

Time passed by slowly as the prince listened to the sounds of war... life and death. Every noise, each movement was a message, a warning that an enemy may be approaching.

Then, after what seemed to be hours of listening to the screaming from the valley, the reinforcements arrived. Though they were well-armed, their formation was lacking.

Arrows zipped through the air from the rangers hidden in the trees, covering the infantry as the lord's reinforcements joined the battle. They crumpled to the ground, arrows poking out of their necks.

'Now, sire?' Markus checked, pushing his shoulders back.

'Not yet,' Harlan ordered as the mist moved over the valley. Screams ripped through the prince as he sat in his saddle, waiting for the right moment. As the final mercenary crossed the mental line Harlan had marked in the valley, he whipped his head to Markus. 'Now!'

A horn blew. The prince drew his sword and kicked the stirrups of his saddle. His horse jumped and galloped down the hill, hooves pounding into the ground. Wheeling around the back of the mercenary forces, the prince and his regiment blocked any chance of escape as Theodor and his men charged down the other side of the valley, filling the spaces between the horses.

Spears poking forward and shields raised, Theodor and his soldiers closed in on the lord's forces, splintering them on their spikes. The mercenaries inside the formation clustered together like panicked sheep being herded to their doom. Blood sprayed through the cold mist; a terrible sight.

A bloodstained knife glinted off the moon as it flew through the fog. There was a strange feeling in the air. The knife stopped an inch from Harlan's nose, the blade pointing to his face.

Harlan noticed a hand holding the knife, having plucked it from the air. His eyes followed along the familiar arm until he was staring at Maldwyn.

'How did you…?'

'Sire!' A sentry, struggling for air, ran up to the hind of the prince's horse. 'The lord appears to be making a break for the keep! He's heading south from that place!'

'Theodor, Markus, with me!' Harlan shouted. One of the mounted soldiers jumped off a grey horse, handing the reins to Theodor and joined the formation of spearmen in the knight's place. 'Erik! I'll need you too!' Harlan called over to Erik, who remained out of danger toward the back of the mounted formation, where Maldwyn was supposed to be waiting. He stared at Maldwyn, full of questions. 'Let's go!'

Harlan rode in the direction of the report, ducking beneath the low branches of the trees as he sped through the woods. The sounds of the battle grew softer and softer. The mist diminished as they rode towards the higher ground. The tangy smell in the air thickened.

Lord Darius and two other riders wearing cloaks could be seen galloping in the centre of a group of soldiers, racing toward the keep. An arrow whistled from a ranger in the trees, landing in the lord's horse, causing it to trip and collapse to the ground, throwing the lord from his saddle. His men gathered around to protect him.

Markus shot another arrow at one of the guards, knocking him from his horse. Theodor threw his spear bringing another steed down to its knees. As the two fallen guards stood up, Harlan sliced through one of them with his sword. The other guard pulled the spear out of the dying horse and used it to knock Theodor from his saddle. Maldwyn jumped from his seat, twirling through the air with expert ease. He landed with a harrumph and seemed to dance around the tip of the spear effortlessly as he dodged the blows. Harlan looked back as his horse vaulted over a fallen tree and saw Erik hanging back, avoiding the fight.

Another arrow shot from the trees and pierced into one of the standing mercenary guards. Harlan jumped off his horse's saddleback when he reached Lord Darius. The lord's two companions stayed out of the way, crouching by a large oak tree.

'You know, if this is because of the assassination attempt, then you should know it was the sloppy work of my wife.'

The unsuspecting Lord Darius wore nothing more than his fine lord's attire with a sword attached to his belt, having been ignorant of the prince's plan to attack. Lord Darius drew his sword and smiled wickedly.

'However, Gerard's betrayal, that was my doing. He came pretty cheaply too. He didn't do it alone for money. He had it in for you.'

Harlan swung his sword with his left hand, clashing with the lord's, eager to silence him.

'You'll die for this,' the lord threatened, glaring through his heavy-lidded eyes.

Lord Darius shifted his weight to his front foot. The prince jumped back, dodging the lord's kick to his shin.

'Do you think that man in the mountains doesn't have his purposes for what's in that mine?' The lord paced, pointing his sword at Harlan.

'How much draconite is there?' Harlan asked in a low voice as he gritted his teeth.

'Loads!' Lord Darius spat. 'You can find it along with the dragon's corpse below the water of the underground lake.' The lord swung his sword in a wide sweeping motion.

The ringing of clashing steel was deafening. Lord Darius pressed harder, cutting the prince's leather sleeve.

Harlan pushed back and yanked his sword free. His steel blade slid along Lord Darius's, slicing the top of the lord's sword hand.

An arrow shot between them from the trees, landing in the eye of a guard behind Harlan. A blood-curdling scream filled the air as the man clung to his face and fell to the ground. Harlan tuned out the noises of the others fighting all around him.

Swift and daring, Lord Darius stabbed the prince. Harlan brushed the move aside with his sword and shoved Lord Darius back a few paces.

With the lord losing his footing, Harlan began an onslaught of heavy, overhead hacks in an attempt to break through his parries. As Lord Darius stepped back from the force of the prince's blows, he tripped over the huge, webbed tree roots and dropped his sword.

'Wait!' The lord shouted, holding his hands up in surrender as he cowered on his knees beneath Harlan's raised sword. 'If you kill me, your father gains total unchecked control of the kingdom. He will continue his quest to exterminate sorcerers and expand his rule. I may be a traitor, but I balance out his power in northern regions. You know it and I know it.' Harlan felt a sickening knot twist in the pit of his stomach and he hesitated. 'Isn't that what you want? You may hate me, you may even hate your father, but this is the price you pay to control him.'

The sounds of the fight around him were a mild distraction as the prince stared at the lord. The fear that Lord Darius was right tormented Harlan as he tightened his grip on his sword. He wondered if the lord was a necessary evil to keep his father's power restrained at the northern border.

'You can't control him without me,' hand raised, Lord Darius smirked, knowing he was getting under Harlan's skin, 'can you, sire?'

He had come too far to do nothing now. He pondered whether he should give Lord Darius a chance to escape. The lord had been effective at keeping a great many details from his father, but his actions were more oppressive and the cost seemed too high a price.

At least people in the capital had better standards of living and were ignorant of his father's actions beyond the city. Glancing around, gruesome scenes of death surrounded him.

Lowering his sword, Harlan stepped away. He looked down to see blood on his hands and he couldn't remember how it got there.

He heard Lord Darius move and suddenly felt as though his body were not his own and he remained frozen. He saw one of the lord's companions quickly jump to their feet, pull out an ornate dagger and stab Lord Darius in the throat. The handle of the knife was red and had silver swirls surrounding a white jade tree. The lord's eyes went wide as blood gushed down his neck. He struggled, clawing at his neck as he collapsed to the ground. Shocked, Harlan could hardly believe his eyes as he watched the lord's life drain away.

Looking at the cloaked figure, a dainty hand reached up to lower the hood. 'Cassara!' Harlan frowned and moved closer. 'You killed him?'

'I had to,' she said in a pleading voice as she dropped the knife, hands trembling. 'I've been here in my dreams. If I didn't act, then he would have killed you and then me.'

She stared over the prince's shoulder, Harlan looked in the direction of her stare and saw Maldwyn watching them as Erik dismounted and began heading over. Theodor and Markus were busy surveying the area, making sure there were no other threats at hand. The ranger that had followed them dropped from the trees to have a few quiet words with Erik.

'It'll be alright. Thank you for saving me,' Harlan mumbled, glancing back at his sister. Her long, glossy hair still shone in the dark and the starlight reaching through the treetops highlighted her cheekbones. 'I shouldn't have hesitated. Are you alright?'

'I am,' her hands were still shaking. 'I protected us and avenged our mother.'

'You're a lot of things, Cassara,' Harlan said in a whisper, 'but you're not a killer. You've never killed before.'

'I'll be fine,' she said in a cold, firm voice as she wiped her hands on her cloak, unsettled by the blood on them.

The other cloaked figure was slow to stand. 'It's good to see you again, Your Grace.'

Harlan cringed at the familiar voice, despite the wheezing.

'Mikel.' Harlan didn't say anything else as he sheathed his sword, remembering that Mikel was the reason for his incarceration in the Anhalt Mountains. 'Erik will take you to the border while the lord's men are occupied,' Harlan told Cassara, sheathing his ornate sword.

'Before we go,' Cassara started, voice tremoring from the rush of her actions, 'there's something else you need to know. Something else that I've seen.'

'What is it?' Harlan glanced over to Markus and Theodor exchanging reports.

Cassara wetted her lips and looked back at Maldwyn, further behind Harlan. 'I know about the spell our mother cast on you.'

Surprised, Harlan frowned and turned his head to the side. Mikel leaned against the oak tree and coughed.

'In the dream I've been having lately, you are a lynx, which means your spell may be triggered soon, and I think it has to do with him.'

'What are you saying?'

'He's not clear in my dream, but I'm sure it's Maldwyn. A crying woman tells me I can't save him.' Harlan recalled Cassara telling him that there was someone her foresight was blind to and wondered whether this was what she had meant. If this were true, then Maldwyn was the person that freed her from her chains. Cassara smiled at Erik as he continued toward them, leaving the ranger. 'I think something bad is going to happen. The awakening is coming.' Lost for words, Harlan managed only a muffled reply. 'It's strange, isn't it?'

'What is?' Harlan asked, resting his hand on the pommel of his sword.

'I've seen so many things that I could never expect. Our mother was a seer. My gift comes from her.' She shrugged, looking sad. 'She saw something about you and wanted to be the one that put you on your path.'

CHAPTER TWENTY-SIX

'She what?' Harlan mumbled as Erik approached and bowed.

'Your Royal Highness,' Erik formally addressed. 'We should leave soon to reach the border before dawn. The sooner the better, to get you farther away from danger.'

The princess smiled and bowed her head to Erik. 'Thank you,' she said in a sincere tone to Harlan, pulling him into a hug. 'Go inside the pit, it's much more than a barracks. You'll find the missing people that worked in the mine. His experiments with the draconite are alarming.'

Pulling away, Harlan wished he had more time as he nodded. 'Take care of yourself.'

Erik led Mikel and Cassara away. The princess paused to look back at the country she was leaving behind. Harlan thought she seemed nostalgic now that she was finally moving forward. In a matter of moments, they were out of sight and Harlan achieved what he had set out to do. The corrupt, tyrannical lord had been stopped and his sister was safe.

'Are you alright?' Maldwyn asked, coming up to his side. The sounds of the battle in the distance were faint.

'Sure.' Harlan feigned a smile, hoping it would convince Maldwyn. 'She'll be safer out there than if she stays here.'

'Sire,' Theodor began, looking exhausted as he bowed. 'I've sent Markus back to oversee the end of the battle.'

'Good,' Harlan replied, crossing his arms.

The ranger walked over and pulled down the hood of his robes. Harlan recognised the square face and cropped hair.

'The sovereign was pleased to be able to honour Kristian.' Jaecen held his bow in a slack grip. 'He wanted me to assure you that you have his support.'

The prince speculated what should happen should he ever lose Jerrik's support. 'I hope this is the start of an important alliance.'

'Our people feel the same.' The ranger bowed his head. 'Until next time, Eminence,' Jaecen said in a soft voice. Harlan got the feeling the remark wasn't directed at him and Maldwyn stood taller on his left.

Theodor glanced at Maldwyn. Harlan felt there was something he was missing.

'It was an honour to fight by your side,' Theodor offered, holding out a hand. 'Your people have incredible skill.'

Jaecen shook Theodor's hand and smiled. 'You're a man of many talents as well.' Theodor chuckled as Jaecen turned on his heel, heading back into the woods.

'A man of many talents.' Harlan mocked, placing his hands on his hips and staring over at Theodor. 'You knew him for less than a week! What did you do?'

Theodor shrugged. 'He likes gambling.'

Maldwyn laughed, shaking his head. Harlan wanted to know how Maldwyn had managed to pluck the dagger from the air on the battlefield, why the Erendil appeared to have a high reverence for him, and what it was that made him invisible to his sister's visions, but there were more pressing matters at hand.

'When the battle is over, we need to finish things and secure the stronghold.'

* * * * *

The prince's men lit torches when the battle was over, illuminating the horror. The lord's men weren't loyal and were quick to surrender, leading Harlan and his soldiers to the lord's pit. The place was a series of mud buildings and tunnels that were dug into the forest and reinforced with a spiked fence.

It was a crude structure that wove through the trees and disordered shrubbery, nevertheless, it was well concealed. The mist lay like a sheer blanket over the stronghold, making it difficult to perceive the exact size of the mercenary garrison. Harlan could see how this place had remained secret for this long.

There was a rotten stench and the prince was told prisoners were being kept in overcrowded cells. It wasn't clear who the prisoners were, given they could barely speak after enduring the lord's cruel tortures, but Cassara had suggested they were the miners who had gone missing around the time the mine was liberated by the Erendil.

Harlan was disturbed to see how extremely thin and unhealthy the people behind the bars were, bones protruding. 'Let them out,' Harlan ordered, noticing their tattered rags for clothes. 'Let them all out. Make sure they are fed and clothed.'

The pit was a series of horrors. There was a smithy, where the prisoners were being used as slave labourers, that tested the strength of new weapons crafted from the steel that had been smelted with draconite. The various weapons were piled together in a disordered mess on a table, next to the forge. The results didn't seem to have yielded much more than a black blade that shimmered in the light.

Deeper into the pit was a small building with mud walls and a grassy roof that was full of apothecary equipment. There was only enough room for one table beneath a wall of shelves, a brazier and one seat, which had shackles on the arms and legs.

On the table was a large granite mortar and pestle beside a stack of ceramic bowls. On a shelf over the table were vials of thick, unknown substances. Pots and pans were hanging overhead and a timber cylinder packed with utensils was placed at the end of the table, near what appeared to be a record book and a box of draconite.

From the entries in the records, the mercenaries had been testing the toxicity and effects of newly developed poisons that were enhanced by the gemstone. The prisoners were forced to ingest the poisons while shackled to the seat.

'How could anyone do this?' Maldwyn murmured behind Harlan, staring at the seat. 'How many people died in his experiments and what did he hope to gain?'

'Forty-two so far,' Harlan mumbled, thumbing through the pages, 'according to the records, but I'm sure it's more than that.' Turning to Theodor, Harlan handed the record book to him and headed to the door to leave the apothecary. 'Bury the bodies. Help the prisoners. Have the draconite sent to the sovereign in the mountains. Then, destroy this place. Burn it to the ground.'

'Yes, sire,' Theodor said to his back.

Harlan left, passing the wagon of bodies beside the apothecary, weaving through the rough buildings and fat trees. Stepping out of sight of his men, he leaned against one of the empty mud structures, horrified by the cruel, twisted nature of this place. How had his father overlooked this much brutality while chasing sorcerers?

'It's not your fault,' Maldwyn said behind him, placing a hand on Harlan's shoulder.

'Isn't it?' Harlan turned, staring into Maldwyn's soft, green eyes that reflected orange hues in the firelight of the torch he carried. 'I sat in a palace and went along with my father's ignorance and listened to the lord's lies for years. I never imagined that it might lead to this. It took my sister coming here for me to even look at this place.'

'You didn't know,' Maldwyn argued.

'More like, I didn't want to know.' Harlan noticed there was still blood on his hands that had dried. He tried to wipe it off, spreading it over his palm. 'He's always been greedy and sought power. I should have known that he was up to something, preparing for a civil war.' Shaking his head, frustrated at himself, Harlan heard his men kicking open a door not far from where he stood. 'That's the only reason he would be building an army and testing poisons. He was probably desperate to get out from under King Filip's control and the only way he could do that without facing execution for treason was to defeat my father and take the kingdom for himself. These are my people and I failed them.'

Harlan rubbed his nose and sniffed. He longed to leave this place and its smell behind. As he saw a group of bony prisoners being led away by guards over Maldwyn's shoulder, struggling to remain on their feet, Harlan thought of the prisoners his father used as labourers. The image of Maldwyn's friends being starved and exploited troubled him.

'If it comes to that, I'll help to free your people and I'll even bring down my father. This can never happen again.' In need of comfort, Harlan leaned in and pressed his forehead to Maldwyn's, feeling the warmth of the flames from the torch. 'I'll arrest Lady Adria for the assassination attempt and treason. Whether or not she agreed with the things her husband was doing, she remained silent and complicit for years. I'll leave Markus in charge of the downs. Then, I'll go back to the palace and confront my father. Will you come with me, or will you return to the Anhalt Mountains?'

'I'll go with you to the capital,' Maldwyn told him. Harlan felt Maldwyn's breath on his face as the torch warmed his cheeks. 'Theodor told me Ailaya wasn't coping with the rumours of my death.'

The battle was over and he had won, but the situation in Karana Downs, the ugliness of this place and the death from the battle in the valley not far from here, made the prince feel unclean.

CHAPTER TWENTY-SEVEN

The Price

SUMMER HAD ARRIVED by the time they reached the capital. It was strange being back in the city after so much time. The cobbled streets seemed more charming than Maldwyn remembered with the evergreen, leafy vines hanging like silky curtains over the timber and stucco houses. The sweet wrens sang to welcome them from the cropped trees as the gentle waves of the shores in the background rolled in to soothe them after their travels. As they rose higher toward the palace, Maldwyn spotted the tawny sails of the ships anchored at sea. The honeyed air seemed more fragrant than Maldwyn remembered.

The horse's hooves clip-clopped loudly as they rode into the open square before the palace. The grey, stone castle walls were masked by the glossy, green vines wrapping around the building. Master Damyan stood with his hands clasped behind his back, waiting at the top of the palace steps to greet them.

'Many happy returns, Your Grace,' Master Damyan said, bowing. His silver streaks were whiter than the last time Maldwyn had seen him and he appeared drained despite his perfect façade.

'I need to speak with my father,' Harlan said abruptly as he jumped off his horse, passing the reins to a nearby servant.

'He's in the council chambers, sire.' Master Damyan told the prince. 'The meeting ended a few moments ago. He should be available to speak with you.' Theodor slipped off of his saddle and glanced up at the sun. It was a hot day.

As Maldwyn dismounted, his golden horse shook its white mane and stamped its hoof. Maldwyn stroked its coarse neck.

Master Damyan approached Harlan, lowering his voice as he moved down the steps. 'Sire, your father has questioned a lot of my staff about the night your mother's pendant went missing.'

'There's nothing to find though,' Master Damyan glanced at Maldwyn as Harlan spoke, 'is there?' Harlan looked over at Maldwyn as well, tightening his brows a little.

'No, of course not,' Master Damyan shook his head and looked at the ground, 'but that foot soldier you sent ahead of you with a message seems unusual.'

'Wait, Your Grace, what soldier?' Theodor asked, frowning at Harlan.

'I didn't send anyone,' Harlan said, concernedly. The bright, hot sun made his hair seem paler. His lightweight, blue leather armour with the rampant lynx must have been uncomfortable in the smouldering heat. 'Does he have a scar on his neck?' Harlan drew an invisible line on his neck with his left index finger.

'Yes, it is quite prominent,' Master Damyan replied.

The rest of the prince's escort was busy passing around orders, readying for a debrief as servants collected their horses for stabling.

'Cassara warned me about him.' Harlan's voice was unsteady. 'That's Mikel's informant! She said he can't be trusted!'

Harlan took off up the steps and ran into the palace. Maldwyn, Theodor and Damyan chased the prince, racing through the expansive palace corridors.

Maldwyn felt out of place in the main halls of the palace. He was used to the small, oppressive labyrinth of tunnels reserved for the staff. The corridors grew wider as they went and the furnishings were more majestic toward the council chambers with striking tapestries of mythological scenes hanging from the walls. The two massive oak doors to the council chambers were manned by the king's sentries, wearing their polished, heavy, golden armour that gleamed under the sunlight pouring into the halls.

The guards bowed as Harlan approached and thrust the doors open, stepping inside. Maldwyn hesitated before entering, considering whether he should wait outside. Theodor went in without pause and the master of the staff signalled for Maldwyn to follow as he passed.

The expansive room was as Maldwyn remembered and the floral air wafting through from the balcony was warm. The long timber table had eight bulky chairs tucked around it.

Candelabras with swirls sculpted into the metal hung from the roof. To the right, beyond an open archway, covered in soft, leafy drapes, was a large balcony and, to the left, was a massive fireplace that had been cleaned. A small room kicked off to the left of the main space with a large, ornate desk in the centre.

King Viktor was sitting behind the desk, writing. The black streak in his grey hair, cutting through the gold, laurel wreath for a crown, commanded attention. Behind the king was a soldier, wearing the basic armour of the capital's infantry. A thick scar ran down the right side of his neck. The man smirked at Maldwyn, as though he had expected to see him here, but Maldwyn did not recognise him.

'Your Majesty,' Harlan started, bowing as he stood opposite the seated king. 'I come with news from the north.'

'You did good work, son,' the king said with a biting tongue. 'Did you find the proof I asked you to find?'

'Lord Darius was a traitor, father.' Harlan glared at the man behind the king. 'He's been in league with King Filip for years, accepting payments from and sharing information about the royal court with your enemy. He was building a mercenary army and I believe he was planning a civil war to overthrow you.'

'That is unfortunate,' the king said, sounding bored, 'and I'm glad you followed my orders this time. It's a pity you weren't able to reclaim the mine while you were there, or locate that pesky sword.' Theodor glanced nervously at Damyan as guards entered through the servant door. 'What of your sister? She was rumoured to be in the area.'

Maldwyn could see that Harlan was careful. The prince pressed his broad shoulders back.

'I never saw her, Your Majesty,' the prince lied. 'However, I should also report that Lady Adria has been arrested and is being held in the dungeons in Karana Downs with the forces I left to maintain the region.'

'Pity,' King Viktor muttered, reclining back in his chair. 'I had hoped to see Cassara. As for the lady of the downs, she's of no concern to me.' Shifting his attention to Maldwyn, the king's face turned cold. 'I know you. You were imprisoned at my son's side.' Maldwyn's stomach tightened and his breaths grew shallow. The guards that had entered through the side door were now standing behind them, chains rattled. 'Yes, you were by his side when he returned from the mountains and you were in the palace the night the princess escaped.' The king stood and circled Maldwyn. Acutely aware of how many guards were in the room, Maldwyn stared at the floor, dubious of what was happening. His power electrified, prickling all over, but he contained it, unsure of the king's point as he circled. 'That was also the night of the theft in the palace.' The king paused, leaned into Maldwyn's ear and whispered, 'I know what you are.'

Maldwyn reached for his gift, except, within moments his arms were grabbed by the guards and his hands chained behind his back. As the shackles locked around Maldwyn's wrists, his power waned. He felt it there, tingling as though it were desperate for release, but it was somehow out of reach. Theodor half drew his sword. Master Damyan began to argue. Harlan stood frozen.

King Viktor stopped to tower over Maldwyn. Uncomfortable, tense and afraid, Maldwyn kept staring at the floor as he felt the tip of a dagger press against his back.

'This man has been very helpful in my search for the thief,' the king said. His breath reeked of garlic and Maldwyn winced. 'He tells me that he saw you attempt to curse the late queen's pendant. He says when the alarm was raised for Cassara's escape, you snuck into my chambers and stole her necklace.'

Maldwyn couldn't bear to look up at the king's smirk. The only way for the man with the scar to have known Maldwyn had been anywhere near the king's chambers was for this man to be the informant that had attacked Maldwyn inside the keep; the man that sifted through his memories. It dawned on Maldwyn that this man was likely the same person that Mikel had used to curse the necklace.

'You're the sorcerer who freed the princess from custody and the thief that stole my late wife's pendant. You will be executed at dusk tomorrow.'

'Father, please,' Harlan begged, sounding panicked as he pleaded. Theodor and Damyan stayed mute, eyeing each of the guards. 'I don't know what that man has told you,' the prince said, pointing at the man behind the desk, 'but it's a lie. Maldwyn's not a sorcerer, nor a thief.'

'You know his name?' The king moved over to lock eyes with his son. Harlan's eyes turned fierce. Maldwyn could see the anger seeping into his blank, royal expression. 'He's nothing but a servant. A waste of space, barely worth existing. You shouldn't acknowledge those beneath you. I raised you better than this.' The king's voice was low and cold. He turned and shook his head, disappointed with his son. 'Take him away!'

Maldwyn struggled against the guards pulling at his arms and locked eyes with Harlan, feeling fear overwhelm him as his power remained out of reach. Though he had little control over his gifts throughout his life, Maldwyn had never felt so powerless.

'Father, you can't kill him!'

'Why not?' The king burst, eyes bulging as he stared at Harlan. Veins popped out from King Viktor's neck.

'I'll do anything you want of me, but please,' Harlan softened his voice, 'don't kill him.'

King Viktor scowled at Harlan. 'I've already made up my mind. Take him away!'

Maldwyn wanted to fight but knew it would be in vain as his power eluded him. The knife pressing into his lower back remained steady as he was guided toward the serving door. He heard Harlan arguing with his father and glanced back, catching a final glimpse of his crystal blue eyes. The door whined as the guards dragged it open and the room fell away as he was pulled into the confined halls, led down the steep steps and brought to the cell that would be the final room in which he would ever lay his head to rest.

* * * * *

The cell was dark and cramped, and the chains around Maldwyn's ankles rattled as he brought his legs up to his chest, burying his head in his knees. Though the heat made the stench of rotting people worse, Maldwyn was slowly adapting to it, with the lingering smell diminishing the longer he sat in his cell. Muck had been left behind by the cell's last occupant and Maldwyn couldn't stop himself from imagining the many sorcerers that had spent their final moments in this cell, in these spelled chains.

The memory of the elderly sorcerer that he had served before execution came to mind. Maldwyn wished he knew his name, but he had never asked.

The hinges on the heavy, timber door to his cell whinged, groaning as the door opened. Maldwyn looked up and saw Theodor standing in the doorway. He looked taller from this angle and his lightweight, brown, leather armour seemed almost black in the dim cell. Maldwyn noted that his sword wasn't hanging from his hip. It was probably a condition for the nobleman to gain entry to a sorcerer's lockup.

'Much appreciated,' Theodor mumbled to the guard with the keys to Maldwyn's prison cell. The door closed behind Theodor as he walked towards Maldwyn. 'I don't know why I thought those chains wouldn't work on you.'

'For some reason, I didn't think they would either,' Maldwyn stretched one leg out as Theodor sat on the ground beside him, leaning back against the wall. 'I guess I brought this on myself. It was me that freed the princess from these chains. I'm the reason she escaped.' Outside, Maldwyn heard the guard dragging someone else to a cell. It sounded like the person was kicking as they resisted. 'I didn't think these would work because I had used my power on them before, but, I suppose, I wasn't the one wearing them.'

'What does it feel like—to wear the chains, I mean?'

'Like I've lost a piece of myself.' Shifting his hands behind his back, Maldwyn pushed himself up to sit taller. 'I can still feel my power, but it's somehow out of reach.' Maldwyn sighed and cleared his throat. 'I know what these chains are now.' Theodor stared at him with a curious face. 'According to legend, Wayland was imprisoned by Hel and her son during the divine wars and forced to work for them. I believe these were the chains that held him. This is why sorcerers can't use magic, can't draw on divinity when they are shackled by these chains.' Pouting, Maldwyn looked over to Theodor. 'It's why I can't use my power.'

'I'm so sorry.' Theodor glanced over to the door. 'I can't help you. Master Damyan and I have never freed anyone from these shackles. The king himself keeps the key to those chains. Besides which, we've never even gotten someone out of the dungeons.'

Maldwyn shrugged, shook his head and stared at his knees. 'I knew I shouldn't have come back here.' He noticed a small tear in his pants to the side of his kneecap. 'I guessed things would end like this, I just hoped I had more time.'

'What do you mean?' Theodor frowned.

A prisoner in another cell coughed loudly. It was a thick sort of cough that sounded phlegmy and diseased.

'Just over a year ago, I served a sorcerer in this very cell. He told me about a prophecy. He called it the Quandiallan Prophecy, or the Awakening of Firebird.' Recalling how happy the tale had made the man, Maldwyn smiled. 'Though I've been reluctant to accept my place in prophecy, I knew that it would come to this. You see the prophecy says that I will burn to death.'

'There has to be a way to save you.'

'I've already lost everything I had. Even if it were possible, if I escaped now, I'd spend the rest of my life running and I'd place the few people I have left in danger.' Maldwyn rubbed his cheek on his shoulder, trying to scratch an itch. 'Besides, that sorcerer made it sound like a good thing.'

Theodor let out an awkward breath, scoffing at the notion of his death being good.

'You should know, the prince begged for your life.' Maldwyn swallowed and avoided looking at Theodor. 'He confessed his feelings for you and he's been confined to his chambers and forbidden from coming here. The king fears he would try to free you, which would taint the image of the royal family further.' Theodor cleared his throat. 'He'll be made to attend the execution to keep up appearances.'

'Ah,' Maldwyn muttered, frowning. 'I suppose that's why you're here, and not him. Can you get Harlan a message for me?'

Theodor raised an eyebrow and grinned at hearing Maldwyn casually call the prince by his name. 'I can tell him anything you want.'

Maldwyn heard doors in the corridor opening. His last meal would be served to him soon and he was running out of time. 'Tell him that man by the king's side is the person that attacked me in the downs, Mikel's informant. He'll know what I mean,' Maldwyn said when Theodor cocked his head, wondering what Maldwyn was referring to. 'He's not just a soldier, nor Mikel's informant, I suspect he's the sorcerer Mikel paid to curse the queen's pendant. Harlan needs to be careful.' Maldwyn checked the door, hearing another cell open and shut. 'That man worships Hel.'

'I don't understand. King Filip, Mikel,' Theodor lowered his voice to a whisper as keys rattled in the lock to Maldwyn's gaol cell, 'they aren't Hel worshippers.'

'They may not know.' The lock clicked over. 'I only worked it out by chance when I saw the marking on his forearm.' The door began to creak open and Maldwyn went silent.

'Food for the prisoner,' the stocky guard called to Theodor and stepped aside.

Staring to the ground holding a bowl of gruel was Ailaya. Her long, wavy, auburn hair was pulled back into a loose ponytail. She was wearing a basic, moss-green-coloured dress. She looked nervously at the guard as she stepped inside and waited for the door to close.

Maldwyn felt his heart racing as he moved, wanting to run over to his closest friend, but his chains wouldn't allow him to move that far. When the guard's feet left the door, heading back down the dungeon corridor, Ailaya raced over to Maldwyn's other side, tears welling in her hazel eyes as she wrapped her arms around him. Unable to return the embrace, Maldwyn tucked his head into her.

'What have they done to you?' She pulled away and stroked his face. 'You need to help him,' Ailaya instructed Theodor. 'We just got him back.'

'He can't,' Maldwyn told her as Theodor looked at her gravely. 'It's okay,' Maldwyn lied to reassure her. 'I'm okay.'

'No… you're not,' Ailaya said, lip quivering as she began to cry. Theodor took the bowl from her trembling hands and placed it on the ground next to him.

'Sure, I am,' he pressed, smiling as a tear ran down the tip of her nose. 'I've lived a pretty full life for someone like us.'

Ailaya rubbed her nose and sniffed. 'I don't accept that,' she said quietly, trying to bury her tears with a smile. 'You're my best friend. What will I do without you?'

What could he say that could take away the pain she felt? How could he comfort her when he wanted to live?

'I'll leave you two to say goodbye,' Theodor said, getting up to stand and bowing before Maldwyn. It was the first time Theodor had shown him the same reverence as the people in the Anhalt Mountains.

'Wait,' Maldwyn looked up at the knight as he moved toward the cell door. 'Can you tell the prince one more thing?' Theodor nodded, standing between Maldwyn and the door. 'Tell him—when they light the pyre—he should close his eyes and look away. I don't want him to remember me like that.'

'I'll tell him,' Theodor said, turning back to the door. He knocked for the guard to return. 'Goodbye, Maldwyn.'

The door opened and Theodor left his cell. Arms shackled behind his back, Maldwyn sat, resting his jaw on the top of Ailaya's head as she clung to him. He sank against her, dreading the moment when she would have to leave and he would remain alone to spend his final moments waiting for death's call.

CHAPTER TWENTY-EIGHT

The Awakening

MALDWYN HEARD THE EAGER crowd cheering in the square as the guards led him up the stairs from the dungeons, toward his pending execution. His chains tolled like bells, ringing to signal the end was nigh as he climbed the steep spiralling staircase. Maldwyn's heart raced as he heard the crowd erupt with excitement. King Viktor must have made his appearance on the balcony that overlooked the square. Harlan was expected to make an appearance as well, and Maldwyn knew that the king would have ensured the crowd got what they wanted. The execution of sorcerers was always turned into a spectacle.

The guards stopped him as they reached the door to the square. 'Since the dawn of time, good men have been oppressed by those who have more power,' the king's voice crept through the door and Maldwyn cringed as his pulse quickened. The people could be heard yelling in agreement. 'Sorcerers have wielded their power like gods, deciding whether regular men will live or die.' The lie was piercing and stirred the rage in the crowd outside. Maldwyn's hands trembled and his palms began to sweat as he listened to the angry mob, waiting to watch the entertainment as a sorcerer burned in the square… as he burned in the square. 'Together, we must rise, and today, we stand against an oppressor. Bring forth the prisoner!'

'For what it's worth,' said one of the guards, a middle-aged man with fine wrinkles and short black hair, 'I remember you as a servant from a while back. You helped me with an errand for the king one time.' The other guard who was younger with a trimmed beard pushed the door open. The crowd sounded louder in the square. 'You saved my skin when you returned with the reports just in time.' The wrinkles deepened as he offered a sad face. 'I'm sorry about this.'

'I guess it's too late to ask you to let me run away from here,' Maldwyn said, shaking. He was terrified of what lay beyond the door as the mob called for his death.

'I can't. I have a family to look out for, but take comfort in that it will be over soon.'

The two guards held him by each arm and guided him through the door toward the square. People lined the courtyard, fists punching the air as the crowd chanted for his death. Soldiers patrolled the space, keeping the hungry pack in line. Angry faces grimaced at him, gritting their teeth. People shouted, accusing him of taking their trades or killing their loved ones. A child threw an apple, whacking him in the collarbone. Maldwyn trembled as he reached for his power in a hopeless attempt.

The stake in the centre of the court poked toward the setting sun and three guards stood around the pyre, holding blazing torches. Everything in him tried to turn back. Someone spat on him as he was pushed forward by the younger guard, thick saliva landing on his cheek.

Glancing up as the guard forced him onto the pyre, tying his chains to the post, Maldwyn saw King Viktor standing on the palace balcony, overlooking the square. Prince Harlan stood at the king's side and looked broken. Maldwyn wondered what his dear prince had endured, being forced to stand at the king's side.

The king waved his arm out wide, pleasing the crowd. 'This man stands before you, guilty of practising sorcery. In line with our just laws, he has been sentenced to death. He will burn for his crime!'

The shackles pinched his wrists as the guards finished fixing them in place. The soldiers moved away and Maldwyn grew short of breath as he saw the flaming torches wavering in the wind. Locking eyes with the prince across the square, Maldwyn said a silent goodbye, begging him to look away when the bonfire at his feet was lit.

'Light the pyre!' King Viktor's voice reverberated around the square. The three guards stepped forward, lighting the dried brush and timbers at Maldwyn's feet. Roaring with excitement the people cheered with crazed faces.

The blaze grew, popping as the heat exploded through the timbers. Flames licked the sides of his pants. Desperate, Maldwyn tried to move away, but the blaze was all around him. He clung to the pole, knowing there was no way out, yet unable to stop trying to escape the rising inferno. The acrid smell of the ash and smoke lined his nostrils.

As his pants caught fire, the flames stung his legs, searing through to blister his skin. Maldwyn looked up at the sky and cried out as he stared at the black ash climbing the darkening sky. He felt the furnace peeling his skin from his bones. The unbearable pain was torture as he filled the square with his screams. Weak he caught one last look of Harlan through the inferno, noticing that he had not looked away. Tears streamed down Maldwyn's face and he closed his eyes, letting the firestorm consume him.

* * * * *

Dead inside, Harlan sank into the soft lounge by the fireplace in his chambers. He was exhausted, having wept in anguish for hours and the summer heat allowed him to suffer in his dark den. He recalled dropping to his knees on the balcony as the fire devoured Maldwyn. His father's guards had dragged him back to his quarters. The sun had left the sky and the stars had come out, shimmering as they wept for the prince's loss.

'Go away,' Harlan told the knock at his door.

'Sire,' Theodor's voice called through the servant door. 'It's Master Damyan and me.'

'Go away,' he said again, agonised as his chest tightened. Tears returned to the prince's eyes and he brought a hand up to his twitching mouth.

'Your Grace, please,' Master Damyan said from behind the small door across the room. 'You shouldn't be alone.'

Harlan didn't want their pity. He wanted to be alone with his sorrow. Taking in a deep breath he stared up at the roof, knowing they weren't going to leave. Wetting his lips, he wiped away his tears and attempted to compose himself as much as possible.

He stood and headed toward the door. The floorboards groaned underfoot. Reluctant, he wrapped his hand around the warm, metal handle and opened the door to let his guests inside.

Theodor's hand was resting on the hilt of his sword and his face was filled with grief. Harlan rubbed his forehead and thought about Ailaya, wondering how she was coping with the misery of losing Maldwyn twice. Master Damyan's sympathetic expression saddened Harlan and brought tears back to his eyes.

'Aw, sire,' Master Damyan said in a compassionate tone as he stepped through the doorway and pulled Harlan into what the prince assumed was a fatherly hug, having never known parental love. Theodor slipped into the room behind Damyan and closed the door as Harlan sunk into the comforting embrace.

Pulling away, Harlan walked over to the lounges and crossed his arms over his chest. 'I had this ridiculous idea that Maldwyn might have somehow gotten away and saved himself. I guess it was because I had mourned him before only to find out that he was alive and well.' Maldwyn's screams rang in Harlan's head. 'There were times he was quite mysterious and I had begun to wonder whether there was something he wasn't telling me… I mean, I saw him pluck a knife from the air like it was nothing. He made it look easy.'

'Your Grace,' Theodor looked worried as he walked by the table towards the windows by the bed, 'did you ever ask Maldwyn about your suspicions?'

'No,' Harlan replied, shrugging. He bit his cheek and swallowed the ball at the back of his throat, trying to bury his heartache. 'I figured he would tell me in time, but I suppose there was nothing to tell.' The memory of Maldwyn burning came to the front of his mind as he rubbed his tired eyes. 'Every time I close my eyes, I see him burning and I hear his screams.' Harlan shook, feeling the tears overwhelm him as he lost his composure. 'I'm sorry,' he mumbled, covering his mouth.

Master Damyan cleared his throat and held his hands clasped behind his back. His shoes sounded on the timber floorboards as he walked toward where Harlan was standing between the fireplace and the lounges. He gently touched the prince's arm and gestured for him to sit.

'Breathe, Your Grace,' Master Damyan said, going over to the prince's set of drawers and pulling out a handkerchief. 'Here, dry your eyes and breathe, sire,' Master Damyan told Harlan.

With trembling hands, Harlan took the handkerchief and patted the skin under his eyes as Damyan plumped the cushions and sat beside the prince on the plush seat.

'I can't unsee it.'

'He didn't want you to watch,' Theodor said to the stars outside.

'I know.' Harlan wiped the drip at the tip of his nose on the velvety handkerchief. 'But I thought he should see someone that cared about him. I didn't want him to feel alone. I didn't want his last sight to be the angry mob and my father's face while I looked away.'

Struggling with the heat in his leather armour, Harlan assumed, Theodor pulled at the collar of his jacket. The room went quiet. Harlan wished he could wind back time. He would leave Maldwyn in Karana Downs and tell him to return to the mountains where he would be safe.

A moment of self-loathing besieged Harlan as he wished he had better listened to Cassara's warning. His arrogance had fooled the prince into taking little notice of her prediction and naively believing that he could save Maldwyn from whatever doom lurked in the shadows of time.

'Sire,' Damyan started, in a low and soft voice, 'they'll be clearing the square shortly. I've asked the servants to gather Maldwyn's remains and deliver his ashes to his mother's grave.' Theodor folded his arms over his chest, staring out the window. 'If you want to visit the square to say your last goodbyes—to have closure—then we should head down there soon.'

'Right,' Harlan muttered in reply and sniffed. His eye ticked and he studied the fleur-de-lis mantlepiece as his breath left him. 'You're right, he should be laid to rest with his family.'

'I'm sorry. Don't feel pressured to go back to the square if you don't wish to,' Master Damyan told him placing a kind hand on Harlan's shoulder. 'I thought you should know, Your Grace, just in case.'

'You don't need to be sorry.' Harlan pinched his mouth inward and held his breath. 'I want to go and make sure that his remains are collected respectfully. He deserves that much. Just, um… give me a moment and I'll meet you both in the hall.'

'Of course, sire.' Master Damyan pushed himself up to stand and gestured to Theodor to leave.

Taking a few minutes to collect his composure, Harlan buried his head in his hands, steeling himself for the horror in the square. A part of him didn't want to go, but he felt responsible for overseeing matters. Maldwyn had no family to take care of such things, nor to mourn his passing.

When he felt ready to face the pain, Harlan breathed a deep breath, stood and joined the others in the servant hall. The corridors were cramped, poorly lit and humid. Staff slowed and bowed as the prince went by, whispering when they thought he was out of earshot.

'Psst.'

The sound came from a nook in the serving hall behind him. Harlan looked back over his shoulder, checking for who had made the noise. He saw a man with a long, grey beard.

'Wait here,' Harlan instructed, heading toward the familiar figure. As Harlan stopped by the alcove, he recognised Gorlois.

'Your Royal Highness,' the elderly councilman bowed, 'I was on my way to your chambers to meet with you. I have been restoring the archives as we discussed and I have found some interesting information.'

Master Damyan cleared his throat impatiently as he waited further down the hall. 'There's something I need to do now. Can we discuss it later?'

Gorlois nodded and scratched his beard. 'Of course, sire.'

'I'll get Damyan to organise a time for us to meet discreetly.'

'Yes, Your Grace,' Gorlois bowed. 'I'm sorry about your friend, sire,' Gorlois added as Harlan went to leave.

'Thank you,' Harlan replied and continued through the labyrinth of halls, ignoring the urge to ask what the Keeper of the Archives had found in his research.

The door to the square was a small timber door at the top of a set of narrow stairs. Beyond the creaking hinges clinging to the door frame was a wide, open space. It was a hot evening.

The quarter moon glowed over the courtyard from the black sky which was speckled with glimmering stars.

Harlan took his time approaching the crumbled mess of charred timbers in the centre of the square. The main post was broken with the shackles hanging from the stake. A few servants, holding brooms were assessing the burned pile of wood. Holding his hands to cover his mouth, Harlan swallowed his tears and held his breath.

Master Damyan stood tall, posture impeccable as always, and walked over to the servants preparing to clear the courtyard. There was a bitter smell in the air and as Harlan stared at the blackened mound of wood, he noted the wing-shaped scorch marks in the cobbled square. He didn't see any bones as he moved closer to the charcoal heap.

'Strange,' Harlan mumbled through his building tears to Theodor, wheeling around the burned mound. 'There aren't any bones.'

'Damyan's servants probably gathered them and set them aside before we arrived,' Theodor offered, crouching to survey the mass.

Harlan leaned closer and saw that the chains were unblemished. There didn't appear to be a single trace of his remains glued to the post. Harlan wasn't sure whether to be relieved that he didn't see any gruesome details, or worried that his remains were dissolved to nothingness and lost to a pile of timber.

It was a still night and as he continued to walk around the timber mound, Harlan noticed a distinct thin, line of ash leading away from the charred stack of wood. With the others focused elsewhere, Harlan followed the ember trail toward a narrow, dark alley.

In the darkness, Harlan's heart jumped in his throat as he thought he saw a form lying on the ground. Apprehensive, Harlan glanced back, seeing Theodor standing near the servants, watching him. Master Damyan was deep in conversation with his staff.

Slow and cautious, Harlan walked down the laneway, following the ashen trail and approaching the figure he thought he saw on the ground. 'Hello,' he called into the dark.

Silence answered him. Rising from the ash trail was the body of a man curled into a foetal position on the ground. 'Are you alright?' The prince asked the silhouette.

Again, there was no response. Crouching beside the naked body, Harlan gently turned the man, slipping his fingers under the man's chin and twisting his face up toward the starlight. The perfect, unblemished, oblong face of his deceased lover stole the air from Harlan's lungs.

'Mal,' Harlan mumbled, lifting his head off the ground to rest in his lap. Hands shaking, Harlan lifted his fingers to Maldwyn's nose and felt the warm breath coursing out. 'You're breathing!' Running his hand down to Maldwyn's chest, Harlan checked the slow rise and fall. 'How are you breathing?' Harlan cupped Maldwyn's face.

'By divinity's grace!' Harlan looked up to see Theodor walking down the lane. 'Is that...' the knight's voice trailed off.

Harlan ignored him and traced Maldwyn's resting face with his hand. His skin was smooth. His dark, walnut-coloured hair remained thick and soft. His head fell back heavily as he lay unconscious in the prince's arms.

Speechless, tears welled in Harlan's eyes as he held Maldwyn tight, placing a gentle kiss on his forehead. Knowing that everything was about to change, Harlan gazed up at the gap above them, staring at the moon and stars watching over them, pondering what would happen next.

ACKNOWLEDGEMENTS

Drafting this book helped me through the last few years as the world seemed to shrink at the same time as becoming more desperate. It's strange to think how the human world seems to be in survival mode around the globe, moving at an impossible speed. It's hard not to feel bogged down and stuck in a rut.

Living at the time in a one-bedroom apartment during Melbourne's harsh lockdowns, unable to step outside for more than an hour, it was hard to feel creative. With a safe, although small, home and working as an essential worker throughout the pandemic, I know I was lucky. But, that doesn't mean it was easy.

Needless to say, working from home in a small place in what was an unhealthy work environment at the time, brought with it many challenges and I certainly had my dark moments.

A huge thank you must go to my family who was faced with my many breakdowns and supported me through the difficulty of living in an apartment that became my hollow and place of despair. These dark times in my mind fuelled some interesting chapters in this book that I had not originally set out to write.

More than perhaps anyone else, I would like to thank my sister who shared in the experience of the Melbourne lockdowns. The amount of time she spent, and continues to spend, listening to my rambling thoughts, reading my earliest drafts, and helping me smile when I felt down, is more than one could ever expect. She has helped keep me sane in an insane world.

I would also like to thank a wonderful family friend and author, who shall always be known as Davin, and who kept inspiring me as he discovered his love of writing. The many moments of picking each other's brains, throwing out ideas, and staying excited about our work kept me motivated to put pen to paper. Thank you, Davin!

Last, but not least, I would like to thank my art and acknowledge the artists that have battled through each day being out of work. As some of the hardiest people who are willing to suffer to continue the craft and often go without payment, let's get back to what we do best and show the people around us our beating hearts.

ABOUT THE AUTHOR

Maddison Greer is an author and poet best known for the *Maldwyn & Harlan Series*. She has written several short stories including *The End of an Era* which was published in the anthology *Reset*, by Hawkeye Books in January 2021. More recently, her short story *Becoming* was published in the collection of stories titled *Jump*, published in 2022 by Hawkeye Books.

Born in Australia in 1994, Maddison Greer has lived in several cities, including Sweden's capital Stockholm where she lived for a few years at the start of her high school education.

Later, Maddison returned to Australia where she completed her Bachelor's Degree at the University of Newcastle. She currently resides and writes in Melbourne, Australia.

www.ingramcontent.com/pod-product-compliance
Lightning Source LLC
Chambersburg PA
CBHW050104120726
47904CB00004B/1214